"Can I kiss you, F

Butterflies took f   ,
she nodded her head. She had been waiting for this moment. Ever since she let her guard down and began trusting him, she had imagined what it would be like to kiss his perfect lips.

Logan reached up, placing one hand under her hair at the base of her neck. Electricity buzzed throughout her body. With his other hand, he cupped her cheek pulling her closer.

Ember held her breath as his lips parted and pressed against hers with the lightest touch. In an instant, their bodies became one. The world melted away. It was just Ember and Logan on the dance floor.

Too soon, he pulled away. Eyes sparkling in the disco light, his tongue darted across his bottom lip.

The kiss was sweet. Perfect. Ember smiled, remembering to breathe.

"You taste better than I imagined." Both dimples asserted themselves as his lips shifted into a devilish grin.

Dead Girl

by

Kerrie Faye

Cover Art by *Kristian Norris*

The Wild Rose Press, Inc.
PO Box 708
Adams Basin, NY 14410-0708
Visit us at www.thewildrosepress.com

Publishing History
First Edition, 2023
Trade Paperback ISBN 978-1-5092-5248-0
Digital ISBN 978-1-5092-5249-7

Published in the United States of America

Dedication

For the real Eric
&
My old Kentucky home.

Acknowledgments

I absolutely must begin by thanking my editor, Kaycee John, and The Wild Rose Press for believing in this story and bringing *Dead Girl* to life.

Thank you to my parents, James and Karen, and to my brother and sister, Jerrod and Sara. And, thank you to my dad in Heaven, Bryce. Your continuous love, tolerance, and encouragement have paved the way for my debut novel.

Next, I thank the early readers and supporters of *Dead Girl*. I will forever be grateful for your insights. You all are the best: Gay, Lyndi, Holly, Kim, Mallory, Cori, Karen M., Tom and Stuart. Special thanks to my Twitter author family, Beautiful Weirdos, for your support and guidance. Additional thanks to my writer friends in SCBWI, RWA, and the Writing Heights Writers Association for mentoring me along on this great writing adventure.

And, to Team Herron, Jesse, James, and Rachel, you are my heart. Thank you for your words of encouragement and giving me the space to write. I couldn't have done it without you. I love you.

Finally, dear reader, thank you for buying this book and sharing your reviews. I am honored to share Ember's story with you. Your support is everything.

And last: If you or someone you know is considering suicide, please don't hesitate to dial 988 or visit the website https://988lifeline.org

You are a gift and a blessing, and you are not alone.

~Kerrie Faye

Chapter One

Teetering on the edge of the diving board, Ember O'Neill's world slowed down. Not like a slow-motion, snail's pace, but the milliseconds-between-seconds kind of slow. Her pupils contracted as her gaze connected with her assailant. She saw his curled lip slide into a sneer from where he stood at the pool's edge. Drops of perspiration beaded on top of his pimpled, freckled nose, like tiny, shiny orbs and his aura flared a dangerous maroon outlined in pitch black.

At that moment she understood that Wayne Wilson wanted to humiliate her in front of everyone at the back-to-school pool party and destroy any hope she ever had of fitting in. Her stomach sank, along with any hope that this year would be different.

His grin stretched as he pulled the trigger. Red paint shot out of the water gun, forming bloody streaks in the air. A cherry rainbow arched across the pool. The first spray splashed across her pale face and white bikini. The liquid felt cool and heavy across her hot skin.

The crowd noise fell into a collective hush while the music blared. Ember's lashes instinctively fluttered closed. Like a hummingbird trapped in a glass cage, wings thumping with no escape, her heart hammered in her chest. She braced herself for the next assault as Maddison Miller's cackle broke through the muffled silence, shattering her last shred of dignity. It was clear her plans for sophomore year were just a fantasy, the desperate dreams of a high school outcast.

White knuckled, her fists relaxed. Shoulders slumped; she released her last breath. Ember O'Neill didn't have a death wish, but it just became her Plan B.

Chapter Two

One Week Earlier

Fingers smudged with charcoal; Ember hurriedly ripped off the insanely optimistic list she made the night before on her drawing pad. She had fallen asleep in her childhood treehouse again. Though little more than a renovated deer stand in the woods behind her house, it was her sanctuary. After being diagnosed with synesthesia, she often felt overwhelmed. Even out in the woods, her high-functioning senses were activated; but the sights, sounds, and scents out there were familiar—not jarring, like when she was at school around others and their auras.

"Seeing colors," as her mom described it, was draining, if not overwhelming.

With her large-breed dog and best friend, Bear, at her heels, Ember jogged into the house. The storm door slammed closed behind them. Her father's morning brew percolated in the chipped carafe by the sink. Without words, he raised his hand in a greeting from the living room. Smoke from his cigarette clouded his aura. He leaned forward in the recliner, listening to the news.

Ember continued into the ranch-style house, yelling, "Birdie Mae! I need your help." Her mother,

Birdie Mae, insisted Ember never call her "mom." She said that it made her feel old, and she was too young to feel old.

Once inside her bedroom, she taped the list to the mirror over her dresser. For her first day of sophomore year, Ember had goals. Her lips slipped into a satisfied smile at her reflection. She popped open the prescription bottles lining her dresser, then swallowed the pills dry. Depressed and dejected, her freshman year had been a nightmare and culminated with her as the joke of Wilson High. So, back to the local doctor, who upped her dosages again.

In three short months of summer, though, Ember had gained some confidence. Maybe it was the pills, but she was willing to give Wilson County High one more shot.

She gazed at her list. Goal number five was written in bold, all capitals: GET A BOYFRIEND. She had drawn hearts around the word. A soft chuckle emerged from her throat. *The pills are definitely working.*

She had sincere hope for goal number one, though: Get a Bestie. Erick Grossman didn't count, and lately, his aura had made her uncomfortable. No, she needed a girlfriend. Someone she could talk with about boys and not worry about hurting their feelings. Besides, all the heroines in her favorite books had a best friend. It would be the perfect way to start sophomore year.

Ember noted the time on her bedside digital clock and rushed to the bathroom, where she washed her face and brushed her hair.

"Yes, baby girl, what's the matter?" Birdie Mae came out of her bedroom at the end of the hall, her bleached-blonde hair in rollers and a lit cigarette dangling between her lips. The beauty shop didn't open till ten a.m.—thank God, because Birdie Mae was not a morning person.

With narrowed pupils, Ember watched Birdie Mae's aura instantly switch from a curious clover green to a cayenne red as she made her way down the hall. Birdie Mae was pissed. Ember had learned at a young age what the colors of auras meant, especially when her dad was back in town.

Birdie Mae yelled into the living room, "God damn it, Billy Joe! Why the hell, every morning, you gotta go and turn off my music videos?"

Ignoring the rant, Ember's dad released the wooden handle on the beat-down recliner, stood, then walked over to the box TV and turned up the volume. Ember noted his aura shifted from his normal congenial yellow-pink sunrise to a concerned indigo as he listened to the newscast.

"*In Chicago this morning, ELL Pharmaceuticals CEO Asher Von Holstein announced that ELL has developed a breakthrough in DNA technology...*" When the news anchor droned on, her dad turned the set off.

"Asshole," Birdie Mae hissed around her cigarette.

"Birdie Mae?" Ember redirected her mom to her room. "I need help. I want to look cooler this year. But all my stuff is old and—."

"And black," Birdie Mae cut her off as she slid hangers up and down the rod. "Shit. Let's go shop from my closet." A cloud of gray smoke blew from her lips. "Next weekend, we are going to Paducah and getting you some clothes, girl."

Birdie Mae's fashion sense came straight from rock band videos. She wore lots of leather, denim, and ripped tees. The women around town loved to gossip about her looks but, by damn, if they didn't keep coming back to Birdie Mae to get their cuts and colors. She was the best in Wilson County—and they all knew it, according to Birdie Mae.

"I don't think I can wear this to school." Ember held up the cut-off denim shorts. "They look too short."

"Oh, hell. It's 1990—not the fifties, for Christ's sweet sake. If you get any shit, you tell that principal to call me." She shoved a concert T-shirt into Ember's hands. "This will look so cute, darlin." Birdie Mae winked. "You'll have them boys dying to take you out, and all those little heifers are gonna be so jealous of you." She pushed her to the door. "Go on, now. Get dressed. That bus will be here any minute."

Ember raced down the hall, stripping out of her clothes and tugged on Birdie Mae's gear.

"Five minutes!" Birdie Mae yelled. "And don't forget your lunch money on the counter."

Ember scanned herself in the mirror one last time, readjusted her ponytail and smiled to herself. Fingers trembling, she took another pill.

"Hey, how was your summer? Yeah? Cool, me too," she said to her reflection.

Breathe in and breathe out. You can do this.

Ember stilled. Her highly sensitive ears picked up on the diesel engine rumbling down the gravel road half a mile away. It was now or never. She grabbed her denim purse and shoved her bottle of uppers into an inside pocket alongside the ridiculous number of tampons and pads she packed last night. She vowed silently not to repeat last year's bloody episode. Ember ran through the house, with Bear lumbering behind her.

She snagged the money on the counter and exited the carport door just as the old, yellow Wilson County school bus came to a screeching halt at the end of her driveway.

"Hey!" Billy Joe yelled from the carport, cigarette smoke trailing from his hand.

Halfway to the bus, Ember turned.

"Remember…*virtus vincit*."

"Got it, Dad." Ember waved back.

Courage conquers. It had been years since he served in the military, but he always had one foot in the past.

Ember stepped onto the bus with her chin up. It was the first day of sophomore year, and she was counting on courage and her plan to get her through it.

****

The bell rang as Ember entered the glass doors of the basic red brick building of Wilson County High. She picked up her pace and slipped through the gym doors. They held the beginning of first hour in the gym for a Welcome Assembly. The array of auras reflecting back at her from the bleachers penetrated her medicinally induced defenses. She looked down, sucked up her nerves, and headed straight for the bottom row. Ember scanned the gym for Erick Grossman, her only ally. Unfortunately, he was helping his dad, the Vice Principal, with the sound system. Ember bit her lip.

The principal tapped the mic, and she looked around and cringed at her seating mistake—too late. She was sitting on the bottom row with the Greenie Freshman, rather than several rows up with her sophomore class. Well, technically, one other person was also sitting in the absolute bottom row with her—a new girl.

Ember studied her profile. She was cute, with brown hair and big, purple-framed glasses. She didn't recognize her from around town. She instinctively breathed in the girl's scent. It was pleasant, like honeysuckle, but not too sweet—a comfortable, familiar scent reminding Ember of summers with her dad. The girl's aura was all over the place. Ember noted that the New Girl was nervous and excited, but also scared and happy.

New Girl gave Ember a meek smile and mouthed *hi*. Ember smiled back. She turned her attention to the principal yammering on about hoping everyone had a great summer and that he's looking forward to the 1990-91 school year. She tuned him out and studied the spectrum of auras flaring from the teachers on the stage, most of them bored.

She was so zoned out that she didn't realize everyone had risen and started clapping. Ember stood. Oh, good, it's over, she thought, and walked away from the bleachers to first period class when out came the cheerleaders bursting from the locker room and turning flips as they made their way onto the gym floor. Maddison Miller's flying leg nearly clocked Ember in the face.

She side-stepped back to her spot on the bottom bleacher. Her face was aflame. Goal number two: Stay off Maddison Miller's Radar, was nearly destroyed within minutes of the first day back at school. The self-anointed queen of Wilson County High could make or break a person's social standing. Until now, Ember had stayed away from Maddison's discerning eye. The queen shot her a glare and chanted with the crowd, "War Eagles! War Eagles! Fight! Fight! Fight!"

Ember winced—the noise was overwhelming. The energy in the gym intensified. Her chest tightened from the suffocating smells of body odor and hormones. The room swam before her eyes. *No, not again. Focus.*

She fumbled with her purse and took out a pill. The doctor had assured her that this new one would dull her senses and make her synesthesia more manageable at school. She swallowed the pill and prayed it would work fast. Over the entire summer, she only took a pill at night and that was to block the nightmares. Now, sweaty and anxious, she plastered a fake smile on her face. You can do this, she coached herself. *Courage conquers.*

New Girl shifted closer, clapped, and smiled. "I don't know the words either. Are you new, too?"

Ember gritted her teeth. "No. I just don't like assemblies."

"Oh." New Girl turned away. Her aura shifted to an embarrassed soft red.

The fast-acting pill kicked in. Relieved, Ember tapped the New Girl on her shoulder. "Hey, sorry. My name is Ember. What's yours?"

New Girl smiled as relief filled her aura. "I'm Hallee Wilson." The crowd roared as Maddison tumbled into the air. "Like Holly, but short 'a,' double 'l,' and double 'ee.' "

"That's different. Never met a Hallee before. Are you related to Wayne? Or Katie Wilson?" Ember asked.

"Yeah, they're both my cousins."

"Oh."

An awkward silence fell between them. The

Wilsons not only had their name on the school and claimed the county's founding, but their numbers flourished well beyond the county line, as well. The name alone sent spiders crawling down Ember's neck. Her number one tormentor was a Wilson and subsequently the subject of Ember's goal number three: Avoid and Ignore Wayne Wilson. She planned to make it her mission to pay no attention to his taunts and pranks this year if it killed her.

Then there was the other Wilson: Katie. Ember noted her bright orange aura, laced with envious green, as Katie smiled at Maddison. Katie was chief consort to Queen Maddison Miller, spreading rumors and shunning the others without thought or remorse. If Maddison and Katie didn't acknowledge your presence, you were a nobody at Wilson High.

Ember was currently a nobody despite her inner longing to fit-in and be popular, which was also goal number four: Become Popular in a Good Way. Lose the nicknames. Or, at least, earn one that carries a positive connotation.

She glanced furtively at Hallee. *Once she gets the lay of the land, she will be like, "See you later, Bloody Ember."*

Hallee shrugged. "My cousins and I aren't close or anything."

"Cool." Her lips jerked into a whisper of a smile. She continued to clap as the cheer squad formed a line. The boys' varsity basketball team, one by one, walked down from the bleachers to be honored. Last year, the team came in runner-up at the state tournament.

"You a freshman?" Ember asked.

"No, sophomore. You?"

"Sophomore." Ember smiled sheepishly. "We are supposed to be seated a whole section up."

Hallee's aura turned a soft salmon again. "What?"

"Yep. We are technically sitting with the Greenies—only we are at the very, very bottom of the Greenie section. We are like totally uncool right now."

Hallee's eyes went wide behind her glasses. "Oh man. No wonder Katie is glaring at me."

"I thought you weren't close."

"We aren't. When I told her this summer I was moving in with my dad and would switch to her school, she gave me strict instructions—don't do anything stupid to embarrass her."

"Oh. Sorry. Yeah, that sounds like Katie—no offense."

"None taken," Hallee replied.

Ember smiled. The pills were working. And she might have just met her new Bestie.

"Oh, wow. He's cute," Hallee crooned as the star basketball player, Kale Martin, was called forward to hold the runner-up trophy.

"Yeah—and he's taken." Ember pointed to the perfect blonde standing next to Katie. "That is Maddison Miller. She's a junior. Kale and she have been on-again off-again basically since middle school."

"So, the cute guy is a junior, and he's like the star of the varsity team?"

"Yep, and everyone thinks they will win state this year and probably next year taking back-to-back titles…" Ember did a weak fist pump. "Go, War Eagles."

"Yay." Grinning, Hallee copied, thrusting her fist in the air.

"Your old school give this much hype to basketball?" Ember asked.

She laughed. "I'm from Kentucky—not Mars. So, yeah. I'm just not into sports that much."

Ember laughed. This Hallee girl definitely had Bestie potential.

"It was a private Catholic school in Paducah."

"St. Mary's?"

Hallee's hand drifted to the gold cross hanging from her neck. "Yeah."

Ember made a fake bow. "Welcome to public school out in the boonies."

"Thanks." Her aura shined a happy, lemon-yellow.

The principal announced that the cheerleaders and basketball team would stay behind in the gym to take pictures for the yearbook, while they dismissed everyone else to first period for the rest of the hour.

"What is your first class?" Ember asked as students started clamoring down the bleachers. Her eyes naturally scanned the room to avoid Wayne.

Hallee pulled out a worn piece of paper. "Let's see… I have World History first hour."

"Really? Me too. C'mon follow me." Ember tugged on Hallee's arm as her eyes met with Wayne's. His brows rose as his gaze dragged over Ember's body. She looked away and quickened her pace.

"Wait,: Hallee said. "You don't know which teacher or the room number."

Ember turned around, "Small school in the boonies, remember? There is only one history teacher."

"Oh." Hallee's cheeks flushed as she rushed to keep up.

Ember's brows furrowed at the droning of the

voices in the hall. The new pill wasn't the miracle she had hoped for. Her overly sensitive hearing picked up everything, and the smells of too much perfume, aftershave, and hairspray spiked in the confines of the tight hallway. She missed the peace of summer and the simple smells of home. She took shallow breaths, but the odors still permeated the hall like a thick soup. She lost her balance, swayed, but caught the wall for support.

Hallee touched her arm, "Are you okay?"

Ember stood straight. "Yeah, sure. Just a little light-headed. I should have eaten breakfast," she lied.

"Oh, yeah, low blood sugar…my mom was a nurse before…" Hallee looked away.

"Did your mom…?"

"What? No. Oh, gosh, no. She's not dead." She fished around in her purse. "Want a banana?"

"No, thank you. I'll be fine. History is just up ahead."

Ember cringed as she heard the whispers in the hall.

"Who's that new girl? And why is she hanging out with Bloody Ember?"

"Oh my God, look at Bloody Ember. What is she wearing?"

Ember glanced back at Hallee. Her aura was unchanged. She clearly hadn't heard them. Relieved, she pressed on to class. If she hadn't felt obligated to get Hallee to the right room, she might have run out the doors and not looked back.

Her goals for sophomore year were fading fast and her courage even faster.

Chapter Three

Walking into class felt like walking onto a stage to sing a solo in front of the entire student body. Or, so Ember thought, as she raised her eyes and saw everyone looking back at her with Hallee in her shadow.

Be brave.

As usual, the cool kids clustered in the back of the classroom, leaving the nerds to fill the seats at the front of each row. Mr. Thompson was dressed in his usual too-tight khakis, button-down shirt, and red sweater vest. If Santa quit his winter gig and became a professor one day, that would be Mr. Thompson, a jolly old elf who loved his history. Ember had him for U.S. History last year and despite nearly failing, she actually liked the old man. His aura was always a bright lemon-yellow happy.

The chalk squeaked against the board as Mr. Thompson etched out his name. With limited options, Ember was grateful to see Erick and his row of empty seats.

He smiled expectantly. "Hey, Ember."

She quickly nodded and motioned for Hallee to sit behind Erick.

Erick Grossman was her only friend at Wilson County High. Years of being outcasts had cemented their friendship. He never once made her feel weird about her abilities, and she accepted his quirky Dungeons and Dragons references and superhero obsessions. The only problem was that his aura was shifting from friendship to something more. She just didn't think of him that way.

The bell rang. Mr. Thompson turned and smiled to the class. "Welcome back, Eagles. I hope you all had a wonderful summer. Did a little traveling, myself. Went to Shiloh with the Boy Scouts. Did a little fishing and camping." The poster of President George H. W. Bush smiled back at Mr. Thompson with approval of his summer exploits.

Ember became distracted. The girls at the back of the room were gossiping about how boring Mr. Thompson was and how his class was going to suck. Her jaw clenched.

"First order of business, books," Mr. Thompson said. "Erick, would you like to help pass them out?"

"Yes, sir."

The girls in the back snickered.

"He must be a Boy Scout."

"Oh, my God. He's such a nerd."

"Did he just salute Mr. Thompson?"

Ember turned in her seat to see who was being so nasty. *Ah, Jamie and Heather.* Those two were on the JV Cheer squad together and were Maddison and Katie's minions.

Ember fumed. One of her goals for sophomore year was to be popular, but not like them. She'd rather be uncool than be a mean girl.

Erick brought a stack of textbooks to the front of their row and passed them back. She noticed he gave her and Hallee the newer texts and the rattier, overused books to the cool kids in the back. She mentally high-fived her friend.

"All righty then," Mr. Thompson said, "Next, the Handbook. Erick, do you mind?"

Erick had just sat. "No, sir, happy to do it." And he was. His aura was almost as yellow as the teacher's.

"In the very back of the handbook, you will find the Code of Conduct," Mr. Thompson said. "You can read through it…for the dress code…" He raised his eyes and looked pointedly at Ember. She squirmed in her seat. "No alcohol…no smoking…"

The girls in the back whispered and joked some more. "Whatever, Grandpa."

"Et cetera, et cetera…just bring it back, signed by you and your parents by the end of next week." Mr. Thompson sat down in his chair. "Okay, next on the agenda is attendance and locker assignments. When I call your name, come up and take this piece of paper. It has your name and locker number written on it." While he called roll, the class talked quietly amongst themselves.

The resident mean girls had now gotten two of the guys, whom Ember recognized as card-carrying members of Wayne Wilson's goon squad, involved in their put-down circle. Jamie and Heather were whining about needing to smoke in the girl's bathroom after class. The guys slipped them a couple of cigarettes. Ember rolled her eyes.

Mr. Thompson called her name, "Ember O'Neill— locker number one hundred thirty-nine."

"Here," she responded and went to the front desk to get her locker assignment while the boys in the back whispered their usual crappy comments.

"Looks like Bloody Ember got a makeover from her mom."

"Dude, her mom is like hot—seriously."

Ember turned and glared.

"Dude, I think she heard you."

"What? No way."

They continued to whisper as Ember sat.

"Dude, I'm telling you, she heard you. Did you see that look she gave you?"

"She's like my grandma. Old bitch can hear everything."

"Whatever. She's a freak."

"Yeah, but at least she got hot over the summer."

"Yeah, she's pretty smokin'. Ha-ha, get it? Ember. Hot Ember."

"Dude…you're an idiot."

"Shut up."

"Whatever."

Ember gritted her teeth. Guys like them were super annoying. She watched their auras shift from eggplant to magenta as their attitudes dipped from ridicule to lust.

Soon, Hallee's name was called, which got the mean girls going again.

"Oh my God, do you see her glasses? They are like from 1980."

"And look at how she dresses. She's like an old lady."

Reaching her limit, Ember turned in her seat. "That's enough. Just stop."

The girls smirked at her.

"Ember, everything okay?" Mr. Thompson asked as Hallee sat down.

"Yes, sorry." She slumped down in her seat. *Ugh. Just ignore them.*

Hallee turned around. "What happened?"

She didn't have the heart to tell her what they said. "Heather and Jamie were not being nice. That's all."

Ember heard them talking behind her again.

"Dude, she can hear you. She has like super-hearing." One of the guys whispered to the girls.

"Yeah, well, if that's true…hey, Bloody Ember…watch your back…it's going to be a long, long year for you. And by the way, you look like a whore," Heather hissed from the back of the room.

Ember unconsciously grabbed the metal support of her desk and squeezed. Triggered by her anger, her unnatural strength bent the metal. It wasn't the first time she'd released her frustration on school property, but she never did it intentionally. And she never, ever spoke back. She kept her eyes locked straight ahead. She was a freak. She knew it. They knew it. But why couldn't they just leave her alone?

The class door swung open. Wayne Wilson walked in, wearing M. C. Hammer pants and a gold chain around his neck. "What's up, Mr. T?" A cheesy grin slid across his freckled, pock-marked face.

"Welcome back, Wayne. I take it pictures are done?" Mr. Thompson asked.

"Yeah, the Wilson County paper wanted to interview us, so it took a little longer. It's cool though. What'd I miss?"

He turned down Ember's aisle and winked. Plopping himself down on the empty chair behind her. His stale, dirty scent coated in Old Spice invaded her senses. He tapped her on the shoulder and whispered,

"Miss me?"

Ember wanted to disappear—like forever. Fortunately, the bell rang one minute later.

"Wayne, come get your textbook, locker assignment, oh, and the handbook." Mr. Thompson attempted to speak over the class as everyone spilled out of the room.

Wayne smirked as he brushed too close against her. "Guess this means we can be study partners, huh, Red?"

"I'd rather be dead, Wayne."

His eyes raked her from head to toe, aura shifting to a passionate magenta. With his goons circled behind him, he licked his lips. The look on his face sent a chill down Ember's spine. "One of these days, Red, you're going to regret saying that."

"Maybe if you weren't such a jerk, I might be nicer." Ember bit the inside of her cheek. She had never stood up to him before.

His brows danced. "We can play nice, if you're into that?" His buddies laughed and gave him high fives.

Erick moved to stand at Ember's elbow as if to protect her, his aura flaring rich red anger. "Leave her alone, Wayne."

"Hey, it's cool, little buddy. I'm not trying to steal your girl—just having a little fun is all."

Mr. Thompson cleared his throat. "Wayne? Your textbook…"

"Sure thing, Mr. T." He turned. "Oh, Bloody Ember…be nice to my cousin." He ruffled the top of Hallee's head. "She's my favorite."

Hallee shoved his hand away and stood. "Oh my

gosh, Wayne. Stop."

"I thought you said that you two weren't close," Ember asked Hallee as they rushed to exit the classroom.

Hallee smoothed her hair. "We're not even—I don't know why he said that. Why did he call you that name?"

Ember flushed, starting down the hall, desperate to disappear. "He says a lot of things that make little sense."

"Hey, wait. What class do you have next?" Hallee asked. "Please say it's Chemistry."

Ember turned to catch Wayne blowing an air kiss at her as he walked by. Her stomach lurched. She swallowed and looked back at Hallee. "Oh, no, sorry. I've got English. But I can show you where it's at."

Erick chimed in behind them, "I've got Chem next, I'll show you."

Hallee beamed. "Oh, great. That's perfect." She extended her hand. "I'm Hallee, by the way."

Erick's aura matched his cheeks. "Hi, I'm Erick."

Ember released the breath she didn't realize she'd been holding. "Perfect, I'm just going to find my locker. See you two later."

"You want to meet up at lunch?" Hallee asked.

"Sure…we don't usually…." Ember noted the expectant look on Hallee's face. "Okay. I'll meet you two at the cafeteria after third hour."

Hallee's aura soared lemon-yellow. "Great!"

"Great."

She watched as Hallee chatted with Erick on their way to Chemistry. She smiled despite her nerves being on edge. There could be something there—a Bestie for her and a girlfriend for Erick—kill two birds with one Hallee.

Ember walked down the crowded hall that had lockers flanking both sides. She wanted to put her history book away before going to second hour. Odd numbers were on one side of the hall, evens on the other. She ignored the gossip as she walked by, scanning the locker numbers. A small clump of students, Jamie and Heather included, stood laughing right where she was headed.

Be brave. Smile. Act confident. Courage conquers. Despite the incantation, her stomach turned to lead. Auras danced the rainbow as she drew near. Ember flinched, listening to their murmurs.

"Wow, she's clueless."

"Shhh...here she comes."

The crowd parted in front of locker one hundred thirty-nine. Ember's knees weakened. Someone had taken a red marker and wrote, *"UR DED RED,"* in sloppy print on the front of her locker. It took everything she had to remain calm. She walked up and opened the door as if nothing was wrong and put her history book inside. The crowd fell into a collective silence, waiting for her reaction, but she refused to give them one. She refused to repeat the colossal failure of last year.

She turned and forced a smile at the girls. Spying Wayne's jackal smile at the back of the crowd, she crushed down the desire to run away crying. She would not let them see her upset. "I guess someone failed spelling." She projected her voice to make sure everyone heard her, including Wayne. "You're missing a few letters."

Heather and Jaimie rolled their eyes, unbothered by the comment, but Wayne and his goons got the message. Snorts and giggles erupted from the circle. She would not be the butt of Wayne's jokes anymore. She would not cower and hide.

Virtus vincit, Wayne.

Ember stiffened her back and pivoted on her heel, ignoring the black haze that now tinged Wayne's aura as the crowd turned on him and laughed at him for once.

****

Second and third hours flew by with much of the same gossip about her clothes and her now graffitied locker. To Ember, it seemed as if nothing had changed since freshman year. She was still a social pariah. Even if some guys thought she was hot, they still avoided Bloody Ember.

Grateful for lunch, she sought her personal sanctuary in the library. Merely steps away, Ember remembered—she'd promised the new girl, Hallee, that they'd meet up for lunch in the cafeteria. Taking a breath, she rolled her shoulders and continued down the hall. She swung by the janitor on the way out and asked Ms. Jackson to do a quick clean on her locker door during lunch hour.

"No, I don't want to report it," she said, after she asked several times. "Yes, I'm fine," she said in response to her next question, followed by, "It's not a big deal," and "It's okay."

Ms. Jackson—she preferred to be called Mama Jackson—was probably well past retirement, but she loved working at the school. She said it kept her young. Ember recalled after she fainted last year, that she had passed the old woman tugging the mop and bucket already on her way to clean up the mess. Ms. Jackson's kind, knowing eyes took in her bloody jeans that day. She said, "Don't you worry, Ember girl, Mama Jackson will take care of it."

Fast forward to Ember's first day of sophomore year, and nothing had changed.

Her forehead creased in concern. "It ain't right how those kids pick on you, Ember."

"I know, Mama Jackson, I know." She took in the old woman's aura that waffled between indigo, purple, and blue. Even though she barely knew Ember, it was clear Mama Jackson cared deeply.

"I'll be fine, Mama Jackson. It's just marker."

The old woman took her hand. "Don't you worry, Ember girl, I'll get that ink right off in two shakes of a lamb's tail."

"Okay, Mama Jackson, thank you." She patted the old woman's hand. "I gotta go."

She smiled and waved her on. "Oh, yes, child. Go get your lunch."

The cafeteria was across the paved lot between the Middle and High school buildings. It was technically the Middle School gym. But with a small enough student population, it served as the cafeteria for the entire Wilson County school system. Ember hated it. Noise echoed off the cement block walls like in any other gym. Add in the constant sounds of loud voices and clattering of dishes, combined with the smells of whatever was being cooked for the day's lunch menu and her synesthesia spiraled. She had found the best way to deal with it was to dip in, get a sack lunch, then go eat in the library.

Running late from her conversation with Mama Jackson, Ember jogged across the parking lot to lunch. Her stomach was in knots from the morning's confrontations. There was no way she could eat. But she refused to let Erick and Hallee down. It was one lunch. She could do it.

How bad could it be?

Chapter Four

Ember felt the noise before she heard it. She opened the door to the cafeteria. The smells and sounds nearly knocked her over. Clenching her teeth, she scanned the room for Erick and Hallee, all the while fighting the urge to turn and run right back out the door. *Where are they?*

She peeked in at the line of students waiting to be served. No luck. She stepped back out and searched each table—then froze.

Hallee sat at Maddison's table. Her cousin Katie was having an animated conversation with the rest of the clique. When Hallee looked up and caught her staring, Ember shook her head and turned to leave.

Hallee stood and yelled, "Ember, wait!"

While Katie pulled Hallee back down, Maddison scooted from the table and marched herself across the room to Ember, her minions, Heather and Jamie, close behind. Ember braced herself against Maddison's aura of hostile, orange-red poppy.

Her chest tightened and every muscle in her body tensed as she prepared for the verbal impact. *This is going to be bad.*

Maddison's petite blonde head bobbed as she pointed a finger in Ember' direction. "You've got some nerve coming in here to eat lunch with Hallee."

"What?" She choked out the word.

"You heard me. How could you be so rude—making fun of Katie's cousin?"

"I didn't—."

Maddison made shooing motions with her perfectly manicured hands. "Go on back to the little hole you crawled out of, Ember O'Neill."

"I don't know what you heard, but I said nothing mean to Hallee."

"That's so not true," Heather piped in, a cruel smile on her face. "Is it, Jamie?"

"She totally made fun of Hallee's glasses. I heard her in first hour."

Maddison's finger jabbed the air. "See. They heard you. So, go on. Git. You. Are. Not. Welcome. Here."

Ember shrugged and turned to leave. She fought back tears and looked over Maddison's shoulder to see that Katie, once again, had pulled Hallee back down as she tried to get up. "Whatever."

"Oh, and Ember?" Maddison crooned.

She didn't bother to turn around.

"Ember? Stay away from Hallee. We don't want her associating with the wrong kind."

Ember walked out the door to the sound of their cackles, so upset she felt like breaking something. Anything.

How could they be so cruel? How? The wrong kind? I'm different. So what?

Plus, that wasn't even what happened in first hour. It was Heather and Jamie who made fun of Hallee's glasses and clothes. Ember's nails dug into her palms, hard enough to make her wince. She looked down and saw bloodied crescent moons weeping from her palms.

Her fingers trembled as she fumbled with the zipper on her purse. Pill bottles rattled. She needed to numb her feelings—her senses—everything. She popped open the bottle and swallowed the bitter pharmaceutical salvation. Her eyes pooled.

"I will not cry over you, Maddison Miller. I will not," she vowed out loud as she zipped up her purse.

"Hey, sorry, I'm late. I had to help my dad. Are you okay?" Erick asked as he neared the cafeteria. His hand reached out, but Ember pulled away.

"Yeah, I'm fine." She closed her purse and turned to walk back to the high school.

"Hey, aren't you going to eat with us?"

Ember paused to study his aura. "Listen…Erick, you don't want to eat lunch with me in there, okay?"

"What do you mean?"

Her laugh was sharp. "Anyone who associates with Bloody Ember…well, it's not pretty. Did you not see my locker this morning? I mean, I know you saw how freshman year turned out. It's only been three periods of the first day of sophomore year…." She shook her head. "Save yourself and go eat with Hallee without me. There is still a chance for you and her to have a normal high school experience."

"I don't care what everyone else thinks, Ember." Erick blushed, his aura turning a bright pink. "You know that. I think you're one of the coolest girls at Wilson County. You play chess and read fantasy. Look…I don't know what happened over the summer, but you came back looking like a real warrior princess—which is totally bad ass, by the way."

The pink in his aura morphed to a passionate red. "I'm rambling, aren't I?" He scrubbed the back of his neck. "Dang it, I suck at finding the right words to say."

She looked in his eyes. She didn't know how to respond. She didn't want to hurt the one person who always had her back but she couldn't encourage that I-think-you're-hot aura.

"Erick, how do I say this? You have been a great friend over the years...But I'm not interested in anything beyond that. I only want to be friends."

"What? Oh. Oh! My aura?" His cheeks to the top of his ears were tinted crimson and his voice pitched an octave higher. "Sorry. Okay, yeah. No, that's cool. Me neither. I mean, I'm not looking for a girlfriend, either."

"So, you're cool with just being my friend??"

"Yeah." His voice cracked, causing his aura to shift to an embarrassed, carnation-pink.

"Good, I mean, that's great." Ember shook her head. "But just so you know, you can always bail if the social stigma of being Bloody Ember's friend gets to be too much this year."

He smiled sheepishly. "Would the warrior prince ever bail on the warrior princess?"

"Of course not. Like never." She laughed—truly laughed straight from her center and the tension melted from her shoulders.

"Well, then let's go hang in the library like usual and read some fantasy, my friend, before lunch break is over. And I'm not afraid to whoop you in a game of chess either, if there's time." His aura shifted to bright yellow, then dipped brown. "Oh, shoot. We forgot Hallee."

Ember glanced back through the cafeteria doors. Hallee was still at the table, smiling and laughing with Katie and Maddison and their minions. She sighed. "I don't think she's going to miss us."

****

The last half of the school day flew by.

Mama Jackson, true to her word, had Ember's locker door cleaned by the time lunch break was over. Gym was not a complete nightmare, but she hit the trifecta when she found Wayne, Heather and Jamie were also in her class. Her medical waiver allowed her to sit out and sketch on the bleachers while everyone else had to prepare for the Presidential fitness exam at the end of the semester. Aside from the occasional sinister glares from her favorite trio, gym wasn't the worst.

Fifth hour was Chemistry. Ember thought it was going to be an easy A. The teacher, Ms. Cooke, had a reputation for being cool. She coached both girls' basketball and volleyball teams. As Ms. Cooke called roll, she asked for each girl in the class to stand. It was as if she was scouting out hidden talent. She eyed each girl from top to bottom. If you met her height requirement—or whatever she was looking for—she'd ask if you were trying out for basketball or volleyball. Ember got the complete scan.

"Ember O'Neill. Ember O'Neill. I don't remember seeing you in the halls…are you new?"

She squirmed under her scrutiny. "No, Coach C. I had a growth spurt over the summer."

Ember heard a couple of girls whisper.

"I can't believe she doesn't remember the bloodbath from last year?"

"I would just die."

"Hmmm…so you trying out for either of the teams?" Coach asked.

"No, sorry, I'm medically exempt from playing sports."

Coached looked Ember over from her desk. "Why?"

She felt the burning stare of every single eyeball. "I have synesthesia."

More whispers hummed behind her.

"She's a bleeder, Coach. You don't want her on the court," one boy joked.

"Well, you got the height. I'll look into this syne—whatever that is." She scribbled a note beside Ember's name. "I expect to see you at tryouts, O'Neill."

Ember sank into her chair. Tryouts? She imagined the number of pills it would take to survive that *special* experience.

"If you are on one of my teams, I got your back." The teacher winked. Ember wished she could turn invisible, not for the first time that day, as her stomach dropped and the outlook for the day continued to get worse.

"All right. That's all I got for Day One. Tryouts for girls' basketball are in two weeks—volleyball the following week. I expect to see you ladies out there." Coach C plopped down in her chair, propping her sneakers onto her desk.

Ember looked down at her own graffitied desk, wondering if someone really needed chemistry to graduate.

Last period, Business Communication, was an elective, and Maddison had already staked out her territory. In the back row, she smacked her gum and leaned flirtatiously onto Kale Martin's desk. Opting for self-preservation, Ember sat in the front row, directly in front of the teacher's desk. She slipped into the cold hard chair and hoping to avoid confrontation.

"Ember, hey." Hallee, looking flustered, rushed in and slid into the seat next to her.

Ember looked back to see if Maddison noticed. Fortunately, she was now in a tongue lock with Kale.

"Hey," Ember whispered.

"Listen, I'm really sorry about lunch." Hallee's aura was a sincere shade of blue.

"I can see that."

Hallee cocked her head, as if confused by what she meant, but continued on. "I'll straighten it out with my cousin. I swear."

"Awesome."

Ember heard Maddison's voice behind her. "That weird skank doesn't know how to listen, and Katie needs to get her little cousin in line and tell her to stay away from the freak."

"Look, Hallee...I think you are super nice," Ember started. "But I don't think you know who you are dealing with. Not everyone here likes me. You might want to get the lay of the land before you decide to burn bridges. You know what I mean?"

Hallee looked over her shoulder. Maddison glared lasers at them. "Oh."

Kale reached over and rubbed Maddison's leg. "Hey, babe, you want to hang out after school?"

Maddison shifted her focus back to Kale. "Yeah, babe."

The two engaged in more tongue wrestling. Ember wondered who had the gum now.

"Yeah, I see what you mean," Hallee said. "I heard how they spoke about...others at lunch." Her aura turned an embarrassed shade of pink. "They are not the crowd I want to hang out with. You and Erick are much more my speed." She pushed her glasses back up her nose.

Right as the bell rang, Erick rushed in and dropped into the desk next to Hallee's. "Hey." He smiled at Hallee and nodded to her.

Ember studied their auras. There could be a little love connection happening between them, she thought.

Everyone continued talking as no teacher had come into the room yet.

"So, anyone know why we don't have a teacher?" Hallee asked.

"Well, it's Ms. Grable," Ember explained. "She's sort of old. Maybe she forgot she was teaching this hour?"

Erick chuckled and adjusted his wire-rimmed glasses. "Yeah—that is a definite possibility."

The classroom door creaked open as the teacher shuffled in, her gray beehive hair leading the charge while the rest of her body lagged behind. People rumored that Ms. Grable had been a student at the school when it was built sixty years ago. She was *old*.

"Morning, class." She shuffled to the board and wrote her name in script.

Ember heard Maddison and Kale laughing.

"Oh my God, she doesn't even know what time of day it is."

"This is going to be an easy A."

"She probably doesn't even know how to turn on these computers."

With all honesty, Ember had to wonder about that as well. Erick and Hallee both looked at each other and cracked smiles.

"Morning, Ms. Grable." Erick cheerfully played along.

She turned, squinting into her thick-lensed glasses. "Welcome back, Eagles. I'm sure you all had a lovely break." She settled into her chair and leaned forward, reading the sheet in front of her. "Ah, okay, Business Communication." Her gray head bobbed. "Let's do roll, shall we?"

It was a small class, maybe fifteen students. She looked up and eyed Erick. "You, young man, why don't you check off this list and see who's here and who's tardy?"

"Yes, ma'am." Erick stood, took the paper, and called roll.

"Oh my God, he's such a Boy Scout." Maddison crooned.

Ember immediately felt flames of anger stoke her insides. She clutched the top of her desk.

Three names in, Erick paused as he looked back at Ms. Grable. She was snoring. He grinned and read the final names, slipping the sheet back on her desk. The class, recognizing their good fortune, quietly chatted amongst themselves.

Erick whispered, "This class could be cake."

"I may regret saying this later...but I was sort of hoping to learn something," Hallee whispered back.

A paper ball nailed the back of Ember's head. She turned around to see who threw it. The obvious culprits were lip locked. Ember opened the paper. It was a terrible drawing of a stick figure girl with blood pooling at her feet with the words *"UR DED RED"* written at the bottom. Ember looked back to see Maddison mime slitting her throat.

Hallee glanced over. "What does it say?"

She crumpled the paper up. "Old news. The option to not be my friend still stands."

Another paper ball came sailing, only this time Ember was ready. *Virtus vincit.* She thought of her dad, turned, and caught the paper wad.

"Nice catch, Red." Kale whispered. When Maddison punched his arm, he looked at her. "What? It was pretty impressive."

Maddison glowered.

"Leave me alone," Ember hissed and squeezed the paper missile into a tighter ball.

"Are you going to open it?" Hallee asked.

"No." Ember fought the burning desire to go back there and slap the smirk off Maddison's perfect little face.

She turned in her seat as another paper bomb sailed her way, only this time, she was ready for it and saw who threw it—Maddison. Ember caught it.

"She's good." Kale nodded approvingly.

"Shut up, Kale."

Ember watched as Maddison tore another sheet of notebook paper. Like a runner on the blocks, waiting for the starting gun to fire, her muscles contracted. She turned just as Maddison tossed the paper bomb. But before it soared over half the classroom, Ember rapidly fired the two she had caught and snagged the one Maddison had just launched. Both of Ember's missiles struck their target: Maddison's face.

Kale's laughter spewed forth like an exploding soda bottle.

"You bitch!" Maddison screeched. "You are so

going to die!"

Ms. Grable snorted awake.

Shit. Shit. Shit. Ember slumped back down into her seat. She shook her head and stared at her desk. Hallee and Erick both looked at her with rounded eyes. *Why did I just do that?*

Day one of sophomore year, not only was Ember on the Queen's radar, but she was now her number one target.

Great. Just great.

****

The phrase "saved by the bell" never felt more true as the school day ended. Ember was quick to escape the classroom. She had stood up to Wayne Wilson and Maddison Miller, but it was time to go home before anything crazier happened. She stepped into the hall and took a deep breath as students filed out of their classrooms. Her anger had boiled before, but it never spilled over like it just did in Ms. Grable's class.

What is happening to me? Could it be the summer training with Dad? The new pills?

"Hey. You good?" Erick tugged on her arm. Hallee slipped in beside them.

"Yeah. I'm fine." She reassured him. "Just ready to go home."

"I'm not sure I get the dynamics…but, just so you know, I'm on Team Ember." Hallee pushed up her purple frames. The sincerity of her aura melted the tension inside Ember.

"Thanks, guys." Ember's ears picked up on Maddison's whiney drawl, getting nearer. She jerked her head toward the doors leading outside. "I need to go catch the bus."

"Oh, hey…I got my license last week. I could drive you." Erick nervously rubbed the back of his head. "You, too, Hallee."

"Okay, yeah, that would be cool." Hallee smiled.

"Ember?" he asked.

Ember spied Maddison coming her way. "Yeah, that would be great. Let's go." Hoping to escape the Queen, she merged into the crowd of teenagers.

But just outside the doors, a logjam of students blocked the sidewalk. Ember peered over the crowd and zeroed in on the problem—Brittany Oliver. If Maddison Miller was the coolest girl at Wilson County High, then Brittany was the most popular girl in the sophomore class.

"Totally!" Brittany's smile revealed a row of perfect white teeth as she handed out flyers. "Just like last year, I'm inviting everyone. Back-to-school pool party at my place! Pass them back."

Erick pressed next to Ember. "What's going on?"

Hallee stood on her tiptoes. "I can't see."

"It's Brittany," Ember answered. "She's handing out invitations to her annual back-to-school party."

Erick pushed the nose piece up on his gold wire-rimmed glasses. "Come on, follow me. My car is parked over by the faculty lot."

"Wait. Don't you guys want to get an invitation?" Hallee asked.

Ember glanced back at Maddison and Kale as they exited the doors. "No. Come on." She laced her hand into Hallee's, pulling her away from the crowd. Hallee reached out, snagging an invitation with her free hand.

"There she is." Erick smiled with pride at the white car with multiple dents and opened the passenger door.

"Welcome aboard, ladies."

"Shotgun." Hallee laughed and slipped into the seat before Ember could snag it.

Instead, Ember settled into the backseat as Erick started the engine.

"I don't get it. Why don't you guys like that girl?" Hallee twisted in her seat as Erick pulled away. "She seems nice."

"It's not so much that we don't like Brittany," Erick explained. "She's actually pretty cool for one of the popular girls. It's just that while she says 'everyone is invited,' she's not talking about us. Right, warrior princess?"

"Warrior princess?" Hallee asked dubiously. "How many nicknames do you have?"

A small smile slashed Ember's face. "Don't ask." She looked out the window as tall corn and dark green soybean fields came into view. "You should go to the party, Hallee. I'm sure Katie will insist on it."

"Then I would be stuck with the cheer squad." Hallee folded her hands together. "Would you two go with me, please?" Her desperate aura eroded Ember's conviction.

Erick looked up at Ember in the rearview mirror. "I'll go, if Ember goes."

She sighed, watching Erick's aura shift as he glanced at Hallee. He liked her. And, honestly, she liked Hallee, too. She definitely had Bestie potential. She wanted to say yes. But she'd never gone to a party before—much less a pool party. She thought of her list for sophomore year as Hallee held up the invitation.

"Please," Hallee pleaded. Her brows arched over her purple frames.

"Okay…but if things get weird, we leave. No questions asked. Deal?"

"Deal." Erick and Hallee responded at the same time, causing them both to laugh.

Hallee gently punched his arm. "Jinx! You owe me a drink."

Erick's aura lit up as he blushed.

Ember smiled. "Can you drop me off first, warrior prince?"

"Sure."

Welcome to Wilson County High, Hallee, Ember thought, as she leaned back in her seat, listening to the two in the front seat banter about Hallee's first day.

And welcome to my freak show.

Her lips jerked up to one side. The first day of sophomore year wasn't everything she had hoped for, but she knew her dad would be proud. *Virtus vincit.*

Chapter Five

The remainder of the first week back at school was surprisingly uneventful. Other than the usual glares, whispers and giggles, Maddison didn't retaliate further. Wayne stared daggers at Ember every chance he got, but he didn't engage, either. While on edge, she enjoyed hanging out with Erick and Hallee. The first week of sophomore year was practically a one-eighty from freshman year, further boosting Ember's confidence to attend Brittany Oliver's pool party on Saturday. But had Ember really thought about it, she would have known that all good things must end…and that end was coming on like a tsunami.

****

Ember's dad angled the old truck at the top of the Olivers' horseshoe drive. His knuckles showed white against the black steering wheel. She noticed his aura was a mix of orange, green, and ocean-blue tinged with its usual golden hue. He was nervous. She was, too.

"Hey, it'll be okay," she reassured him—and lied her ass off. "Yesterday was like the easiest day ever at school. No one said a word. Plus, my friends will be there, Erick and that new girl, Hallee. Everything is going to be fine. No. It's going to be great. *Virtus vincit*, right?"

He lit a cigarette and blew smoke out the open

window. She noticed a slight tremor in his hand.

She leaned over and touched his arm. "You okay?"

He coughed and cleared his throat. Looking over, he gave her a reassuring grin. His aura turned a warm red trimmed in gold. "Shit. Everything's fine. I'm just an emotional old fart." He reached over and took her hand. "You're growing up, Ember Eve." He shook his head. "It's hard to believe. Here we are. I thought—well, hell, I thought we had more time."

"What do you mean?" Ember gave his rough, calloused hand a squeeze.

"Aw, nothing. I got a call...another job...running down to New Orleans after I leave here." Smoke drifted as he exhaled. "Be back in a couple of weeks or so."

A car pulled up behind the truck. Billy Joe looked up in the rearview mirror and gave a half wave to the driver behind them. "Don't you worry about me. Go on and have fun with your friends. Erick gonna give you a lift home?"

"Yes. Thanks, Daddy." She gave his hand one last reassuring squeeze and grabbed her purse and bag, jumping down out of the truck.

"Ember."

She turned. "Yeah?"

"Ah, hell, nothin'. You go have a good time."

"I'll try, Dad. Love you. Have fun in New Orleans for me." She saluted and walked up the path to the Oliver's front door.

Billy Joe's rusted blue truck didn't move till Ember was safely inside.

****

Her heart raced as she pulled the glass storm door open. The Oliver's home was a brick ranch, like

Ember's; but on the inside, it was much nicer. The hardwoods gleamed. Not an ounce of dust sat on the blue ceramic lamps with their crisp white linen shades. Wood and glass coffee tables flanked two Victorian armchairs and a plush floral sofa. They even had one of those new TVs that didn't need an antenna. It stood looming large across the room like a bouncer. Her nerves catapulted and her feet froze as the storm door slammed closed behind her.

"Come on in," a warm female voice called. "Party is in the back."

Ember stood there, taking in the smells of a clean home and food cooking in the kitchen. No leftover cigarette smoke hovered over the room like fog. No dirty glasses littered the end tables. Dust didn't drift like snow on their TV. This house was spotless.

A plump blonde woman with rosy cheeks and an aura of bright lemon-yellow stood in the archway to the kitchen. "Well? What are you waiting for?"

"I wasn't sure if I was supposed to take my shoes off?"

The woman's blonde brows arched. "What?"

Ember pointed to the floor. "It's so clean."

"Oh, don't be silly. Come on in." She motioned for her to follow. "You must be Ember."

"How did you know?"

"I'm Mrs. Oliver, by the way." She looked Ember over. "Brittany has told me all about her friends."

Ember's cheeks warmed at the potential stories Brittany had told her mom.

"I was just mixing up some dip to take outside. You hungry, sweetheart?"

"No, thanks."

41

"Well, all right then." She turned to the counter to stir a creamy white mixture in a bowl. "You can throw your things in Brittany's room down the hall. She's out back setting up."

The intoxicating smells of food baking in the oven, the cookies and pastries spread out on the table, laced with the aroma of a clean house were overwhelming, but in a good way. Ember's stomach rumbled.

Mrs. Oliver turned. "Sure you're not hungry?"

"No, ma'am, I'm fine."

Ember pivoted on her heel and went down the hall. Family portraits lined the walls in gold gilded frames. They looked like the perfect All-American family. Brittany, the youngest of the family, was in pigtails. The father stood proudly with his arm around Brittany's mother. Graduation photos of her three older brothers surrounded the larger family photo. In an instant, Ember imagined Brittany's future: high school graduation, off to the University of Kentucky, sorority life, and then marrying her college sweetheart. Brittany's world was so different. So perfect.

Everything Ember longed for: a normal existence.

She closed the bathroom door and checked herself over in the mirror. Her long auburn hair was pulled up in a ponytail. Her golden, almond-colored eyes looked sorrowful. She took in a deep breath. *You can do this, Ember. Courage conquers.* She reached down into her purse and pulled out a pill bottle. Fingers trembling, she popped one into her mouth and swallowed.

She sifted through the swimsuits in her bag that Birdie Mae got for her. Slim pickings, she'd said—end of summer and all. So, she got what was still left on the clearance rack at the store. Her mom found two choices in her size: a very conservative, color-blocked red and black one piece that she imagined a mother of two would wear to the community pool. The other choice was a slinky string bikini in white. Ember stared at the two choices in her hand.

While both screamed "look at me," one whispered, "Hi...I'm a lame prude." The other literally yelled swimsuit-magazine-cover-wannabe teen edition.

She stared at the tiny two piece, thinking of her list taped to her bedroom mirror and went for it. *Go big or go home.*

Once dressed, she borrowed a towel from Mrs. Oliver and headed outside.

Brittany was talking to a couple of boys under a pool umbrella. Ember straightened her back and attempted to walk over with confidence.

"Oh, my God! There you are!" Brittany beamed. Ember stumbled and turned to see if Brittany was talking to someone else.

"This is my friend, Ember. Ember, this is Anthony. He and I met over the summer, modeling at the mall." Sprayed tan and bleached blond, Anthony smiled.

"Hey." She waved shyly.

"And you already know, Derek, my older brother." Ember swallowed. Derek was two years older and was still the hottest guy she had ever seen—and was one of the nicest, too. He was a rare package.

Derek smiled. His dimples sunk into his cheeks, revealing his perfect white teeth. But Ember's gaze hung on his lips as they puckered into a whistle. Brows arching, he laughed, "Don't tell me this is Bloody Ember?"

The nickname coming from Derek's lips stung. She

felt her face burn.

"Oh my gosh, you idiot." Brittany elbowed Derek in the chest. "Shut up."

"Ouch, what? Ember got hot. It's true." His denim eyes flashed with teasing humor, but his aura danced with heated, red lust.

Beneath his scrutiny, flames licked her skin and sweat flowed in a beaded stream down her back.

Brittany steered her away by the shoulders. "Ignore that moron. C'mon, let's lay out over here."

Several white plastic chaise lounge chairs were lined up along the side of the pool. Ember had never swam in an actual pool. The water looked so clear and refreshing.

"Here, you take this one." Brittany directed her.

Ember hesitated. "Why are you being so nice to me?"

Brittany flipped her hair over her shoulder. "Duh, you're my guest. Well, technically, the first guest, Anthony, just got here, but he's going to help DJ. He got here early to go through my cassettes and work on a playlist."

"Okay." Ember bit her bottom lip. "So, it's cool that I came?"

"Yes—totally. Maddison said that Katie said you might show up with Hallee. It's totally cool." Brittany wore the concentration of an animal in heat as she stared at Anthony across the pool deck. "Isn't he like the cutest ever?"

Ember glanced back over at the boys. "Yeah." Anthony was cute, but her eyes lingered on Derek. He smiled, catching her stare. She shifted her eyes away, wishing she could crawl into a hole.

"Should I play the music?" Anthony yelled over.

"Sure!" Brittany yelled back. "Thank you, *A*!"

"Of course, *B*!"

"Aren't we the cutest?" she crowed in that irritating girly squeal. "It's like our pet names…*A*, *B*."

"Yeah, that is so cute. So, are you two official?"

"I mean, like he hasn't asked, but there is still the winter modeling season coming up. So, I'm sure it will happen."

Ember chanced a look over Brittany's shoulder. Derek winked. Ember was certain waves of heat were now emanating off her body. "Can we get in the pool?"

"Oh, yeah, sure." Brittany hopped up. "But I don't want to get my hair wet."

Ember slid down into the cool water. It felt amazing. Brittany stood by the stairs, not wanting to get below waist deep. Over the music, her ears picked up the sound of a vehicle pulling up the drive. "I think you have another guest coming."

"I do?" Brittany twisted around. Playing the perfect host, she climbed up the pool steps. "I'll go check."

Ember watched her towel off and walk with runway model form into the house. Everything about Brittany was perfect. From her looks to her attitude, she was everything Ember was not.

The slam of vehicle doors closing caused Ember to stiffen. *Great. Time to shine.*

"Cannon ball!" Derek ran and jumped into the deep end. Waves of pool water splashed against Ember's chest. His long, lean body carved effortlessly through the water like a shark zeroing in on its prey. A sandy blond head broke through the water, revealing Derek's brilliant white smile, forcing his twin dimples to come out of hiding. "Did I get you wet?"

Positive her face was on fire, Ember couldn't focus. He invaded her personal space in the best-worst way. "Oh." She looked around, searching for words. "No, I mean, I was already wet." She gently splashed the water to prove her point.

"Yeah, cool." He studied her face. "Wow, like, you look so different from last year. Sorry about earlier."

Ember tried to look anywhere but his eyes; dark as the ocean, she could get lost in them. She instead looked down and flushed, entranced by his sculpted abs. Ember quickly looked up, hoping he hadn't caught her, but Derek was still staring at her. He licked his perfect pillow lips as red singed his aura. Her nostrils flared as she inhaled his delicious chocolatey scent.

"So, are you dating anyone?"

The absurdity of the question made her laugh out loud. "What? No." She had to get away from him. She moved back toward the wall as his eyes raked over her.

"That's good to know."

"Ember! Hey!"

She snapped out of her trance to see Hallee and Erick walking up. She was so mesmerized by Derek that she hadn't sensed her friends were close.

"See you later, Em."

Derek turned and swam a lap to the deep end. Anthony tossed him the pool basketball. He didn't miss a shot, Ember noted, and he called her Em.

"Hey." Ember tore her eyes away from Derek's perfection and waved to Hallee and Erick.

Her friends stripped down to their suits. Ember smiled inwardly as they both chuckled when they realized they were both wearing purple. Hallee blushed and took off her glasses, setting them on the lounger. Erick's eyes rounded behind his own as he saw Hallee for the first time without them. Their auras reflected their mutual embarrassment and attraction as they slipped into the water.

Hallee shivered. "Oh, my gosh! It's so cold."

Erick's voice cracked. "Yeah, it's a little chilly."

"Cute suit," Hallee said.

"Thanks. You guys didn't tell me we were supposed to wear purple."

"It was a total accident." Hallee blushed.

"Well, purple is the color of royalty." Erick pointed out, straightening his pale, boney-white shoulders.

"Whatever." Ember splashed water his way.

"Hey! Watch the glasses!" Erick splashed back, getting Hallee by accident.

"Take that, Prince Erick!" Hallee sent a bigger splash his way.

Mayhem ensued as they fell into a splash war. Ember was lost in the moment, having fun, until the high-pitched voices of the cheer squad cut through her joy. She froze, then looked up to find Maddison and her minions hovering poolside.

Maddison stood there, leering like a lion, observing its prey. "Glad you could make it." Her perfect, red-stained smile didn't reach her eyes.

As Maddison's aura soared in an aggressive, orange-red, she spun on one heel and sauntered off in her red string bikini.

An icy chill ran down Ember's spine.

That's not good.

Chapter Six

Ember looked away as the cheer squad gathered up their chairs into a semi-circle to get the best angle for the sun. "Well, this should be fun."

"Maybe they won't get in the pool," Erick offered.

Hallee scoffed, "We can't stay in here forever."

"It's me she's after," Ember said.

Erick shrugged. "I don't get what her problem is."

"I do. I retaliated. No one has ever gone against Maddison Miller." Ember sighed. "Till now."

A shadow fell over the trio. Derek leaned over the edge of the pool. "Hey, Em, you want a drink?"

Her heart galloped. His scent reminded her of freshly baked chocolate chip cookies, sweet and decadent. His blue trunks hung low on his hips, causing her gaze to drift lower.

"Do you?" he asked again.

Crap. Crap. Crap. Ember realized she was staring. "Yeah, that would be great." She swirled back around to face her friends as Derek walked away.

"Oh, my gosh." Hallee cooed. "He's cute."

"Oh no. Not girl talk." Erick rolled his eyes and made his way to the pool ladder. "I think I'll go get some sunscreen from Mrs. Oliver."

"That's Brittany's older brother, Derek." She spoke low, looking over Hallee's shoulder as Derek walked over to the beverage table. Beads of water glistened along his tan Adonis backside.

"So, what's the story?" Hallee pushed.

"Nothing really. This is the first time I've seen him since he graduated."

"So, you guys never dated?"

That question elicited a heavy eye roll from Ember. "What do you think?"

"Well, I think he's into you."

"I'm into him," she confessed, causing Hallee to giggle."Unh oh, he's coming back," Ember hissed. "What should I do?"

Hallee pushed her toward the stairs, laughing. "Go get him, Tiger."

She gave her new friend the side-eye as she climbed out of the pool.

He handed her a fizzing cup. "Hey, hope this is okay?"

"Yeah, sure, it's great. Thanks." She took a tiny sip.

He grinned as his eyes slid over her body, taking her in from head to toe. "That bikini looks good on you."

Ember thought her heart might stop. "Thanks." She took another tiny sip. "You look great, too, I mean."

She stiffened. She heard her name being spoken. She glanced in the direction it came from. *Maddison.*

Shit. Shit. Shit. She's coming this way.

Ember unconsciously squeezed her cup. Soda spilled over her hand, down her arm, and onto the concrete like a brown waterfall.

Why can't I be normal and not have the strength of five men in my fingertips?

"I'm such an idiot," she mumbled at the mess.

Derek looked down. "Shoot. Let me get you some napkins." He turned right into Maddison's perky chest.

"Derek." She wrapped her arms around him. "I've missed you." She latched onto his arm and steered him away. "Have you been working out?" Maddison looked over her shoulder and stared daggers at her.

Derek turned and mouthed "sorry" as Maddison commanded his attention back to her while Ember looked down at her sticky mess.

Hallee rushed over with napkins. "So, fill me in. What did he say?" She dabbed at the spilled soda spots.

Ember took some napkins and soaked up the brown puddle on the ground. "Not much." She looked over at his bronze back and Maddison's perfectly manicured red claws, still clutching his arm. Maddison's aura was a deep, determined red.

"There. I think we got it all." Hallee looked over to see what Ember was staring at. "Well, what did you talk about?"

She shrugged. "He said he liked my bikini."

"Okay, that's good. No, that's great!" Hallee pushed her glasses back up her nose and waggled her brows. "He was totally checking you out."

"But then Maddison immediately came over and stole him away," she said, nearly spilling more soda as she squeezed her cup.

Hallee gently pulled the warped cup from Ember's grasp. "Let's go throw this away and get you a new one."

"Okay, yeah, thanks."

The pair walked over to the beverage table. Erick stood nearby in animated conversation with Mrs.

Oliver. Groups of more students arrived high-fiving and jumping into the pool.

"So, now, suddenly, Maddison is into Derek?" Hallee poured fresh drinks. "I thought she was with Kale."

"Not exactly. Remember when I told you that her and Kale had been on-again off-again since middle school?"

"Yeah?"

"Well, when she was off Kale, she was on Derek."

"Oh." Hallee shook her head. "That's not good."

"Yep. Basically, I just moved up on Maddison's hit list." Ember took a long swallow. Her hands trembled. "I need to go get something in my bag."

"Cool, I'll go with you." Hallee sat her drink down. "I really need to pee anyways."

****

Ember's stomach flopped. Maddison Miller, the Queen of Wilson County High, was gunning for her. It was obvious. It was only a matter of time before the Queen made her move.

She reached into her bag and pulled out the bottle of pills. Technically, she wasn't supposed to take them on an empty stomach or doses this close together, but she needed reinforcements—badly. If her comfort zone was being at home in her treehouse in the woods, this was completely the opposite. She was just treading water, barely afloat, untethered in a foreign ocean without a single soul or island in sight. And there were sharks, a blonde one named Maddison Miller.

She eyed the pink princess telephone on Brittany's nightstand. It would be so easy to call the beauty shop. Birdie Mae would give her hell for messing up her schedule, but she'd come and rescue her. Ember could be home in her nest…safe…in a matter of minutes.

"Hey, you coming?" Hallee poked her head in the doorway.

Ember studied Hallee's aura. In one short week, Hallee had proven to be a better friend than all her classmates combined—excluding Erick, of course. Hallee hadn't bailed at the first rumor she heard about her, nor had she buckled under the peer pressure from her cousin, Katie.

No, Ember decided instantly, she would stick it out at the pool party, a little longer, for Hallee and Erick.

"Yeah, sure." She followed Hallee down the hall to the kitchen where Erick was helping Mrs. Oliver carry more snacks outside.

"Hey." His crooked grin lit up his face when he saw Hallee and Ember. "Want some chips?" He held up a supersized bag of ruffled style chips. "I'm taking these outside."

They followed him out to the snack table. More people had arrived. Brittany hovered around Anthony and her clique of friends under the umbrella table. It was obvious that Brittany was on proverbial cloud nine as Ember took in her bright yellow aura.

She scooped up some dip and chips onto her paper plate. Butterflies took flight in her stomach. She smelled him before she saw him. Ember turned, locking eyes with Derek as he walked over. "Hey, sorry about that." He scrubbed the back of his hair. "You good?"

"Yeah. I'm totally fine. Thanks."

Awkward silence filled the void between them. His dark blue eyes seemed to pierce her protective walls. *Why does he smell so good? Is it the pills?* Ember blushed. The male teenage scent was usually too pungent and always a turnoff.

"So, you and Maddison…" She tilted her head towards the cheer squad.

His dimples winked at her. "Nah, that's old news."

"Cool." She struggled to meet his eyes, but looking down at his toned stomach only made her blush more. "So, you still doing baseball?"

"Yep." He stole a chip off Ember's plate. She tracked it like it was the last bite on Earth as his lips parted. She watched as he licked the salt off his lips, then fingers. "Playing at Murray State."

"Cool."

What is wrong with you? There are more words in the dictionary than "cool."

She scanned the pool area, trying to come up with something better to say when Wayne Wilson sauntered by, goons in tow. Ember shrank.

Derek noticed. "What's up?" He touched her arm. She audibly gasped as tingles rippled across her arm from his fingertips. "You okay?" She looked at his aura as it shifted to a dark indigo matching his eyes. A cute boy had never looked at her like that—ever.

"Yeah…it's nothing…just…" His smell, those eyes…she had trouble stringing words together.

He searched her face. "Is something wrong?"

Wayne Wilson walked up and put his arm around Ember's shoulders. Grinning like the Cheshire Cat, he tilted his head to Derek. "What up, D-Money! Hope you like sloppy seconds."

Wayne's goon squad slapped palms as they walked away. "Eww, burn! Don't you mean bloody seconds?"

She saw fire—lakes of it. She clenched her fists.

Her nails bit into her palms.

Derek's flawless forehead creased. "I'm confused. Did you two date?"

"No. Wayne's just making it up."

Derek scrubbed the back of his hair. His aura clouded with concern. "That's not how it sounded."

"I can explain."

"Attention, everyone!" Brittany stood on the diving board. Anthony lowered the volume on the music.

"In keeping with the tradition of last year's Back-to-School party, we will kick things off with a swimsuit competition and…"

The boys hooted and whistled, while Ember's stomach plummeted to her feet.

Chapter Seven

Ember's attention darted among her classmates whose auras flared with emotions ranging from excitement to lust. Her confidence sank like a toy into the deep end of the pool.

Brittany smiled and waved her tan arms to hush the crowd. "And…after that we will have the boys compete for best dive!"

"How about cannon balls?" one guy yelled.

Brittany laughed. "Cannon balls count too, right, girls?"

Most of the girls cheered in response.

"Okay, five minutes, girls!" she added.

A collective crescendo of high-pitched chatter rose, causing Ember to wince. The cheer squad fell into action, fixing ponytails and slathering on tanning oil *en masse.*

Ember turned to finish her conversation with Derek, but he had already walked away.

Hallee rushed over, panic on her face. "A swimsuit contest? No one told me we would be parading around being objectified."

"Me neither, Hallee. Me neither."

Ember searched the pool deck for Derek. The crowd had grown. It seemed like the entire school was there now.

Her focus darted to the cheer squad when Maddison squealed, "Oh my God, Kale! You're finally here!" Maddison rushed to him, wrapped herself around him and kissed Kale's cheek as if she wasn't flirting with Derek Oliver just moments before.

"Well, that should solve your problem with Derek, right?" Hallee mused.

"Nope. Wayne, your favorite cousin, basically told Derek that we had been hooking up."

"Oh no." Hallee's eyes rounded. "Why would he do that?"

"Oh yes, and don't ask." She shook her head. "Then Derek left before I could explain."

"Oh, man, I'm sorry, Ember. I'm sure you can find him and talk to him later. And I can tell him it's not true, too, if you want?"

"No, it's okay. Nothing would have happened between us, anyway."

Erick sauntered over; a huge grin split his face. "So, which of the two of you wants my vote?"

Hallee crossed her arms. "I'm not doing it."

Erick looked disappointed. "Ember?"

Virtus vincit. As she glanced over at the cheer squad, her attention snagged once again on Maddison. "I'll do it."

"Yes." Erick's fist pumped the air. "Let's go, warrior princess!"

Hallee rolled her eyes. "Calm down, mister warrior prince."

"What? She's the underdog. You always have to cheer for the underdog."

Ember raised an eyebrow. "Are you saying this warrior princess is the underdog?"

"I mean, no…I just…" Erick fumbled his words.

She cracked a smile. "I'm just teasing."

He wiped his brow. "Whew! I was afraid for a second that I had actually pissed off my warrior princess."

Ember chewed her bottom lip and spread her arms wide as Bon Jovi blared in the background. "Kidding aside—Hallee, how do I look? Seriously?"

Hallee scanned her up and down. "Let's see…take down your ponytail. Okay…smile, give me a pageant wave."

She shook out her long auburn hair.

"Yeah, like that." Hallee smiled, then scowled. "For the record, I don't support the objectification of women. That being said…I like your odds."

"Okay, everyone line-up!" Brittany yelled across the pool area.

Ember saw Derek under the umbrella with Anthony. Her heart fluttered, then crashed to the pit of her stomach. "I can't do this." She shook her head. "I changed my mind."

Erick pushed her forward. "Oh, no you don't."

"Ember, get over here," Brittany called and waved her over.

"Go," Hallee pressed. "If I'm only watching, I need a horse in this race."

Be brave. She swallowed her fears like bitter cough medicine and marched forward.

"You're really going to let a whore participate?" Wayne Wilson yelled loud enough for everyone to hear. His buddies laughed.

Brittany scowled. "Shut up, Wayne."

"She's such a slut," he hissed.

Brittany guided her into the line. "Ignore him."

Heat rose to her cheeks. Sounds muffled as the extra pills she'd taken earlier kicked in. She steadied herself when her limbs became liquid. The smell of hormones and suntan oil permeated the air. She glanced around at her classmates. Wayne's wicked, lusty glare caught her eye. He blew her a kiss. The chips and dip that she had consumed earlier rose to the back of her throat.

"I'll be your emcee, guys!" Derek announced, standing on the diving board. "And Anthony, over there, will be our DJ!"

The guys booed and chanted. "We want the girls!"

"Okay, okay. Calm down," Derek said. "Ladies, one at a time, you will walk down the side of the pool. Step up here and walk down the diving board, spin, and walk back down and over to the other side of the pool and stand in line."

Derek flipped off the diving board and swam to the other end. The waves of nausea intensified in Ember's belly as he stepped out of the pool and shook off the water, looking straight at her. "Ready ladies?" His crooked grin made a single dimple pop. When the girls cheered, he yelled, "Okay, hit it, DJ!"

Warrant's "Cherry Pie" blared from the boom box as Anthony pressed play.

"Perfect!" Derek said. "First up, we have the reigning Homecoming Queen, Maddison Miller!"

Ember fought down her gag reflex as Maddison sauntered along the pool.

Kale blew a piercing loud whistle and yelled, "That's my girl, right there!" She blew him an air kiss as she effortlessly twirled on the diving board.

One by one, the girls paraded around the pool to the whoops and hollers of the guys. Jamie nearly lost her balance on the diving board, but quickly recovered—unfortunately, Ember thought. Numbers dwindled and she was both grateful and stressed that Derek hadn't called her up yet. Then, it was just her and Brittany left. Derek winked at Ember and called out his sister's name. Brittany smiled and walked smoothly to the music, displaying her summer of mall fashion show modeling experience.

"And we saved the best for last, boys! Ember O'Neill!" He put his fingers to his mouth and whistled. "Give it up for the hottest girl here!"

Flames of embarrassment engulfed her cheeks. All eyes were on her. She instinctively scanned the crowd for Wayne. She couldn't see him, but she could smell him. He was there.

The music suddenly switched. She looked over to see Wayne's goons scuffling with Anthony at the boom box, causing her to pause.

The boys on the pool deck yelled, "Keep going!"

Kale's aura was a passionate red. He whistled and cheered the loudest, causing Maddison to stare at him in disbelief. Ember walked briskly and almost tripped but caught herself as she stepped onto the diving board. It was her first time being on one, and she wasn't expecting it to bounce and sway as she walked to the end. Fortunately, she remembered Jaimie's near fall and steadied herself.

She looked over at Derek. His dimples stood at attention as he yelled and cheered. Ember blushed and smiled. She could only imagine what her aura looked like. Pink? *No, it must be yellow.* Ember was happy.

59

She'd done it.

Despite her nerves almost getting the better of her, she didn't run away. She was brave, and she did it. Dad would be so proud, she thought as she carefully turned on the diving board. Hallee yelled and cheered with Erick. Her heart felt as if it would burst. It was nice to have real friends.

Just as she was ready to dismount, she froze as Hallee's aura visibly muddled.

What's wrong?

Hallee's eyes widened. She screamed, "No!" She was looking at something behind Ember.

Wayne Wilson stood at the edge of the pool holding a super soaker water gun. With an aura coated in black, he leered like a hyena salivating at its dinner. This was the retaliation she'd expected from the first day.

Wayne raised the gun. The world slowed. The crowd went silent. The music was a buzzing hum in her ears. Evil, unlike any she'd ever seen, coated his aura like a black cloud. He wanted payback, and he wanted it to be public. Gazes locked, he sneered and pulled the trigger, spraying her from head to toe with crimson paint. A bloody rain of red streaked down her white bikini. Stunned, she just stood there.

Wayne leaned closer and shot the remaining ounces across her chest. "Slut." The word cut through the muffled music like the crack of lightning.

And like the thunder that follows, Maddison's laugh carried across the pool as she slowly clapped for Wayne's red rain of terror.

Shock and horror etched the faces of her friends. Ember couldn't move. She couldn't think. She couldn't

breathe. She just wanted to disappear.
    Ember wanted to die.
    So, she fell into the pool.

Chapter Eight

Indistinct sounds echoed under the water as she sank to the bottom of the pool. A red cloud of diluted paint blossomed above her. She was numb. Her feelings—her body—everything. She fought the desire to breathe. She didn't want to come up for air. She just wanted to sink to the bottom and die.

Closing her eyes, she begged for the darkness to overtake her. Images of last year flashed through her mind…her bloodied new pair of acid-washed jeans and the circle of students laughing at her as she fainted in the hall. Wayne's leering sneer as he coated her in the red paint.

Her chest burned. She forced herself to stay down. This is it, she thought. *This is how it ends.* No matter how hard she tried, she could never shake being the freak, the weirdo…Bloody Ember. Her pulse slowed. Her lungs filled with water. She drifted to the concrete floor of the pool. Splayed out like a starfish, her body came to rest just above the pool drain.

****

Though her eyes were closed, she saw a dim light coming into focus. So, I am dead now, she thought. *This must be the so-called light everyone sees when they die.*

The most beautiful man she had ever laid eyes on

materialized in front of her. His aura glowed a blinding, shimmery gold. "Daughter of Eden," he said.

"Are you God?" she asked.

The beautiful man chortled, a deep and resonating sound. "No, Ember, I'm not God, but I work for him. I am the Archangel Michael."

"Oh." She studied his perfect face, eyes, and hair. He wore blue jeans and a white tee. He could have been a model for a Calvin Klein ad. "I thought angels had wings and wore white robes."

His laugh erupted even louder. "Humans have the best imaginations."

She blushed. "I guess this means I'm dead, huh?"

He shook his head. "On the contrary, Ember, your true life is just beginning."

"What do you mean?" Flashes of the red pool, Wayne Wilson's leer and Maddison Miller's sneers ran through her mind. "I can't go back there."

Archangel Michael's eyes crinkled at their corners as his smile gentled. "It is difficult being different, I know—down there on Earth."

"You have no idea."

His smile faded. "There isn't much time, Ember."

"I don't understand."

The white nothingness flashed to a dark world of smog. It was difficult to breathe. The ground was covered in a dark gray soot. She felt heartache and pain. She looked over at Michael. "What happened? Where are we?"

His Adonis-like face turned sorrowful. "There is a war coming, Ember. The question is which side will you be on?"

"What do you mean? What war?"

Ember looked around. The scenery changed. She saw a city scape coming into view. A tall silver spear of a building overshadowed all. She heard babies crying and women wailing. In a flash, she was in a gray, stainless-steel operating room. A woman was giving birth. Sweat streamed down her cheeks as she screamed with one last push.

"A boy," the doctor announced, then handed the baby to the nurse. "Test his blood."

"Please, can't I just hold him?" the mother begged.

"No." The doctor curtly answered. "Clean her up and get her back down to breeding." The woman's wails echoed in the operating room.

Ember grabbed Michael's arm. Electricity pulsed at her touch. "We have to stop them."

"I cannot control the future." Michael shrugged as the room morphed again into white nothingness. "Only you can stop this, Ember."

A chill raced down her spine. She hugged herself. "How?"

"Take the oath." A golden sword appeared in his hand. The blade vibrated with energy.

"What oath?"

The archangel suddenly looked around as if confused. "We are not alone." His face turned stony. He took Ember's wrist. Electricity sizzled up her arm. "*Eligere,*" he commanded as his image dissipated.

"What? Wait! Come back!"

The white world around her morphed again. Ember was standing in a garden now, alone. The air was pure. The grass was green. A stone wall enclosed the beautiful sanctuary while roses perfumed the air. Across the garden, a stone bench rested beneath the arms of a swaying willow. It was paradise.

"Is this Heaven?" She looked around. It was like her own secret garden—like the book.

"Do you like it?" A warm, rich voice floated across to her. The voice was young and male—and not the Archangel Michael's.

She turned, looking for the source as fear slid into her heart. "Who…who are you?"

"Don't be afraid." The male's warm tone cooed and soothed. "I sensed you. I sensed your fear. I sensed your panic." The voice enveloped her, sending warm shivers over her skin. The distinct scent of chocolate and whiskey tickled her nose.

"Show yourself. Who are you?" she asked again.

The voice sounded amused. "I could ask you the same."

Annoyed, she demanded, "What is your name?"

"Call me…" The voice paused. "Call me Adam."

"That's not your real name."

"Maybe. Maybe not. What is yours?"

"What happened to Michael?"

"Michael? Who is this, Michael? Is that your boyfriend?"

She spun around, searching for the source of the voice. "I don't have a boyfriend."

"Really? You are so beautiful. Why do you lie to me, angel?"

She squeezed her fists. "Who are you?"

"Ah, that's better," the voice crooned. "You are very sexy when you're mad."

"Get out of my head. Whoever you are…just stop."

"Sorry, angel." Adam chuckled. "Don't you like the garden? Isn't this from one of your favorite childhood books?"

"How do you know that?" Fear crept into her voice. "Am I in Hell?

"Hell?" The voice of Adam chuckled. "No, my angel. You are definitely not in Hell."

"Stop calling me that."

"What should I call you then?"

She tried to think of something clever.

"Ah, yes, I will call you Eve. I like it. You—me—in the garden, a little cliche, but it will work."

"Get out of my head!"

"Why? I can help you, Eve." He let the name drawl.

"I just want to go home." She shivered despite the perfectly warm breeze gently swirling around her.

"Do you really, Eve?" Another pause. "I don't think you like your current existence that much."

Ember wanted to run—anywhere—to just get away from this Adam voice. "Leave me alone."

"You can't hide from me, Eve."

"Michael!"

"Who is this, Michael, Eve?" Another pause. "You are blocking him from me. Why?"

She looked around and imagined being in her bedroom. "I don't know what you're talking about. I want to leave this garden, Adam."

"Ah, this is...quaint." Adam remarked as the garden morphed into her tiny bedroom.

"Leave me alone." Ember repeated as she sank into her bed and pulled the covers up to her chin.

"Eve, let me help you." His voice sounded strained. Pained almost.

Ember looked over as her pill bottles materialized

on her nightstand. Her life was a nightmare. Wayne's sneer as he sprayed red paint over her rushed back. The overwhelming desire to end it all came down hard. She picked up the pill bottle, cracked it open, and tossed back pills one at a time.

"Who is this Wayne, Eve?"

She took another pill.

"You don't need those." She ignored him. "That won't work."

Adam's voice sounded bored. She shrugged and kept taking more. "First of all, we are in a dreamscape."

Ember paused. Shoulders slumping. Somehow, she knew he was right. She didn't want to trust him, but somehow, she knew taking more pills would not end this mirage or her miserable life.

"Secondly, we can't die."

She looked up. "What do you mean?"

"I mean. We. Can't. Die."

The garden morphed into a white blankness again.

"I'll be seeing you again, Eve." Adam's voice grew faint as her eyes cracked open.

****

"Clear!" The paramedic's face was etched in panic as he held the paddles above Ember's chest.

A machine toned. *Beep. Beep. Beep.*

"Wait! Stop. We've got a pulse." The female paramedic crouched over her and shined a light into her eyes. "Can you hear me, honey?"

Ember coughed. Water leaked out of her mouth. She tried to sit up. A tangle of wires snaked from her body. A siren blared, a radio chirped and crackled in the background. She was alive—in an ambulance—and strapped to a gurney.

"Ember, it's going to be okay." The female EMT looked over at her partner, her eyes watering. "It's a miracle, Don. She's alive."

Don, the paramedic, looked just as shocked and surprised but instantly sprang into action checking her vitals.

"What happened?" She struggled to get the words out. Her throat was raw.

"Do you know your name?" the female asked.

"Ember Eve O'Neill." She was able croak out the few syllables. "Hurts to talk."

Don's forehead wrinkled. "Probably raw from the chlorinated pool water."

Don crossed himself, then kissed the crucifix hanging from his neck. "Let's keep monitoring her vitals and let the ER docs do the rest."

Chapter Nine

From her hospital bed, Ember glanced out the window that overlooked the parking lot. The setting sun reflected off the glass and metal of nearby structures like a shimmery lake. It had been several hours since her epic dive into Brittany Oliver's pool. Wires roped from her body and connected to the beeping monitors that flanked both sides of her bed. Distant sounds of medical chatter and the hospital paging system filtered through the walls to her hyper-sensitive ears. The thin hospital gown and sheets were less than insulating against the cool sanitized air of the hospital room. She just wanted to go home, get in her nest, and snuggle with Bear.

I just want to forget this day ever happened.

Rubber soles squeaked against the linoleum tile and stopped at the doorway. Ember heard the shuffle of papers as the door eased open. A tall man, graying at his temples, flipped through a chart as he walked in. He looked up and smiled when he saw her sitting up.

"Oh good. You are awake." His bushy brows rose above his thick, black-rimmed glasses. Ember noticed his aura was a sincere, concerned indigo blue.

"Hi." She tried to wave, but tubes and wires prevented much movement.

"I'm Dr. Peters. I am the attending physician on

call." He looked down at his clipboard. "And you are Ember, correct?" He sauntered over and looked at the digital readings on the monitors.

"Yes."

He wrote some information on her chart. "How are you feeling?"

"Fine."

He studied her like a scientist analyzing a new species. "No headache? Nausea? Anything feel off or unusual?"

"Nope. I feel okay." She smiled, hoping it would reassure him. "Can I go home?"

Dr. Peters' aura changed. "I'd like to keep you overnight, monitor your vitals, just to be sure everything is working as it should. You are one lucky young lady." He tapped his pen on the chart. "I'll get your mother. She's eager to see you."

Before he could do much more than that, the door flew open. A bloodshot Birdie Mae stormed in with a flustered-looking nurse on her heels. "I'm so sorry, Dr. Peters. I tried to stop her," the young nurse said.

Birdie Mae rushed to Ember's bed, leaned over the side rail and hugged her. Her tanned arms squeezed so tight around Ember's torso that she could hear her mother's racing heartbeat. "Ember Eve O'Neill!" she chided, cupping Ember's cheeks in her palms. "You are never allowed to go swimming ever again. You hear me?"

"Sorry, Birdie Mae."

She looked away. She had never seen her mother's aura so distressed—and was surprised to see that she cared so much. With a laugh, Birdie Mae swooped in for another suffocating hug. "Oh, sweet baby girl, I ain't mad. Just worried sick is all." Her mascara had run, creating two dark patches beneath her eyes. "They are saying you were dead for over twenty minutes!"

"What?" Ember figured it was just Birdie Mae exaggerating again.

"Yep." Birdie Mae's head bobbed like one of those dolls. "The Oliver boy pulled you out of the pool, did CPR till the ambulance arrived. Then the paramedics took over. Said you came back to life on the way to the hospital."

She felt the weight of her mother's words, and her mind reeled.

I died. So, how did I see those visions? Were Michael or Adam even real? Did the pills cause me to hallucinate? Or was the vision just something my brain created to cope with the stress.

****

As darkness fell over the hospital room, Birdie Mae left, promising to reach her dad and let him know what happened. Ember wondered what her friends were thinking. Did Wayne regret what he did? Was Maddison gloating? And what about Derek? He was the one who dove in to save her.

A soft knock on her door interrupted her thoughts. "Come in…"

Eyes rimmed in red, Hallee peeked her head through the crack. "Is it okay if I come in?"

Ember smiled. "Hey, yeah…come in."

Hallee shuffled in. Her eyes rounded as she took in all the wires and tubes, and Ember saw fear licking at her friend's aura. "It's okay. It's just monitors. I'm okay, really."

"You sure?"

She motioned to the lone visitor's chair. "Yeah, come over and have a seat."

"Thanks."

"My mom just left."

"Yeah, she's the one that said I could visit. Erick is out there, too. And Mr. and Mrs. Oliver, Brittany, and Derek."

"Oh, wow."

"Yeah, everyone wants to see you, but the doctor said only one at a time—if you are up for it?"

She rolled her eyes and put on a smiling face. "I'm totally fine."

"I'm so sorry." Hallee's eyes watered. "I didn't see Wayne till it was too late."

She steeled herself against the memory flooding back. "I'm fine. Really."

Hallee looked up, hopeful. "Seriously?"

"Yes, I mean…" She looked around, realizing that she felt great. "I feel better than ever, actually."

Relief seemed to roll off Hallee's shoulders. "I'm so glad." She looked around the room and shivered.

"Don't like hospitals?"

Hallee gave a soft laugh. "You could say that."

She tried to lighten the mood. "So, I was told that Derek is the one who saved me?"

"Oh my God, Ember! Like, if it was so, like, not real. And you, you know, weren't dying—it would have been, like, so romantic."

"Wish I could have seen it."

"It was totally like on TV. And, Ember, he totally wouldn't stop CPR till the paramedics got there. He was pretty amazing."

"Guess I owe him big time, huh?"

"He's super worried about you, too, Ember." She looked down at the floor. "We all are."

Another knock came from the door. Erick poked his head in. "It's the warrior prince's turn."

"Seriously, Erick?" Hallee pleaded. "It hasn't even been five minutes."

"I've been friends with her longer."

"That's not fair. I just moved here."

Grinning, Erick opened the door wider. "Not my problem."

Hallee turned back to her. "Do you think you will go home tomorrow?"

"Yeah."

"Okay, cool. I'll call you tomorrow, then."

"Sure." Ember's heart warmed. She'd never had a girlfriend call just to talk.

Erick pointed at the chair. "May I?"

Ember cracked a smile despite herself. "Sure."

"What? Something on my face?"

"No, I mean, just your hair. It reminded me of a doll."

"Wow. Just wow. My best friend, who I'm man enough to admit I cried over, comes back to life after drowning, and the first thing she does is make fun of me?" He put his hand to his heart. "That hurts. Right here."

Ember laughed so hard her jaw hurt. "Sorry. It was the first thing that came to mind."

"Okay, ouch. You can stop now." Erick laughed with her. His aura glowing a brilliant yellow.

"Sorry."

"It's fine. Just glad you are alive." His aura shifted to a sincere purple. "That was insane, Ember."

"Yeah. I know."

"So, what happened? They said you must have slipped on the paint and hit your head on the diving board. I guess I blinked cuz I just saw you just sort of go down and then not come back up."

"Erick, I…"

She saw his concern, but she couldn't tell him the truth. She couldn't tell him she wanted to die—that she had wanted to drown. That she wanted it all to end. She couldn't tell him, or anyone—ever. No one could ever understand what it was like being her—the broken freak that was Ember O'Neill.

So, she lied. "I don't know. I think I was just in shock and lost my balance."

"Yeah, sure." He punched his fist into his palm. His aura charged an angry red. "Monday, I'm going to put Wayne Wilson in his place."

"Erick, no. Wayne is a complete douche, but he's not worth getting expelled over."

"He can't get away with it, Ember. It's not right."

"Hey, I'm the victim here. Wayne has always been a bully, especially toward me. I should have seen it coming." She shook her head, remembering the look on his face—his black aura. She cringed at the thought of seeing him at school on Monday. "He's a sicko but I can handle him. Honestly, it's Maddison I'm more afraid of."

"He should pay, Ember. At the very least, make like a public apology." Erick stood as another knock tapped lightly on the door. "That's probably Derek." Erick nodded. "I'm sorry I didn't dive in like he did, Ember. I just sort of froze." He shoved his hands in his pockets. "I'm sorry."

"Erick, don't be sorry. It was an accident. I'm fine. I'm a warrior princess, remember?"

He cracked a tiny grin. "By the power of Skull Mountain!" He held up his mock sword.

She laughed.

"Hey, can I come in?" Derek's denim blue eyes zeroed in on her. The world disappeared except for those two beautiful orbs.

"Yeah, sure." Erick backed away from her bedside. "See you Monday." He nodded and shuffled out the door.

"Hey."

"Hey." Derek's tall frame was covered in a navy-blue Murray State hoodie and khaki shorts. Ember watched as he slowly walked over to her, analyzing the wires and tubes.

"They are just monitoring me." She felt the need to explain. "I'm fine. Same old Ember."

"Yeah." He ruffled his sandy blond hair on the back of his head. "I just wanted to see you with my own eyes." His aura was a deep purple as he reached down to take her hand. "I thought you weren't going to make it."

Ember felt like her whole body was on fire. His hands were calloused, but gentle, as tingles trailed up her arm as he stroked her fingers. "Thanks for saving me." She didn't know what else to say.

His dimples danced as he smiled. "I'm not sure I actually saved you. I think the professionals deserve the thanks." He squeezed her hand. "I just did what I could till they got there."

"Yeah, well, either way...thanks for trying."

"Em, are you okay?" He pulled his hand away and

scrubbed at his hair again—a habit she found totally endearing. "I saw everything."

"Yeah. I swear that I'm fine."

"It's just I remember what the kids used to call you last year. And then Wayne…" He clenched his fists. "Do you want me to kick his ass?"

"What? No. I'm fine, Derek. I swear."

"You sure?"

"Yep, totally. What he did wasn't cool, but the whole thing was an accident." She shrugged trying to sell it. "I'm fine. Totally fine."

He let out a soft sigh. "I have to go back to Murray tomorrow."

Another knock sounded at the door. Brittany popped her head in. "Hello? I've been waiting."

"Sorry." Derek turned to leave. Ember didn't want to see him go.

He gave a half wave as Brittany barged in. "My turn," she said and gave him a little push out the door. "Oh my God! Ember, you like totally scared all of us! And there are, like, so many reporters and news crews outside!" She took in all the wires with stride and plopped down in the chair. "I totally thought you could swim." She pouted. "Thank God, Derek was there. It was insane." Brittany quickly shifted gears. "Well, so you might want to turn on your TV."

"Why?"

"Because I'm totally going to be on the ten o'clock news!" She tossed her blonde hair over her shoulder. "They wanted an eyewitness to tell what happened. And, of course, who better than, *moi*?" She smiled, showing her perfectly straight white teeth.

Ember shrank into the bed. Everyone in the tri-state

was going to know about Wayne's prank. She hadn't even thought about Monday at school. She could handle Wayne, but what about the looks? The stares. The gossip. It would be worse than last year. There would be no escaping her freak status.

Sophomore year was toast.

"Hey...don't be worried." Brittany paused her diatribe. "You're like going to be so famous!"

Ember cringed. "But not in a good way."

"What are you talking about?" Brittany's blue eyes flashed. "We're going to be on the news! Well, I am, but I'm sure they will want to interview you someday, you know, when you're ready. They are calling it a miracle. But, anyway, it's like the news! Eek! I need to call my agent." She stood up. "This is like so big time!"

Ember winced as the door slammed shut behind Brittany.

Why doesn't this feel like a miracle?

Chapter Ten

Despite being exhausted, Ember did not want to sleep. As she watched the black hands of the wall clock creep around the face, her eyes grew heavy. She immediately snapped her eyes open. Without her pills, she was too scared to sleep. Plus, what if she dreamed of that Archangel again or heard the voice of the guy who called himself Adam? She didn't want to risk it.

Her gaze drifted to the TV; her freshman year school picture filled the screen: stringy hair, pale face dotted with a sea of pimples, and dark circles looming beneath her sad eyes. The headline read, *Up Next: Local teen drowns and lives to talk about it.*

"No. No. No." She pulled the sheet up over her head. "This can't be happening."

She pulled the sheet back down as the news came back on. From outside the hospital, a reporter offered an update. *"Yes, Tom,"* she said into a microphone, a look of dead seriousness on her model-beautiful face, *"the medical people are calling it a miracle. Local teen, Ember O'Neill, was attending a back-to-school pool party at a friend's house when the unthinkable happened."*

The screen then shifted to prerecorded footage with what looked like an earlier interview with Brittany. The brunette reporter tilted the mic toward Brittany. *"Can you tell us what happened to your friend, Ember?"*

Brittany smiled and looked into the camera. *"So, like we were just having fun, and someone sprayed a water gun on Ember. She slipped, hit her head, and like, fell into the pool."*

"Someone sprayed water on Ember?"

Brittany rolled her eyes. *"Well, it was really red paint. Anyway, my brother dove in and pulled her out of the pool. He did CPR till the ambulance got there."*

"So, your brother...what's his name?"

"Derek."

"Your brother, Derek, may have been the real hero of this story."

Brittany's brows furrowed. *"Yeah, sure, maybe. But she was like totally dead. Not breathing. No pulse."*

She shivered.

The screen went back to the same reporter live outside the hospital. *"Sources tell us Ember O'Neill was considered dead for twenty-one minutes, Tom."*

"Wow, that is a miracle." The gray-haired broadcaster shifted his glasses. *"How is Ember doing now?"*

"We hope to have an interview with her tomorrow. Sources say she is doing great, and they expect her to be released to go home within the next twenty-four hours. Authorities have confirmed that no charges have been filed against the parents who hosted the back-to-school party." The reporter tapped her earpiece. *"I'm sorry, Tom, I am getting an update. Producers are saying..."* She paused, eyes growing wide.

"Tom, sources are saying that the classmate that sprayed paint on Ember is now missing. Police are searching for Wayne Wilson, a fellow Wilson County

student and resident."

The news anchor nodded to the camera. *"Thank you, Bonnie. We look forward to hearing more as the story unfolds."* He shuffled papers on his desk. *"Up next…will the University of Kentucky Wildcats' new recruit live up to expectations?"*

After the broadcast cut to commercial, Ember clicked off the TV. Her fingers twitched. She missed having her pencils and sketch pad nearby. With a moan, she pulled the sheet back over her head. Between the constant orchestra of beeping and humming from the medical equipment and the sporadic cries and wails of patients, it was going to be a long night.

The sounds reminded her of the woman in her vision crying for her child. Ember bit her lip, willing the sun to rise sooner. She just wanted to go home.

Chapter Eleven

The next morning, with no warning, Ember's hospital door swung open and Birdie Mae rushed in. She quickly shut it and leaned her back against the door. Her frosted blonde hair was pulled back with a blue bandana. Her white T-shirt rose and fell with each ragged breath. A denim skirt and a worn pair of sneakers completed the unconventional ensemble.

Birdie Mae rifled inside the fringed leather bag she was never without and swore. "Shit." When she looked up, her aura was all over the place. She pulled out a pack of cigarettes. "Can I smoke in here?"

Ember sat up. "What's wrong, Birdie Mae?"

"Shit. Shit. Shit. I left my lighter in the car." She slipped the cigarette back into the pack, walked over and plopped into the chair. "Hell of a night. I didn't get any sleep. Phone kept ringing. I finally took it off the hook. Then I get here and there's every Tom, Dick, and Harry out there, wanting to interview me." She stuck one finger into her mouth and began to chew on her nail. "A total cluster fuck."

As if remembering why she was in the hospital room, she glanced at her only daughter. "Guess you didn't get much sleep either, huh?"

"Nope." Ember shrugged. "Without my pills, it's really hard."

"Damn. Sorry, baby girl. Mrs. Oliver gave me your stuff last night." She tilted her head at the fringed bag. "I figured you could just put back on the clothes you wore over there."

Her fingers clutched the sheet. "Can I have my purse? My pills should still be in there."

Birdie Mae got up and handed her the bag.

Fingers trembling, Ember rifled through the bag to get to her purse and find her medication. It had been hours, and she craved the numbness the pills brought. She popped open the bottle and took two. Within minutes, the sounds of the hospital grew fuzzy. Her muscles relaxed.

Her mom pulled out a brush and started detangling Ember's hair. She tensed at the gesture. She imagined Birdie Mae was just doing what came naturally, fixing hair. Plus, it kept her hands busy since she couldn't smoke. But all it did was make her feel awkward.

A gentle knock interrupted the uncomfortable silence. Dr. Peters stepped into the room. He looked the same as yesterday—white lab coat over the same shirt and glasses. She wondered if he ever went home.

"Doc! Come in." Birdie Mae smiled and put away the hairbrush. "Tell us some good news. Can Ember go home now?"

Dr. Peters adjusted his glasses and nodded. "Mrs. O'Neill. Ember." He flipped open her chart and checked off some items with his ball-point pen. He walked over and looked at the monitors and shook his head.

"What? What is it?" Birdie Mae's forehead lined in concern. "Is it bad?"

He looked up and smiled. "Oh, nothing is wrong.

Sorry. Everything is perfectly normal."

Birdie Mae's aura shifted to yellow. "Great. Does that mean she can go home?"

"I just have a few questions." He glanced down at the chart. "Your blood work came back unusually high for…" His brows rose over his glasses as he looked down at Ember. "…Temazepam and Fluoxetine."

Birdie Mae asked, "What the hell is that?"

"Are you taking any anti-depressants or sleep aids?"

Ember's eyes darted to her purse.

Birdie Mae blurted, "Oh! Yeah, our family doctor prescribed her some pills for her synesthesia."

"Synesthesia?" Dr. Peters flipped through the chart. "There is nothing here about that condition in the records." He looked up. "When were you diagnosed?"

"When I was little," she answered.

His brows scrunched. "And they gave you pills for this condition?"

"Yeah…she said she was seeing colors," Birdie Mae shared. "They was prescribed the drugs so she could focus better."

The doctor's aura shifted to a curious, lime green. "Tell me what you see, Ember."

She hesitated. For years, she had stuffed that part of herself way down inside. She never talked to anyone about it—occasionally Erick, but that was it. She was broken. A freak. When her symptoms flared last year, the doctor just raised her dosages and added the sleeping pills.

"Tell him, Ember," Birdie Mae pressed.

"I…see colors around people," she admitted.

"Okay." The doctor wrote on the chart. "Anything

else that you see or feel?"

She wasn't about to share anything more. "No."

"So, you don't associate a color with a number? Or day of the week?"

"No."

He scribbled down more notes. "Do you see colors when you listen to music?"

"No."

"Doc, I don't understand." Birdie Mae's foot started tapping the floor. "Why all the questions?"

"Well, I'm not convinced Ember has synesthesia."

"What?" Birdie Mae and Ember asked at the same time.

Birdie Mae stood. "Then what's wrong with her?"

"Describe what you see, Ember," Dr. Peters said. "When you look at people."

She cringed, ready for the freaked-out look she was about to get from the doctor. She twisted the sheets in her hands. "I just see like this rainbow-ish cloud around people."

"And do the colors stay the same? Or do they change?"

She nodded. "They shift with how the person is feeling…what they are thinking."

He looked up and then wrote more on the chart. "Auras." He mumbled to himself. "And how do you know what they are feeling?"

"I don't know. But I can guess what they are probably feeling."

The doctor studied her, rubbing his jaw. "And what colors do you see around me?"

She peered at the green and aqua-blue haze that surrounded him. "Your colors are wavering between blue and flickers of green."

"And how do you interpret that?"

She blushed. "I think you are sincere, concerned, and maybe curious."

The briefest of smiles creased his lips as he jotted a few more notes. "Hmm. Interesting."

Birdie Mae crossed her arms, tapped one foot and demanded, "So, what is it, Doc?"

"I'm not sure." He shook his head. "I'd rather not speculate." He scribbled on a prescription pad and ripped off the sheet, handing it to Birdie Mae. "That is a referral for a colleague of mine at the university. He's a psychologist whose special interests lay with the…what you might term the unexplained." He paused and looked over to Ember. "You don't have synesthesia."

She shook her head. "I don't understand."

"A psychologist?" Birdie Mae crumpled the paper in her fist and tossed it to the basket. "You think she's crazy, huh, Doc? Well, I got news for you—she ain't."

"Now, Ms. Oliver, I didn't say that. I said she doesn't have synesthesia. I am not an expert in that field, but it's obvious her brain works differently than ours." He glanced over at the trash. "I recommend you make that appointment with Dr. Kayce. He can help your daughter, Ms. Oliver."

He looked back at Ember. "No more pills." He tapped the chart. "Temazepam, that sleep aid, is highly addictive. And the fluoxetine, for the anxiety, can cause you to have suicidal thoughts. It's a dangerous combo." He gave Birdie Mae a pointed look. "Your daughter is a walking miracle. Take care of her."

"I know how to take care of my own daughter, Doc. Can I take her home now?" Birdie Mae's aura had turned flaming red, meaning she was pissed.

"Yes, Ms. Oliver." He turned on his heel to leave.

"Dr. Peters?" Ember asked.

"Yes, Ember?"

"Do you know why I lived?" She looked down. "I mean, why didn't I die and stay dead?" Adam's voice echoed in her mind. *"We can't die."*

The doctor turned back to her. His aura turned a curious, greenish-yellow. "We're not sure. There have been cases, rare, but it has happened before. The medical field has dubbed it the Lazarus Effect or Lazarus Syndrome." His brows scrunched together. "In each case, the subjects were pronounced dead and minutes later they reanimated, no explanation. Thus, the term, Lazarus."

"Okay." Ember wasn't sure what she was hoping to hear, but his answer left her feeling unsatisfied. The doctor turned towards the door.

"Thank you." She whispered as the door closed behind him.

"Oh, thank God!" Birdie Mae erupted. "The nerve of that man. I'm so over his know-it-all ass." She pulled out a piece of gum. "You want one?"

"Nope, I'm okay."

Birdie Mae chomped furiously, pacing the room and muttering under her breath about damn hospitals, money, and doctors not knowing shit.

A knock on the door paused her in her tracks. A young nurse peeked her head in. "Sounds like someone is getting to go home today. Ready to get unhooked from all that wiring?"

She nodded. "Yes, please."

Birdie Mae's eyes darted between the two. "I'm

just going to go out and see if I can bum a light off someone. I'll be right back. Okay, baby girl?"

"Yeah, sure."

Birdie Mae left as the nurse got to work unhooking cords and wires. After a moment, she said, "Okay, Miracle Girl, you are all set." She stepped away from the bed and left the room.

Ember grabbed her bag of clothes, glancing at the wadded-up paper Birdie Mae had tossed to the wastebasket but missed. The crumpled paper lay on the tile floor, beckoning her to pick it up. She walked over and smoothed out the blank prescription pad paper to read the doctor's note. "Dr. Edgar Evans Kayce, Professor, Department of Psychology, Murray State University." She carefully folded it up and placed it in her purse.

Her skin danced with goosebumps as she changed into her old clothes. She sat down on the edge of the bed, waiting for Birdie Mae to return. Her mind tumbled through everything Dr. Peters said. The pills weighed heavy in her purse. *I'm not addicted. I need them.* Anyone would have suicidal thoughts if they were a freak like me, she told herself.

Birdie Mae burst through the door looking ten times happier and calmer. "Ready to go?"

Ember was more than ready to get home. "Yeah."

Chapter Twelve

Leaving the hospital was a nightmare. News crews and reporters hovered outside the entrance, waiting to pounce. "Ember! Ember! Can we get a quote?"

"How does it feel to die?"

"Did you see a white light?"

"Why did Wayne Wilson spray paint on you? Was he your boyfriend? Did you break up?"

"Ember! Do you believe in God?"

"Ember! Ember!"

Despite her petite size, Birdie Mae plowed through the mob like a linebacker, carving a path straight to her old, rust bucket of a car. She slammed the door shut, twisted the key in the ignition, and waited for the engine to rumble to life. "You all right, baby girl?"

"Yeah." She looked out the window as photographers ran alongside with cameras flashing.

Birdie Mae let the tires squeal as she sped out of the hospital parking lot. "Damn reporters."

"Did you ever reach Dad to tell him what happened?"

"Nah, just left a message at that number he left."

Disappointed, she watched the scenery blur by as Birdie Mae flew down the gravel covered back roads. She drummed her fingers on the steering wheel. "I'm sure he'll call once he gets word."

Ember shrugged. "Sure."

She was grateful to be out of the city and that concrete hospital building. The familiar scents of ripening corn fields and pig farms wafted through the air vents. As much as she savored going back home, the doctor's words kept tumbling back to the forefront of her mind.

"You don't have synesthesia."

****

The crunch of gravel never sounded so good as when Birdie Mae pulled up to the house. Lola, her dad's old hound, greeted them with howls as they exited the car. Seconds later, Bear, Ember's oversized dog, bounded down the drive, tongue hanging crooked and loose. Ember met him halfway and fell to the ground letting the fluffy fool drown her in kisses.

Birdie Mae watched the pair. "Shit, I don't ever get that kind of greeting. You'd think you'd been gone forever."

The dog's aura was a brilliant yellow. He was so happy to see her. "I missed you so much, Bear-Bear."

From inside the house, the phone rang. "Goddamn it," Birdie Mae growled and stormed inside.

"Come on, Bear. Let's go get in our nest."

By the time Ember and the dog were inside, Birdie Mae had already lit another cigarette and was pouring her signature rum and soda drink. Since it was only ten a.m., Ember cleared her throat.

"What?" Birdie Mae turned. "It's not like I got to go to work today or something." She took a sip. "My schedule is clear today because of you." Her shoulders relaxed like a deflating balloon after one swallow. Birdie Mae tilted her head to the marigold yellow phone on the wall. The handset hung dangled from the base. "I unhooked the line, too."

"What about Dad? How will he reach us?"

Birdie Mae blew gray smoke and placed her tarot cards onto the table. "Ain't I good enough? He knows you're fine. I said so in the message." She slumped down at the kitchen table, cigarette teetering on the edge of her pink painted lips. "Go on and get some rest." She shuffled the cards and placed them one by one onto the table. Her aura shifted darker and more muddled with each card.

Inside her room with the door shut tight, Ember threw her purse and bag down on the floor while Bear leaped onto the bed. "Scoot over, you big oaf." Ember nudged his big body hard enough to make Bear roll over and expose his belly for a scratch.

"You are so spoiled." She happily reached down and gave him some love. "Bear...if I don't have synesthesia, then what is wrong with me?" She looked over at the pill bottles lined up on her nightstand like an army of soldiers waiting for battle. "Bear..." She whispered. "Something very weird happened when I, you know, died."

Bear whined as she got up and pulled her sketch pad and pencils out of her closet. "Don't worry, I'm coming back."

She blew a fine collection of dust off the sketch pad and flipped it open. She settled back into her bed. She had been so busy, she hadn't once felt the urge to draw till now.

"It's been a while." She glanced at her previous sketches as she turned to a blank page.

Her mind raced as she tried to mimic the look of

the Archangel Michael in her vision. His penetrating eyes and Greek God-like build. Her hand flew trying to recreate the memory. She shook her head. It wasn't nearly as accurate as her mind remembered, but it would have to do.

She studied his face. "Who are you?" Then, "Bear, do we have a Bible anywhere around here?" His ears twitched at the sound of his name.

She flipped the page and began drawing Michael's sword. She tried to capture the size and weight of the luminescent weapon. There were etchings on it. Symbols, maybe. She couldn't remember exactly.

"What does it mean, Bear?"

She turned to another blank sheet and sketched the dark skyline she'd seen with Michael. She added the dark tower that loomed over the other city buildings. Where is this? She wondered. Hurriedly, she drew the cold stainless-steel room with the woman lying on the table giving birth. She looked up and told Bear, "If anyone saw these, they would for sure think I was crazy."

She concentrated on the scene in her memory. *Anything else? Anything that hinted about where they were?*

She sketched the doctor and nurse, the bloody baby, and then her mind saw it—the clue she needed. The name tag of the nurse. Her name wasn't clear. But she could make out a logo on the tag. Ember furiously sketched. It was an apple sliced open, exposing the core and seeds. The stem seemed to be alive. *No, wait.* Ember erased the stem and started over. There was a snake intertwined with the stem. The image sent an icy chill down her spine. At once, the image felt wholly wrong and familiar, but she couldn't place why.

Frustrated, she drew the garden in which she first heard Adam's voice. It was the easiest to remember. She drew the weeping willow and bench first. The lush rose gardens were next. She could almost smell it. Then she drew herself. Her long auburn hair reached just to her elbows. She smiled and added a warrior princess sword. Erick would love this sketch, she thought.

Ember tried to imagine what Adam looked like. Was he tall or short? She sketched his frame but became frustrated and erased him altogether.

She looked back at the sketch of Michael. *What was it he said?* The word came echoing back to her. *Eligere.* Ember wrote the word beneath his drawing, unsure of the spelling.

"*Ell—eh—jer—ee.*" She sounded the word out. "It sounds like a foreign language, huh, Bear?"

Her buddy snored in response.

"How did my brain come up with this? None of it makes sense. But if these visions were induced by the pills when I died, then in theory I will not have any more." She shrugged and looked at the pills. "Unless, you know, I die again."

Then she remembered Adam's last words to her, *"We can't die."*

That's crazy. What happened to me was a fluke. Everyone dies eventually. None of it was real.

Flipping through her sketches, Ember grew tired. The weight of the last thirty-six hours finally took their toll. Before she could think about taking a sleeping aid, she was fast asleep with Bear by her side.

Chapter Thirteen

The night felt heavy.

The clouds hung low, as if attempting to shelter the stars from what was about to happen below. Despite being late fall, the humidity was thick in the air over the Kentucky river bottoms. Ember immediately regretted wearing her volleyball jacket. She stripped the red and black monogrammed satin off her body and tossed it in the bushes as she ran. Making the team had been unreal. But now, none of that mattered.

Occasionally, the moon peeked through, revealing itself and casting light on her path. Her heart raced and her arms stung as the bare branches of the overgrown trees and bushes slapped her bare skin. Autumn's cast-off brown leaves crushed and crackled under her worn, knock-off sneakers. Her hair slipped free from her red and black matching elastic band and whipped behind her like the tangled mane and tail of a wild stallion. She was searching for someone. Desperately searching. Time was running out.

Deep in the woods, she stopped. She didn't want to, but only for a split second, she had to.

In seconds, she had run faster and farther than humanly possible. She had to pause to get her bearings. She controlled her breathing and listened. In the distance behind her, she heard someone yelling out her name. "Ember, wait!"

Following her scent, Bear crashed through the woods behind her. She sensed his feelings. He was anxious. He wanted her to slow down so that he could lead and protect her, but Ember's instincts were strong. Her body had changed. She was no longer the weak little girl who hid in her room, living her life through books. She was no longer lonely, desperate to end the relentless teasing from her classmates.

She had changed. She was something else.

And she embraced it.

Nostrils flaring, Ember smelled the air. Dank and musty. The faint hint of something dead lingered in the air. The river wasn't far. The path leading to the cabins in the river bottoms was seldom used.

Locals just pulled their trucks up to the boat ramp and parked alongside the river while they fished. Back in the 70s, some rich farmer built those cabins thinking he'd make an extra buck or two off the tourists who came to Kentucky. The cabins were now dilapidated, and the stuff of teenage pranks and lustful rendezvous.

The area was familiar to her. She had spent last summer camping with her dad down in those bottoms, not too far from the cabins. She recalled the mosquitos were brutal.

Ember narrowed her focus. Dark shadows cast by the bony tall trees surrounded her. Her dad had taught her how to track prey. She looked for fresh disturbance on the trail: broken limbs or bent branches. Sweat beaded along her brow and snaked down her spine. Her unnaturally powerful senses pierced through the decay and the last remnants of dying honeysuckle as mists formed throughout the river bottoms. Bear charged through the woods behind her, trying to catch up.

A ribbon of sensation slithered over her body. She wasn't alone. She sensed the presence of someone. Ember inhaled. There were two humans ahead. She could almost taste their salty sweat and smell the fear permeating from one and the overconfidence oozing from the other. Both scents were familiar. The pounding of their hearts pulled her forward like a magnet. A boat engine suddenly roared to life in the distance.

Damn it.

Ember sped forward.

She reached a clearing on the bank of the Mississippi. The water gently lapped against the sandy, rocky shore belying the dangerous current that flowed beneath its inky surface. There, almost in the center of the river, she spied the boat.

A girl's screams carried over the water. A shadowy figure tossed something large overboard, then sped away.

It's the girl.

Ember didn't hesitate. She ran into the cool water and dove. The swift current pulled her away from her target. Using her superhuman strength, she battled the current and surged forward. She fought her instincts to breathe and used her enhanced vision to find the sinking body.

The river pulled against her as she dove deeper and deeper and farther out. Debris and broken branches obscured the murky waters. She focused her senses. The girl's heartbeat faded. Gargled sounds blended with the rushing water as the girl's lungs filled with fluid.

"No!"

****

Ember's body jerked forward in her bed as she screamed. Heart pounding and drenched in sweat, she made a visual search of the room. The bedside digital clock shared the time. It was a little after ten. She'd slept for almost twelve hours.

A chill danced along her spine. Her sketchbook had fallen to the floor and flipped open to one of her drawings from last year. The sketch of the river bottoms and the drowning girl came from the same nightmare she'd suffered from for more than a year.

It was the same ending. No matter how fast she ran, no matter how fast she swam, Ember was always too late. The girl drowned.

During her entire childhood, she'd experienced bad dreams. None felt as real as this.

Chapter Fourteen

Ember reached over and popped open the pill bottle. She took one and swallowed it dry. Bear lay at her side, paws twitching. Deliberately, she slowed her breathing and stroked the dog's fur. Soon, the pill numbed her. But not the memory of the nightmare.

Her eyes flew open when the slow squeal of the carport storm door alerted both her and Bear that someone else was awake. The dog snapped to attention; a low growl rumbled from his chest. Outside, Lola howled, her chain clanging. She tensed and listened intently. The booze usually knocked her mom out by that hour. The ten o'clock news anchor droned on in the living room.

Her heartbeat quickened. Birdie Mae would never switch off her music videos. Only her father watched the news. Ignoring the upset dogs, Ember jumped up. *Dad came home.*

Still in the clothes she'd worn for the last two days, she quickly slipped on her shoes. With Bear at her heels, she was careful not to wake Birdie Mae who was indeed passed out on the couch. The cigarette in the ashtray had long burned out, and her glass was empty.

But the cloying smoke hung in the air rising from a lit cigarette resting in an ashtray next to Billy Joe's recliner. *He's home.* All the lights were off, only the glare from the TV lit the path to the kitchen. Ember ran to the door. Bear's growl grew deeper.

"Shhhh, Bear. You're going to wake Birdie Mae. It's okay. It's just Dad."

Even as she said it, she sensed that something was off, too. Lola yelped and fell silent. Her hand froze on the door. Something was wrong. Instinctively, her nostrils flared, inhaling the humid, late August night air. Her father's familiar scent lingered, but there was something else.

A foul odor. The hairs on her arms stood on end. It smelled rotten, like something dead.

Just as she pressed on the door to open it, her heart nearly stopped as her father slid in front of the screen. His blue eyes wide, with a finger to his lips, he motioned for her to stay. Her blood pounded in her veins, watching his aura flare both love and fear. She slowly nodded. Bear let out a soft whine at Billy Joe's retreating frame. Her hand drifted to calm the dog as her gaze snagged on the gleaming blade in her father's hand. He inched away from the door towards the backyard. Ember couldn't breathe. Whatever was out there, it had her father scared.

Over the past summer, her dad had trained her in hand to hand combat, small arms, tracking and hunting. She felt well prepared to fight. But in her mind, it was always Wayne or some imaginary bully she was fighting. At the pool party, though, her fighting instincts had failed her. She'd done nothing to cause it but when faced with her attacker, she had literally done nothing. She had just wanted to die.

Now, real danger lurked. Something bad. She felt it in her bones. It felt evil. She would not fail her father.

She would not let him face it alone. Ember pressed against the door slowly, trying to stifle the squeaky hinge. Sounds of a struggle pierced the night. She eased the door open, just far enough for her body to slip through, but Bear barreled past her legs and out the door. Barking viciously, the dog charged into the backyard. She abandoned all caution and ran after him.

Fear sliced through her heart. A monster of a man tore into her father's shoulder with his teeth like an animal. Bear barked and nipped at the giant's calves. The man's aura was all wrong, like nothing she had ever seen before—black smothered in rusty red.

Her father fell back. The blade tumbled from his grasp. Bear lunged. The man growled, undeterred, and tossed Bear aside with inhuman strength. The dog yelped in pain as he landed awkwardly. It wasn't a man. It was something else. The beast chomped down on Billy Joe's prone form, ripping flesh.

Without thinking, Ember ran forward, plucking the knife from the dewy grass. The metal seemed to glow in response to her touch. She stabbed the monster in the back repeatedly. An unnatural shriek erupted from it as it arched its back with each blow.

After releasing Billy Joe, the monster turned its attention to her. Drool and her father's blood leaked from its lips as it snarled at her. Ember braced herself when it lurched toward her. She ducked, avoiding its claws, took advantage of the opening and aimed the knife at the beast's heart, stabbing its chest. The blade struck true.

The creature staggered and clutched at the weapon briefly before its corporeal form dissipated, leaving a rusty, dark cloud in its wake. The blade hung in the dust cloud for a split-second, then fell to the ground.

Ember bent over her father to assess his injuries. He bled from multiple bite wounds; the neck wound looked the worst of all. Breathing ragged, he winced as she pressed her hand to his neck to apply pressure in an effort to stop the spurting blood.

"You're going to be okay, Dad." Tears leaked from her eyes. "He got you pretty good, but I will get help. Just hang on."

Her father's bloody hand clasped her wrist. "No."

"Don't talk." Sobs threatened. "Let me get help."

"No—not enough time." He choked out the words as blood leaked from the corner of his lips. His grip loosened. "Listen to me. Take the key. Find him." His right hand gestured to the chain around his neck, his military tags.

"Dad, no. You are going to be okay." Ember said the words even though she knew they weren't true. The rhythm of his heartbeat had already slowed. Not only could she feel it beneath her fingertips, but the familiar beat had lost its tempo.

"Demons." His eyes jerked to where the weapon lay. "More coming." His eyes widened briefly, then fluttered closed.

Demons?

"Dad—no!" She clutched the front of his shirt. "Dad! Please! Don't go!"

His aura flashed a brilliant gold, then disappeared all together. His body relaxed, then went limp.

As a fist, cold and cruel, squeezed Ember's heart, she mourned the loss of the only person who had ever truly seen her—and loved her for who she was.

Chapter Fifteen

The community and news crews flocked to the funeral home. It wasn't enough to see the man savagely killed by a rabid bobcat—a conclusion by the the sheriff and coroner, despite Ember's insistence it was something else. Plus, everyone wanted to get a look at the Dead Girl.

It was a two-for-one show, something no one in the small town could pass up. Birdie Mae burned through nearly half a carton of cigarettes and an entire quart of rum before the day was over. Co-workers from her salon arrived, smoking and drinking in solidarity with offers to take her out to the bars across the river in Cairo, Illinois after the funeral.

Birdie Mae didn't think twice. As soon as Billy Joe was six feet under, she left Ember without a word. Eventually, the crowd dispersed, leaving only Erick to give Ember a ride home.

He glanced furtively over at her as he pulled off the gravel drive looping through the cemetery and onto a paved road riddled with potholes. "Sorry," he said under his breath as the car creaked with each impact.

She bit her lip as the cemetery disappeared out of view. "It's okay."

Silence filled the void between them like steam filling a room. Soon, one of them would have to open a window and say something before the pressure became too uncomfortable. Ember was the first to crack the window. She eyed his aura and took a breath. "It wasn't a bobcat."

His head swung in her direction. "What was it?" His Adam's apple bobbed as he shifted his eyes back to the road.

"I don't know exactly." She twisted the stray black thread that had come loose on the hem of her shirt. To say out loud that it was a demon, sounded insane even to her own mind. "It wasn't a bobcat. That much I know for sure."

"You know I'm an Eagle Scout." His lips raised slightly. "I can look at the tracks, maybe identify it."

"I don't think you'll find anything helpful."

He tilted his chin. "Doth me lady doubt my special skills?"

She shrugged. "Knock yourself out, Sir Scout."

****

Moments later, they pulled up to her house. It had been one week since her dad had been murdered, and it still didn't feel real.

"Around back." Ember motioned with her hand as Bear limped down the drive to greet them. The dog briefly greeted Erick then quickly diverted around him to nuzzle on her, giving her slobbery kisses.

She kept her distance while Erick disappeared around the back of the ranch house. Bear hovered close at her heel. Ember slipped inside the house, retrieving her dad's blade. It was something he always wore on his hip. His handgun always sat on one side of his belt and the knife on the other. The blade felt heavier than it did that night—the metal cool to the touch. It didn't glow, either. *I must have imagined it.* She traced the intricate swirls and patterns etched along the blade with a lone fingertip.

Her father had never let her hold it until last summer, when he taught her how to use it. Even then, he kept the lessons brief with the blade, explaining it wasn't a practical weapon. Instead, he'd had her work with a smaller switchblade, *"easier to conceal and just as deadly,"* he'd said.

She walked back out onto the carport just as Erick came around the corner. He stroked the three chin hairs that he refused to shave. "I don't get it. I can see signs of a struggle, but no animal tracks other than the dogs'." His eyes drifted to the knife. "Is that your dad's? Is that what you used to kill the animal?"

She nodded, handing it to him. Erick's eyes widened as he took in the blade. "I've never seen one like this before." He ran his finger along the swirls. "Is that a foreign language?"

She shrugged. "I don't know."

He looked up. "So, tell me what exactly happened. What do you think killed your father? And why did he choose to use a knife instead of that gun he always wore?"

She bit her lip. "Come inside."

Erick handed her the blade and followed her to her room. Ember slipped it under her pillow and sat cross legged on her bed. Bear whined as he attempted to join her. She figured it was because the pain in his leg prevented him from making the leap. She leaned over and patted his head. "It's okay, Buddy."

Erick then pulled out her rickety old desk chair and straddled it, resting his arms on the back. He pushed up the nose piece on his glasses. "So, tell me." His aura soared lime green and sky blue. "Judgement free zone, right here."

"I know." She sighed. "There's so much I need to tell you. I don't know where to start."

"Just start from the beginning." He cocked his head, grinning. "Once upon a time…"

She returned the smile. It was one of their favorite pastimes they'd concocted during recesses and lunch breaks. They made up fantastical stories with insane monsters and brave heroes.

"Once upon a time," she began, "there was this girl named Ember…"

She bit her bottom lip but forged on, telling Erick everything. From the visions she'd had while she drowned, to the doctor telling her they had misdiagnosed her, she spared no detail. But when she came to her dad and that night, it was more difficult. Erick moved from the chair to the bed and held her as she told him between tears what had happened.

He stroked her hair as she sniffled on his shoulder. "It's going to be okay, Em. I promise. We'll figure it out together."

She pulled back. "You don't understand. This could be dangerous. My dad said more were coming. You saw the knife. No blood. That thing just evaporated into dust."

Erick fingered his chin hairs. "Demons." He let out a low whistle. "Definitely not a bobcat."

"You don't think I'm crazy?"

"It's possible the vision you had when you drowned was drug induced. That is a plausible explanation. But your dad…you can't deny what he said and what you saw." He glanced at the pill bottles on her nightstand. "We need to see this, Dr. Kayce. Find out if you really need all these pills. If you don't need them, then once you are off them, it will be quite telling if you have more visions or not."

Ember's fingers trembled, clutching the quilt on her bed. "I don't think I could manage not having them, Erick."

"And that's okay if that's the case. But don't you want to know why you see auras? Why your senses are more advanced than the rest of us Neanderthals?"

She nodded.

"It could help answer why you have so many nightmares, too."

Ember winced.

"Are they getting worse?"

She gripped the quilt and looked away. "I get so close, but I can't ever save her."

Erick reached over to rest his hand on hers. "You're not alone. I'm here, and I'll help you."

A single tear escaped. "I know. I know that. I'm sorry I didn't tell you sooner."

He wiped the tear away and pointed to the chain hanging from her neck. "Is that your dad's?"

Ember looked down, forgetting she had put her dad's military tags on that morning.

"Yeah."

"Want to see what that key opens?"

"I already know." She slipped off the bed and pulled her dad's army footlocker out from under it. She had retrieved it the night before from her parent's closet but had not had the nerve to open it. She rested it on the mattress between them. "It goes with this."

"Have you opened it yet?"

Ember shook her head. "No. I was too nervous."

"Want to do it now?"

She slipped the chain over her head. The metal ID tags shone in the fading afternoon light. She took the small metallic key sandwiched between the tags, slid it into the lock, then turned until she heard the click. With a deep inhale, she pulled the lid open. Her shoulders slumped as she eyed the contents. She wasn't sure exactly what she hoped to find, but military gear wasn't it. She riffled through discharge papers, certificates of commendations, and military ribbons.

"I don't understand."

Erick sifted through the papers. "Perhaps there is a clue in some of these documents."

"No, wait."

Ember lifted a faded picture of her dad and another soldier, each showing off newly inked tattoos. *Virtus vincit.* Her eyes pooled. It was only last summer when Billy Joe had shared the story.

"This." She tapped the photo. "This is who he wants me to find."

Chapter Sixteen

Summer Before Sophomore Year

Ember took a deep breath to settle her nerves.

She had expected the gun to feel heavy and awkward, like how an axe must have felt to a medieval executioner. Yet, the weapon felt cool and light, as if it was meant for her hand. She didn't need her extraordinary senses to feel her dad's watchful presence looming behind her. The smell of cigarettes and sweat permeated the air in an invisible cloud around his body, invading her space.

She knew if she turned around to look at the hardened man, she'd see a rainbow of anxiety and fear flaring throughout his aura.

Her dad had been training her for weeks in the Mississippi River bottoms that formed the western border of Wilson County. Desolate, quiet, it was the perfect vacation from the miserable freshman year that had just ended. The afternoon July sun gleamed across the river and onto her backside, causing sweat to travel in rivulets under her T-shirt.

Her dad's gruff smoker's voice barked out orders like a military drill sergeant all day long. It was no secret that he intended to immerse her in his own version of a physical and psychological boot camp.

Freshman year had been the worst, and it seemed to Ember that he was determined to get her mind off it one push-up at a time. But rather than be frustrated or annoyed with her dad, the strategy worked. She was happy. Not only did the exercise feel great, but she had also never gotten to spend that much uninterrupted time with her dad before.

The long days of running, tracking, and training always ended with a lesson in weaponry, her favorite part. Finally, he handed over the Colt 1911. Up to this moment, the gun rarely left the holster on his hip.

Her pale arms, now tan, had lost their ghost-like appearance. Her body had welcomed the strenuous activity and blossomed under the pressure. Affixing her gaze on the target, she raised the gun.

Billy Joe's breathing slowed as if it was his finger curled around the trigger instead of hers. He leaned in and spoke softly. "Relax your arms. Let the gun become an extension of your hand." His calloused fingers coaxed her elbow down. "Breathe, Ember."

She hadn't realized that she had stopped. "Okay." She whispered and relaxed her shoulders. A delicate breeze wafted strands of her hair into her eyes. She puckered her lips and blew the hairs away.

Billy Joe took a step back. "Now, once you get the target lined up, gently squeeze the trigger."

Her vision narrowed on the target, a rusted beer can resting on a fence post about thirty yards away. She squeezed the trigger.

Pop.

The can fell to the ground. Ember's shoulders dropped as she lowered the gun. She looked over her shoulder and saw the stunned look on Billy Joe's face.

He let out a low whistle and winked. "Damn, girl. You nailed it on your first try."

"Can I do it again?" she asked, a smile spread across her face.

"After you line up more targets." He took the gun from her. "Go on!"

****

Arching above them, the Milky Way strutted her cosmic gauze while pinpricks of starlight danced against the dark night sky. The campfire crackled and popped. Sparks and smoke wafted up, obscuring the view. Ember studied her father across the flames. It was their last night camping before school was back in session. Her gaze darted to the fence line. In the distance, her inhuman sense of hearing picked up the soft sounds of music and laughter.

Her dad's military training kicked in as his hand shifted to hover over his gun. "What is it?"

Ember poked a twig into the fire. "Nothing. Just thought I heard music."

Billy Joe scratched at the stubble on his cheek and spit into his dip cup. "Probably some of your...friends from school..." His eyes narrowed. "Want me to drive you over there?"

"Me? No." She sighed into the flames. "I'd rather avoid school and the people from it for as long as possible."

His brows knitted, like he didn't believe her. A long silence hung between them before he spoke. "You know, there were times in the Army that I wanted to quit. Times where I was seconds away from saying, 'Fuck it.' I knew it was just going to be a few years...but sometimes those years feel like lifetimes."

Ember looked up from the flames. "Why didn't you? I mean, why didn't you quit?"

His head cocked to the side. The fire danced in his eyes. He tilted the cup to his lips and spat. "Did I ever tell you how I got this tattoo?" He sat the cup on the ground and unsnapped the button on his sleeve, rolling it up to his elbow. He rotated his left arm, revealing the dark blue lines of words written in Latin.

"No." She swallowed and waited. Growing up her dad had kept that part of his life hidden. The few times she had mentioned his military past he would clam up or change the subject. It became understood over the years that it was just something he didn't want to discuss.

"*Virtus Vincit.*"

"What does it mean?" she asked.

He cleared his throat and spat into the cup. "Courage conquers."

She leaned forward on her stump, eager to hear more.

"Things happen when you are at war, Ember. Terrible things." He looked up. "Things I don't want to remember."

Ember nodded softly, not wanting to interrupt.

"Me and my platoon got this tattoo after one of those terrible things happened." He flexed his hand into a fist. A muscle in his jaw twitched as his eyes drifted back to the fire. "We were out doing recon. Should have been a simple in and out." He reflexively spat in his cup. "My second and I were taking lead. The rest were behind us." He looked up, locking eyes with Ember. "I'll spare ya the details; but about an hour into the jungle, the shit hit the fan."

She noted the slight tremble in his hand. "It's okay, Dad. You don't have to tell me."

"Shit. I'm fine. It was years ago." He spat into his cup. A thin smile stretched across his lips. He got up and pulled another log onto the fire. The flames licked higher into the night sky as if emboldened by his memory.

He sat back down. "Long story made short, we found ourselves surrounded. We tried to call for aerial support, but communications were down. Men under my command were riddled with bullets." He paused, as if reliving the harrowing moment. She waited.

"We were running light, not much ammo among us. We hunkered down. Grenades came flying in." He looked up into the sky, then back down to the flames. "Then there were just three of us." He spat in his cup. "No one was coming to save us. We had to save ourselves." He took a deep breath. "On my lead, I got us out. Two of us."

He looked across the flames at her. "The third didn't make it. We carried him as far as we could. Got nearly to camp before we realized he was already gone."

Ember swallowed, seeing the flicker of sorrow envelop his aura.

"Hell, none of us should have made it. My superior said it was either courage or stupidity that got us out." His lips cocked to the side. "Me and my second chose to believe it was courage."

"So, when you said that you and your platoon got that tattoo…"

"It was just the two of us. And after that, that soldier became like a little brother to me." He spat in

111

his cup and looked at her. "Courage, Ember. Courage conquers. Don't let fear keep you from living. Don't let those little shits at school get to you."

"*Virtus vincit.*" She stumbled over the unfamiliar words.

Maybe she should have been overcome by his bravery, or perhaps enough time should have passed since she was last bullied at school; but regardless, she failed to feel encouraged by his story. She had had so many successes over the summer. But they paled in comparison to the halls of Wilson County High. Hitting a target or tracking prey was a great distraction, but not very useful when you are the social pariah of the school.

"*Virtus vincit.*" She repeated the motto and nodded. She was a terrible liar, and they both knew it; but she would try—for his sake, at least. "I will, Dad. I will try to be brave like you."

She watched as his aura swelled with pride. "Sounds like a good plan, kiddo." He tossed his dip cup into the flames.

"How about we work on your nighttime navigation? Tell me where the North Star is."

Ember smiled and pointed. The rest of the evening was spent talking constellations and reviewing the survival skills he had taught her over the summer. It was a night she'd never forget.

****

"Courage conquers," she said aloud to the photo of the two young, haggard, but happy looking men. But her attention was drawn to her dad's friend, the one who became like a brother to him. He had kind eyes and auburn hair. *Who are you? What is your name?*

"This is the guy." She pointed to the soldier whose arm was around her dad's shoulder. "I think this is who he wants me to find."

"Do you know his name?"

"No." Ember set the photo aside, then sifted through the box. At the very bottom, a small black box about the width of two fingers rested on its side. She pressed on the edges until a small compartment slid open and exposed a small silver key inside. The inscription read: Bank of New Orleans. She slipped the key onto her dad's chain.

"Could it be a key for a safe deposit box?" Erick asked.

"Maybe. But why New Orleans?" She eyed the photo then placed the picture on her nightstand.

"You've said that your dad often went there for jobs. Maybe he opened an account?"

She looked up at her friend. "Perhaps...but Birdie Mae is from New Orleans. Maybe it's hers?"

"Maybe, but why would he have it locked away?"

"I don't know." She reached over and squeezed Erick's hand. "Thanks for not freaking out."

"That's what friends are for." He smiled. "Would it be cool if we brought Hallee into the loop?"

She swallowed. "You realize she must be questioning our friendship at this point and probably devising a brilliant strategy to escape the Dead Girl's circle of crazy?"

His lips twitched. "She's not like that. You should talk to her more. I actually think she would make a great asset to our team."

"Our team?"

"Yeah, we can make shirts."

She tossed her pillow at him. "Whatever."

"Easy, warrior princess." He laughed and held up his hands in surrender. "Honestly, I think she's cool."

"I know you do." Ember rolled her eyes as Erick flushed. "Okay, we'll ease her into it. See how it goes."

"Cool." He reached out his hand.

"Cool." They shook on it, but something told her it was a mistake to bring Hallee along.

Something didn't feel right.

Chapter Seventeen

The next day at school, Ember and her dad were no longer the hot topic in the halls. The high school rumor mill churned with new gossip. Old Ms. Grable had taken an unexpected leave of absence. Stories circulated she was finally dead. While others heard she had taken off to retire in Florida. Regardless, Ember was grateful to hear that Wayne was still missing.

Her ears perked up, though, when Heather and Jamie brushed past her on their way to their seats in first hour. "He's like so hot," Heather said and fanned herself.

"I totally call dibs on this one." Jamie slid into her seat and glared at Ember. "What are you looking at?"

Ember turned back around. Her face was aflame. They didn't bother to lower their voices.

"She is such a freak."

"Anyways, I wonder how old he is?"

She breathed a sigh of relief when Hallee and Erick walked in together. "Hey, Ember. How are you doing?" Erick's warm brown eyes filled with concern.

"I'm okay. It's weird being back at school." She didn't want to talk about herself. Everything was still too fresh. "I hear we got a new teacher for Business Communications."

"Not only that. There is a new student, too!" Hallee

gushed. "I'm no longer the 'new kid' anymore."

Erick pushed his glasses farther up his nose. "Yeah, he was in the office getting his schedule this morning."

"Wow. A new teacher and a new student—all in one day." Ember's eyes widened. "Guess I'm definitely old news then."

"Wait. Why were you in the office?" Hallee asked Erick.

He slid into his seat. "Oh, you know, hanging with my dad, helping Ms. Evelyn file stuff…just killing time till school starts."

Ember rolled her eyes. "The perks of being the Vice Principal's son."

His aura shifted to pride. "And my mom is a counselor at the middle school, too, don't forget."

Ember feigned worship, waving her hands. "Yeah…I know. We're not worthy."

"Wow. I never made the connection…the last name and all." Hallee's aura turned pink as she blushed.

"Yeah, I'm big time." Erick popped his collar. "Stick with me, ladies."

"Whatever." Hallee and Ember jinxed and laughed in unison.

It was the first time she had truly laughed since her father died. Erick was such a good friend. He had stood by her side over the years, even when it meant being shunned by the cool kids. She knew she could count on him to not freak out about everything. But Hallee…she was still unsure about her.

As much as she wanted to pretend that a demon didn't kill her father, she couldn't stop reliving the moment. She needed to find answers not only about herself, but also about her dad and the demon. And she would need her friends' help to do it.

"Hey, guys, at lunch, I need help with something," she said. "Can we meet up in the library?"

Erick answered immediately, "Sure. What's it about? Is it what I think it is?"

Her eyes flicked to Jamie and Heather. "I can't tell you here."

"Okay, cool. Yeah. Got it."

Hallee's aura flared to a sincere blue. "Of course."

"Thanks." Ember shifted back into her seat.

The bell rang and everyone settled. Mr. Thompson scratched the day's lesson across the chalkboard as the door suddenly cracked open. A sandy blond head dipped inside—the new boy.

"Mr. Thompson?" His voice was smooth and deep with a southern drawl.

"Yes? Yes, come in. Class, this is our new student." Mr. Thompson gestured for him to enter.

The new boy stepped fully into the classroom. Ember's mouth fell open. Not only was he gorgeous, but his aura was tinged golden like her dad's.

No one. Absolutely no one she had ever met had an aura like that. Ember's pencil dropped out of her hand, breaking the silence of the room as it rolled off the desk and landed on the floor. New Boy looked in her direction. His eyes were a dark chocolate brown. He winked at her. Her stomach flopped.

Did he just wink at me?

Mr. Thompson continued. "Logan? Logan Lauder, yes?"

The new boy nodded. "Yes, sir."

"Well, take a seat." He gestured toward the class.

"Anywhere is fine."

The girls behind her started to whisper all over again. Ember's nostrils flared. Their pheromones filled the classroom, but her eyes slid shut as she zeroed in on this Logan Lauder's scent and inhaled. He smelled like strawberries and chocolate. Her mouth watered at the decadent thought.

Her eyes flew open, locking with his. She tried to look away, but she couldn't. His energy drew her like a magnet. He was tall, and by the way the pink T-shirt clung to his arms and chest, Ember knew that the body underneath was chiseled. His light blue faded jeans hugged in all the right places. Her heart pounded in her chest, and her mind reeled as he walked in her direction.

"Hey." Logan paused beside her desk and picked up her pencil off the floor. "I think you dropped this."

She snapped out of her trance. She was sure the AC had quit. Sweat beaded down her back. "Thanks." Fire crept up her face as her fingertips touched his hand. His touch was electrifying.

"You're welcome."

Ember had to remind herself to breathe as he slipped into the desk behind her.

"Logan, before we get started…Erick, can you give Logan a textbook?" Mr. Thompson asked.

"Yeah, sure." Erick dutifully took a book from the shelf.

"While he's getting that, Logan, would you like to share a little about yourself?"

She shifted up in her seat, eager to learn about the new boy.

"Yes, Logan, tell us." Ember heard Jamie drawl

from across the room.

"He is so cute," Heather cooed, probably echoing the thoughts of every girl in the classroom.

Ember felt the warmth radiating off his body as he stood behind her. "Sure thing," he answered.

She didn't dare turn around, but from the corner of her eye she saw his aura. He was calm—not nervous at all. "Just moved from New Orleans, but I've lived all over…mostly the Midwest. Played football and was on the swim team." He paused. She felt a pulse of electricity buzz between them. "And I'm looking forward to getting to know everyone."

He slid into his seat behind Ember as Erick handed him his textbook.

"Thanks." His warm breath tickled the back of her head, causing a tingle of desire and temptation to sizzle down to her core.

A sharp crack broke the silence. Hallee turned around in her seat, looking at Ember. They both looked down. She had snapped her pencil in two.

Hallee looked up at her with concern and mouthed, "You okay?"

Ember waved her off. "Yeah." And shivered when she heard Logan's deep inhalation of breath behind her.

Mr. Thompson instructed the class to open their books.

Like static electricity, she felt a spark as Logan leaned forward and whispered into her ear. "You smell nice."

She choked on her own spit—and not like the clear-your-throat kind of choke. This was a full-blown hack-attack. Her eyes watered as she fought not to cough, but she couldn't stop.

Mr. Thompson paused. "Ember, are you all right? Want to get some water?"

Everyone looked at her.

She shook her head viciously and croaked, "No." She fought another cough. "I'm fine."

She heard the soft rumble of a chuckle come from behind her. Logan was laughing at her.

Mr. Thompson continued his lecture.

She slumped down into her seat, scared that a river of sweat cascaded down her back and certain her pits were twinning dark pools. She did a quick sniff test on herself. *Damn it*. The day she forgot to put on deodorant had to be today. *I'm not sure what he's smelling, but I definitely don't smell nice*. Ember tucked her arms in tighter to her sides, fearing her natural scent might escape. *Why is first hour always the longest?*

Conscious of the slowly ticking arms on the clock, she found it impossible to concentrate. The energy coming off Logan both attracted and repelled her. On one hand, she was dying to know more about him. Why was his aura like her dad's? And his smell was undeniably delicious. Her stomach growled.

On the other hand, he made her feel so weird, so off-balance in a matter of minutes. It was unnerving. There was an undeniable spark there, but Ember wasn't sure if it was a good or bad thing. She nearly jumped out of her chair when the bell rang.

"Hey, need help finding your next class?" Erick stood and turned towards Logan, essentially blocking her exit from the row.

"Yeah, that would be great."

He stood so close to Ember their arms were nearly touching. She found herself studying his aura. It was beautiful...so many colors, but the gold—it made her miss her dad.

His hand reached out and touched her arm. "Hey, you're the Dead Girl, right?"

She jerked her arm back from the shock.

"Sorry, must be static electricity. You okay?"

She looked up at his warm eyes and his concerned aura. "Yeah, sure." Flustered, she took her books and pushed past them into the aisle. She had to get away. His whole vibe was too overwhelming.

"Ember, hey, you all right?" Hallee called after her as she brushed past her.

She couldn't talk. She had to get away from Logan.

"Okay, then...see you at lunch," Hallee said to her retreating backside.

Ember slipped into the hall, where the slamming of lockers and loud voices were a welcome relief.

Who is Logan Lauder?

She clutched the chain at her neck and decided to add him to her list of mysteries to solve as she headed to English. She was relieved to find that Logan wasn't in either of her second- or third-hour classes. As soon as the bell rang for lunch, Ember jogged over to get her sack lunch from the cafeteria. She was anxious to meet with Erick and Hallee.

She took one of the pre-made bags of peanut butter and jelly sandwiches from the counter and stood in line to pay, grateful for Birdie Mae's jar of tip money hidden in the corner cupboard in the kitchen. The sounds of trays clashing on tables and the loud chatter of students accosted her senses, but one voice stood out from the rest.

She focused on Logan Lauder's warm baritone

coming from his seat at the cool kids' table. He smiled and laughed with Kale Martin while sharing high-fives. Maddison Miller looked like a cat ready to pounce while, of course, her two minions, Heather and Jamie, ogled the fresh meat as well.

It was Ember's turn to pay for her lunch. She took one last glance at Logan and got caught. He was looking directly at her. She felt herself go up in flames as he smiled and waved. His aura was a smoldering red trimmed in gold.

She nodded and rushed out of the cafeteria glass doors, releasing the breath she had been holding.

Logan Lauder is interested in me.

Chapter Eighteen

Ember entered the library and was grateful to see that her friends had already claimed the back table in the library. The rows of shelves stacked neatly with books were like her very own sanctuary from the chaos. Cozy and quiet, it was the only place she could relax at school.

"Ah, there she is." Erick waved her over. "Now the Lunch Club is complete."

"Lunch Club?" Ember tossed her sack lunch down and slipped into the hard wooden chair. Hallee was already half finished with her ham and cheese loaf sandwich.

"Yeah, ya know, like that movie, "The Breakfast Club." Erick's brows bounced over the rim of his glasses.

"I'm obviously Clark," he said.

Ember laughed. "No. He was the jock."

"Don't be rude. I just haven't explored my talents within the field of athletics yet."

Looking excited, Hallee's brows rose. "Wait. Can I be the girl, Ali?"

"That's Alison," Erick answered confidently. "And, yes, you may. Just don't steal my stuff."

Hallee reached over and attempted to swipe his chips.

"Guys. Guys. Can we focus?" Ember asked. "I have a serious question."

"What?" they said in unison.

"Do I smell?" They laughed. "What? I'm serious."

Erick straightened in his chair. "Well, from across the table, I can say with all honesty that I cannot smell you, but Hallee may have a different opinion. Hallee?"

Hallee hesitantly leaned in closer to her and sniffed. "Nope. I smell nothing."

"Why?" Erick asked.

"What about now?" She raised her arm.

"Oh, no, you don't." Hallee pushed Ember's arm down. "I am not going in. You can't make me."

Laughing, the tension in Ember's shoulders relaxed a little.

"Did someone forget to put on their deodorant today?" Erick looked over his wire-rimmed glasses.

"Maybe?" She squirmed. "So, what do you all think of the new kid?"

"He's cute," Hallee gushed.

Erick's aura turned into an annoyed peach tone as he rolled his eyes. "He's nice. He asked a lot of questions about you on the way to second hour."

Her heartbeat quickened. "Really?" She picked off the crust of her peanut butter and jelly sandwich.

"Yep, said he saw you on the news." He took a bite of his sandwich.

She cringed, remembering that her freshman year school picture had been on full display for the world and Logan Lauder to see and her appetite withered. *He's curious about the walking dead girl. That's all.*

"So, what is it you wanted to discuss?" Hallee asked.

Ember pulled out her sketches from home and unfolded the sheets, shifting them, pressing them flat for Hallee and Erick to look at.

"Whoa. Is this what I think it is?" Erick pushed up his glasses.

"Did you draw those?" Hallee asked.

Be brave. Courage conquers.

"Do you like mysteries, Hallee?" Ember asked.

"Yeah, totally. I love Nancy Drew, and I've probably seen every episode of Scooby Doo." Her cheeks flushed at the admission.

"I drew these after...you know, I drowned." She glanced furtively at Erick and Hallee as they looked at the drawings.

Hallee examined the picture of Michael. "Who is this? Is this person a model?"

She shrugged. "I don't really know who he is or what any of it means." *Here goes nothing.* "I saw them in a vision." She nervously watched Hallee's reaction. "I saw them in a vision—" She took a breath. "—while I was dead."

To her credit, Hallee didn't immediately freak out. But the silence was deafening.

Hallee looked over at Erick. "She already told you, didn't she?" Her eyes shifted back down to the drawings as he nodded. "So, you saw all of this while you were technically dead?"

"Yep." She pointed to the picture of Michael. "Don't laugh; but I saw a white light, and this guy appeared."

As Hallee's mouth hung open, the silence slowly melted from seconds into hours—or so it felt to Ember. "Okay. I said don't laugh, but...please, say something."

"I don't know what to say," Hallee said.

Ember gathered up the drawings. "I knew this was a mistake. Just forget it."

"Wait," Hallee said. "You're telling me that's God?"

"What?"

Hallee reached over and pulled the sketch of Michael to the center of the table and pointed. "Him. Is that God?"

Ember pulled the drawing back. "Forget I said anything."

Hallee stopped her from moving the paper. "I'm not joking." Hallee's aura was a sincere plum and blueberry. "Is that him?"

She found it hard to speak. The words stuck in her throat. If Hallee didn't already think she was crazy, then she would for sure after she told them who "he" was. "No. He said he was the Archangel Michael."

Erick stroked his chin hairs. "He's like a warrior angel, I think."

"Wow." Hallee looked up at her. "This is amazing. You went to Heaven, Ember."

"Not exactly," she said and retold the entire vision to her friends.

****

"And that's not all." She swallowed and bit her bottom lip. "A bobcat did not attack my dad. It looked like a man, but my dad said, before he died, that it was a demon." Because Hallee hadn't picked up and run out of the library, Ember told the rest. "After I stabbed it in the heart, it turned into dust."

She watched as Hallee processed another crazy truth bomb. Eyes rounded, chewing furiously on her nails, Hallee was either about to proclaim that Ember was crazy, or perhaps she was thoughtfully mulling over it. Either way, she could barely breathe waiting to hear her response.

Erick waved his hand around his body. "I think you should tell her about the other stuff, too."

Hallee looked pale, but she was willing to risk it all and open herself completely for a loyal friend...a possible best friend. "There is one more thing," she said. "I have synesthesia. I was born with it. Well, actually, the doctor at the hospital said that I was misdiagnosed. According to him, it's not synesthesia but something else...he referred me to a Dr. Kayce in Murray."

"What is synesthesia exactly?" Hallee finally spoke, her brows popping over her purple frames.

"My senses are heightened. I see colors...around people."

Erick shook his head. "But this doctor says you don't have that."

"Yeah, he said I see peoples' auras. That it is rare, but it's not synesthesia."

"What about the other stuff?" Hallee asked. "Your other senses?"

Erick cleared his throat. "You should probably tell her about your dad, too."

Hallee's aura flared a brilliant green. "What about your dad?"

Ember fingered the chain around her neck. "My dad...before he died, he also told me to find someone. Someone he was close to in the army, I think—a soldier. I believe my dad thought this guy can help me—with everything."

Ember watched their auras shift as she continued. "So, I need some help to try to figure out what all this means: the vision, my abilities, the demon and my dad, and his friend." She motioned to the drawings. "I can't go to Birdie Mae. She's on the verge of a mental breakdown herself and is drunk more than she's not."

She looked up at Hallee and Erick. "I need to meet with this Dr. Kayce and figure what is wrong with me. And I need to find this soldier from my dad's past." She plastered on a fake smile. "So, Hallee? Want to help? Or do you think I'm totally crazy? It's okay to say, no. I get it. It's a lot. Plus, it's weird."

"A misdiagnosis? Visions? Demons and a mysterious man you need to find? C'mon, what's weird about that?" Erick stood, scooted his chair back, and walked around to stand next to Ember. With a dramatic bow he said, "I am at your service, my liege. It would be my honor to serve you on this quest."

Ember and Hallee giggled.

"Ladies…ladies…we're in the library. Shhhh. Please." Erick scolded while smiling ear to ear himself.

"And what say you, Hallee?" she asked.

She reached her hand over the table for Ember to shake. "Duh, I'll be the Watson to your Holmes."

"Thanks." Relief flooded her just knowing that she wasn't alone, trying to figure it all out and that Hallee was still her friend. She shook Hallee's hand. "Welcome aboard the crazy train."

"Don't say that." Hallee gently squeezed, her aura dipping dark blue. "You're not crazy."

The bell rang.

Erick pointed to the drawings. "Dang it. I was ready to go all super nerd on you and start looking up languages of origin for that word on your sketch."

"There's always tomorrow." Hallee gathered up the trash from their lunches.

"Can you guys meet after school?" Erick asked.

"Sure," she answered. Hallee nodded.

Erick's aura bloomed a happy lemon yellow. "We need to come up with a mission code name."

Ember grinned. "I thought you wanted to make T-shirts?"

"A code name and T-shirts," he clarified.

"See you in Business Communication," Hallee said over her shoulder as she left the library.

Ember picked up her drawings and folded them into her purse.

"Hey…it's going to be okay." Erick stopped her. "We'll help you get to the bottom of everything."

"Yeah, I know. Thanks. It means a lot. It's just…" Ember gestured to the papers in her purse. "It's just…I wish I knew what it all meant."

"Don't worry…I'm like really smart—really, really smart. Last year, I totally crushed the hopes and dreams of this kid who kept trying to beat me in chess."

She punched his arm. "Hey, that was me."

He flipped the collar up on his polo shirt. "Exactly. I will be the brains of this operation. I got this."

She laughed and followed him out of the library. She couldn't get her mind went off the sketches. There was so little to go on. And uccess seemed unlikely.

Chapter Nineteen

Everyone was lined up and dressed out in the regulation gym uniform of gray T-shirts with Wilson County High in bold red letters across the front and gray shorts. As usual, Jamie and Heather clumped together, whispering and giggling. Ember didn't need to see their auras to know the topic was boys.

Her breath caught when her eyes settled on the gym teacher talking to Logan. She was halfway to the bleachers, doing her best cat burglar impression, when Mrs. Hall blew her whistle. "You're late, O'Neill."

Logan grinned and arched one of his perfect brows at her.

"Sorry." Ember ducked her chin and headed straight for the bleachers.

Mrs. Hall handed Logan a set of gym clothes and sent him to the lockers to change. Ember flipped her notebook open as Mrs. Hall called roll. Icicles snaked down her back as the teacher called Wayne Wilson's name. She looked up at the vacant spot in the line, grateful that Wayne was still missing.

She turned to a blank page and sketched her vision again, hoping something new would come to mind. Mrs. Hall blew her whistle, cueing the class to take laps around the gym. When Heather and Jamie lagged, doing more talking than running. Mrs. Hall yelled at them to get a move on.

Ember continued to sketch the skyline from her vision. She closed her eyes and meditated on the image, but it was impossible to focus with the gym noise constantly interrupting her thoughts. Alerted by his odor, she looked up to find Logan peering over her shoulder. "What's that?" he asked.

A thousand tiny fires erupted all over her body. "What?" She struggled to utter the single syllable.

"What are you drawing?" he said more slowly.

Ember's eyes hung on his perfectly formed lips as he spoke each word.

"Lauder!" Mrs. Hall yelled. "Get moving!"

"Later." He left Ember alone—and smoldering. Her stomach liquified into mush.

She refused to get caught looking at his perfect body, but she couldn't help but sneak furtive glances as he went through the motions with the rest of the class. Logan didn't break a sweat. The muscles in his arms rippled with each effortless push up. His sit-ups were quick and flawless while even the athletes in the class were struggling.

Mrs. Hall blew her whistle and tossed basketballs out to the class. She told them to warm up. The last half of the class would be scrimmages. Ember fought the desire to look up. She could hear the commentary as both the girls and the guys were in awe of his natural basketball skills. He was sinking threes with ease.

Ember finally glanced up. Logan dribbled down the court, jumped at the free-throw line, releasing the basketball so that it arched into the hoop seamlessly. You didn't have to be a psychic to know that Wilson County was going to love Logan Lauder.

She ignored her original plan to spend class sketching her vision, and, instead, she watched Logan as the class broke off into two teams. Both groups played to win, but he was unstoppable.

Instinctively, she drew his form. She tried to capture his smooth transitions with the ball sketching his long frame as he dribbled down the court. In the end, his team dominated. Mrs. Hall blew the whistle for everyone to go change.

She looked down at what she had drawn and flushed with embarrassment. It was the perfect action shot of Logan sinking another three. She quickly closed her notebook as students filed past her on their way to the locker rooms. The guys clustered around Logan as he made his way towards her. He gave them high fives as they walked past.

"So, what was that you were drawing?" His brows scrunched together.

"Nothing." She was proud that she was able to get the two syllables out. Her nostrils flared in and out as she inhaled his delicious scent.

He reached out for her notebook.

"What are you doing?" She felt tiny little sparks as her hand grazed his.

He pulled his hand back. "Whoa. Relax. I was just curious. No big deal. Just that sketch reminded me of Chicago. You know, the Sears Tower."

"Oh, sorry." She worried her face was now the color of a ripe tomato.

"I gotta change. See you later, Ember." He winked and left her to melt in his wake. She replayed the sound of her name on his lips. There was something about Logan Lauder that turned her world upside down.

She wanted to dig a hole and bury herself. Why did he make her brain function at sloth level? And why the wink? Ember hugged her notebook to her chest, grateful he didn't see her sketch of him. The bell rang and she couldn't get to Chemistry fast enough...until she remembered Coach Cooke was the teacher.

He basically called her out in front of everyone, saying that she checked her file and found nothing in there to prevent her from playing sports. So, unless Ember could provide some documentation, she expected to see her at volleyball tryouts. Ember spent the entire hour, once again, wondering if she really needed chemistry to graduate.

It was with great relief when Ember walked into last hour and did a double-take as she slipped into her chair. The new teacher was young—and male—nothing like old Mrs. Grable. Mr. Greene had wavy, sandy blond hair, eyes the color of the sea, and a sexy five o'clock shadow that did nothing to disguise his chiseled jawline. She studied his aura as he smiled and spoke softly with Hallee. There was an edge of nervousness to his aura with dark blue intent. She picked up his scent...licorice and leather.

"What's that about?" she asked Erick.

"Apparently, if you are first to class, you get to be his helper." Erick shrugged. His aura flared an annoyed, peachy-orange.

"Don't be jealous," Ember teased.

"What? No, I'm not jealous." His cheeks turned red as he brushed his glasses up his nose. "It's not like that."

"Admit it, he sort of looks like that hotter, younger star on that TV cop show based in Miami."

Erick rolled his eyes. "You can stop now."

When the bell rang, Hallee returned to her desk.

"Saved by the bell." Ember's lips lifted into a crooked grin at Erick. "I was about to finger-drum the intro to the show." She waggled her fingers above the desk.

Mr. Greene stood, cleared his throat, and smiled. Before he could utter a word, the door flung open. Kale Martin and Maddison Miller walked in with Logan in tow. Ember slumped in her chair and let her hair fall forward. She did not want to make eye contact with Mr. Wink.

"Welcome. Come in." Mr. Greene's voice was as smooth as silk.

Kale jerked his thumb toward Logan. "Sorry, teach—new student, here, was lost."

"No worries. Take a seat. I know how it is." He turned and wrote his name on the chalkboard. "I am Mr. Greene. I will be taking over all of Mrs. Grable's classes."

"RIP, Mrs. C.," someone chirped loudly.

Everyone laughed. Mr. Greene blushed but did not address the outburst. "As I was saying, I am new to Wilson County, but I'm from Cincinnati, so not too far away." He walked around to the front of the desk and sat on the edge.

Ember bit back a laugh when she noticed that the teacher was not wearing socks with his loafers. She tried to make eye-contact with Erick, but he was solely focused on the new teacher. Her attention soon became distracted by the whispers emanating from the back of the classroom.

Maddison was grilling Logan about his "situation.

"So, no girlfriend waiting for you back in New Orleans?" she purred.

"Nope."

"I don't believe you."

"It's hard to have a relationship when you move around as much as I have," he said.

"Oh, that's so sad."

She rolled her eyes. *How could Kale stand to listen to her flirt with Logan?*

"How about we start with this row?" Mr. Greene looked pointedly at Ember.

"I'm sorry?" Her cheeks warmed. "What?"

"Wow. I've already lost the front row, and I'm just doing introductions." He smiled. "I'd like you to go first." He emphasized the "you" and picked up his paper and pencil. "Go on."

Ember felt the eyeballs of everyone staring at her. "Oh, okay."

Someone faked a cough and said, "Dead Girl."

Every pore on her back opened and released a river of sweat. Seconds felt like centuries. "Do you want me to stand?"

He smiled and jotted something on his notepad. "Only if you want to."

"My name is Ember O'Neill."

She searched her mind, desperate for something interesting to share. Logan's scent wafted to the front of the classroom. She didn't want to say something stupid and further cement his idea that she was a complete idiot. Her palms grew moist. *Shit. Shit. Shit.*

Every recent bad memory flooded to the forefront of her mind. Bloody Ember. Wayne Wilson. Dying. The demon. Her dad…Her eyes watered. But then memories of last summer in the river bottoms rushed forward to replace them. She swallowed.

"And...I like to go camping?" She didn't mean for it to come out like a question, but she looked up to see Mr. Greene smile as he wrote something down.

"Thank you, Ms. O'Neill. Next?"

Ember slumped back down in her chair, grateful to be out of the spotlight. She zoned out until it was Logan's turn. Determined not to turn around like everyone else in the front row. She sketched in the margins of her notebook but listened keenly as he spoke.

"Hey, I'm Logan Lauder. Just moved here from Louisiana. And I like to go camping, too."

Her head shot up. She refused to turn around. *Was he serious? He likes to go camping?*

Hallee reached over and tapped her with her pencil. "I think he's looking at you."

Ember felt her cheeks pink. She absolutely was not going to look.

She turned and looked. His gorgeous face stared straight at her. He winked and broke his gaze away first, sitting down in his chair. Ember spun back around in her seat dropping her chin. His aura was a passionate red. Her body went into flames. She couldn't think. She couldn't breathe. She felt like she could pass out.

"I think he kind of likes you, Ember," Hallee whispered across the aisle.

Ember raised her hand, "Mr. Greene? Can I get a drink of water?"

The new teacher sat up straighter in his chair and glanced down at his paper. "Ms. O'Neill, correct?"

"Yes, I just need to get a drink."

He tilted his head at the door. "Okay. You've got five minutes."

She tripped getting out of her seat. She felt the heat of everyone's stares.

"You okay?" Hallee whispered.

"Yeah." Ember hauled ass to get out of the classroom. As soon as the door closed behind her, she instantly felt better. She heard Maddison introducing herself. She rolled her eyes and broke away from the door, walking down the hall to the water fountain.

She was annoyed with herself for not thinking to take a couple pills from her purse before she got up to leave the classroom. But, at least, the water was refreshing.

The scuffle of feet and the swishing of a broom echoed down the hall toward her. Mama Jackson swayed her direction. "Ember girl. How are you, child?"

"I'm okay, Mama Jackson. Just getting a drink."

"No, I mean, how are you? I saw you on the TV and I says to myself, 'That girl, right there, is tough.' I ain't surprised one bit that you survived that drowning…and your father…he was a good man."

"Thanks, Mama Jackson. I'm okay really."

"Just between you and me…" She leaned in conspiratorially. "I heard the sheriff got a tip, and they done found that no-good, Wayne Wilson. So, don't you worry about that kid no more."

Ember nearly choked on her drink of water.

Mama Jackson reached out to squeeze her hand. "You one of the good ones, Ember girl. Don't ever change." She waved her broom. "Best get back to work."

"Yeah, I need to get back to class."

"Take care, child."

"I will. You, too." Her aura was a soft yellow. Ms. Jackson was a naturally cheerful soul.

She reached for the doorknob to the classroom. *Be brave. Courage conquers.* It was only a few steps to her seat in the front row. She could do this. She opened the door.

"Ah, Ms. O'Neill. Everything okay?"

She slipped into her seat. "Yep."

"Good. We finished the introductions. Just letting everyone talk amongst themselves, since we don't have much time left." He nodded to the clock.

Thank God, Ember thought.

Hallee turned in her seat towards her and whispered, "You good?"

"Yep. Just needed a drink."

Hallee's eyes rounded behind her glasses. "So...you missed it."

"What?"

"Apparently, Maddison likes to go camping, too."

Ember snorted. "What?"

Hallee grinned. "Shhhh. I know, right? I don't even really know her, and I know she's lying."

She shook her head. "Whatever."

"Can you imagine if she actually went camping?"

Erick leaned over Ember's desk. "What are we talking about?"

"We are trying to imagine Maddison camping in the bottoms," Ember answered.

"Oh, yeah, that." He shook his head and peered towards the back. "Yeah, that's not happening." His voice dropped low. "Don't look now, but the pretty new boy is coming this way."

"Hey." Logan grabbed a chair and sat down, straddling it backwards.

"Hey," Hallee responded softly.

Erick lifted his chin. "What's up?"

"Nothing. Just seeing if you were going to the bottoms this weekend. They were just telling me that's where everyone hangs out." He motioned to the back of the room.

"The bottoms? Us?" Erick's eyes went wide. "You do realize we are the nerds at this school?"

Hallee leaned over and kicked Erick in the shin. "Speak for yourself."

"Okay, okay, sorry."

Logan grinned and looked at Ember. "So, Saturday night? You guys going?"

"We actually have a thing on Saturday." She noticed his aura shifted to disappointment.

"Oh, okay."

"We do?" Hallee asked.

Ember tilted her head at Hallee. Her eyes shot daggers at her new friend.

"Oh, yeah. That thing…" Hallee tried to retract.

The bell rang. Logan got up. "Hope I see you there." Ember looked up just in time to catch another wink as he walked away.

Hallee and Erick both gathered their things.

"I think he just asked you out," Hallee whispered to her as they walked through the door.

"He asked *us*," Ember pointed out.

"Whatever. He is totally into you," she insisted.

Erick held the door open as they exited down the hall to the library.

****

Fingering the sparse hairs on his chin, Erick recalled that the root of most languages was Latin, but there were no Latin translation books in the school library.

"What if we killed two birds with one stone?" Ember asked.

He closed the massive dictionary he had been flipping through. "Okay, I'm listening."

"What if we went to Murray State on Saturday? We could meet with this Dr. Kayce and use the university library."

Hallee nodded. "Sounds like a good plan to me."

Erick grinned. "I'm always surprised when you speak so smart."

Ember smiled. "Funny. Real funny."

"You know, my uncle is a priest," Hallee said. "Would it be cool if I asked him about the Archangel?"

"Totally."

"I could ask my preacher, too." Erick's aura soared as he smiled at Hallee. "See what he knows."

"That would be great." She hugged her friends. "Thank you."

"So…we have a plan for Saturday," Hallee said.

Erick's aura shifted, matching the color of Hallee's cheeks. "Yes, it's a date."

Ember cleared her throat. "Thanks, guys, for supporting me. I mean it."

"Hey—would Watson abandon Holmes?" Hallee waggled her brows over her purple frames. "I don't think so."

"Hey, she's a warrior princess," Erick teased, brandishing his invisible sword. "And I'm a warrior prince."

"Whatever, mister warrior, think you can give us a lift home?" Hallee asked.

"Of course, my ladies…" Erick pulled out his keys and jingled them. "Your chariot awaits."

Ember and Hallee both exchanged looks and laughed. "Come on, let's go." Ember took her new best friend by the hand, realizing in that moment that Hallee really was her BFF.

One of her goals for sophomore year had been accomplished.

Chapter Twenty

Ember's head jerked up as she heard Birdie Mae's car rumble down the gravel county road. She glanced at her digital clock. It was already eight thirty. She looked out her bedroom window. She'd been so focused on her math homework that she hadn't realized how dark it had gotten outside. The sun was setting earlier and earlier.

Leaning back, she flicked the switch on to her reading light. Bear's ears twitched at the sound. She picked up her dad's blade gleaming on her nightstand and shoved it under her pillow. She liked to keep it close…just in case.

"Wake up, Bear." She nudged the giant ball of fur with her foot. "Dinner is coming."

She folded her homework inside her textbook and walked down the hall with Bear by her side. The carport door creaked open. She smelled the chicken before she heard the swish of bags as Birdie Mae made it inside.

"Hey. Need help?" she asked.

Birdie Mae had her hands full with a sack of groceries and a bag of takeout from Linda's Restaurant. She rushed over before she could respond and took the sack of groceries from her.

"Thanks." Birdie Mae set the food on the counter.

Ember noted the bags under her eyes and the V between her brows. "Everything okay?"

"What? Oh, yeah, baby girl...just a lot on my mind. Ya know, the beauty shop...getting caught up on all the appointments I had to push out because of the funeral."

Ember put the groceries away: milk, bread, cereal, a two-liter bottle of soda and a carton of cigarettes—the necessities, she noted.

"Picked up some tenders...and before you ask, yes, she gave you extra ketchup and house dressing. She didn't even charge me." Birdie Mae shook her head as she poured rum into her glass of soda. "I swear these people think we are a charity case now."

Ember sat down at the kitchen table. Her stomach rumbled as she cracked open the container of food. Bear sat dutifully by her chair. Birdie Mae skimmed a fry and sat down across from her. She lit a cigarette and took a drag. "Gawd, it feels good to get off my feet." She eyed Ember. "How was school?"

She finished chewing her bite to answer. "Good. We have a new student and a new teacher."

"Oh yeah, I heard." Birdie Mae leaned in on her elbows. "The word is old Mrs. Grable done went cuckoo and had to be sedated. They put her in the nursing home down in Bardwell."

"Wow, that sucks." Ember drowned a chunk of chicken in the dressing, then popped it into her mouth. A tiny whine escaped Bear's salivating mouth. "Okay, buddy, hang on." She pinched off a bite and handed it to him.

Her mom rolled her eyes. "That dog acts like he's starvin'."

Birdie Mae opened her to-go box. She had gotten her signature salad with grilled chicken and dressing on the side. She often told Ember she refused to get old and fat like the rest of those Wilson County heifers. "So, tell me about the new kid. I hear the uncle rented the old Thompson farm just on this side of the county line. Happened real quick, too, from the sound of it. Paid big money, cash, to move in on Sunday."

"Uncle?"

"Well, you know how those old hens gossip…who knows what's really true, but supposedly the kid's parents died in some terrible accident years ago and the uncle has been raising him since."

"Oh." Ember thought back to how Logan, as the new kid, seemed so calm and sure of himself. He had been through a lot, it seemed. "That's sad."

"Yeah, word is that the uncle has some big job out of Chicago and makes real good money." Birdie Mae's brows raised. "So, what's the kid like? Hear he drives a real nice car." Her head tilted. "Like real nice."

"He's okay, I guess."

"Okay? Hmmm…all right then. Well, them old biddies say the uncle looks like a movie star." She waggled her brows. "So hot." She took a bite of her salad.

"Ewww. Gross." She tossed a fry to Bear.

The phone rang on the wall. Birdie Mae jumped out of her seat. "I'll get it. Better not be one of those damn reporters again."

"Hello?" Ember heard Hallee's voice on the other end. "Yeah, sure. Hold on." Birdie Mae covered the phone. "It's your friend, Hallee." She put extra-emphasis on the word "friend."

Ember got up and took the phone. She walked around to the hall as far as the phone cord would reach. "Hey, what's up?"

"So, I talked to my dad and stepmom…we are good to go on Saturday…"

"Okay, great…I still have to ask my mom. Hang on…."

"Wait! There's more…do you want to sleep over Saturday night?"

She froze. She had never, ever, had a sleepover or been invited to one. Part of her was excited, but she was mostly scared. What if she had a nightmare? "I don't know, Hallee…"

Birdie Mae called from the kitchen, "What she want?"

Ember cringed.

"Just ask her," Hallee pleaded.

"Okay." She walked back around to the kitchen. "Hallee, Erick, and I have a project…is it cool if we go to Murray to use the university library on Saturday? Erick said he could drive."

"Ask her about the sleepover," Hallee insisted.

"And…she wants to know if I can sleep over afterwards?"

"What? Of course, baby girl. I think that's wonderful." Birdie Mae's aura flashed a happy shade of yellow that Ember hadn't seen in days.

She relayed the news to Hallee. "She said yes."

"Yay! I'm so excited! We can plan everything tomorrow at school."

"Okay, yeah, sure."

"Oh, and is she cool with Erick driving us to Murray?" Hallee asked.

Kerrie Faye

Ember looked at her mother. "What about Murray State? Is it okay if Erick drives us?"

Birdie Mae shoved a bite of salad in her mouth. "Oh, yeah, sure. That kid is as straight as an arrow."

"It's a go," Ember shared.

"Yay! Perfect!"

Ember winced as a child screamed in the background. "Everything all right?"

"Oh, yeah, it's fine. That's just my little brother. He's throwing his Legos at my little sister. It's totally fine. But I should probably go stop him. See ya tomorrow, Em!"

"Okay, yeah, sure…bye." She hung up the phone. A small smile stretched across her lips. *Em.*

"Look at you…someone is getting popular," Birdie Mae sang.

"I wouldn't go that far." She plopped down at the kitchen table. She studied Birdie Mae's aura. "Are you sure it's all right?"

"Shit, Ember Eve." She chomped down on a bite of salad. "It's about damn time you got a friend that wasn't Erick. And, yes, I'll be fine. Hell. By the time I was your age, I had lots of girlfriends and several boyfriends, too." She waved her fork in the air. "Anyways, I've got a wedding this weekend. Damn near forgot. Doing hair and makeup for the bride and all the bridesmaids. I'll be in and out." She took another bite. "Just find yourself a ride home on Sunday. I ain't gonna do shit once that wedding is over."

"Okay." She took the last bite of chicken and split it with Bear. "Promise you'll feed Bear for me?"

"That damned dog ain't gonna starve. Look how fat he is." Ember watched as Birdie Mae's aura shifted as she looked down at Bear. She didn't mean it. Love glimmered in her aura.

"Birdie Mae…if for some reason he starts growling, don't go outside. Call the sheriff." Ember bit her lip. Talking about what happened to her father was a touchy subject with her mom.

Birdie Mae jabbed her fork in the air. "Listen, I ain't no fool like Billy Joe. So, don't you even worry about me."

"Birdie Mae…" She had already tried to explain what she saw to her mom after the incident, but she just dismissed her like the sheriff had.

"You listen, here. Your father was an idiot for going out there and getting himself killed." She lit a cigarette and blew smoke with a slight tilt of her head. "I ain't stupid like that." Her fingers trembled. Her aura became muddled—probably too much rum.

Ember eyed the empty glass and spat, "Dad wasn't being stupid. He was trying to protect me."

Her mother's eyes narrowed. "Yeah, well, maybe if you'd stayed in your room that night, he might be here right now."

Ember's eyes watered. "Don't say that."

"Don't say that he cared more about you than he did his own safety? That maybe if he wasn't so wrapped up in protecting his broken baby girl, he might be here right now? Well, it's the God damned truth. He was always too obsessed with protecting you, and it got him killed." She poured more rum on the ice left in the glass and took a long swallow.

"It wasn't like that."

"Hell, once you were born, you became his entire world. I was fuckin' chopped liver. Everything was about you. Men are users, Ember Eve." She stabbed the air with her fork. "They take what they want and move on to the next one. Billy Joe wasn't perfect. And, as soon as you accept that, you'll realize how much better off we both are without him."

Furious, Ember shot to her feet. "That's not true."

"Isn't it?" Her aura was completely muddied now. Nothing good ever happened when it clouded over like that. Birdie Mae was drunk.

"I'm going to my room."

"Good. Stay there. Maybe your precious daddy would still be here if you'd done that last weekend." Birdie Mae tilted her glass, draining more rum.

Ember bit back the sobs that threatened to escape until she was in her room. Her mother's words cut deeper than she even knew. Exhausted and upset, she shoved her books out of the way and fell asleep, forgetting to take her pills.

Chapter Twenty-one

As Ember raced through the woods, branches scraped and slashed at her arms. She had to stop to get her bearings. It was the same nightmare. She knew what she had to do next: she needed to find the river.

If only she could track their scent, she could find them, the man and the girl. She knew she could do it. Her nostrils flared. Decaying earth and the faint sweet scent of honeysuckle hung in the air. There! The scent of fear mixed with adrenaline wafted her way. She lifted her chin, inhaling. She looked down for signs of tracks. The smell was faint, but not old. They couldn't be too far ahead.

Her thoughts were interrupted. Someone was there. She felt him—smelled him, actually—chocolate and whiskey. It was Adam.

"Why do you do this?"

Ember jumped and spun in circles, looking for him. "How are you here?" She peered into the woods, torn between her desire to engage him and to track her target.

"We can dream-walk, remember?"

Ember turned, annoyed. "Show yourself."

"I'm unable to show myself, Eve." Her name slowly slid off his tongue, like honey off a biscuit.

"You mean you can't, or you won't?" Her heart

pounded. "I can't talk." She turned to run and instantly felt a tug on her arm.

"What are you doing?" His voice was thin with frustration.

She hissed at the invisible restraint. "I need to save her."

"Tsk, tsk, Eve. This isn't real. Well, technically, it hasn't happened yet. You cannot save her."

A boat engine ignited to life in the far distance. "What are you talking about?"

"Look around you," he insisted.

Ember tried to pry the invisible hand from her arm. "I have to go. Let me go."

A warm breath tickled her ear. "Eve, look." Although he physically wasn't there, she felt his warmth on her neck as if he stood too close, invading her personal space. "Look around you. See. The edges are fuzzy. That's how you know it's a premonition and not a dream from your imagination."

Ember scanned the perimeter. Beyond the immediate woods, everything was hazy, fuzzy in fact.

"If it was a dream, your mind would have filled in the entire landscape—no fuzzy edges."

"How do you know?" she questioned.

"Eve, think back to when we first met…you were able to recreate your entire bedroom with just a thought. This scene…it hasn't happened yet. Your mind is only picking up snippets of the future."

She slowly turned, scanning the dark, dank woods.

"No matter how hard you try…you will never get there in time. What happens…happens, Eve."

She vehemently shook her head. "No, I can't believe that. I need to save her."

"Who do you need to save, Eve? Is it your mother? Your sister? Your friend? Who?"

Ember shrugged. "I don't know. I don't know who it is, Adam."

"Don't be sad." She felt his warm hand cup her cheek. "Let me help you."

"How?" She felt his touch trace along her arm. She shivered. "Don't do that."

Ember blinked. Suddenly, the dreamscape changed to her secret garden. "How did you do that? How did you get inside my mind? How did you get in my dreams? Who are you, Adam?"

"Tsk. Tsk. One question at a time. But first we make a deal. I will help you now...but you must promise to help me later...someday when I ask."

She wasn't sure why, but Ember felt like she was making a deal with the devil. *Maybe it's because I'm in a garden. I'm pretending to be Eve, and he's Adam.*

Adam chuckled. "I'm no devil, Eve. I promise you I have no ill intent. I just want to help. And maybe, someday, you could help me."

Against her better judgement, Ember agreed, "Okay. We have a deal. So, who are you?"

"I am like you, Eve. I have abilities. I can see and do things most humans can't even imagine."

"Like what?"

She felt his warmth beside her. "I can read people—their auras."

Her heart beat faster. "Me, too."

"I can dream-walk," he said.

"Obviously. What else?"

He leaned closer to whisper in her ear. "I can make people do things."

Rivers of ice flooded her veins. "What do you mean?"

His voice lightened. "Oh, you know, I can suggest to someone that they open a Christmas gift early. It's something they've been tempted to do but their better nature has stopped them. I can loosen their free will, so to speak. And then they open the box."

"Wait. That's like mind control." Ember shook her head. "That's wrong."

"Is it? It was already in their head to open the box. I just give them a little nudge."

"So, you can only make someone do something if they have already thought of it."

"Yes, the seed is there. I just water it and fertilize it till it grows."

"I guess that is not too bad." Ember wished she had that ability, too. Life would be so different if she was able to convince Wayne to leave her alone once and for all, but then he'd have had to have already thought to do that. Unfortunately, Wayne was not one to just leave her alone, ever.

"You can. I'm sure of it." The confidence in his voice slithered around her.

"Can, what?" she asked.

"Do it, too…" His tone turned cocky.

"Okay, Rule Number One—stay out of my head, Adam." She put extra emphasis on his name.

"Okay, okay…whatever you wish, angel."

Ember sat down on the garden bench. "So, how do you do it?"

"Honestly, I'm not sure. I'm only just exploring my own abilities."

Her shoulders slumped.

"Eve, before I can help you…train you, I need to know who your parents are. Can you tell me about your father? Your mother?"

"Why do you need to know that?" Unease danced down her neck as she sensed him sit down on the bench beside her. He smelled so good; she could almost taste him.

"I think it will help explain who you are and where your abilities come from."

"My parents don't have any abilities." Ember looked away. "I was born with synesthesia." She stopped herself. "Well, that's what the doctor said when I was little. Dr. Peters, at the hospital, said it was a misdiagnosis. I don't know how I got this way or what made me like this."

She jumped off the bench, realizing the answers were a breath away. "But you do. Right? Tell me. How? How did we get like this? How did you get your abilities, Adam?"

But before he could answer, she felt his presence dissipate. "Adam? Adam!"

He'd left her. Alone…with more questions than answers.

****

Ember woke. It was dark outside her bedroom windows. Bear snored at near epic decibels next to her. She slipped her hand under her pillow, grasping her dad's blade. She wanted to trust the mysterious Adam; but, until she got answers, she would never feel safe in her own home again. She lay wide-eyed until the sun came up.

Chapter Twenty-two

The rest of the week flew by. Gossip about the Dead Girl had ebbed to a rare, comfortable murmur.

She credited the new boy, Logan, and the new teacher, Mr. Greene, for the favorable change in the rumor mill. Maddison and her minions were obsessed with Logan while the guys were in awe of his skills on the court. Rumors of winning State was all they could talk about. While the new teacher was easy on the eye, he quickly became the coolest teacher at Wilson County High with his young vibe and lenient grading policies.

Saturday finally arrived and Ember felt her stomach twist into knots. She peeked out the window. She heard Erick's car come down the road before she saw it. Anxiously, she rechecked her overnight bag for her pills.

"It's one night, Bear." She bent to hug him. "I left you extra food and water, just in case." He whined. "I know. I know." He rolled over, exposing his belly. She quickly scratched his tummy. "Okay…okay…I got to go."

Erick's car pulled up into the drive. Bear followed her out to the carport. Erick stepped out of his car. His gold-rimmed glasses glinting in the sun. His aura soared when he spied Bear.

"Hey, Buddy." Bear limped at a quick trot down

the drive to Erick who kneeled down so Bear could give him licks. "Still jealous that you have a dog." He patted his head. "Got to go, buddy."

He slipped into the driver's seat. His fingers danced on the steering wheel as they pulled away from the house. He shot a quick glance over at Ember. "So, did you hear about Wayne?"

Ember picked at a loose thread on the seam of her jeans. "No, I mean…Mama Jackson told me they found him."

"My dad said he won't be coming back to the school for a while."

"Why? What happened?"

"The sheriff arrested him."

"Because of what happened at the pool party?"

"I don't know the details, but my dad said that he was found with death threats and that he was building a bomb. They think he was planning on blowing up the school."

"A bomb?" Ember was dumbfounded. "Why? That's insane."

Erick shrugged. "I don't know. Dad said that he was being held in the county jail, but he expected the judge to send him off to a juvie facility in Hopkinsville."

"Wow. That's crazy."

"Yep. Look, he was a complete douche bag to everyone. And he was a complete dick to you for years. I say good riddance." He turned on the radio and began twisting the dial. "Want to listen to music?"

She shrugged. She was too shocked by what Erick had just shared. Wayne Wilson was a bully, but she never thought he'd actually try to kill people.

Moments later, they arrived at Hallee's. "Here we are," Erick announced. They pulled up a gravel drive leading to a brown, double-wide mobile home. Hallee waved to them as she walked out the front door. Ember got out and gave Hallee a hug.

"Eek! I'm so excited to go Murray." Her cheeks pushed up the large plastic frames of her glasses. "Shotgun!" She called as she deftly pushed around Ember and slid into the front passenger seat.

"Nice. Real nice." Ember rolled her eyes.

"What? With two younger siblings, you learn quick."

She crawled onto the backseat. "I see that." She really didn't mind. In fact, she was happy to see both of their auras glowing a bright yellow.

****

Erick parked across the street from the Education building on the Murray State campus. Ember eyed the plain brick building surrounded by large oak and maple trees. Their leaves were shifting into autumn's colors. A handful of students passed by along the sidewalk. She wondered if Derek was on campus this weekend or if he had a ball game.

The creak of Erick's driver side door broke her train of thought. "Okay, ladies...we are here." He stepped out of the car. "My mom called ahead. She said Dr. Kayce has office hours today—second floor. So, he should be in there."

"I've never been to Murray," Ember shared as she exited the car. She breathed in the unfamiliar scents wafting in the air. The air was crisper and clearer in Murray—no pig farms or chicken barns close by.

"My mom and dad brought me here a few times for

games. And once I got to sit in on one of my mom's continuing education classes," Erick said. "That was cool."

"I have a cousin who used to go here," Hallee added. "It's a nice campus."

"I feel like I've never been anywhere but Wilson County," Ember said under her breath as she looked up at the imposing building. "Okay, so what do we do? Just go in and knock on the door?"

"Pretty much. My mom had Dr. Kayce years ago for one of her classes. She said he's nice, just a little quirky."

"Well, let's do this." She led the trio across the street to the building.

Inside, a wide staircase greeted them. Ember had imagined what a college campus looked like, but it wasn't quite like this—so clean and relatively quiet—not at all like Wilson County High. Flyers of all colors were posted on a bulletin board just inside the entrance announcing intramural sports, sorority and fraternity events, and various organizations to join. Vending machines for soda and snacks sat in a small alcove with a few tables and chairs nestled nearby. College had seemed so foreign and unattainable, but this place seemed benign and, maybe even fun, for a normal person…someone like Derek Oliver, she thought.

"C'mon." Ember shrugged off thoughts of Derek and climbed the stairs. She noticed the faculty tag at the end of the hall. "This way."

The hall split in two. The entire wing was for faculty. She let her instincts take over, choosing to turn right. They passed by several closed doors labeled with professor's names until they came upon a corner office with the door held open by an overflowing box with a sign taped above that read, "papers," and an arrow pointing down to the box. It was Dr. Kayce's office.

She looked back at her friends and rapped her knuckles gently on the door. The strong odor of oils and incense tickled her sensitive nose.

"Hello? Dr. Kayce?" Ember peeked her head in.

An old man with unkempt, wild gray hair sat behind a desk cluttered with piles of paper. He leaned over a stack on his desk, reading intently through thick lenses as he waved his hand. "Just put it in the box. Thank you."

Ember stepped into the office. Framed photos lined the walls of a younger man, much like the professor. Yellowed with age, newspaper clippings of the same man were stuck along the walls. A few newer articles, lighter in color, stood out amongst them...one catching Ember's eye.

The photo was of Dr. Kayce shaking the hand of a handsome younger man. The headline read, "ELL Pharmaceuticals Funds Research at Murray State University." The logo of the company sent a chill down Ember's spine.

It was the same apple split in half with the snake on its stem. It was the logo on the doctor's badge in her vision. She froze in place.

Erick brushed past her and cleared his throat. "Excuse me, Dr. Kayce?"

The old man looked up; his black-framed glasses enlarged his eyes behind the lenses. "Yes?"

"Sorry to bother you. My mom, Karen Grossman, called. We are the students from Wilson County High."

Dr. Kayce's eyes darted amongst them as if trying

to make sense of what Erick said. His lips puckered together as he looked up at the ceiling. Ember watched as his aura flickered between blue, pink and green as he recalled the conversation. His eyes landed back on them. "Ah, yes. Sorry, I forgot." He tapped his graying head. "The old noggin' doesn't quite work like it used to." His smile was benign. "What can I do for you, kids?"

She swallowed. "Dr. Kayce, we were hoping you could tell us about unusual abilities? My doctor, Dr. Peters, suggested we reach out to you."

His wide eyes scanned her from head to toe. "Do you have special abilities?"

Ember nodded. "Yes."

"Please sit down." He gestured to the two chairs littered with files. "Oh, sorry." A small chuckle erupted from his chest. "Just set those on the floor."

"I'm fine. You two go ahead." She crossed her arms. Her eyes returned to the photo of Dr. Kayce and the ELL logo.

The professor rifled through his piles of papers and books on his desk till he found a yellow notepad and pen. "Tell me, young lady, what is your name?"

"Ember…Ember O'Neill." She walked closer to the wall, studying the clipping.

"Now that name sounds familiar…" He looked up once more to the ceiling as if searching for the answer.

"I was just on the news. I'm the girl that died."

"Oh. Yes! That's it. And…your father…quite tragic…" He peered across the desk at her.

She turned to face him. His aura was sincere, but it was unnerving to see it tinged in orange…as if he was excited, too.

Erick redirected the conversation. "Dr. Kayce, what can you tell us about people with the ability to see auras?"

"Is that your ability? Seeing auras?" the old man asked.

Ember nodded.

"Now that's exciting." His aura flared as he wrote notes. "And how long have you been able to do that? Was it after your drowning that you gained the ability?"

Despite her racing heartbeat, Ember replied evenly. "I have been able to see auras my whole life."

"Did you have a difficult birth? Did something happen to you as a child?"

She shook her head. "No. Nothing unusual that I know of."

"And anything else that you see or can do?" His pen paused above the paper. "Something that is unusual, I mean."

Her teeth dragged over her bottom lip, unsure of how much to share. Hallee looked at her expectantly.

She let out a breath. "I have been experiencing nightmares...lately they seem real...like something that is going to happen."

Dr. Kayce looked up. "Go on."

"My senses are more heightened. I smell, see, and hear things most people don't. And, most recently when I drowned, I had a vision...I met an angel."

Dr. Kayce's pen dropped as his mouth fell open. He quickly got ahold of himself, and a smile spread across his sagging cheeks. "Ember O'Neill...I have been searching for someone like you my entire career."

"You have?"

The doctor sprang from his seat with more vigor

than one would have assumed of someone his age. He walked around his desk and hugged Ember. She stiffened at his touch but allowed his grasp. Just as quickly, he released her and began gesturing to the walls.

"My father was like you." He pointed to the faded news articles and photos lining the wall. "Well, almost like you." His hands steepled as he returned to sit behind his desk. "We never understood where his abilities came from. He asserted an angel came to him when he was a child." His eyes glazed over. "But no one believed him. My father became known as the Sleeping Prophet for his ability to foretell the future. People came to him from across the world to see him and to get answers."

He returned his gaze to Ember. "It is what has driven my research...to try and understand how? Why was my father able to do this? Why not me, his son? Was it really an angel? Was it a cosmic anomaly? Why is it that some humans can see auras while others can't? Why do some have psychic abilities? Others don't. I have been trying to unlock these mysteries of the mind my entire career."

"Have you ever met someone who could compel others...like mind control?" Ember asked, thinking of Adam. Hallee and Erick both jerked around in their seats, eyeing Ember.

The doctor's brows arched above his glasses. "No...not yet, but my research has never included someone like you. Can you do that?" He licked his lips and began writing on his notepad.

"I'm not sure. Tell me about your research with ELL Pharmaceuticals, Dr. Kayce. What is it you do for them?" She gestured to the photo.

"Do?" He looked up at the ceiling. "Do? Well, I share my research with them. They are very interested in the mysteries of the mind, you know."

Erick leaned forward. "Why is a company that makes medicines interested in people who can see auras?"

"Well, I wouldn't know exactly…that's their business. They fund my research, and I share my findings."

"And what kind of research are you doing?" Ember asked.

"I test people for abilities. If one is found to have a special skill, we experiment and explore their capabilities and limits."

Ember's gaze was drawn to the caption of the photo: Chicago magnate, Asher Von Holstein, of ELL Pharmaceuticals, continues his father's legacy by funding medical research grants across the United States.

The room suddenly felt too small.

"I need to go." She turned on her heel, exiting into the hall, and ran down the steps till she was outside. Behind her, Hallee and Erick yelled for her to wait.

Her breaths were shallow as she bent over trying calm down. The dark vision of the woman screaming for her child echoed in her mind. A shiver ran down her spine. She winced, reliving the woman's anguish as her baby was torn away from her.

"Ember?"

She turned to the familiar voice. Derek. Her pulse quickened as he walked toward her with a backpack slung across his shoulder.

"Hey. I thought that was you. What are you doing here?" His piercing blue eyes seemed to see right through her walls and into her soul. "Hey, are you okay?" He closed the distance and reached out, touching her arm. Tingles of electricity erupted from his touch.

Ember jerked her arm away. "I'm fine." She didn't want him to see her upset like that and forced a smile. She gestured to Erick and Hallee exiting the building. "I'm here with my friends doing some research."

Derek scrubbed the back of his head. "I heard about your dad, Em. I'm sorry"

"Hey." Erick tilted his chin at Derek.

"What's up, Big E." Derek slapped palms with Erick.

"Nothing much."

"Hallee? Right? Good to see you again." Derek nodded at Hallee eliciting a severe rash of pink to bloom across her face and aura.

"We were just headed to the library." Ember arched her brow at her friends. "Right?"

"Yeah, that's right." Erick pushed up his glasses.

"Okay, cool. Need help finding it?" Derek asked.

"Nope. We are good. Bye, Derek." Ember took her friends' arms, steering them away.

"Okay, bye, then," Derek said to their backsides as she picked up the pace.

Once they rounded the building out of Derek's view, Ember released them and stopped. "I don't know where the library is."

"Yeah, I know." Erick's brows pinched together. "Mind sharing what that was all about back there? Running out of the office? Brushing off Derek? I thought you liked him?"

She scanned the tree lined quad. A handful of students were crossing the green space to other buildings. Her heart thumped in her chest. "Let's just get to the library. I'll explain everything there."

Chapter Twenty-three

Once inside the library, surrounded by the familiar smell of leather and the soft whispers of pages turning, Ember felt more at peace. She chose a table hidden deep inside the library between stacks of dust covered shelves. Her friends looked at her expectantly as they joined her at the table.

"Remember my vision about the woman delivering a baby and the nurse taking it away?"

They both nodded. Ember pulled out her sketches and spread them out. She pointed to the name tag she had drawn from the memory. "One of the pictures on Dr. Kayce's wall had this in it. It is the logo for ELL Pharmaceuticals." Her brows drew together. "ELL's doctors are taking babies from mothers and…and testing their blood. That's what I saw in that vision."

She swallowed. "And they're funding Dr. Kayce's research. It all must be connected." She pointed to the sketch of the city skyline. "Logan said this looked like Chicago. This must be where ELL is headquartered, Chicago."

"Logan? When did you show him your sketches?" Hallee asked.

"I didn't. He looked over my shoulder and saw it." Ember tugged on the chain around her neck. "This must be what the Archangel was trying to show me."

Erick steepled his hands. "Look, Em, we know nothing. Your vision still could have been from the medication in your system."

"You can't tell me it's a coincidence, Erick. I have never seen that symbol in my life. The vision is real. It must be."

Hallee reached over and squeezed her hand. "I believe you."

Erick sighed. "It's not that I don't believe you. I know you believe what you saw. It's plausible that you might have seen that symbol subconsciously. ELL Pharmaceuticals make a lot of products. Maybe the logo reemerged in your psyche when your body was under duress. Regardless, we must take a scientific approach. One variable we need to prove or disprove is the medication you're taking. Will you consider going off the meds just for a day?"

Ember nodded. "Yes, but I'm telling you, it's not the pills. Adam visited me again."

Hallee's mouth fell open. "What?"

Erick pushed up his glasses. "Okay…what happened."

Hallee flipped open her notebook, pencil at the ready.

"I was having the usual nightmare," Ember said, "running through the bottoms trying to rescue the drowning girl when his voice broke into the dream."

Erick interrupted. "And you had not taken any pills?"

Ember looked away. "Not any sleeping pills."

Erick pointed to Hallee. "Write that down."

"He offered to help me figure things out," Ember said.

"Let's just say he's not a figment of your imagination, how do you know you can trust him?" Erick asked.

"I don't."

Erick leaned back in his chair. "Okay, tell us exactly what he said."

She spent the next few minutes sharing everything that Adam told her.

"So, if this guy is for real…somehow he senses you and can dream walk." Erick ticked off his fingers. "He can get inside your mind. He can compel people to do things." He leaned across the table. "He sounds dangerous, Em. And, I hope, for your sake, that it's all up here." He tapped his temple.

Ember suddenly felt defensive of Adam and herself. "Are you saying I'm dangerous?"

"No. Of course not, that's not what I meant," Erick said and looked to Hallee for help.

Hallee leaned forward. "I think what he's trying to say is that we don't know this Adam guy. But we know you. You would never do anything to hurt someone. This Adam…we don't know what he is capable of. Just be careful, Em."

She watched their auras shift to pure concern. "I'm sorry. Yes, I will be careful, of course." She looked down at the sketches. "Until we know more, though, I am staying away from Dr. Kayce." Ember crossed her arms. "We will figure this out without him. Okay?"

Erick raised his palms up. "You'll get no argument from me. The guy was a bit off, ya know?"

"Exactly. We can totally do this without him." She pointed to the sketches. "Let's see if we can figure out what that word *Eligere* means"

"I know just where to start. Follow me." Erick pulled back from the table and led them to an enormous book resting on a podium in the center of the library.

"It must be in here. It totally sounds like Latin." Erick flipped pages till he landed on the right one. His finger trailed down the page.

"I see it." Hallee reached over his shoulder and pointed. "*Eligere*." She read aloud. "It means to choose." They both looked at Ember.

"So, I am supposed to choose…" Ember's voice trailed. "That sort of makes sense because…" She lowered her voice to a whisper. "He said that I needed to take the oath."

Erick leaned in. "Yeah, but what oath?"

"I don't know," Ember answered. "He basically said that only I could change the vision of that dark future, but I would need to take the oath, I think." She rubbed her temples. "It's all becoming so hazy."

"Hey, let's split up and do our own research," Hallee suggested.

****

"So, we have some information to share about the Archangel," Erick offered once they were seated back at their original out-of-the-way table.

"Yeah? What did you find out?" Ember asked.

He motioned to Hallee. "Ladies first."

"Well…" Hallee flipped back several pages in her notebook. "I spoke with my uncle, Tom, who is a Catholic priest. He said the Archangel Michael was like a warrior angel. He's mentioned a few times in the Bible, but most significantly, he is known to lead the angels in their fight against Satan in the Book of Revelation."

"Satan?" Ember felt the hairs on both arms stand on end.

Looking up from her paper, Hallee nodded. "The cool thing is that my uncle did this paper on the Order of Saint Michael. It was like this group who were knights in France who did these crazy things like murder in the name of the Archangel. The King eventually disbanded them, but my uncle was able to trace some of their leaders to the United States where they settled in and around New Orleans." Hallee's brows bounced above her purple frames. "He believes the Order is still around today, acting in disguise."

Erick leaned back in his chair. "That's cool."

Ember crossed her arms. "Yeah, but I'm not sure what it has to do with me?"

"Maybe…your dad was one of these Order members and that demon was trying to kill him?" Hallee offered.

Her brows shot up. "Whoa. I think I would have known if my dad was some psycho Order member."

"Okay, whatever, it's just a theory." Hallee shrugged.

Ember massaged her temples. "What did your preacher say, Erick?"

Erick stroked his chin hairs. "Not a lot. But it was more about what he didn't say that got me to do my own digging."

Curiosity piqued, Ember leaned forward. "Go on."

"He mentioned the Archangel is only referenced in the Old Testament like three or four times. And that people associate him more with the End Times." He reached into his backpack, pulling out copies of scripture. "So, I did some research in our church library and found this from the Book of Enoch." He pushed the papers across the table to Ember and Hallee. "It's controversial, but from what I gather, some people believe the Archangel petitioned God to save the Nephilim."

"Nephilim." The word stuck on Ember's tongue.

"Yeah, so this is where it gets controversial. Before Lucifer was thrown out of Heaven, he oversaw these angels, who were supposed to help and guide man on Earth. According to this book, Lucifer and those who were loyal to him rebelled against God and went against him, including having sex with humans." Erick's cheeks flushed. "That union created these human-half angel beings called Nephilim."

"Wow." Hallee's eyes widened, looking at the copies. "It says they were like giants."

"Yeah." Erick pushed up his glasses. "God's not happy, right? So, he casts Lucifer or Satan into Hell along with his legion of angels creating what are known as demons." He looked at Ember. "God then sends a great flood to wipe out the Nephilim."

"Noah and the Ark," Ember breathed.

"Yes, exactly. So, according to this…" He pointed to the document. "In the Book of Enoch…which by the way is not accepted to be legitimate scripture…but in Enoch's account, he says that the Archangel Michael petitioned God to save the Nephilim race, arguing that it wasn't their fault that the angels went against God's word."

"So, what happened?" Hallee asked.

"Well, the flood was legit. It lasted forty days and forty nights. Noah, the Ark, etc., they survived." Erick leaned forward. "But what if the Nephilim did, too?

What if the Archangel was successful and God spared them? What if these half human-half angels survived?"

Hallee dropped her pencil and looked at Ember wide-eyed. "What if you're Nephilim, Em?"

She released a nervous laugh. "Do I look like a giant? Besides, I think my parents would have told me, especially my dad."

"Would he?" Erick asked.

Ember's hand reflexively fingered the military tags around her neck. She wasn't sure of anything anymore. "This is crazy." She brushed the papers back to Erick.

"Is it?" Erick pressed. "Any crazier than a demon attacking your dad? Any crazier than you having visions? Any crazier than you coming back to life after being dead for twenty-one minutes?"

"Okay. Okay, I get it." Ember sighed. "Anything is possible at this point, I suppose." She thought of her dad's photo. "We need to find the soldier who served with my dad. I feel like he is the one with all the answers."

Erick gathered the papers, putting them in his backpack. "Agreed. I'm just not sure how we do that though."

"Maybe my dad can point us in the right direction," Hallee said. "He served in the Army Reserve. Maybe he has some ideas on how to track this guy down."

Ember smiled. "Ah, brilliant idea, Watson."

"Well, thank you, Holmes." Hallee dipped her head.

"Hey, what about me? I did all this research on my own." Erick pouted, but Ember saw his happy aura.

"Good job, warrior prince," she teased. "Proud of you. That must have been difficult with your big ol' muscles and tiny brain."

"Ouch. Are you making fun of my massive muscles?" Erick flexed.

"Yep." Ember said, letting the "p" pop. "And your tiny brain."

"Who won the last chess match? Hmmm?"

"C'mon, let's go." She tossed her sketches into her purse.

"Hmm-mmm. Exactly. That's what I thought." Erick placed his backpack over his shoulder. "In case you were wondering, Hallee, it was me. I won our last six matches."

"But who's keeping count, right?"

She rolled her eyes. No matter what their investigation turned up, she was grateful to have them both in her corner. "All right, let's get out of here."

Chapter Twenty-four

Ember threw her bag down on the floor of Hallee's room. She spun, taking in the lilac walls and eggplant colored comforter. A purple stuffed bear rested on a purple pillow. "So, your favorite color is…"

Hallee laughed. "Yep, purple, you guessed it." She pointed to the poster taped above her bed. "And my favorite singer is Prince."

Ember's eyes floated to the wooden bookshelf, leaning awkwardly in the corner. It was crammed full of books with an assortment of troll dolls scattered here and there. A jam box and a stack of cassettes rested on her small nightstand. She noted the collection of eyeshadows and lip glosses organized on her dresser. The room was eclectic and totally Hallee.

She turned to her new best friend. She could see Hallee was nervous, perhaps even more nervous than she was. "I love it! Your room is amazing!" She pointed to the bookshelf. "I'm jealous…all those books. What do you like to read?"

Hallee's nervous aura was immediately replaced with lemon yellow joy as she plucked a book. "I read a lot of romance." She waggled her brows. "This one is really good."

She read the title, *Sweet Savage Eden*. The cover showed a man with coal black hair and bulging muscles

173

and holding a swooning blonde in his arms. "Oh, wow. Cool."

"I also like…" She paused and blushed.

Ember moved closer. "What else do you like to read?"

"I'm, like, really into the paranormal—angels, vampires, werewolves."

Ember laughed. "No judgement here." She raised her hand. "I'm totally into fantasy—more Tolkien, epic type fantasy. But, yeah, that's totally cool." Ember's eyes snagged on a book about aliens. "Aliens, too?"

"What?" Hallee's face turned crimson. "No." She took the book and shoved it to the back of the shelf. "That was my mom's."

"Oh, sorry."

Hallee turned and sank onto her bed, hugging her stuffed bear. "No, it's okay."

Ember carefully sat on the bed beside her. "You don't have to talk about it. I get it. Trust me."

"No, it's fine. It's just—I don't really know how to tell someone that my mom is crazy." Hallee tucked her chin into her bear.

"Hey, you just did, and I'm still here." Ember tried to console her.

She looked up over her glasses. "My mom started having these blank spots in her memories—that's how it started. She wouldn't have any money to pay rent or buy groceries, and she couldn't explain where the money went. Soon, she stopped going to work. She claimed the aliens were messing with her brain and doing experiments. She became obsessed."

Her eyes darted to the bookcase. "When my dad saw how bad things had gotten, he took custody of me and had my mom committed to a facility."

"Wow, I'm so sorry, Hallee. That must have been so hard."

Her forehead crinkled. "Yeah, they said it was a form of early onset dementia."

"When's the last time you saw her?"

"About a month ago...end of July." Her eyes filled with tears. "She was so drugged up, Em. She barely acknowledged that I was there."

"I'm so sorry, Hallee."

Hallee sniffled. Reaching over, she took a tissue from the box on her nightstand and blew her nose. It sounded like a foghorn. "Sorry about that. I never learned to blow my nose like a proper lady."

That made Ember laugh. "Yeah, me neither."

"So, there you have it. My mom sees aliens. You're not the only cool one, Em."

Ember's face turned serious. "Can I ask you something?"

Hallee nodded.

"Do you think I'm imagining everything? Do you think maybe it's just all in my head?"

"No. And I'll tell you why." Hallee got up and pulled out her notebook from her purse. "Number one...and probably the most important reason, because it comes from the hospital doctor who released you and said you are perfectly healthy. You do not have synesthesia. And he said you should consult another medical professional who specializes in unique cases like yourself—but we are scratching Dr. Kayce from that list." Hallee paused and looked up at her. "Would you like number two?"

She grinned. "Sure."

"Number two…when evaluating said auras your assessments are usually spot on." She raised her brows. "Number three…." She looked up. "Technically, I don't have a number three written down, but I believe you." She reached over and hugged Ember.

It felt good having her support. Ember pulled back. "Thanks, it means a lot."

Hallee leaned back on her pillows. "So, you want to explain why you completely blew off the hottest guy on campus today?"

"Derek?"

Hallee's aura flashed pink. "Yeah, who else?"

"I just didn't want to have to answer questions about why we were there. You know?"

"I get it." She picked up the stuffed animal. "What about tonight? Are you sure you want to go to the bonfire?"

A nervous tingle ran down her spine. Ember wasn't sure, honestly, but she wanted to get answers. "Yeah, I think Logan Lauder used to live in Chicago. Maybe he might know something about ELL? Birdie Mae made it sound like his uncle was a big shot executive from there. Maybe he's heard something. It's worth a shot, anyway."

Hallee grinned. "Not to mention, he likes you."

"No, he doesn't. He's just curious about the Dead Girl. Once he hears all the rumors, he will be on to someone else, like your cousin, Katie, for instance."

"Speaking of which, Maddison will probably be there tonight."

"Yeah, I know." Ember tugged on her dad's chain. *Virtus vincit.*

Chapter Twenty-five

The sun was just setting as Erick pulled up. Hallee's dad gave him a grilling that Ember knew her dad would have respected. Hallee was mortified, but Erick handled it like a champ.

The last time Ember had been down to the river was at the end of July with her dad. She reached up and touched the military tags and keys hanging from her neck but refused to let her mind go there.

Tonight, she was going to be a normal teenager and hang out with her friends. And, if things went well, she would pick Logan Lauder's brain about Chicago and ELL. She looked at Hallee and Erick's auras glowing a flirty pink as they argued the pros and cons of classic rock artists from the seventies and eighties. Erick turned down a road that barely earned that distinction from a well-worn path—no gravel, just bumpy, hard-packed earth and weeds growing between a tire-carved trail.

It was completely dark now. A chill ran down her spine as thoughts of her most recent nightmare filled her mind. She reached down into her purse and took two more pills. Tonight was not the night to have a sensory overload.

Erick slowed the car down to a crawl as they neared an enormous bonfire glowing up ahead. Old trucks and cars, mostly rusted clunkers, were parked every which way, making it look like a used car lot in the middle of nowhere. Country music blared from the cab of a truck. Tailgates were dropped and plastic cups were in hand as classmates sat sipping beers and mixed concoctions.

One vehicle stood out—Maddison Miller's—the object of desire for most of the school. And when they were on-again, Maddison let Kale Martin drive it. Ember's stomach flopped at the thought of seeing the queen. Hopefully, she'd stay off Maddison's radar tonight.

Erick pulled the car to a stop and pushed his glasses up. She noted that he had dressed up, donning a new pair of acid-washed jeans with his favorite polo shirt and sneakers. "Okay, gang. We're here."

"Yay." Hallee's aura wavered between excitement and fear, and Ember felt the same way.

"So…" Erick let out a breath. "All for one, one for all?" His hands squeezed the steering wheel as he looked in the rearview mirror at her.

She thought of her list. Number five…become popular…in a good way. She needed to be brave. She was no longer "Bloody Ember." She was the Dead Girl, but maybe…just maybe…it could change. Maybe she could just blend in or just maybe be the "Cool Girl" for once. *Virtus vincit.*

"Three musketeers?" Her lips shifted into a smile. "Really?"

Erick shrugged and grinned.

She opened the car door and braced herself like a soldier going to battle. "Okay, let's do this."

Hallee walked alongside her, with Erick following

behind. Flickering flames cast a shifting light amongst those standing around. She quickly noted the silhouette of Kale with his arms around Maddison, who sneered at Ember across the fire.

Redirecting, she headed to the opposite side of the flames. Katie was locking lips with some boy she didn't recognize. Heather and Jamie were dancing to the music with members of the cheer squad. Their beers sloshed and spilled with every hip thrust. Ember received a few nods from some, but several arched their brows at her appearance.

A familiar "Eek!" screeched ahead. She looked over to see Brittany breaking from her group of friends and bouncing toward her. "Ember! Oh my gosh, I didn't know you were coming." The red plastic cup dripped as she sloshed its contents over the side. "Oops." She held up a cup. "Want some?"

She recognized Brittany's glossy eyes and muddled aura. She was drunk. "I don't know..." She had never partied before.

"Come on...don't be lame."

She looked at Hallee. She was no help. "Okay...just a sip." The liquid burned as it went down her throat. She coughed. "What is this?"

"Jack and cola. You'll get used to it." Brittany took her hand and pulled her over. "Come hang out with us."

She looked back at Erick and Hallee. They shrugged and stayed back by the fire. She felt torn but told herself it would just be a few minutes, then she'd go back to the fire with her friends.

"Guys, Ember is here." Brittany announced to the sets of unenthusiastic eyes, taking her in from head to toe. She questioned her own outfit as she scanned the girls in return. They were wearing Daisy Duke shorts and various Wilson County High War Eagle shirts and jackets, with matching red bows adorning their ponytails.

"Ember, meet the newest members of the Wilson County High JV Cheer Squad! I made the team!" Brittany's aura glowed as her tan legs bounced up and down.

"Congrats." She smiled and nodded, not sure why Brittany was acting so friendly.

The girls mumbled thanks shifting away from her.

"We're celebrating! Want one?" Brittany didn't wait for her answer. She pulled a drink from the cooler and began mixing in a brown liquid. She proudly handed her the mixed drink. "Bottoms up."

"Thanks." Ember took a sip and immediately thought her throat was on fire. Liquor. Her eyes watered.

A set of headlights glared in their direction as a vehicle pulled up. "Oh, my gawd. It's Logan!" Brittany gushed and grabbed her wrist. "How do I look?" Ember took a large swallow of her drink. "You look cute."

"Good. I need you to come with me. I heard he was, like, totally curious about the Dead Girl. So, I thought who better to introduce him to you than me? I can tell him everything that happened, okay?" Brittany pulled her toward Logan as he exited his car.

Logan Lauder was wearing faded blue jeans and a black T-shirt that clung in all the right places. Their eyes met—flames erupted—and her bones melted. There was no denying the chemistry between them.

"Hey, what's up?" He nodded to Brittany, then looked directly at Ember. "Glad you came."

"Look at you, you handsome stud." Brittany's drunken drawl drew out the "u" in you. Her brilliant smile flashed in the moonlight. "I'm Brittany, by the way, and this is the Dead Girl." She waved her hand back at Ember. "You are going to die when I tell you what happened at my party." Brittany steered Logan past her to her tailgate and the flock of cheerleaders.

Left standing there alone, she took that as her cue to rejoin Erick and Hallee by the fire.

"Well, that was quick." Hallee tilted her head towards Logan.

"Yeah, that didn't go exactly as I imagined, but the night is still young." Ember raised her cup. "Want a sip?" She offered the drink to Hallee.

She shook her head. Erick's aura and look screamed disappointment.

"What? When in Rome…" She took another sip…this one went down much smoother.

He raised his hands. "Hey, judge-free zone here. You've had a lot on your plate."

She took another swallow. "Thanks. I really needed that reminder."

Sparks glowing like fireflies wafted up into the night sky. She studied the endless sea of sparkling stars until the smell of strawberries and chocolate broke her concentration.

Hallee elbowed her. "Guess who's coming over?"

She glanced over her shoulder. Something about Logan Lauder was magnetic. It felt natural, instinctual, and totally scary.

Hallee pinched her arm. "Ember! He's coming to talk to you."

She peered down at her friend. "How do I look?"

Behind her glasses, Hallee's eyes enlarged as she scanned her over. "You look great." She cocked her head. "I knew purple would look good on you."

"Hey, what's up?" Logan nodded and raised his palm to Erick.

His gaze drifted over Ember from head to toe, eliciting a crooked grin to slide across his lips. Hallee reached down and squeezed her hand. In the distance behind Logan, she saw Brittany staring at Logan's backside.

"You and Brittany have a nice chat?" Ember tilted her head.

His brows raised. "Jealous?"

As much as she wanted to disappear into the earth, she instead gulped more of her drink before she answered. "What? No. Why would I be jealous?"

"Relax, O'Neill." He winked. "I'm just messing with you." He nodded to the fire. "Haven't been around a fire since boarding school."

"Boarding school?" Erick said what everyone was thinking—no one ever goes to boarding school, especially not anyone from Western Kentucky.

"Yeah, when I was younger…it's a long story." He looked over to Ember. "So, what do you do for fun out here?"

"Don't ask us," Erick shared. "We're the nerd squad, remember? This is our first time."

"Hey! Brought you a drink!" Brittany interjected herself beside Logan. "And a refill for you, Ember."

"Thanks." He took a sip. "Whew! That is a heavy pour." When he winked at Brittany, her aura lit up like a magenta Christmas tree.

"Erick…Hallee…sure you don't want one?"

Brittany asked. "We are celebrating! I made the JV squad!"

Ember raised her brows, eyeing them both.

"When in Rome?" Hallee shrugged and followed Brittany to the tailgate.

"I'm just going to make sure she doesn't pour the whole bottle of Jack into Hallee's drink." Erick left, leaving her and Logan alone.

Logan's eyes flicked to her chest. She watched in horror as his hand reached out towards her boobs. She swatted him away. "What are you doing?"

"Relax, Ember." He chuckled, stuffing his hand into his tight jean pocket. "I was just curious about that chain."

Her cheeks grew warm. She took a sip of the new drink. It was even stronger, but she was grateful for the liquid courage. She studied his aura over the edge of the cup. It was a confusing mix of curiosity and affection. "It was my dad's."

His aura shifted to indigo. "Sorry, Brittany told me about that."

Erick and Hallee walked back over easing the tension. Erick raised his cup. "Believe it or not they actually serve water over there."

Across the bonfire voices rose, causing heads to turn. Maddison and Kale were fighting. Her ears burned. Maddison was pissed because Kale said Ember was hot. Then he accused her of throwing herself at Logan. Ember looked at Logan trying to figure out if he knew what they were saying.

He caught her staring. "Guess there's trouble in paradise."

As Katie consoled Maddison, Kale walked over to

the fire. Kale glanced at her as he palmed Logan.

"Hey, Kale." Erick bumped fists with him.

Logan took a sip and nodded. "Girl problems?"

"Yeah, it's whatever. She's pissed. And now we are broken up…again." He shook his head. "She's hot, but she's as moody as hell, man." He took a sip of his beer. "Trust me, you don't want none of that."

Logan nodded, "Noted."

The fire seemed a thousand degrees hotter as Ember took in the view of Logan Lauder and Kale Martin standing side by side. Kale caught her eye and his aura soared magenta. She looked away; confident she was now a human puddle.

"So, congrats on making the team," Kale said to Logan.

"Yeah, thanks." He kicked a rock with the toe of his shoe. "It's not really my sport, but I'm learning."

"Give it a few practices…Coach will have you playing varsity with me."

Hallee leaned in towards Ember and whispered. "I'm definitely going to enjoy watching basketball at Wilson County High."

Ember flushed. "Yeah, me, too."

"Erick, my man, we still need a manager…" Kale shoved Erick on the shoulder, nearly knocking him down.

"I don't know…" His voice cracked.

"Dude, you know you'd be good at it. Plus, there are some perks." He nodded to the cheer squad, getting sloppy drunk.

Erick took a sip of his water. "I'll think about it."

Hallee beamed up at Erick. "That would be so cool if you became the team manager, Erick."

He pushed his glasses up his nose. "Yeah, maybe."

Kale's gaze shifted to Ember. "So, you guys want to come with us to go check out the cabin Wayne Wilson was holed up in?"

A cool shiver washed over Ember. "What?"

Kale put his fingers to his mouth and blew a shrilling whistle. Heads jerked in his direction. "Time to go!" He circled his finger in the air. "Get your shit—lights, drinks—and let's go."

Kale pulled a flashlight from his back pocket and looked at her. "You down to go check it out?"

She drained the last of her drink. "Yeah, sure."

"Cool. You're with me."

When he reached out his hand, she hesitated. Hallee elbowed her into action. She took Kale's hand. It was warm and soft.

"Let's reload our drinks…it's a long walk," Kale said and tugged her forward.

Ember looked over her shoulder at Hallee, who gave a little wave and a thumbs up. She inhaled Kale's scent. It was nice…probably some cologne Maddison bought him, she thought. But it was nothing like Logan's natural scent or…Adam's.

You are an idiot. The star basketball player is holding your hand. She looked up and smiled at Kale. *And you're thinking of Adam?*

"Thanks."

"For what?" He refilled her cup as she felt the eyes of the entire cheer squad burn holes into her backside.

She looked up into his warm brown eyes. "For being nice to me."

He crooked his finger, motioning for her to come closer. "That's because I like you." He reached down and cupped her cheek.

A boy had never looked at her that way. His eyes traced her face, landing on her lips. "You want to kiss me," she whispered, shocked at the realization. *Kale Martin wants to kiss me*.

"Yes, I want to kiss you very much, Ember O'Neill." His voice was husky as he leaned forward.

She stepped back and shook her head. "I must be drunk."

"Excuse me…" Brittany batted her lashes. "Everyone is ready to go now, Kale."

He flipped on his flashlight. "Yeah, sure." He turned and yelled, "Follow me."

Ember's eyes snagged on Logan, who had Maddison hanging off his arm.

That didn't last long. She rolled her eyes and followed Kale.

****

Ember wasn't exactly afraid of what they would find at Wayne Wilson's cabin hideout. She was more on edge about being in the woods in the middle of the night at the river bottoms. It echoed too close to her nightmare, and with each step, they snaked deeper and deeper into the woods. Being there heightened her senses and multiplied her fear, despite the alcohol wrecking her inhibitions.

Kale pointed out that the old path led to several abandoned cabins he said his grandad used to rent out. They caught Wayne hiding out in one of them, he explained. Ember followed closely behind him. She tried to focus on Kale and the path ahead, but Maddison's whiney voice kept interrupting. Ember got more and more annoyed with the Queen of Wilson

High as she gushed over Logan.

"Here it is." Kale shined his flashlight on a dilapidated shack. Police caution tape, strung between several trees, effectively fenced it in. Kale lifted the tape for her. "Ladies first."

Her heart thumped as she moved closer to the cabin. The last time she saw Wayne, he was spraying red paint at her.

She stopped. Erick and Hallee had caught up to them. Hallee touched her arm. "Hey, you okay?"

"Yeah. You know, it's just sort of creepy."

Kale pushed the door open. The hinges creaked. He stood in the doorway and slowly angled his flashlight around the room. "Oh, shit." He shook his head and backed out the door. "This was a mistake." He took Ember by the elbow and tried to turn her away.

"What? What is it?" she asked.

"You don't want to go in there."

Her classmates brushed past them. She could hear the hisses and laughter. "Kale, what is it?"

She knew she shouldn't do it, but she walked ahead and stepped inside the cabin. She shuddered. Graffiti lined the walls in red, dripping spray paint.

"UR DED, BITCH. UR ALL DED."

The words…the letters…reminded her of her locker. She raced out of the cabin. Her head pounded. All the liquor she had consumed was now forcing itself out of her body. She bent over and vomited violently.

"Shit." Kale rubbed her back. "You all right?"

"No." Ember brushed the back of her hand over her mouth. The bitter vomit taste clung to her tongue.

His brown eyes softened. "Let's go back. We'll get you some water."

187

Ember heard the conversations behind her. Maddison argued Wayne's side, saying, "I don't blame him. The whole thing was blown out of proportion."

Erick came up to her with Hallee at his side. "Hey…you okay?"

Kale put his arm around her. "We're headed back. She's not feeling well."

"Okay, cool." Erick brushed his glasses up. "We'll follow."

****

They walked in silence with only the crickets and the distant chatter of her classmates to serenade them. Ember shuddered at what Wayne had written. Despite all his harassment, she never truly felt threatened by him, not like that. She shivered. Now she knew that sometimes there was more behind a person's aura than what she could see.

A strong scent of death wafted across their path. Like evening dew, the rotten odor settled around them—*a demon.* She reached out her hand motioning for her friends to stop.

"What's wrong?" Kale asked.

The muffled sound of a girl yelling echoed down the path from the direction of the bonfire. Ember didn't pause to explain what she had heard. She just left them behind and ran back through the woods with unnatural speed, tracking the screams. Kale yelled in the distance behind her to stop, but she couldn't.

She had to save the girl.

Ember reached the bonfire inexplicably fast. She scanned the area. Rot hung in the air, along with the smell of lustful pheromones. She ran to the truck, ripped the door nearly off the hinge, and pulled the attacker off the girl.

Ember slung him to the ground, then slammed her fists into his face. Bones crunched and blood splattered as she broke the attacker's nose.

Katie Wilson slid out of the cab of the truck. Her Wilson County High cheer shirt was torn. Mascara tinted tears streamed down her cheeks as she screamed for Ember to stop.

But she couldn't. She wouldn't let this demon hurt anyone again. Logan's strong hands pulled her back.

"Let me go," she gritted between her teeth.

"It's okay. It's okay, O'Neill," Logan said. "You stopped him. Look at me."

She looked up. His piercing eyes broke through her murderous rage.

"Oh my God." She looked over to see the boy, not a demon, curled on his side and coughing up blood.

Kale ran up with Hallee and Erick just behind. "What the hell happened?" He looked between Logan and Ember.

"That crazy bitch just went nuts," the boy exclaimed with blood spurting from his nose into his mouth.

"Katie?" Hallee gasped as she took in the scene. "What happened? Are you okay?"

Katie snapped out of her trance as Hallee reached over and hugged her cousin. The boy brushed the dirt off his shirt, revealing the logo of Hickory High, a rival school from the next county over. "We were just having some fun."

"You were hurting her, you asshole," Ember gritted between her teeth as Logan used force to keep her from pouncing on the attacker again.

"I think you better leave, Chad." Kale stood firm. "Now."

The boy raised both hands. "Whatever, man. Just a big misunderstanding." As he walked away, he yelled over one shoulder, "Hey, Katie...call me!"

Before Ember could react, Kale Martin tackled the guy. Fists flew, and both boys rolled on the ground.

"Shit." Logan hissed under his breath. "Stay here," he commanded Ember.

She watched as he easily pried the boys apart. Her classmates had finally made their way back from the cabin and gathered in a ring around the entangled boys.

"Kick his ass!" One encouraged Kale.

Kale was breathing hard. He spit blood from his mouth. "Don't you ever touch Katie again. You don't call her. You don't know her. Got it, Chad?"

The boy put his hands up and slowly backed away. The crowd collapsed on Kale giving him high fives.

She turned to Katie and Hallee. Katie was shaking, but her tears had stopped. "Hey..." She reached out.

Katie looked up. Her aura was a mix of emotions. She didn't say anything. She just hugged Ember quickly and whispered, "Thanks."

Kale broke free of the crowd. "Hey, you all right?" he asked Katie.

Katie nodded her head slowly.

"We should get you home," Hallee said.

"Yeah, I can drive." Erick dangled his keys.

"You and I need to talk." Logan leaned into her ear. "I can drive you home." He looked down at her. "If that's okay?"

Her heart thumped loudly in her chest. "Actually, I'm sleeping over at Hallee's."

Kale stepped forward, wiping blood from his split lip. "I'm taking Katie home." He pulled her into a side hug and whispered something in her ear. She nodded, said goodbye, and left with Kale. Ember watched Maddison stare daggers at the pair.

"All righty then..." Erick broke the silence. "You know...I think this party is over, anyway. You ladies ready to go?"

Hallee nodded. "Yeah."

"Mind if I drive Ember to your house, Hallee?" Logan asked.

Hallee's head bobbed in a circle. "Yeah, that's cool."

"Ember?" Logan's deep voice purred in her ear, sending tingles down her spine.

"Sure."

Deep inside, she knew being alone with him was dangerous territory. As much as she knew she should say no, her body begged for more time with Logan Lauder. But she justified the alone time since she still needed to ask him about Chicago.

Chapter Twenty-six

Erick and Logan exchanged a few words while Ember stood by Logan's shiny black sports car. She could just hear the murmurs spreading that the Dead Girl was leaving with Logan Lauder.

Maddison stormed over to her vehicle and turned on the ignition so that the headlights blared right at Ember, then yelled for Heather and Jamie to come with her. They obediently ran over and hopped into her ride. She spun the tires, causing rock and dirt to churn. The guys cheered her dramatic exit as she slammed the vehicle from Reverse into Drive. Maddison's middle finger jabbed out the window as she roared past Ember, leaving her in a cloud of dust.

Ember coughed and waved the dirt cloud from her face. *That went well.*

Logan walked over. His scent was overpowering as he leaned in and opened the passenger door for her. "Well," she said, brows raised. "Logan Lauder is a gentleman. Good to know."

He grinned, forcing a dimple to pop out. "Always." He shut the door and deftly slipped into the driver's side. He turned the ignition, and the car purred to life.

"What kind of car is this?" She asked as the console lit up. She noted the interior was all black, and the radio was digital with one of those built-in new CD players. The car smelled like leather and Logan.

"It's new—only a few in production." He shifted it into gear. "My uncle bought it for me." He nodded to Erick's car pulling out. "We're following Erick. He needs to get gas in Bardwell before he takes Hallee home."

"Okay." Her stomach flopped as the drive just got longer.

He gave her an appraising glance. "So, O'Neill, who taught you how to fight like that?"

"My dad...this past summer. We did a lot of hunting and fishing...and training."

"Training...with your dad? Is that a Kentucky thing? Fathers teaching their daughters how to kick ass?" His head tilted and grinned.

"Well, it's sort of a long story, but if you haven't heard already...last year sucked royally for me." Ember squirmed in her seat and looked out the window.

"Go on," Logan encouraged.

"My dad just thought it would be good for me. Get out of my head and be in nature."

"And was it? Was it good for you?"

Ember studied his aura...her gaze hung on that golden hue like her dad's. Tears misted her eyes. "Yeah. It was the best summer of my life."

He reached over and squeezed her hand. Electricity sparked between them. Ember jerked her hand away. "Sorry." His brows formed a *V*. After a brief pause, he continued. "So, Ember O'Neill can kick ass. She also kicked death's ass. She can run like hell." He glanced over at her. "Got any other cool tricks up your sleeve?"

She felt sweat erupt in all her cracks and crevices. Something about him made her want to spill the beans about everything. But she knew the moment she did, it would be the last time Logan Lauder looked and spoke to her in the way he was doing right now. No, she would never tell him her secrets.

"Nope. That's all I got, Lauder."

"Okay, O'Neill." His dimples stood at attention as he glanced over at her. "Why don't I believe you?"

Beneath his scrutiny, a blaze of fire roared through her body. "So…how about yourself? You were pretty impressive out there. You were nowhere, then suddenly you were pulling me off that Chad kid. You didn't even seem winded. Care to share your secrets?" She looked down at her knuckles, still red from the contact with Chad, the almost-rapist's face.

Logan's aura shifted and swirled, coral kissing blue and red. He was uncomfortable. His face fell, causing Ember to regret the question. "There's nothing to tell." His fingers drummed over the steering wheel. "Tell me about growing up here. Your parents…what are they like?"

"Okay…" They were now turning onto paved roads leading back to civilization. "Let's see…it was me and my mom…and my dad…"

He noticed her pause. "I'm sorry. Stupid question."

"No, it's fine." Her chin dipped. "It's always just been the three of us…and the dogs, of course."

His head cocked to the side. "What kind of dogs?"

"Lola was a bloodhound. My dad got her in New Orleans and trained her from a pup." Ember paused. "She died during the attack on my dad."

"I'm sorry."

"It's okay. My dog, Bear, is an Ovarka Caucasian Mountain dog."

"A what?"

She laughed. "He's a unique breed. Basically, he looks like a dog-bear, big and fluffy, and he's super protective and loyal."

He nodded. "Good to know, if I ever decide I want to sneak into your bedroom."

Her face went up in flames. She couldn't look at him. He's just joking, she told herself.

"I'm familiar with bloodhounds, though." His lips twitched. "They are a good breed to have around."

The car stopped. They had reached the one stoplight in Wilson County.

"You know, this town is growing on me. It's refreshing—no traffic." He motioned to the stoplight. "It's peaceful. I can see why people choose to live here."

Erick's car idled in front of them. She chanced a glance at Logan. He reached over, picked up strands of her auburn hair, and twirled a piece between his fingers.

"And, of course, there is you. I've never met anyone like you, Ember O'Neill. You fascinate me." He reached up. His thumb vibrated with energy as he stroked her jaw. His aura was magenta and gold. Ember swallowed.

The light turned green, and he pulled his hand away. The moment was broken. He steered the car into the gas station behind Erick. She could see Hallee sitting in the front seat through the rear glass.

"So, tell me…why does a girl who is obviously fast, strong, and maybe immortal, not participate in gym class?"

"What? Okay…well…" Ember squirmed, not sure how much to share. "First of all, I'm not immortal. The whole 'drowning' thing was a fluke. As for gym…my senses operate at a higher frequency than most people's. So, being around loud noises can become too intense. I don't do gym or sports." Afraid to see his reaction to that, she looked out the window. "At first, I could barely attend school. I used to wear my dad's construction earmuffs to block the noise—it was not a popular fashion choice, even in elementary school."

She turned to find his aura was only curious, flaring various shades of green. He wasn't laughing at her. "This doesn't freak you out?" She couldn't believe his neutral reaction.

He grinned, "Not in the slightest." Erick had finished filling his tank and pulled out of the gas station. Logan followed.

"Well, that's good to know." She smiled. "In middle school, I was prescribed pills that helped dull my senses. Now, being at school doesn't bother me so much. And I don't need earmuffs."

"That all makes me wonder why don't you participate in gym. If the pills dull your senses…" He flicked on the blinker as they turned onto the gravel county road leading to Hallee's house.

Ember shrugged.

He gave her an appraising look. "Aren't you curious what that body of yours can do?"

Ember felt hot under his scrutiny.

"Girls volleyball tryouts are next week. You should go for it."

"Yeah, about that…Coach C is my chemistry teacher. If I want a good grade, I don't really have a choice but to try out."

"Good! You should. No more sitting on the

bleachers in gym, either." He slid his hand onto her thigh and squeezed, sending flames licking up to her center. "The world should see what I saw tonight, O'Neill." He looked over at her and winked.

Ember didn't know how to respond. Words, breathing…they were an afterthought as she studied his hand resting on her thigh. Moments later, they pulled up to Hallee's. She wasn't sure if she was disappointed or grateful to have the drive end.

He put the car in Park and reached up and stroked her cheek. He was looking at her like she was the only person on the planet—like nothing else existed but her. His eyes explored her face. Logan leaned in. His warm breath treaded the inches between them.

Ember jerked back. "Sorry," she said, embarrassed. *Logan Lauder likes you. What is wrong with you?*

"Sorry for what?" He leaned in closer stroking her hair. His smell was intoxicating. "You smell so good, O'Neill."

"You do, too."

She felt the buzz of energy spark as he inched closer. Ember bit her lip. Her heart raced as he licked his lips.

"Can I kiss you?"

"Yes." Ember gulped as he leaned in. "I mean, no." She backed away against the door. "I'm sorry. I-I barely know you." Her heart pounded in her chest. "Why do you like me, Logan?" She spat out the question that had been nagging at her.

He pulled back, resting one forearm on the steering wheel. "These kids…they've really done a number on you." His lips shifted into a lopsided grin, forcing a dimple to pop. "I like you, Ember, because you are different. You are hot, sexy, and you don't even know it. The things you're insecure about are what make you special." He leaned towards her. "I see you, and I'm not afraid nor freaked out. You can trust me." Sincerity oozed from his warm chocolate eyes, and his hungry aura melted all Ember's barriers.

"Okay." She let words slip between her lips without thought. "I will trust you."

Erick's engine cranked to a start. Logan nodded at Hallee's front door. "Guess this is goodnight."

He got out of the car and walked around to the passenger door. Energy sizzled between them as he pulled her close to his hard body. His warm brown eyes glowed molten in the moonlight. "Anybody ever tell you that you look like an angel?"

"No, not exactly." Adam's voice calling her "angel" echoed in her mind. She pulled back. Her heart galloped. "I need to go." She released his grip and headed to the door.

"See you on Monday, O'Neill."

His soft baritone voice reached Ember as her hand gripped the knob on Hallee's front door. She glanced over her shoulder. He leaned against his car watching her leave. She turned the knob and felt the cold shock of the AC cool her sizzling body. She gently closed the door behind her and rested against it, letting out a long exhale. *See you on Monday, Lauder.*

Her heart was still racing from him—from her almost-first kiss—when Hallee peeked her head around the hall corner. Her aura soared a happy yellow. She grinned ear to ear. Hallee put her finger to her lips and motioned for her to follow her to her room. She gently closed the bedroom door behind her.

She plopped down on the bed next to Ember. Her eyes rounded in excitement behind her purple frames. "So? What happened? Did you ask him about Chicago? Tell me everything."

"No." She bit her lip. "There really wasn't an opportunity."

"Well, what did you talk about?"

Her brows furrowed. "He asked a lot of questions about me…"

"Okay, that's good, right? He's interested in you."

"Yeah." She fingered her dad's chain. "Or, he's just into freaks."

"Stop." Hallee squeezed her knee. "I don't need special abilities to see how he looks at you. He likes you, Ember…and…so does Derek."

"Derek is just concerned about me because of what happened at the pool party."

Hallee rolled her eyes. "Keep telling yourself that. I saw how he looked at you before."

"I can't even think about boys right now." Ember ran her fingers across her knuckles. The bruising had already faded.

"Are you thinking about what happened back at the bonfire with Katie?" Hallee asked.

She looked away. "I thought it was another demon. I swear I could smell it." A shiver ran down her spine. "And then, I heard the scream…I didn't think. I just ran. I had to stop it." Her fingers trembled at the memory.

"Hey, it's okay." Hallee reached out and squeezed Ember's arm. "Katie was lucky you were there tonight. We all were. Because of your good hearing, Katie wasn't raped."

Her hand curled in a fist. "I know…but I almost killed him."

"Hey. Don't. Don't do that. You were a hero tonight. I know that. Katie knows that." Hallee's lips twitched. "And I bet Chad never tries to hurt another girl again. You did a good thing tonight."

She rubbed her temples. "Two things…one, can you remind me not to do the whole when-in-Rome thing and just say no."

Hallee smiled. "Sure."

"Two, can you tell Katie to put in a good word for me with Maddison?"

Hallee released a sharp laugh. "I don't think it will help, but sure."

She fell back onto the pillow and exhaled. "Speaking of your cousins…"

"Wayne?" Hallee curled up beside her. "I'm so sorry, Ember. I don't get why he has it out for you."

Ember rolled onto her side, facing Hallee. "It's my fault, really."

"How? How could any of this be your fault?"

"I…had a dream. Sort of like this recurring nightmare with the girl drowning, but not nearly so scary. It was seventh grade. I kept dreaming that Wayne asked me to the school dance. I said yes. And we were out on the dance floor. He tried to kiss me, and I pulled away. The whole school laughed at him." Ember paused, wincing at the memory. "I didn't want to hurt him."

"But that was just a dream."

"Until it wasn't."

"Go on." Hallee encouraged.

"We were on break outside. I went to my usual

spot under the tree. Wayne walked up with a group of boys. He asked me to go to the dance. When I turned him down in front of them, it was like something snapped. The boys laughed, calling him a loser. The next week, rumors spread about me and Wayne. They called me, 'Easy E.' He claimed we made out and had sex."

"Oh, no."

She nodded. "Yeah."

"I'm so sorry, Em."

Ember shrugged. "Honestly, I got used to it. But, for some reason, I thought it would be better in high school. I thought, you know, people would be more mature and have more important things to think about and do, but…"

"Yeah, you said freshman year was bad…what happened?"

Ember closed her eyes and took a breath. "I got my period and bled all over myself. I didn't even realize it until it was too late. I had taken so many pills that I was numb." Hallee reached over and held her hand. "I didn't know what was happening to me. Birdie Mae never talked to me about it. I thought I was dying and fainted right in the middle of the hallway. Everyone saw me. Saw it. Saw all the blood." Ember paused, reliving the moment. "When I came to, everyone was looking at me. It was the worst, Hallee. I just wanted to disappear."

"I'm so sorry, Em."

"Yeah, well, it just gave Wayne one more thing to harass me about, and unfortunately, I did that one to myself."

"He's locked up and can't bother you anymore."

Ember squeezed the pillow. "True."

"Mind if I change the subject?"

"Please."

Hallee's cheeks flushed. "I sort of have a crush on Erick."

Ember smiled. "I thought so."

"Oh." Hallee pointed to the air around her. "My aura?"

"Yep. And he likes you, too…in case you were wondering."

"Eek!" Hallee squealed into her pillow.

"Shhh." She teased.

Hallee looked up. Her face grew serious. "Have you…and…Erick…?"

"Have we what?" Ember watched as Hallee's brows bounced over her purple frames.

"You know…kissed?"

"What? Ew, that's so gross. No. He's like a brother. "

"Okay. Good." Relief flooded Hallee's aura.

"He's the best, Hallee. And I think you two would be perfect for each other."

"Thanks."

After they changed, Hallee turned off the light, but Ember lay there looking out the window. The demon scent was still fresh in her memory. She fisted the quilt and watched the patch of moonlight shift along Hallee's floor. She couldn't sleep.

Chapter Twenty-seven

The bell rang just as Ember walked in the school doors with Logan Lauder at her side. He had been waiting for her. The hot new boy had been waiting for her. She couldn't believe it. The halls swarmed with her classmates darting to make first hour on time. And she was walking in, holding hands with Logan.

She couldn't help but notice the change in auras as people saw her with him. The few times she heard her name mentioned, it wasn't in a negative manner. It was as if she was accepted—just another student at Wilson County High. Logan kissed her cheek as he left her to go to his locker. Her shoulders shifted down and her neck muscles loosened. The instinct to armor herself from her classmates melted away. She smiled as she slipped into her chair for World History.

Hallee and Erick walked in together. Ember noticed their auras...carnation pink and lemon yellow. They were smitten with each other. She could see it and smell it.

"Hey." Erick and Hallee said simultaneously to her, then busted out laughing as they both said, "Jinx!" at the same time.

Ember laughed at her friends as the scent of chocolate and strawberries wafted her way. Her eyes shifted to the door. Logan gave a high-five to Kale

Martin as they parted ways in the hall. Her stomach flopped as she took in his tall, lean body. Even though she had just been with him, it was like seeing him again for the first time. He was mouthwatering.

Speaking of being smitten, Ember teased herself. Their eyes met as he entered the classroom. She felt the familiar buzz of electricity as he passed by her seat saying hi to Erick and Hallee.

The heat of his breath tingled her neck as he leaned forward and whispered in her ear, "Miss me, O'Neill?"

His words melted her.

The bell rang and Mr. Thompson wasted no time getting class started. Throughout the hour, Logan played with her hair hanging down from her ponytail. It was distracting in the best way. Jealous whispers from Heather and Jamie traveled across the room. For once, Ember did not let their words bother her. It was Logan and his touch that promised to be her undoing.

The bell rang, disappointing her. Class seemed to fly by. She didn't want to part from Logan. He tugged at her hand as she stood to go to second hour. His chocolate brown eyes were molten as he reached up, fingers trailing along her cheek. "Can't wait to see what you got in gym, O'Neill."

Certain her body was up in flames; she could barely form a response. "Yeah, me too?"

She glanced over his shoulder to see Hallee waggle her brows and mouth, "See ya."

He tipped her chin back and studied her face. "Your eyes are mesmerizing."

"They are?"

"They are like amber…almost golden."

Mr. Thompson cleared his throat. "Don't you two

have somewhere to be?"

Ember was confident her face was a new shade of red as she rushed to leave the classroom. Logan's fingers lingered on the small of her back as he guided her out into the hall, walking her to her locker. Her heart pounded as she opened her locker door. She had seen this sort of thing acted out countless times in the hall. Boys lingering at their girls' lockers. Make-out sessions interrupted by bells. She didn't know what to do now.

"Hey." He leaned in, touching her arm. She looked up. "You good?" His aura was lit with concern.

"Yes, of course. English is next, and I can't remember if I actually did my homework," she lied.

His fingertips tilted her chin up. "You're a terrible liar, O'Neill." He smiled. "But I like you anyway." His head tilted down, and his lips brushed her cheek with a feather-light kiss.

Her heart raced as she watched him walk away. *God, Logan Lauder is hot.*

He looked over his shoulder and winked. "See you later, O'Neill."

She felt the eyes of everyone in the hall looking at her. She quickly got her textbook and rushed to English class. Within seconds, looks turned into rumors that circulated down the hall and spilled over into classrooms.

"Logan Lauder is totally into the Dead Girl."

****

Shoulders back, Ember swallowed her pride, fears, and anxiety, along with another pill, and walked up to Mrs. Hall to request gym clothes. The teacher looked at her as if she had grown two heads, but then retrieved a

Wilson County High T-shirt and shorts for her to wear. Ember smelled Logan before she saw him. She chanced a quick glance back, catching his wink as he walked in.

She tried to calm her nerves as she entered the girls' locker room. She had never changed out for gym. She had never taken part in gym. Sweat beaded on her forehead. *What are you doing, Ember? There is a hot guy out there who likes you. Shake it off and be brave.*

She blew out her breath and changed into the tight-fitting gray shirt and shorts. Ember groaned at her reflection in the mirror above the sink. You could see everything. Her boobs had grown over the summer along with her legs. She would have to ask Mrs. Hall for larger sizes. She took a deep breath and pushed open the door to the gym. *Be brave.*

Mrs. Hall blew her whistle, indicating it was time to run laps. Wrapped in a magenta and gold aura, she caught Logan's approving look. Ember smiled.

"Let's go, O'Neill," Mrs. Hall yelled.

Ember shook off her nerves and joined the trail of students lightly jogging the perimeter of the gym floor.

Logan ran up beside her. "Damn, O'Neill. You got me having regrets."

Ember didn't know what to make of the comment. She looked at him sideways. "About what?"

He smiled and shook his head. "You have no idea, do you?"

"I don't know what you are talking about." She glanced around the gym. Heather and Jamie said her name between huffed breaths.

"What's wrong?" She questioned.

"You are without a doubt the hottest girl in this school. And, in that outfit, you are going to have a line of guys wanting to take you out." He winked. "I don't need that kind of competition."

"Ha. Ha. You're funny." Ember let her eyes slide over his physique, setting off butterflies in her stomach.

"I'm not joking." His dimples danced as he fought a grin.

"Okay, whatever." She actually enjoyed the jog. It felt good to stretch her legs and get her heart pumping. She picked up the pace and ran ahead.

He caught up. "Whoa. It's not a race, O'Neill."

"I know. It just feels good. I think I enjoy running." With each breath, she felt more energized—more powerful, even. It reminded her of training in the bottoms with her dad. The freedom to just *be* felt intoxicating.

He grinned. "You look good doing it."

She rolled her eyes.

"Let me take you out this weekend. How about Saturday? A date?" he asked.

The butterflies were now breakdancing in her belly. She had never been on an actual date, ever.

Virtus vincit, Ember. "Okay."

His aura lit up like a neon sign. "Be prepared to have the night of your life, O'Neill."

Her face flushed at the thought of what that could mean.

Mrs. Hall blew her whistle and put them through the motions of push-ups, crunches and wall sits. Ember's fears dissolved with each one. It felt good to push herself. Occasionally, she'd catch Logan watching her. It made her feel good to see his admiring looks.

The last half of class was dedicated to volleyball. Ember cringed when the teacher assigned teams. She had no clue what she was doing. Fortunately, Logan was on her team, and he calmly explained the rules to her. More than once she nearly took out the lights with her serves, causing glares from Mrs. Hall, but her blocks at the net were perfection. At the end of class, he said she was a natural and that he was confident she'd make the team at tryouts that week.

In the locker room, Ember ignored the looks and commentary from Heather and Jamie and changed back into her clothes. A small part of her enjoyed that for once it was jealousy that their auras were oozing and not mockery.

Logan met her outside the gym and walked her to her locker. She wondered if he could feel the electricity pulse between them, too.

"So, if I'm planning the perfect date—say, in the big city of Paducah—what would that look like for you, O'Neill?" He leaned in against the lockers.

She surveyed his chiseled jaw and perfectly arched brow. "Surprise me, Lauder."

"Wow. Not even a favorite food or restaurant?"

She leaned forward, inhaling his sweet aroma. "I like chocolate." She unconsciously reached up and pushed a lock of his hair back into place.

A sound like a growl purred from his throat. He muttered. "I can definitely work with that."

She pulled away, stunned at her own familiarity but loving his reaction in response. "I'll see you in last hour, Lauder."

She noted that his breath caught, and his heart thumped faster. Ember savored the effect she had on him and tossed her ponytail over her shoulder. It felt good to have a boy look at her like that.

Chapter Twenty-eight

She found it hard to concentrate on chemistry. Her nerves were on edge at the thought of seeing Maddison, Kale, and Logan next hour. Coach C confirmed during roll call she had Ember signed up for tryouts that afternoon, making the chemistry lesson even harder to focus on.

She wanted to do well at tryouts, primarily, so she could get a good grade. But what if she actually made the volleyball team? Ember wasn't sure if she could handle that. She checked her pill bottle in her purse. It was getting low. She bit her lip. She had to space them out better if she was going to make it through the week.

Her heart fluttered when she saw Logan waiting for her at her locker after class. His aura was a sunny yellow, trimmed in gold.

"Hey." His dimples popped with his smile.

"Hey, yourself." She teasingly arched a brow. "You stalking me, Lauder?"

He chuckled. "Maybe? Can't blame a guy, can you?"

Kale Martin walked by, punching Logan in the shoulder. He nodded to Ember and continued to walk down the hall, stopping to talk with Katie Wilson.

Ember swung her head back around. "So, is that a thing now? Him and Katie?"

He shrugged. "I don't know. Just glad he got the message."

Her brows scrunched together. "What message?"

"That you're off the market."

Her cheeks flushed as he leaned in and brushed a soft kiss on the top of her head, sending a warm tingle down to her toes. "Oh."

More than one person whispered her name as Logan escorted her to class, and it had nothing to do with being the Dead Girl and everything to do with being Logan's girl. Her heart felt like it might burst from happiness. But that quickly changed as they walked into Business Communication.

Maddison's sour face and aura glowered in the back of the classroom. Kale sat next to her, giving her the cold shoulder. Her eyes darted between Ember and Logan as they entered, soiling her aura, shading it even darker. A shiver snaked down Ember's spine. Maddison hated her.

Hallee and Erick were already seated. They nodded to them as they took their seats. Mr. Greene sat behind his desk reading a book about business. He wore a button-down baby blue shirt. Sleeves rolled up to the elbow with brown Docker slacks. She couldn't help but glance at his feet to see if he was still sock-less.

The teacher cleared his throat and stood as the bell rang. Ember looked over, catching Logan staring at her. She mouthed, "Stop." But he just winked in response.

"As you know, this is another busy week at Wilson County High. And it has fallen on me to help with the extracurriculars. Along with assisting with the girls' volleyball team, I will be your new business club advisor. As such, I am encouraging all my business students to join and consider running for an officer position." Mr. Greene looked pointedly at Erick, Hallee, and Ember in the front row.

Her stomach flopped as she realized that she now had two teachers coaching volleyball.

"All clubs will meet during last hour on Friday. Our first business club meeting will be in here. I hope you will join, but I get it—free period, last hour on a Friday—I would be the first student to skip back in my day." He smiled. "So, to further motivate participation, I will give extra credit to those who join and attend meetings. Dues are twenty bucks…looks good on your college apps especially if you hold an officer position…so think about it…" He smiled and turned, writing the assignment on the board.

Maddison made a snide comment about it being just a club for nerds. Ember rolled her eyes. She didn't know where she'd get the money, but she was happy to join a club that Maddison Miller would not be in.

The hour flew past too quickly for Ember and not because of Logan. Her heart hammered when the bell rang—time for tryouts.

****

Ember said goodbye to Erick and Hallee. They each wished her good luck. Logan walked her to her locker. She fumbled with the latch.

"Hey, don't be nervous." He reached over, a buzz of energy tingled down her arm from his touch.

"Yeah, no, I mean…I am nervous, but it's not like a big deal if I don't make the team, right?" She tossed her things in her locker.

Logan's dimple peeked out as he smiled. "Ember, you are amazing. You are going to make the team." He checked his watch. "Speaking of…" He jerked his chin over his shoulder. "I've got to get to basketball practice." He leaned down and gave her a peck on the cheek, sending tendrils of heat down her neck. "See-ya later." Both his dimples popped as he smiled and turned, leaving Ember to melt in his wake.

She took a deep breath and began the long walk over to the middle school gym. She toyed with the thought of bailing and just taking the bus home instead, but she didn't want to disappoint her friends or Logan. Plus, she really needed an A in Chemistry.

Coach C was standing by the door in her standard red and black tracksuit talking to Mr. Greene as Ember entered the gym. With all the cafeteria tables put away, she noted that the gym looked bigger.

Coach C nodded. "O'Neill." She marked Ember's name off her list.

"Hey, Ms. O'Neill." Mr. Greene smiled warmly. "Didn't know you were trying out."

"Yeah, I told her not to let her disabilities hold her back. I mean, look at that height." Coach C's brows raised. "She could be great on the net."

She squirmed. *That's not exactly what you said in class, Coach.*

"Disabilities?" His brows inched together.

She flushed under his scrutiny. "It's nothing."

Mr. Greene's aura lit up in excitement. "Well, good luck out there."

"Thanks."

"Have a seat, O'Neill, on the bleachers with the others. Oh, and no jewelry." Coach C pointed to the chain around her neck. Ember nodded and pulled it over her head and placed it in her purse.

She took a deep breath and squared her shoulders, walking forward. *Virtus vincit.* Ember scanned the clumps of girls sitting around talking to each other. Her eyes snagged on one group in particular.

Sitting on the top center of the bleachers was senior, Ashleigh Gardner, who was flanked by two sophomores, Nina Halloway and Missy Wilkers. They each wore their jerseys from last season and were laughing at something one of them had said. Ashleigh was the female equivalent of Kale Martin on the basketball court, but she dominated volleyball, as well. It was expected that upon graduation, she would get a free ride to any school in the SEC. Combined with Nina and Missy's emerging talent, Coach C had high hopes for the State finals this year—so she had said countless times in class.

Ashleigh's chin tilted as she scanned Ember from head to toe. Her aura was steeped in curiosity. Ember looked away and found a spot as far away as possible from the dream team. Her fingers squeezed the hard plastic bleacher as she overheard the soft whispers of shock and surprise from the other girls.

"All right, ladies. Today, we'll be working on conditioning." A groan from the girls behind her sounded.

"Yeah, yeah…it's part of it, ladies. Tomorrow, we will test your volleyball skills. But, today, it's conditioning."

"Mr. Greene, here, will be assisting this season. Our goal, if we are lucky, is to have a JV and varsity team this year." Murmurs erupted from the bleachers. "Mr. Greene will coach JV, and I will continue to coach the varsity. Any questions?" She paused, eyeing the girls. "All right then. Let's get moving. Twenty laps." Coach C blew her whistle. "Let's go!"

Like gym class earlier, Ember fell into the pod of classmates jogging around the gym. The running helped calm her nerves. She fell into a rhythmic pace at the head of the group. Ember received an approving nod from her business teacher. Twenty laps felt like nothing.

She was disappointed when they were instructed to stop. Coach C had them line up arm's length apart and drop, completing as many push-ups as they could in one minute. Several students groaned as Coach C blew the whistle. She was shocked at her own endurance, as each push-up felt effortless. Next were crunches. Muscles releasing and contracting, she enjoyed the motion. She chanced a glance at Ashleigh, who was hissing through pursed lips with each crunch. Mr. Greene caught her eye and gave her a thumbs up. Her cheeks flushed.

Tryouts lasted a little over an hour. While most everyone was sweaty and complained about how hard it was, Ember felt really good—actually great. She took her purse off the bleachers and walked out the gym with her head held high. She was halfway out the door when an unfamiliar voice called out her name.

She turned to see Nina Halloway's tall frame behind her. "Hey, you trying out again tomorrow?"

She wasn't sure how to respond. "Yeah."

Nina's aura was sincere, and so was her tone. "Good. I hope you make the team, Ember."

"Thanks."

"See ya tomorrow." Nina turned away to grab a drink from the water fountain.

Ember walked dumbfounded through the parking

lot over to the high school student lot. She was confident Nina Halloway had not spoken a single word to her during their entire school career. Not that she was mean to Ember or ignored her. Nina and Missy were always too busy together competing against each other. It was probably what drove them both to be such talented athletes. When other girls were having sleepovers and playing dress-up, those two were always at the softball fields or in the gym. She chewed her bottom lip. If Nina was giving her the stamp of approval, then maybe she had a legit shot at making the team.

A shiver ran down her back, she turned, looking behind her. It felt like someone was watching her, but there was no one there. She froze, smelling the air seeking out the all too familiar demon scent of death and decay. The air smelled of dumpsters and rotten food.

She quickened her pace unable to shake the feeling that someone was stalking her. She decided to cut through the buildings rather than go around the school. A car's engine roared to life, startling her. She looked back. It was Mr. Greene. Relieved, she slowed her pace.

He rolled his window down as he creeped the car alongside her. "Need a ride, Ms. O'Neill?"

"No, my—" Ember caught herself as she almost called Logan her boyfriend. "No, my friend is giving me a ride."

"You sure? I'm happy to do it anytime."

"Nope, I'm good. Thanks." She turned, ready to walk away.

"Ms. O'Neill?"

"Yes?"

"I'm curious…you seem like a natural athlete. Why didn't you ever play before?" His aura was an odd mix of curiosity and a shade of red that she usually associated with anger.

She shrugged. "I just didn't know that I could."

He nodded as if he understood, but she doubted he knew exactly what she meant—that without the meds she'd be curled up in a corner crying from the overstimulation.

"All right then. Glad to see you out there. Have a good night, Ms. O'Neill." He gave a quick wave and drove away.

Ember quickened her pace to the high school parking lot, relieved to smell the sweet scent of chocolate and strawberries on the air. She jogged between the buildings and spied Logan leaning against his black sports car. A few other basketball players stood talking nearby. She noticed that Katie was sitting on Kale's tailgate as he talked with the guys. Kale waved at her, causing Katie to turn. She smiled at Ember and waved, too. Her aura bloomed a happy pink and yellow. Ember never thought she'd see the day when Katie Wilson would happily acknowledge her presence.

"Hey, you," Logan called out to her, "need a ride?" Both dimples popped at his full smile.

"Hey." She spoke into his chest as he pulled her in close.

Her body instinctively stiffened, then melted into his. He felt good. Real good.

Logan inhaled deeply. "God, you smell…almost delicious."

She laughed and pushed him away. "There is no

way that I smell that good."

He opened the door for her. "So...how did it go?" Ember watched him walk back around to the driver's side. Muscles flexing in his forearm, he turned the key in the ignition. The car purred. "I want to hear everything."

She examined his profile as he maneuvered around cars to exit. Her heart raced. She really didn't know what he saw in her, but today, in that moment, she felt like she was in a dream—the very best dream. She wasn't the freak that Wayne Wilson harassed over the years, or the weirdo people ignored. She wasn't Bloody Ember from freshman year that people pitied. Very few of her classmates even referred to her as the Dead Girl anymore.

She was becoming the Ember O'Neill she had always wished to be. People who used to ignore her now smiled at her and waved. She owed that to Logan. He looked past what others thought. He saw her for who she was or rather what she could be—like her dad.

He looked over and grinned, making his right dimple reappear. "What?" he asked as he pulled out of the parking lot.

"Nothing." She didn't understand what he saw in her, but she was grateful to him. She knew his attention, alone, totally flipped the switch on how her classmates viewed her. Not to mention, how he made her feel gave Ember confidence to push past her comfort zone to participate in gym and try out for volleyball. Being around Logan Lauder made her better, braver.

"I don't know how you ended up at my school, but I'm happy you did."

She watched his aura shift, flashing from a cheerful

pink and yellow to a muddied mocha. He reached over and squeezed her hand, sending warm energy pulsing up her arm. His reaction was confusing. Usually, that murky tone meant someone was hiding something, like when her dad would lie to Birdie Mae about getting laid off from a job.

She dismissed it as his aura quickly shifted back to a passionate magenta pink, outlined in his signature gold. She must have misread the tone.

"So, you going to tell me about tryouts?"

Ember shared how good it felt and that she was surprisingly looking forward to the next day. She was nervous, of course, but she felt really confident. She listened as he told her about basketball practice. Her heart felt so happy that she didn't want the car ride to end. It was as if they were an actual couple. She didn't know where his head was on it, but she would one hundred percent say "yes" if he asked her to be his girlfriend.

Too soon, they arrived at her house. Ember didn't know if she should invite him in or just say goodbye.

He turned off the ignition. She watched as he licked his lips. He reached over cupping her cheek, sending tingles from her head to her toes. He looked like he was going to say something. Perhaps something important by the shade of his aura. Ember bit her lip. Her thoughts flew through the possibilities and landed on her previous thought—he was going to ask her to be his girlfriend. She swallowed, ready to say yes.

Suddenly, the tap of paws on the door and a deep growl jerked them both apart as Bear stood on his hind legs, staring at Logan through his driver side window.

"Oh! I take it that's Bear."

"Bear! Down." Ember commanded. The dog whined, but obeyed. She shook her head. "Sorry."

"I don't think he likes me," he confessed.

She felt the burn in her face. "He's just not used to seeing me with someone...like this."

He shifted back towards her, scanning her face like she was a rare jewel, eyes settling on her lips. "I'm glad."

"You're glad about what? That I've never had a boyfriend?" Ember wished she could take back the omission. She looked away.

"Hey." His fingertips grazed her chin, turning her head back towards him. "I meant that I'm glad he's here to protect you, since your dad's not able to." She watched his aura shift from a sincere blue to a deep indigo. He reached up, brushing the auburn strands at her temple, pushing them back into place. "I will protect you, too, Ember." The sincerity and intensity of his gaze started a fire in her veins. She boldly leaned forward. Logan moaned softly. His aura shifted, as if he had competing thoughts.

"It's okay," she whispered.

Bear jumped up on the driver side window again, barking and growling, causing him to pull away completely.

"I think I like him more than he likes me."

"Bear, down," Ember hissed. The big dog whined again, but this time he sat there panting with his tongue hanging out crooked. Ember knew he was just happy...probably feeding off her energy.

He twirled a piece of her hair. "So, can I pick you up in the morning and take you to school?"

"Sure...seven thirty?"

He leaned forward and kissed her on the forehead. "I'll be here."

Ember walked away, knowing that today was the best day of her high school career—maybe even the best day of her life. It tickled the back of her mind though that Logan now seemed reluctant to kiss her, but, then again, that was all her fault.

She was the one who initially pushed him away.

Chapter Twenty-nine

Ember and Hallee had agreed to do a double date for their very first, *first dates*. Erick drove his vehicle since Logan's sports car wasn't exactly made for backseat passengers. Ember sat in the rear seat with Logan and was immediately aware of his presence. He wore his faded light blue jeans that she noted hugged in all the right places and a crisp white polo shirt with a small green alligator on the chest. When he took her hand, lacing his fingers with hers, electricity buzzed between them. He smelled of cologne, but it didn't mask his natural scent that she much preferred.

His eyes appraised her as he smiled, causing two dimples to form on his cheeks. "You look good," he said. His aura bloomed magenta.

She blushed and self-consciously touched her hair which she had pulled up in a bright yellow scrunchie per Hallee's advice. Her emerald green T-shirt hugged tight around her curves, but Hallee assured her it highlighted her golden eyes making them pop.

"Thanks. You do, too." He squeezed her hand in response.

"So, ladies…prepare to be amazed." Erick grinned into the rear-view mirror. Yours' truly and that guy, back there, have planned an exquisite first date."

Logan looked down and winked mischievously at

Ember. "That's right and don't ask. It's a surprise."

Hallee groaned from the front passenger seat. "I don't like surprises."

Erick started the car and turned on the radio. "Oh, I think you'll like this surprise."

Hallee brushed his hand aside. "Fine, but I get to pick the station."

The car filled with the jarring sounds of Def Leppard as they drove to Paducah. Ember smiled as the two of them bickered like an old couple. Despite the fuss over which band was better, their auras mirrored each other's, carnation pink and lemon yellow.

Ember was eager to see what the boys had planned for them. It surprised her when Erick veered off the highway toward Lone Oak, a small town adjacent to Paducah. Birdie Mae rarely went shopping in that part of town, and her dad had always avoided crossing the county line altogether. She wondered what kind of surprise lay in wait for them.

They drove by busy store parking lots and cars snaking around fast-food restaurants. Erick turned on his blinker and pulled into Bob's Drive-in, a quaint "mom and pop" restaurant with a giant soft serve ice cream cone on its sign.

"Ladies, prepare your taste buds for the most amazing burgers and fries of your life, topped off with the most amazing ice cream to ever bless the tri-state," Erick said, as his brows danced over his gold wire-rimmed glasses.

Hallee slid sideways in the seat, taking both boys in with one look. "I was worried you guys booked us at The Pines—and we are totally not dressed for that kind of fancy."

"The Pines?" Logan looked down at Ember, eyes turning molten. "I'll have to remember that for the future."

Erick parked and placed their orders at the speaker menu. Shortly, their food arrived, and Ember had to admit that it tasted really good. After they ate, Erick teased that he hoped they still had room for more because the next stop would definitely have endless options to *tempt their palates*.

Her heart raced in delight when she saw where they were headed to next. The setting sun cast a warm yellow glow over the large Ferris wheel in the center of the McCracken County fairgrounds. Ember's nose flared as she inhaled all the familiar scents of kettle popcorn and cotton candy. It had been many years since she had gone to the fair and the memories flooded back. She remembered squeezing her dad's hand after he won her a little toy at one of what he called "sucker games." Unconsciously, she squeezed Logan's hand. It was one of the few times her dad took her into town.

He tilted his head to her. "You okay?"

"Yeah." Her eyes became glassy as tears pooled. "The one and only time I came to the McCracken County Fair, I was with my dad. I was probably ten years old."

"Oh." He stroked her cheek, sending prickles of energy dancing down her neck. "We don't have to do this if it's upsetting."

"No, it's fine. I'm fine. Just memories, good ones, that's all." She shook her head and smiled.

After a while of exploring all their options, they decided to split up. Each couple bought their own tickets. Logan insisted on paying for everything, for which Ember was grateful. She thought he was cute, when he claimed every game was rigged because he couldn't win a prize for her. He especially had to swallow his pride when she beat him in the strongest man contest and won a giant stuffed panda.

Ember and Logan eventually met up with Erick and Hallee at the concession stands. They shared about having seen Mr. Greene wandering the fair alone.

Hallee's brows pinched above her purple framed glasses. "I feel so sorry for him. He looked so lonely." She looked over at Erick. "It's difficult being new. I hope he finds someone…to be friends with."

Erick blushed and pushed his glasses up his nose. "So, you ladies want some refreshments? Dessert? Ice cream?" He gestured to the sign above the food truck.

"I don't think I could eat another bite." Hallee rubbed her midsection.

"How about you?" Logan leaned over and whispered in Ember's ear. "You hungry for anything? Chocolate perhaps?"

Ember's stomach did somersaults as her mind went to places it shouldn't. Heat flushed her cheeks. She couldn't form words and nodded "yes."

"I know just the thing." His dimpled smile turned her into jelly as she watched him walk away to order.

She forced herself to stop staring and joined Hallee and Erick at a nearby picnic table, placing the giant panda on the bench beside her.

"He's cute. Did Logan win it?" Hallee asked.

Her lips slid into a lopsided grin. "Nope. I did."

"Way to go, warrior princess," Erick voiced his appreciation.

Hallee leaned over. "Should we do it now?"

Ember gulped and nodded. She had forgotten about their plan. She cupped her hand and whispered back to Hallee. "When Logan comes back."

"What's with all the whispering?" Erick slurped up his cherry iced beverage.

Hallee blushed. "You'll see."

Logan returned, smiling ear to ear with a chocolate fudge sundae. "I wasn't sure if you liked nuts or not, so I erred on the side of caution and went no nuts and extra chocolate with whipped cream."

Ember's mouth watered. "Ice cream? Feels like we should be celebrating something."

Logan scooted the dessert between them. "We are. Congrats on making the volleyball team."

"Yeah, congrats, Ember. I know that wasn't easy for you." Erick nodded. "I think your dad would be proud."

"Thanks." Tears threatened again. "I think so, too."

"Ladies first." He gestured with the red plastic spoon.

She scooped up a spoonful. Her eyes closed. It tasted like Heaven. When she opened her eyes, her face turned crimson as she realized Logan had sat the spoon down and was just watching her eat.

"It's really good." She jabbed her spoon into the plastic bowl. "You should have some before I eat it all."

"Eh-hm." Hallee cleared her throat and looked pointedly at Ember.

"Ah, yes...there is something we need to ask you both." Ember's eyes darted to her best friend.

They had decided it would be safer and less embarrassing to do the deed together on their double date. Logan and Erick both looked like they had just inhaled an unpleasant smell…confusion and concern danced in their auras and on their faces. She motioned with her fingers counting down…three…two…one.

In unison, Hallee and Ember asked, "Will you go to the Sadie Hawkins dance with us?"

Erick laughed. "Oh, wow…I didn't know what you were going to ask. You both got so serious."

Logan winked at her. "Yeah, you had me worried, O'Neill."

Hallee shot Erick a pointed glare. "Well…?"

His forehead became a map of lines. "Well, what?"

Ember looked down at the melting ice cream too nervous to meet Logan's eyes and muttered, "Will you guys be our dates?"

Logan placed his hand on the small of her back and leaned over, kissing her temple. "Always."

"Of course." Erick's voice cracked, causing a burst of red to flush his cheeks.

Hallee let out a breath. "Oh, thank goodness! I couldn't eat all night."

Erick's brows raised. "So, now you want food?"

"Yes, please. I want what they're having." She motioned to the sundae.

"Okay." Erick rose to get in line at the ice cream food truck.

Hallee followed him. "But I call dibs on the cherry."

Ember chuckled at her best friends.

"They're cute together." Logan took her hand and traced her palm with his finger.

She turned to face him, studying his strong jawline and perfect sandy blond hair. She wondered what it would be like to run her fingers through the silk-like strands…to kiss his soft, pillow-like lips.

"You're doing it again." The neon lights from the fair twinkled in his eyes.

"I'm doing what?" Ember asked softly.

"You're making the world stop." His fingers lightly stroked her jaw. "Everything falls away when you look like that."

"What do I look like?" she asked.

His thumb outlined her bottom lip, sending a bolt of desire to her very core. "An angel."

She stiffened, but not because of what he said. Her instincts took over. The smell of cotton candy, licorice, popcorn, and hot dogs permeated the air—nothing unusual for a carnival, but she sensed something was off. Like a rabbit sensing the hunter, she froze, seeking the predator.

"What's wrong?" Logan asked.

"I don't know." While scanning the crowd, she gripped his hand. Wayne was in jail, she reminded herself. Whatever it was, it didn't smell like the rot of demon.

Her gaze snagged on Mr. Greene, talking to a classmate by the concessions. Their eyes met. He smiled and waved. Ember nodded and averted her eyes, looking for something…anything that was wrong.

Assured nothing was amiss, she forced a smile and squeeze his hand. "It's nothing. Everything is fine."

Erick and Hallee returned to the table with their sundae. Ember shook her head and laughed with them as the two bickered over who was eating more.

No, it is more than fine, Ember thought. *This night is perfect.*

She ignored the tiny prickle that nagged at her

brain, refusing to let it ruin the night. It was her first date, ever, and it was with Logan Lauder, the hot new guy at Wilson County High. Her life didn't get much better than this.

Chapter Thirty

Ember studied her reflection in her dresser mirror. After just a few weeks, volleyball conditioning had caused the roundness of her cheeks to thin out, thus accentuating her high cheekbones. Her arms were more toned. Her auburn hair had grown longer and thicker since summer, and her amber eyes seemed brighter, almost golden.

She cringed when she thought about last year's Sadie Hawkins dance. It was the first dance of her freshman year, and everyone was excited. Of course, Ember wasn't going. There wasn't a boy at school who she was interested in, and none who were interested in her. She told herself she was okay with it, but internally she wished she could have been more like Brittany Oliver.

Brittany's face had flushed pink on the bus as she told everyone the story of how Michael Brown had said yes when she asked him to the dance. Instead, she suffered through laughs and jokes at her expense as Wayne announced on the bus that Ember wasn't going to Sadie Hawkins because literally every guy she begged said no. She recalled curling up on the bus seat, wishing she could just disappear as the guys laughed and made fun of her.

Surveying her reflection, Ember straightened her

back and dropped her shoulders. So much had changed. She was no longer that tortured, nervous girl on the verge of ending it all. She glanced at her list of goals, still stuck on her mirror from the first day of school. It felt like eons ago since she'd written them.

She had a new best friend in Hallee. Her grades were perfect. She and Logan were on the fast-track to relationship status. She had made the volleyball team, and she had joined the business club. And, as far as popularity went, she felt she was moving up the ranks. So many people from school now looked her in the eye and smiled.

No longer were there averted glances and whispers of Bloody Ember or Dead Girl in the halls. If anything, the guys gave approving nods and commented on how lucky Logan was. Excluding Maddison and her cheer squad pack, Ember felt she had somehow cracked the girl code and was part of the "in" group. It had been weeks since she had eaten lunch in the library. She missed her lunch club with Erick and Hallee, but her new friends on the volleyball team were fun to hang out with, too. For once in her entire life, Ember felt peace and acceptance at school.

She looked down at her dad's chain hanging around her neck. She reached up and squeezed the tags and keys. It didn't really go with the ivory dress, but she didn't care. In her mind, it symbolized her dad— like a piece of him was still with her. Her eyes watered. She knew he would be happy to see her now.

When volleyball season was over, she vowed to get to the root of things. But, for now, her life was just too important. She couldn't screw it up. She rattled her pill bottle. It was getting low, but tonight was too important to screw up. She took two pills, then glanced at the clock. Logan would arrive soon.

She gave Bear a hug. He rolled over, exposing his fluffy underside, and begged for Ember to scratch. Her eyes darted to her bedroom door. She heard his car driving down the gravel road to her house.

"Wish me luck, Bear. It's my first dance," she whispered. The purr of the car's engine shut off. "Got to go." She gave Bear one last scratch. He whined and batted her hand with his paw. "Sorry, Bear-bear." The dog sat at attention and growled.

"It's okay. Logan is a friend."

Ember checked her reflection one last time and smiled. For once, she felt pretty.

****

Her heart fluttered when she saw her date walking up the drive. The sun was just setting, casting a warm glow on Logan's chiseled features. He wore tobacco-colored pants and a pink button-down shirt with brown leather shoes and belt. He stopped walking. His brown eyes turned molten as his gaze devoured her from head to toe. His aura burned a dark magenta. Ember bit her bottom lip.

He whistled. "Damn. You look hot. Oh, I almost forgot." He turned and rushed back to the car, opened the door, and pulled out a small box.

"This is for you." He pried open the lid, revealing a red rose corsage adorned with ivory ribbon that matched her dress and shiny rhinestones. Logan cleared his throat and, for once, his confident aura wavered. "I wasn't sure if I was supposed to get a corsage for you or not. I've never been to a Sadie Hawkins dance."

"Me, either." Ember's smile fell when she inhaled

the sweet rose scent. It reminded her of Adam and their secret garden. She had hoped she would have heard from him by now, but he hadn't returned.

He closed the box. "I see."

"See what?"

"Your face. I can tell you don't like it."

"What? Oh my God, Logan, no. It's beautiful. I love it. Please help me put it on."

His brow furrowed. "Are you sure?"

"Yes, please," she reassured him.

His fingers left a buzzing trail along her wrist as he closed the clasp. She raised the rose to her nose and inhaled deeply. She opened her eyes to see him studying her face. "What?"

He leaned forward, cupping her chin. "You are so beautiful, Ember. I could look at you all night."

She glanced away. The husky sound in his voice made her knees weak. She swallowed and willed herself to meet his gaze. Pulse throbbing in her veins, she prepared for her first kiss. His eyes dipped to her lips. Her breath caught. This was it. She leaned forward. Just when she thought their lips would touch, he pulled away, clearing his throat.

"But I would be a terrible date if I did that instead of taking the most beautiful girl at Wilson County High School to the dance. So…" Logan quickly walked to the passenger door and opened it for her. "Would you do me the honor, Ember O'Neill?"

She slipped into the passenger seat, disappointed that he didn't kiss her. But one quick look at Logan was all the reminder that she needed. She was living her wildest dreams. He really liked her. She really liked him. If it was a dream, she did not want to wake up.

Chapter Thirty-one

No matter how well things had been trending, Ember still had to convince herself to be brave as Logan opened the doors to Wilson County High. Music echoed inside the gym. The thumping, vibrating base of a Def Leppard number caused her to squeeze Logan's hand a little too hard. He looked down and smiled reassuringly at her. The medication dulled her senses, but even with two extra pills in her system, the music was overwhelming.

"I'm not sure I can do this," she said.

"I won't leave your side, O'Neill."

Ember straightened her back and took a deep breath. *Be brave. Courage conquers.* She forced a smile. "Okay."

Her eyes widened at the transformation of the gym. The business club sponsored the Sadie Hawkins dance every fall. While Ember had been at volleyball practice all week after school, Erick and Hallee had been helping plan and decorate for the dance. She was surprised to see how much they had done in so little time.

Hay bales lined a makeshift dance floor and served as seating around tables on the far side of the gym. Centerpieces of daisies and sunflowers rested in the middle of each table draped with red gingham. On the stage, a DJ booth was set up to the side. Erick and Hallee stood on stage talking with the DJ. At the center of the stage, they had set a red photo backdrop up with cornstalks and hay bales. A floral arch crowned above the gold glitter sparkling dance sign, Sadie Hawkins Dance 1990. Behind the photo backdrop, concessions were being served by parent volunteers.

The lights were off in the gym and lit in their place were several strands of white lights suspended over the dance floor. At the center of the ceiling, a disco ball hung causing splashes of light to flicker around the gym. She caught Hallee's eye up on the stage and waved. Her aura was a sunny yellow. Hallee elbowed Erick, directing him to look out onto the gym floor. He spied her and waved back. They both looked so happy. She noticed that they both wore purple—Hallee in a purple silk shirt and lavender and gray plaid skirt and he in a lilac button-down shirt and gray pants. Ember smiled; *he got the "wear purple" memo.*

Logan tugged on her hand, directing her through clumps of classmates laughing and talking together. He waved and nodded at his teammates from basketball. Ember noted the smiles and approving auras as she walked by. She felt the tension in her shoulders relax as the pills settled in. Hallee and Erick took a shortcut through the stage door down to the gym floor and emerged to meet them. Hallee waved and motioned them over to a table in the back.

"We saved this table for us," she yelled over the music, hugging Ember.

"It looks amazing, Hallee." She gestured to the dance floor. "You guys did a great job! It doesn't even look like a gym anymore."

"Thanks." Hallee and Erick said in unison. They looked at each other and laughed.

"Jinx! You owe me a drink," Hallee teased Erick.

Erick pushed his wire-rimmed glasses farther up his nose. "Speaking of…can us gentlemen get you fine ladies a beverage?"

Hallee's brows danced. "Oh, yeah, a soda, please."

Logan leaned in and asked softly. "Ember? Would you like me to get you a drink, or would you rather I stayed here with you?"

Ember flushed from the warmth of his breath on her neck. "It's okay. A drink would be great."

A single dimple popped from his crooked smile. "Soda?"

"Sure."

"Okay, be back in a jiffy, ladies." Erick saluted, guiding Logan up to the stage.

She looked out at her classmates. The usual cliques formed around the gym. The cheer squad was dressed in various shades of plaid flannel and cut-off jean shorts. She noted Kale Martin was Katie Wilson's date. But she didn't see Maddison. So far, she hadn't made her grand entrance yet.

"I see it's official…your cousin, Katie, and Kale, huh?" She angled her shoulder so Hallee could see.

"Yeah, you were right. Kale and Maddison run hot and cold. I'm hoping they stay cold." Her brow arched. "I could get used to seeing hot Kale with Katie at our family gatherings."

"Hallee, stop."

"What? He is hot, and I appreciate his hotness." Hallee's eyes lowered into slits behind her purple rimmed glasses as she surveyed the small group entering through the gym doors. "Speaking of hot…did Brittany invite her model friend, Anthony? Oh. Oh, no. Is that…Derek…with Maddison?"

She fought the urge to turn around in her seat and gawk. But she lost the internal battle and casually glanced over her shoulder, only to lock eyes with Derek from across the gym. His denim eyes sparkled in the disco light. He smiled and winked at her. Ember flushed and turned back around.

"Ember O'Neill, did Derek Oliver just wink at you?" Hallee gushed.

She picked at the gingham tablecloth. "Me? No, I'm sure he was looking at someone else."

"Well, it wasn't me." Hallee smiled. "I think someone has a fan club."

"Whatever." Ember scanned the stage, looking for the guys.

"It's like one of my romance novels where the guy saves the girl, and they fall in love." Hallee's brows arched. "Only you are dating Logan, so…plot twist!"

"Hallee, stop." She pulled a daisy from the vase and tossed it at Hallee.

She raised her hands in surrender, laughing. "Okay, fine…but I still think he likes you."

"Whatever. If he likes me so much, why is he here with Maddison?" Ember sighed.

"Ah-ha! You do like him." Hallee teased.

"Oh, hey, look…" Ember tilted her head. "It's our dates that we invited to the dance…coming back with our drinks."

Hallee took the cue and twisted back in her seat as the boys returned. Logan and Erick sat down, passing the girls' drinks across the table.

"Logan and I took the liberty of requesting a few songs for later." Erick pushed up his glasses and smiled at Hallee. Her aura flashed pink.

"I think you'll like what we chose." A singular dimple popped as Logan leaned across the table, his fingertips grazing the red rose corsage on Ember's wrist.

The music stopped and boos ensued. The DJ got on the mic. "I know. I know. I hate to stop good music too, but it's time for your official welcome speech from tonight's dance sponsor, business club advisor...Mr. ..." The DJ paused, looking down at an index card. "Mr. Greene! Mr. Greene, would you please come forward?"

He sauntered across the stage in his leather loafers, no socks, khaki pants, white button-down, and brown tweed jacket. His hair was trimmed and slicked back. He looked every bit the cool young college professor and nothing like the typical middle-aged Wilson County High teacher.

The crowd cheered as he took the mic. "Welcome! Welcome!" He waved his hand. "I'm so glad everyone could come out and support the club." Ember noted his aura, a sincere blue and happy lemon yellow, and his licorice and leather scent. "Just a quick reminder that we will be crowning the king and queen of tonight's dance in an hour. So, please don't forget to cast your vote up here by the concessions."

She felt Logan's eyes studying her. "What?" she mouthed across the table.

He winked and said, "I just voted for you."

Ember blushed and turned back to the stage.

"Also, I'd like to thank our parent volunteers—

without your support, none of this would be possible."
A mild clap echoed throughout the gym. "Okay, enough
of all that." Mr. Greene smiled and motioned to the DJ.
"Hit it, DJ."

Bass vibrated through the speakers, causing several
couples to shift back to the dance floor.

Hallee looked over her glasses expectantly. "Who
wants to dance with me?"

"I got this." Erick stood. "Prepare to be amazed."

Ember watched as her friends moved out onto the
dance floor.

Logan's fingertips slid to Ember's hand softly
stroking each knuckle, sending tingles down her arm.
"Want to dance, O'Neill?"

"I don't know how," she answered honestly.

Suddenly, the rush of arms hugged her from
behind. She stiffened. But Logan's dimples popped as
he smiled at the invader. Missy Wilkers swung into
view and plopped onto the hay bale beside her. She
relaxed, seeing her teammate. Missy's toothy smile
seemed too big for her face. Her aura was ablaze with
mischievous green and happy yellow.

She punched her arm. "Why aren't you dancing
with the team?"

Her eyes darted between Logan and Missy. "I don't
think dancing is really my thing."

She tossed her crimped blonde hair over her
shoulder. "Whatever. You didn't know volleyball was
your thing till you tried it."

"True," Ember acknowledged.

"It's so much fun…here." Missy pulled out a silver
flask from her back pocket. "This your drink?" She
asked, pointing to her cup.

Ember nodded, and Missy poured the brown liquid from the flask into her drink.

"Liquid courage." Missy nodded to the cup. "It helps. Want some?" She tilted the flask to Logan.

"Nope, I'm good. I enjoy dancing."

"You do?" Ember asked.

She remembered her first—and last—time drinking alcohol. She had promised Hallee that she wouldn't drink anymore, but it helped numb her senses. She glanced at her classmates having fun on the dance floor and vowed this time not to go overboard. She would pace herself. Ember tilted the cup.

"Bottoms up." The now familiar burn of alcohol slid down her throat.

"Okay, then, let's dance!" Missy took her hand and led her onto the dance floor. Logan smiled, following behind the girls.

Ember stood awkwardly as her teammates slipped into rehearsed dance moves. Missy and Nina led the dance circle. Nerves cemented her feet. She looked at their happy auras and felt like she didn't belong.

Nina's warm brown eyes connected with hers. "Don't worry, O'Neill. I'll teach you."

Logan pressed his hand against her back. "Go ahead. I'll go over with Erick. I can teach him some of my moves."

Nina took her hand and led her to the group. "Just copy me." She gestured. "Kick your foot out, then in, on the beat."

Ember studied Nina's motions and tried to imitate her smooth transitions.

"Yes, that's it. Now bring your arms forward, then back." Nina encouraged.

It was awkward, at first, but soon she got the hang of it. She smiled and received high fives from Missy and Nina as the song ended.

"See. That wasn't so bad, was it?" Missy beamed.

"Cool. Yeah, it was sort of fun," she conceded. The alcohol was beginning to kick in.

The music transitioned to a slow song, causing another round of boos from the dance floor. Missy and Nina's eyes both widened slightly, looking over her shoulder.

"Don't look now, but I think your date is coming for you." Nina grinned. Ember felt the sizzle of Logan's fingers on her arm.

"Ladies." Logan nodded to Missy and Nina. He leaned down close to her ear. "Ember, will you dance with me?"

The girls wiggled their fingers goodbye, leaving her alone with Logan on the dance floor. Prickles of fear and excitement raced down her spine. She inhaled his berries and chocolate scent. She had never slow danced with a boy. The thought of being that close, parts intimately touching, made her breathing hitch. She nodded "yes," as he reached down and took her hand, leading her to the center of the dance floor.

Ember felt like all eyes were on her. Logan put his hand on her lower back and pulled her in close. Electricity crackled from his touch down her spine. His heartbeat raced wildly, like her own. She looked up into his chocolate brown eyes. He smiled crookedly, causing a dimple to pop. Her heart melted. She was certain that if she actually died a second time, this would be the highlight of her life, right here, in this moment, on the dance floor in Logan's arms.

He grinned sheepishly. "I like this song."

Ember listened, recognition quickly flashing across her face as the lyrics registered in her memory.

"Is this the song you requested?" she asked.

"Yeah, it's deep."

Ember wasn't sure if he was being serious or not. "You think this song has a deeper meaning? I thought it was just about roses and thorns." She swallowed hard when he shifted his hands, caressing her waist with his fingertips.

"Yeah, but if you listen closely, there is more to it." He tilted his head, studying her face. He reached up and gently shifted her chin to make her look at him. "Danger often hides behind a mask of beauty."

"That is deep." The intensity of his stare made her feel awkward. She forced a smile. "I thought it just meant be careful when you pick a rose."

A laugh rumbled from his chest.

"What? I did." Ember giggled with him, glad to break the tension.

"I love that." He reached up and pulled a piece of hair away from her cheek. "I love your innocence. I love your hair. And those eyes…don't get me started." He ran his thumb gently across her bottom lip. "And these, right here." His voice dipped low. His tongue darted across his lips as he looked into her eyes.

"Can I kiss you, Ember O'Neill?"

Finally. Butterflies took flight in her stomach. Slowly, she nodded her head. She had been waiting for this moment. Ever since she let her guard down and began trusting him, she had imagined what it would be like to kiss his perfect lips.

Logan reached up, placing one hand under her hair

at the base of her neck. Electricity buzzed throughout her body. With his other hand, he cupped her cheek, pulling her closer.

She held her breath as his lips parted and pressed against hers with the lightest touch. In an instant, their bodies became one. The world melted away. It was just Ember and Logan on the dance floor. Her greatest wish for the night was coming true. She was kissing Logan.

Too soon, he pulled away. Eyes sparkling in the disco light, his thumb dragged across her bottom lip. She wondered if he could feel her racing pulse.

The kiss was sweet. Perfect. Ember smiled, remembering to breathe.

Both dimples asserted themselves as his lips shifted into a devilish grin. "You taste better than I imagined."

Her face flushed crimson. An invisible flame licked across her body at his words. He took her hand and led her off the dance floor. She hadn't realized the song had even stopped. Numb and in a trance from the kiss, she barely caught the approving looks of her teammates and classmates as they made their way back to their table.

Hallee rushed forward before Ember could sit down and tugged at her wrist. "I need to tell you something."

Ember glanced at Logan. "Okay."

"Go ahead. I'm going to go say hi to the team." He nodded to the basketball team gathered by the bleachers.

"Over here." Hallee tugged her a few steps away from the crowd into the corner.

"What's going on?" she asked.

"Well, a couple of things." Her brows raised above

her purple frames.

"Okay, go ahead."

"First, you are getting a lot of votes for queen!" Hallee squeezed her hands.

Ember looked at her friend like she sprouted two heads. "What? That can't be possible."

Hallee's head bounced. "It's true. Mr. Greene just told me."

"Okay, but we all know Maddison will win." She rolled her eyes.

"I don't know, Em. He said you were in the top three."

"Okay, what else did you want to tell me?"

"Your mom is here?" she whispered.

"What? What do you mean, she is here?" Ember turned, scanning the crowd.

"She's up on the stage helping...sort of...her and her friend Sherry. Your mom is being extra friendly with Mr. Greene..." Hallee let her voice trail off.

"She's probably drunk."

"Sorry, I just thought you should know." Hallee's eyes widened. "Wait." Hallee leaned in and sniffed her breath. "Have you been drinking?"

She shrugged. "A little. Missy poured something in my drink."

"What about our pact?" Hallee gripped her friend's arm. "If you get caught, you could get expelled."

"Relax, Hallee. Everyone is doing it."

Hallee placed her hands on her hips. "We promised each other not to drink anymore."

"It's not a big deal. If anyone checks my drink, I'll just say it is my mom's. Everyone will believe me." She smirked, but Hallee's lips formed a straight line.

"Not funny. But as your best friend, if anything happens, I got your back."

The medication and alcohol settled in her bloodstream. She felt nothing. Not even remorse for breaking her promise to Hallee. She let the numbness envelop her. "Nothing is going to happen. Help me find my mom?"

"Sure."

As they turned to go up the gym stairs, the distinct scent of chocolate chip cookies wafted their direction. She looked over her shoulder to find Derek Oliver two steps away. His deep blue denim eyes penetrated her very soul. Ember froze. As he stepped forward, a smile slowly spread across his face. "Hello, Em."

Her eyes darted about the crowded room. "Where's your date?"

"She went to go freshen up. Something about looking camera ready for the crowning." He took one hand out of his pocket and rubbed the hairs on the back of his head.

Ember nodded and rolled her eyes. "Sounds like the Queen."

His gaze slowly dragged over her, lips parting. Their eyes met. His aura flared magenta. "I noticed your date left you, too." He moved closer. Ember felt the heat emanating off his chiseled frame. Her teeth raked against her bottom lip, reminding her of the kiss she just had with Logan.

She tore her eyes away and looked over his shoulder. "My date will be right back."

"I'll just go...find your mom...by myself." Hallee awkwardly slipped away.

Derek's fingertips drifted to her hand, bridging the

distance between them. His thumb stroked her knuckles. "If you were my date, I'd never leave your side." His touch collapsed any resistance she had left. Derek was different. He made her feel different, at her very core.

Ember searched his eyes. She wanted so badly to know what he was thinking. Something about him felt safe and perfect. It was as if he was the North Star her soul navigated to. She wanted to know if he felt the same way, too. She told herself that it was just some protective savior complex that made his aura flare like that, but what if it wasn't?

Men are users, Ember Eve. Birdie Mae's cutting words echoed in her mind.

She needed to know if Derek truly liked her. Ember unconsciously leaned into her desire. She slipped into a gray space where their energies and minds intertwined. She saw everything and felt everything Derek was feeling. He cared for her. More deeply than she dared hope for. His thoughts skipped about. He wanted to kiss her. Take her away from the dance. But he saw how she looked at Logan. He didn't think he had a chance.

Her breath caught. The realization of what she had done shocked her. She pulled back, breaking the connection.

I just entered Derek's mind.

Her eyes rounded as Logan's silhouette came into view behind Derek. He walked straight for them. Forehead lined in concern, he clamped his hand on Derek's shoulder. "What's up?"

"Nothing." Derek blinked, still staring at her. "Just saying hello." He pulled his hand away and brushed the back of his hair. "See you around, Em." She watched him slowly make his way back to Maddison's cheer table. His aura shifted to a regretful eggplant tone.

Logan cocked his head, fist flexing. "Was that guy bothering you?"

Ember shook her head slowly, still dazed, watching Derek's retreating silhouette. *Derek Oliver really likes me.*

He took ahold of her arms, shifting her focus back to him. "Ember, hey, you okay?"

"What? Yes, everything is fine. Derek was just saying hello."

"Yeah, that's what he said." His jaw ticked repetitively. "Maybe we should go sit down." He led her back to their table.

Moments later, Erick landed onto the hay bale next to them, wiping the sweat from his brow. "Dancing is a great cardiovascular workout." Breathless, he grinned and took a sip of his drink.

"Depends on what kind of dancing you're doing." Hallee rolled her eyes, sliding onto the bale beside Erick. She arched her brows at her. Ember snorted. The alcohol had definitely kicked in. She took another swallow.

"What? I don't get it. Dancing is like exercise." Erick pushed up his glasses. "Ooooh, you mean slow dancing…" His cheeks turned cherry red. Hallee and Ember giggled.

"These two are real funny." Erick thumbed his hand in the girls' direction.

"Attention! Attention!" Mr. Greene announced on the DJ's mic. "This is your fifteen-minute warning. Voting will close in fifteen minutes." He paused and grinned. "And Hallee Wilson…this next song is for you. Thanks for all your hard work chairing the dance committee." Her favorite singer's number one hit played throughout the gym.

Hallee's face lit up. She reached over and hugged Erick, fiercely kissing him on the cheek. His cheeks to his ears turned a new shade of crimson.

Adam's apple bobbing, he gulped. "You're welcome?"

"Come on. Let's dance!" Hallee pulled Erick's hand. Ember got up to join them.

"You go ahead. I'll be right back." Logan waved her on.

"Okay…" Ember joined her friends, forgetting about drunken Birdie Mae on stage. She forgot about invading Derek's mind, knowing his feelings. She fell into a sweet spot of numbed sensations. Carefree and happy.

The dance circle of volleyball girls expanded to let them join. It made Ember's heart soar to see Erick and Hallee have fun with her teammates. Sweat began to pour down her back as she tried to keep up with the new dance moves. The DJ played a trio of Prince songs causing Hallee's aura to soar the lightest, happiest shade of yellow.

The DJ cut in over the music. "And now what we've all been waiting for. The votes are in. Your newest King and Queen of Wilson County High's Sadie Hawkins dance are…drumroll, please…" The DJ pressed a button and prerecorded drums blared across the gym speakers.

"Kale Martin and Ember O'Neill."

****

Confused and lightheaded, her feet planted in place. There must have been a mistake. Her pounding heart muffled the cheers and applause that erupted around her. Her eyes darted amongst the crowd, seeking out Maddison. There was no way she had won. There would be a recount. Maddison would be named queen. That was the natural order of things.

Panic set in as all eyes landed on her. It was a mistake. It had to be a mistake. Hallee squished her in a tight hug. "I knew you could do it."

Erick walked up behind Hallee and pushed up his glasses, smiling. "Well done, warrior princess."

"Thanks, but this can't be right."

Logan's dimples danced as he joined them, smiling down on her. "Don't question it, O'Neill."

A loud shriek pierced the crowd noise, followed by the sound of glass breaking. Ember turned to locate the source. Maddison had taken a vase off the table and smashed it on the bleachers. Shattered glass reflected in the disco light on the gym floor.

Maddison stood there, trembling in anger. Her eyes were like daggers as she plastered a fake smile across her face and mouthed, *"pity vote."* Ember shivered. The cheer squad surrounded Maddison, consoling her. The disdain rolling off Maddison's aura was palpable. She turned, sensing Kale Martin as he walked up to Logan and shook his hand.

"Hey." Kale's warm brown eyes crinkled at the corners as he smiled. "Guess we better go get our crowns, Queen." She robotically took the hand he offered. The shock of being named queen had not yet worn off. It didn't feel real to her. Kale parted the crowd, leading her up on the stage.

She fought back tears as everyone clapped while they placed the crown on her head. Kale squeezed her hand. Ember looked up at him, grateful for his kind eyes and strength.

"You deserve this." He smiled down.

"I can't believe people voted for me." The yearbook staff moved in, taking photos of the newly crowned pair.

"And now, a song for our king and queen." The DJ announced.

"This way, my Queen." Kale took her hand leading her back down to the dance floor.

Ember's heart raced as Kale put his arms around her. She couldn't help but compare his touch to Logan and Derek's. His hands were warm, and his touch was soft, but she didn't feel the same sizzling connection that she did with both Logan and Derek. His fingers squeezed gently around her waist. Kale looked down into her eyes. "What are you thinking, my Queen?"

"I'm thinking Maddison is going to have my head." Ember bit her lip. "Marie Antoinette style."

Kale's deep laugh resonated in his chest. "Maybe?" His brows darted up as his gaze searched the bleachers. "Don't worry, I'll be here all night to protect you from Maddie." His lips jerked to one side. "Her bark is worse than her bite, trust me."

"What about Katie? Will she be mad about this?" Her eyes floated to the crown on his head.

"Nah. Katie is cool. Hell, she voted for you." He grinned at her shocked face.

"She did?"

"You've got more friends than you realize, Queen."

Tears formed at his words. "Yeah?"

"Yeah." He tucked his chin, looking over her head. "Looks like the president of the Ember O'Neill fan club is heading over." She turned to see Logan make his way through the swaying couples.

"He's a good guy, Ember." Kale gave his stamp of approval.

"Yeah, he's a keeper." She smiled.

"Mind if I cut in?" Logan's deep voice sent shivers down her neck.

"Anytime, Lauder. Take care of my Queen." Kale teased and walked away.

Logan was just reaching to put his arms around her when he quickly jerked away.

"What?" She looked up.

"Don't look now, but I think your mom is coming over with Mr. Greene."

"Oh." Ember swiveled to see a drunken Birdie Mae weave her way through dancing couples. Her cup sloshed in one hand and a cigarette smoldered in the other. Her teacher followed closely behind, concern etched deeply across his face and aura.

"Queen? Shiiiit. I never would have called it," Birdie Mae slurred, wrapping her golden tanning-booth arms around Ember. Her frosted blonde tips appeared gray in the disco light.

"Thanks, Birdie Mae. What are you doing here?" Ember tried to steer her mom off the dance floor, but she wouldn't budge.

Instead, her mom turned, letting her hand linger on Mr. Greene's arm. "This handsome fella came into the salon today needing a cut for the dance." Birdie Mae shifted her other hand on her hip. "How come I had to find out about this dance from one of your teachers?"

"I'm sorry. I should have mentioned it." Ember eyed her mom's muddled aura. "Let's get off the dance floor, Birdie Mae."

"What? I'm not good enough for you?" Her Louisiana drawl was even thicker when she was drunk. " 'Fraid people gonna think something? I'm not the freak. You are."

"Birdie Mae…" Her voice failed her as the sting of her mother's words cut to her core.

"Mrs. O'Neill, the dance is almost over. Would you like a ride home?" Mr. Greene rested a hand on Birdie Mae's shoulder.

Her aura immediately shifted as she focused her attention on the handsome teacher. She took a drag off her cigarette and blew smoke to the side as she slowly eyed Mr. Greene from head to toe. "Why, Ryan, you of all people know I ain't married no more. Call me, Birdie Mae." His aura flashed a carnation pink at the evaluation.

The song switched to something more up tempo, causing the couples to transition off the dance floor leaving Ember, Logan, Mr. Greene, and Birdie Mae in the spotlight. She bit her lip as Birdie Mae leaned into the teacher. "Ryan, you handsome devil. I would love it if you gave me a ride."

"Birdie Mae—" Ember interjected.

Mr. Greene cleared his throat. "No, it's okay, Ms. O'Neill. I'll be happy to give your mother a ride home." He emphasized the last word.

Birdie Mae's muddled aura flashed magenta at his words. She slipped her hand around his arm, completely ignoring Ember and the destruction she left in her wake as she steered Mr. Greene off the dance floor.

She exhaled a breath she didn't realize she'd been holding once they were gone. A single tear escaped as she fought back the urge to cry on Logan's shoulder.

"Hey." He reached down and wiped the tear from her cheek. "Let's go sit down."

He guided her through the gyrating students. Ember noted that the cheer squad was no longer at the dance, and neither were Maddison and Derek. She straightened her shoulders and put a smile on her face as classmates congratulated her as she passed by. She refused to let her mom ruin her night.

She picked up her drink off the table and drained it as she sat down next to Logan. "Sorry you had to witness that. Birdie Mae can be intense."

"Yeah, sort of like you?"

"Me?" She snorted. "We are nothing alike."

"Hmmm...I disagree. In some ways, you are similar."

"She's confident. Popular. Everyone likes Birdie Mae or wishes they could be like her with her blonde hair and tan body. She looks more like my older sister than my mother."

"Exactly. I think you two are more alike than you think." He cocked his head.

Ember rolled her eyes. "I'm not confident or popular."

"So, says the girl who just got crowned queen."

"I..." She couldn't argue his point. Realization sank in. She was popular now...and not in a bad way.

"Okay, but I'm still not confident." Ember said.

"That will come, Queen."

"Whatever." She scoffed, although she sincerely

wished that were true.

"Hey." He tilted her chin towards him. "Forget about your mom. You're the Queen." He leaned forward, dropping a quick peck on her cheek. "I'm the luckiest guy at Wilson County High. What do you say we go out there and show Hallee and Erick a thing or two?"

Ember looked into Logan's eyes, hoping it was true—that he really did feel like the luckiest guy. But as badly as she wanted to know his true feelings, she would never slip into his mind to confirm it. What happened with Derek was an accident. Just because she could do it didn't make it right. Logan's aura matched his words. That should be enough. I don't need to slip into his mind to know how he feels, she told herself.

Ember chewed her bottom lip. *Birdie Mae was wrong. Not all men are users. My dad was a good guy, and so is Logan. I trust him. And besides...Derek left with Maddison.*

She took his hand. "Okay, Lauder, let's dance."

Despite Hurricane Birdie Mae's trek out onto the dance floor earlier, Ember knew hands down that this was the best night of her life as she danced with her teammates, best friends, and her date, Logan Lauder.

Chapter Thirty-two

The door was unlocked when Ember returned from the dance. Greeted by the sounds of the TV and no Bear, her brow furrowed. Bear always ran to her when she came home. But it was late, almost midnight and Birdie Mae was passed out on the couch. Infomercials blared from the box TV in the living room. Everything felt off. Normally Birdie Mae fell asleep watching the music video channel. She walked over and turned down the volume.

Ember nearly stumbled as she walked into her room. Bear was unconscious on the floor right inside the door. She panicked and dropped to her knees, yelling, "Bear! Wake up!"

He didn't budge. She stroked his fur and realized he was just in a deep sleep. Relieved, she scratched behind his ears. He didn't crack an eyelid, as if someone had drugged him.

"Wow, Bear. Did you get into Birdie Mae's rum?"

A soft rumble of a growl escaped his throat, paws twitching as if he was chasing something in his dream. She shook her head. Whatever he had gotten into, he appeared to be okay. It was late. She yawned and stepped over the sleeping giant.

Ember looked at herself in her mirror. It was like a stranger stared back at her. Despite being tired, she had a healthy glow to her skin. Her eyes were brighter, and her cheeks had color. Her fingertips trailed across her lips where Logan had kissed her. The entire night was magical, except for Birdie Mae's outburst. She hung the plastic gold crown on her bedpost and quickly changed. She was anxious to get in bed and sketch her memories from the dance.

She parted the clothes hanging in her closet and reached into the back for her sketchbook. But her grasp came away empty. Her drawing pad wasn't there. She walked to her bed. Sometimes, when she was too tired to put it away, she would slide it under her bed. She kneeled and lifted the bed skirt—nothing but dust bunnies and dog fur. She looked between the mattresses. It wasn't there.

Ember slowly spun, scanning the room. Where was her sketchbook? Her pulse raced as panic set in. Someone had been in her room. She looked at her nightstand. It was bare.

Realization sank in. It wasn't just her sketchbook that was missing. Someone had taken her pills, too. The misalignment of everything since she got home now stood out like red flags. The door was unlocked. Birdie Mae fell asleep to the wrong channel. Bear was knocked out. Her personal items were missing.

A chill ran down her spine.

Why go through the trouble of knocking out Bear to just take nothing of value…only her things? Who would do that? Wayne? But he's in jail. Maddison was mad because she lost being named Queen but why would she take anything of mine? She's rich.

She looked at her digital clock. It was two a.m. Ember bit her bottom lip. Of all nights, she really needed to talk to Adam.

Someone had invaded her home and stolen her sketches and pills. At the dance, she had slipped into Derek's mind, and she didn't know how she did it. But Adam would know. She was convinced, with no doubt, that he was real. He could help her.

Curled up in her bed, Ember slipped her hand under her pillow, clasping her father's blade. She closed her eyes, meditating on Adam. She tamed her chaotic thoughts. For weeks, she had tried dream walking to reach him with no success. With each breath, her focus narrowed. She could almost hear his smooth, deep voice and smell his tempting scent.

****

Ember opened her eyes. She was no longer in her bedroom. She was in a room—an office. It was cold and gray, modern. A man sat behind a glass desk. He wore a tailored black suit and shirt, no tie. His hair was as dark as coal and slicked back. He sat with his hands steepled as if contemplating a decision.

Across from him, a boy sat in a wheelchair. He, too, wore all black. They were both pale and handsome, with chiseled jaws and piercing green eyes. Her nose flared as she inhaled their scents. One was familiar and intoxicating, chocolate and whiskey. The other was new—wintergreen, like the gum. Ember hated that smell.

She looked around them. The edges of the room were hazy. She was in a dreamscape. Her mouth fell open. She had done it. She was in Adam's dream. Not just a dream, she was in his premonition dream. She studied both males, not sure which one was Adam.

Seconds crawled as neither said a word. It startled

Ember when the man finally spoke—but it was not Adam's voice. "You realize you have no allegiance to her? She is nothing. Not your family. Not your friend. She is nothing but a tool to be used."

The boy sat silent.

The man lost his cool and stood, knuckles white as he leaned forward on the desk. "Answer me."

The boy's face remained emotionless, seemingly unaffected by the man's outburst. This was Adam. "Yes, Father."

Her eyes rounded with the realization.

The man's jaw muscles pulsed as he clenched his fists and came around to the front of the desk.

"Yet, you still hide her. Protect her." The man pulled his arm back and punched the boy across the face.

Ember screamed, "No!"

Adam's head swung around. His eyes sparked as blood trickled out of his nose.

"Eve?" The dreamscape immediately changed to her secret garden.

Ember reached up to touch his face, but he jerked his head back. He was no longer seated in the wheeled chair from his dream but stood in front of her, calm, as if his father hadn't just hit him. She pulled her hand away. His face was unharmed. The blood was gone.

"Adam? Are you okay?"

"It's nothing." He cocked his head, eyeing her. "Someone's been testing their new skills."

Ember blushed at the accusation. She studied his frame, his size. He stood taller than her. He wasn't as muscular as Logan, but he was clearly strong. She noticed the way the tight black tee hugged his torso. His dark hair was thick and slightly wavy. She imagined running her fingers through the raven strands. His soft lips jerked up in a smirk, green eyes sparkling. She breathed in his intoxicating scent.

"Who is Logan?" Adam asked.

"What?" Her cheeks flushed, realizing he had been in her head. "Stop, Adam. We had a deal. No more getting in my head."

"Angel, it is difficult to resist when you leave yourself wide open like that." He touched her arm, sending a pulse of heat radiating up to her shoulder. She jerked away and turned, surprised to see her weeping willow tree was now strung with a rope swing.

"What happened to my bench?" Ember turned to face him.

"Swings are more fun." He tilted his head. "Want to try? I'll push…"

"No. I don't want to swing." She rolled her eyes. "I want answers, Adam."

"Okay, fine. I'll swing." He sauntered over and sat down on the swing pumping his feet. "It really is so much fun." Sheer pleasure filled his face.

She couldn't help but be taken in by his happiness. He was mesmerizing. She found herself watching him, enamored by him. Adam was beautiful.

He slowed the swing and stared at her. "No, you are beautiful, Eve."

His tone. That look. Flames erupted at her core. Spreading, it enveloped her.

"I've never met a more beautiful being." He stopped the swing and stood analyzing every inch of her.

Under his scrutiny, she felt laid bare. Exposed. As

if he could see past her clothes, his eyes caressing every curve. Adam walked towards her like a predator stalking his prey. His steps were smooth. She couldn't hold his gaze. She looked away. She was not beautiful. She was broken, a mistake. She was a joke, a messed-up freak.

He reached out. But as if he thought better of it, he pulled his hand back. "Someday, you will trust me and believe me when I tell you that you are beautiful," he said and returned to the swing. "I was once like you."

Ember looked up.

"It's true. My family treated me like I was broken, a burden. Still do. They underestimate me, Eve." The hardness in his voice made the hair on her arms stand.

"Before, in your dream…that was your father, right? Does he hit you like that a lot?"

Adam looked away. "It's becoming a bad habit of his as of late." He tilted his head. "Did you find out anything about your parents?"

"I told you before. My parents don't have 'this'— whatever 'this' is. My mom does hair and acts like a teenager." Ember rolled her eyes. "And when my dad was alive, he used to work on a riverboat…if he wasn't laid off." Ember's voice trailed. "Neither one is different, like you or me."

"You sure about that? No special abilities?"

Ember thought about her dad's aura and its unusual golden hue. "I guess it's possible he didn't know that he was different?"

Adam's brows rose. "Interesting…" He rubbed his jaw. "What did it look like? His aura?"

"I didn't say anything about his aura." Her lips drew into a hard line. "You did it again, Adam."

"Sorry."

"Your father? He's like us? He can read minds?"

His voice steeled. "No, and yes. His abilities are, shall we say, limited?" He looked away. "My father has more than one nasty habit."

"And your mother?" She hoped that was a better situation.

Their eyes met. "Dead."

"Oh, I'm sorry."

She walked over in front of him, blocking his ability to swing. Her heart split in two as she imagined what his life must be like without a mother and an abusive father. He looked up. "Don't." He got up and brushed past her. "Don't pity me."

"I'm not." She swallowed. "My father died recently…that's all." She turned to follow him but stopped.

He toyed with a rose bloom and pricked his finger. "Damn." Blood seeped from the wound. He turned, smiling sheepishly. "I was going to pick it for you…"

She walked over. "Let me see your hand." She reached out. A sizzle of energy passed between them as she held his finger in her hand. She looked up to see him examining her face.

He leaned forward. "Do you feel it, too?"

She ignored the question and looked at his finger. His scent was overpowering. She bit her lower lip, wrestling with a deep desire that longed to be set free. She jerked her hand away.

"It should be fine. The thorn isn't stuck in there." He lifted his finger to his mouth and sucked the blood away. Eyes locked, his gaze pierced her defenses.

Ember backed away and sat down on Adam's

swing. His emerald eyes lit when she pushed herself back. She let the swing go. The warm scented garden air flowed through her hair. She smiled. He was right. It was fun. Plus, it was a distraction from Adam and his tempting scent.

"I knew you would like it." He walked confidently behind her, giving her a push.

"I don't need your help." The sizzle of his hands sent trails of electricity down her spine.

He walked around to face her, arms crossed. "Ah, but you do. Isn't that why you are here?"

"Whatever. You know what I meant." She rolled her eyes, going higher and higher.

"Come here, Eve." She tilted her head and immediately stopped the swing. She had this unbelievable desire to please him...to do whatever he wanted.

She walked over and stood in front of him, compliant.

"Do you want to learn new tricks?"

She slowly nodded.

"In the beginning, you will need to use touch to get into someone else's mind."

He reached out and held both of her palms. She looked down, fascinated by the warm, pulsating energy that rolled between them. His hands were soft, yet firm. She felt her cheeks warm as her thoughts drifted, imagining his touch on the nape of her neck and at the curve of her waist. He released one hand to cup her cheek. "Do you want to kiss me, Eve?"

Despite being consumed with embarrassment, she answered honestly and nodded. "Yes."

He cocked his head, eyes searching hers. "I know."

His green eyes sparkled as she lifted her hand to touch his pale, sculpted jaw. Before she could register his movement, Adam's hand wrapped around her wrist.

"Not yet, angel." His lips twisted into a crooked grin.

As if someone had thrown cold water on her, she gasped. Released from the thrall of his influence, she jerked from his grasp. Adam had compelled her.

"Stop it." She pulled her arms close around her, hugging herself.

He smirked and stepped around her, walking to the swing under the willow. He sat down and pumped his feet, sending the swing into motion. The aroma of chocolate and whiskey engulfed the garden.

"I can't make you do anything you don't already want to do. Remember that, Eve." His eyes danced in merriment.

The truth in his words made her flush. She had wanted to kiss him. Ember crossed her arms. "This isn't playtime, Adam. Teach me what you know."

A smile teased at his lips. "Perhaps not for you, but it is playtime for me, my angel."

"Whatever." Ember tossed her hair over her shoulder in frustration. "I need your help, Adam." She dropped her hands and walked closer.

"Eve, were you not listening...in the beginning, you will have to use touch to enter a person's mind. Then—"

She cut him off. "I know...I mean, I get it. It happened by accident tonight at the dance. How do you control it?"

"Control it?" His chin dipped. "Why would you control it? Release your powers, Eve. Would you never open a gift? Set it on a shelf, forgetting it existed?" He pumped his feet, sending the swing higher. "No, you wouldn't. And you shouldn't. Don't be embarrassed or ashamed, Eve. And don't deny what you are. Never forget, I am just like you." His gaze pierced the distance between them.

Ember winced and rubbed her temples.

"Have I upset you?" He stopped the swing and studied her face. "That wasn't my intention. I'm sorry, angel."

"No, I get it. I see your point. It's something else. Tonight, when I got home…" She took a deep breath and explained what had happened during the evening.

He raised a single brow. "At this dance, did anything unusual happen there?"

"No, I mean…I was crowned the Queen." Her mind drifted, thinking of the kiss from Logan.

A muscle ticked in Adam's jaw. "Queen, hmmm…and this Logan? Was he crowned King?"

"What? How?" Ember stomped her foot. "I never said his name. Get out of my head, Adam. And, no, he wasn't. Logan was my date. Kale was named King."

The jaw muscle ticked more rapidly as his brows drew together. "So many suitors…should I be jealous, angel?"

"Suitors? No. *We* are not a thing. Suitors? Who even uses that word?"

His lips jerked into a crooked smile. "Your lips say one thing, but your scent says something else." His nostrils flared.

"Adam, just stop. Please. I'm scared. I tell you someone broke into my house and all you want to do is joke and talk about the dance. My dad was killed by a demon in our backyard. What if one got inside my house?" Ember turned and swatted at the willow branch hanging in her way.

She started when his hand clasped her wrist. She hadn't realized he had moved. He spun her around to face him. His eyes scanned her from head to toe. "Did the demon hurt you, Eve?"

"No. Let go of me." She wrestled her hand out of his grasp. "I killed it with my dad's knife." His face was expressionless. "You are not surprised."

"No, I'm not surprised. The question is who sent the demon and why?" His eyes narrowed. "Show me what happened."

"Show you?" He cupped her cheek. Instantly, she closed her eyes and was back to that night, reliving her father's death. She trembled under Adam's touch.

"Shhh. It's okay, angel. I've got you."

Ember opened her eyes. Adam's hard body was pressed against hers. He held her tenderly, stroking the strands of her hair. The air hummed with electricity between them.

"I am sorry, Eve. I felt your distress that night. I tried to reach you." His fingertips outlined her jaw, sending tingles down her neck. He wiped away the single tear that escaped. Her cheek drifted into his caress. But Adam quickly pulled his hand away and stepped back. He searched her face, spun on his heel, and promptly paced the space between them.

"I'm not in a position to protect you yet." His fist clenched. "But I will be soon." He paused his pacing and faced Ember. "That knife…always keep it with you. It is an angelic blade." He winced as if feeling pain. "It will kill any type of demon."

"Wait. What?" Her brow furrowed. "What do you mean, angelic blade?"

He waved off her comment. "It's no ordinary knife, Ember. And your father was no ordinary human."

Her mouth fell open. "What do you mean?"

His lips twitched. "Did I fail to mention that we're not human, Eve?"

"I'm human," she insisted.

Adam laughed. "No. You're not. And your father was Nephilim."

"That's not possible…."

Adam cocked his head. "Isn't it though? You saw your dad's aura. Those with angelic blood have golden auras."

"Do I have a golden aura?"

His brow arched. "Angel, your aura shines like a golden star."

Ember sat down on the swing. Her mind churned.

"Your father never told you?"

"No."

He walked closer to her. "Well, that was incredibly reckless of him."

"He always made me feel special, like there was nothing wrong with me despite what others said…"

"That's nice, but he left you vulnerable with no training and no information."

"That's not true." Ember squeezed the rope. "He taught me how to use weapons."

"But nothing about your heritage…or demons."

"No." She muttered. She knew her father loved her, but why wouldn't he want her to know those things? It would have made her life so much easier.

"Would it? Would it have made life easier, angel?"

His lips twitched. "I know it all, yet your life seems ten times better than mine."

"You're kidding, right? My life sucks." Ember stood from the swing, frustrated.

"We don't have time for pity parties, angel." His face grew hard. "Keep that blade with you at all times. There are several types of demons. The one you destroyed was a lower-level type—highly aggressive, but not much going on up here." He tapped his temple and paced once more. "Someone is on to you. It's possible they sent the demon to test your skills or your defenses…or just to eliminate your dad. Either way, we need to up your skillset and quick." He stopped pacing. "Can you handle nightly lessons?"

She nodded.

"Good. Training begins now." He sat down on the swing. His fingers picked at the rope. "First step. Stop taking the meds."

Her brows drew together. "Considering they were just stolen. I'd say that won't be an issue, but how do I handle the sensory overload? The noise? The smells?"

His lips twisted. "Does a dog have trouble inhaling and discerning all the surrounding scents? Hearing all the noises of the world?"

She slowly shook her head.

"Correct. A dog can focus and weed out what's important and what's not. Our senses are better than any canine, and so is our control." His pupils narrowed.

"How do you know?" she asked.

Adam cocked his head and cracked his neck as a scowl fell across his face. "Trust me, I know. My loving father, remember?"

"Oh." She twitched at the image of Adam being

punched.

He smirked looking at Ember. "Exactly. I learned very quickly how to break connections and how to create them."

"So, how do you do it?"

"Well, at first, when I was younger, I learned how to connect through touch." His brow arched. "Which, I believe, you have mastered."

"Sort of…"

"Now you must learn to connect to others without touch. See my aura?"

"Yes."

"You must imagine a string connecting it to you and pull on it. Bring it to you. Step into it. Let it become a part of you."

She closed her eyes, trying hard to imagine the string connection. She gasped. She felt him. She felt Adam. Ember opened her eyes. Not only could she see what he was feeling through the colors of his aura, but now she could feel those same feelings, too. "I can feel you," she whispered.

"And how do I feel, angel?"

"Proud. Maybe happy?"

"And what am I thinking?" he asked.

Ember closed her eyes, focusing on the connection. But it was like there was a wall…a very tall wall. She opened her eyes. "It's like there is a wall."

"Good." He began to swing.

"Good?" Her voice rose. "How am I supposed to get into people's heads if I can't get into yours?"

"Tsk. Tsk. Don't lose your temper, angel. The humans will be easy to tap. I have protected myself for a long time. My walls are quite high." He shot up off the swing. "I must go now, angel." He ran his fingers through his raven hair.

"But how do I cut off all the noise? The people? Their auras?"

He made a cutting motion with his fingers. "Snip-snip."

"And how do I protect myself?" Worry crept into her voice.

His emerald eyes softened. "I will protect you."

"No, I mean how do I build a wall to protect myself from…from…"

"From someone like me?" His smile didn't quite reach his eyes. "Angel, I doubt you will ever meet anyone as skilled as me."

"But how?"

"Brick by brick."

"But what about Logan?"

"What about him?"

"He has a golden aura, too."

"He does…" Adam's pupils narrowed. His hands flexed into fists and then relaxed. "It is possible that he doesn't know. Many Nephilim are lost little lambs and are harmless, their powers so diluted from breeding with humans that it's not detectable. But until we know more about who sent that demon, keep your distance from this Logan boy." A sly grin slid across Adam's face. "See you tomorrow night, angel. Class is dismissed." His glowing eyes dissipated with his body.

Ember vowed to learn quickly as she was left alone in the dreamscape. Someone was messing with her, and she was determined to find out who it was.

Chapter Thirty-three

Ember walked into Wilson County High with her chin up and her shoulders relaxed. She practiced most of Sunday latching onto Birdie Mae's aura and then repeatedly cut the connection and mastered the process in no time. Now she felt so much lighter, not having to feel everything at such a heightened level, and without pills. Ember, for once in her life, felt unburdened and empowered.

Before first hour, classmates brushed by, smiling, and congratulating her as she and Logan made their way to their lockers. With her clipping the invisible threads that connected her to their auras, she realized this must be how everyone else sees and hears things in the world. It was near bliss. She no longer heard the whispers or saw the auras. It was better than taking the medication.

Ember was now able to mute everyone around her with only a thought.

Logan gave her hand a quick squeeze before she released it to open her locker. Breaking the aura connection had also shut off the buzz from his touch. She missed it to a point, but appreciated the freedom of not seeing, feeling, and hearing every little thing. Besides, Adam was right—she needed to keep her distance from Logan till she knew more.

"How does it feel to be queen, O'Neill?"

He leaned against the lockers as she pulled out her books. Her eyes grazed the interior. She knew better, but she had hoped to see her sketchbook tucked away inside the locker. A small shiver snaked down her back.

His fingers tilted her chin up, forcing her eyes to meet his. "What's wrong?"

Ember studied his warm, brown eyes. She didn't need to connect to his aura to see he was concerned. She didn't believe he could have had anything to do with her missing things.

"I, this Saturday…after the dance…" Ember could not finish as Hallee and Erick rushed forward.

"Ember! Hey, I tried to reach you all day Sunday."

She winced as she saw and felt the onslaught of Hallee and Erick's emotions. She quickly clipped the connection. "Sorry. Birdie Mae had a massive hangover. She took the phone off the hook."

Logan palmed Erick. "Hey, what's up?"

"We've got some bad news," Erick said, looking pointedly at Ember.

"My cousin is back." Hallee's face flushed behind her purple frames.

"Which cousin?" Logan asked.

"Wayne." Erick and Hallee said simultaneously.

She leaned back against the lockers, hugging her books to her chest.

"I thought they sent him to juvie," Logan said.

"My dad says that some hot-shot lawyer out of Cincinnati took on his case and petitioned a judge. He presented evidence that showed Wayne was set up."

Ember just rolled her eyes. Hallee reached out and squeezed her arm.

"Look, Em, he's a complete douche bag…I talked to my dad. He's going to see about moving Wayne out of the classes that you and he have together, okay?" Erick pushed his glasses up his nose. "It could take a couple of days to get it sorted out, though."

Ember let out a breath she didn't realize she had been holding.

"Don't worry, warrior princess, we've got your back." Erick's smile didn't quite reach his eyes.

Logan's hand formed a fist. "I dare that prick to try anything."

Ember lifted her chin and straightened her back. She wasn't the same person who took Wayne's harassment day after day, year after year without fighting back. She was stronger now. She had power over her abilities. "Okay."

Hallee's brow arched over her glasses. "Just 'okay'? That's it?"

"Innocent or not. I'm not afraid of Wayne Wilson." Ember wasn't sure if she truly believed the statement, but it sounded good. *Virtus vincit.*

Logan put his arm around her and squeezed. The bell rang. Her heart hammered in her chest.

Erick tilted his head to the classroom door. "He's already in there."

She took a deep breath and turned. "Okay."

"Wait." Hallee grabbed her arm. Everyone turned to look at Hallee. "Oh, just Ember. One sec…we'll meet you inside. It's about the thing we talked about," she said to Erick.

"Oh, yeah…" Erick saluted and turned toward World History.

But Logan hesitated to leave. Ember nodded,

assuring him she'd be okay.

"What's going on?" She searched Hallee's face. She was so used to relying on people's auras that it tempted her to reconnect with Hallee just to have a clue.

"So, the reason we were trying to reach you on Sunday was also this." Hallee lifted a fat folder stuffed with loose papers.

"What is it?" she asked.

"Erick and I began comparing notes on Sunday…we have some theories…about you."

The tardy bell rang.

"Okay, let's talk about it later."

"But Em—" Hallee continued.

"Look, whatever it is…it can wait. Right now, I've got your cousin to deal with."

"Okay, later." Hallee exhaled and reluctantly followed Ember into the room.

****

Mr. Thompson's aura bloomed into a concerned indigo as he watched Ember walk into the classroom. He smiled briefly at her and turned back to the chalkboard, writing the day's agenda. Ember snipped her connection to him, and the rest of her classmates, cutting off their whispered words and clouded auras—until her focus locked onto the seething cayenne aura at the back of her row. It belonged to Wayne Wilson.

She watched Wayne's smirking lips mouth the words, "I'm back, bitch. Miss me?"

A sliver of fear raced down her spine. Ember immediately cut the connection and dropped into her chair. For the next hour, she fixed her eyes on the clock, watching the hands tick slowly around the dial. While the room turned hot and stuffy, her mind kept snagging on the negative energy that rolled off Wayne.

Finally, the bell rang. She felt Logan's familiar heat as he rose to stand by her. His body stiffened as Wayne walked up the aisle toward them. Logan angled himself protectively.

"What are you looking at?" Wayne sneered.

She gripped the desktop. Waited.

From the corner of her eye she saw Logan's lips tilt into a lopsided smile. "I can't decide what's going on here. You seem like a dick," he started, "but maybe asshole is more accurate."

Wayne stepped up, just inches apart from Logan. "Why don't you meet me outside after school and get a closer look?"

"No." Ember stood to place herself between the two boys. "Leave him alone, Wayne." She locked eyes with the bully, connected to his aura and for a moment pushed into his mind. His eyes widened, then relaxed.

"I said leave him alone," she said slowly, emphasizing each word.

"Whatever." Wayne shook his head and stepped back, brushing past a gawking Hallee and Erick.

"Wayne?" Ember called out. He turned at the door. His eyes slid to hers. She felt his anger and confusion.

"What?" he gritted.

"When did they let you out?"

"Saturday." His lips curled into a menacing smile. "Sorry, I didn't have enough time to make it to the dance, Queen."

Ember lost what little control she had and walked toward Wayne, a lioness stalking her prey. She tightened her grip on his mind. His body stiffened. She leaned in and spoke low beside his ear. "Stay away from my home, my family and my friends." She inhaled his putrid fear and exhaled. "Or else."

His face paled, eyes watering. "I'm sorry," he whispered.

With that, she released her grip on his mind and aura. He stumbled backward into the hall. "You're fucking crazy, bitch!" he screamed and quickly scrambled out of sight down the hall.

"That was hot." She jerked when Logan spoke. She hadn't realized he'd moved up behind her. "Wanna share what that was all about?"

A small smile lined her lips as Logan handed her books to her. "Wayne Wilson shouldn't be a problem anymore."

As Erick's brows pressed together in concern, Hallee moved to her side. "Em, we should really talk."

"Later." She brushed past her friends into the hall. "We are going to be late for second hour."

Erick shrugged as he and Hallee exchanged looks. "Later."

****

As the last bell of the day rang, Ember gathered up her things. Wayne Wilson was a no-show for the rest of the classes that they shared. She smiled at his empty seat. Adam was right. Their powers were a gift.

Hallee came up to her, giving her a pleading look. "Hey, Ember, can we talk now?"

"Yeah, warrior princess," Erick said. "It's kind of a big deal."

Not needing any special powers to sense the intensity of their thoughts, she slumped back into her chair. "What is it?"

Erick's eyes darted around the room. "Maybe we should go to the library?"

"Do you mind?" Maddison huffed as she brushed past Erick, causing him to flush crimson.

Other than nasty glares, the queen of mean and her crew had essentially given her the cold shoulder all day. She watched Maddison float over to Mr. Greene's desk and was never more grateful for her newfound ability to shut off her connections to others. Listening to Maddison flirt with her coach and teacher was the last thing she wanted to do.

"Okay, sure," she said. "Let's go to the library."

Logan leaned in and kissed her on the temple. "I'm going to practice."

Ember felt warmth rush to her cheeks as Maddison and Mr. Greene caught the interaction. Maddison glared and leaned in closer to the teacher, distracting him with her cleavage.

Mr. Greene cleared his throat as Ember reached the door. She looked over.

"See you on the court in fifteen, Queen." He smiled. Maddison crossed her arms and rolled her eyes.

"Yep." Ember let the "p" pop as she walked out the door. Erick and Hallee shifted anxiously in the hall waiting on her. "I've only got like ten minutes."

"Trust me, we know, Queen," Hallee teased, leading them into the library.

Inside the library, Mama Jackson hummed to herself as she steered the loud commercial vacuum between bookcases. She immediately snipped her connection to the woman, causing the noise in the room to lower to a comfortable level. Hallee led them to their lunch club table in the back of the room. She dropped the thick file folder on the table. Ember stood as her friends slid into the wooden chairs.

"You should sit down," Hallee said, nodding to the chair across from her.

"I don't have much time," she insisted.

"She's right. You should sit." Erick's voice cracked, causing him to flush.

"Okay." Ember rolled her eyes and sat down. "What did you figure out?" She drummed her fingers, looking at the wall clock in frustration.

Hallee flipped open the file folder and sorted through photocopies until she came to one with a drawing of a sword. Her eyes widened. It was very similar to the one she had seen when she had drowned in the pool. It was exactly like the Archangel Michael's sword, but at the top of the hilt were engraved wings.

She used a lone fingertip to trace the sword. "Where did you find this?"

"It is from my church's archives. It's the symbol for the Covenant Knights." Hallee pulled out another sheet and set it beside the other. "And this is the symbol for the Order of Saint Michael, a heretical sub-sect of the Covenant Knights."

Ember leaned forward, pupils narrowed, as she studied the subtle differences.

"Do either look familiar to you?" Erick leaned across the table. "Did your father have any tattoos like this? Or wear any jewelry with this symbol on it?"

"No. I don't think so."

He slumped back into his chair.

She pushed the papers back to Hallee. "What are Covenant Knights?"

Her friends exchanged glances. Erick pushed up

his glasses and crossed his arms over his chest. "You said you wanted to tell her."

Avoiding any eye contact, Hallee shifted the papers on the table. "Okay…so, remember we read about the Nephilim in the Book of Enoch?"

The hum of the vacuum stopped as Ember felt the tug of a new energy entering the room. "Why, Mr. Greene! I didn't see you there." Mama Jackson's warm voice carried through the stacks. "How you liking Wilson County High?"

"Good. Good, thank you." Ember turned to see the teacher not six feet behind her. His aura flared an upset, orange-red as his gaze shifted from her to the table. His lips fell into a tight line. "Were you planning on going to practice today, O'Neill?"

Surprised by his angry aura, Ember quickly snipped the connection and stood. "Sorry, Coach. We were just working on a project."

"I can see that," he said. A muscle ticked in his jaw as he stared at the sketches and copies on the table. When Hallee quickly picked them up and placed them back in her folder, Mr. Greene's face shifted. He looked up and smiled warmly at her. "And you, Ms. Wilson, let's schedule a time to meet." He winked, causing Hallee to blush. "I like how you handled the dance committee." He moved in closer to the table. "I think we should discuss expanding your role in the club…more responsibilities, etcetera."

Hallee beamed. "Okay, yeah, sure."

"And O'Neill…" He slid one arm across Ember's shoulders, sending a shiver down her spine. She instinctively pulled away. A muscle ticked in his jaw.

"Yeah, Coach?"

"If I beat you to the Middle School gym, it's extra laps for you and the entire team." He cracked a smile at her panicked face. "I'm just kidding." He turned and winked at Erick and Hallee. "Or am I?"

Ember took the hint. "I don't want to find out." She said her goodbyes and hustled out of the library with Mr. Greene slowly following behind.

Chapter Thirty-four

Ember sensed Coach Greene was picking on her at practice. Though he ran both JV and varsity practices, he critiqued her nonstop. No matter how high she jumped or how much she sacrificed her body diving for the ball, he found something wrong with her technique.

She understood he was under a lot of pressure. He was a new coach, and their first game was coming up on Saturday; but she didn't appreciate being singled out. Halfway into practice, he moved her to do three-on-three drills with the varsity team and senior, Ashleigh Gardner, a one-woman powerhouse on the volleyball court. She didn't go easy on Ember, either.

Ashleigh looked like she descended from Vikings. Twin braids held her long, blonde hair back off her face. Over six feet tall, Ashleigh was a wall at the net. She smiled at her through the volleyball net. Ember shook out her hands and bent at her knees, sinking into a ready position.

"Good luck," Ashleigh mouthed to her. But as soon as the whistle sounded, Ashleigh's face hardened.

The ball flew over the net. A teammate lobbed the ball to Ashleigh. She smacked the ball hard over the net and into Ember's face. She wasn't used to such power and reacted barely in time, sending the ball out of bounds.

"Point," Ashleigh shouted, smirking at her. She gave high fives to the girls on her side.

"Again," Coach yelled and blew the whistle.

Time after time, the same scenario played out until she figured out the right position to return the ball. As soon as she was convinced that she knew how to defend Ashleigh's spike, the senior switched from her dominant hand to her left, sending the ball sailing into center court. Ember whiffed on the miscalculation and smacked air.

"Point!" Ashleigh palmed her teammates.

Coach blew the whistle. "Break for five. O'Neill, over here."

Her shoulders slumped when she saw his disappointment. "Yes, Coach?"

"What's going on? I know you can do better."

She looked away. "I'm not sure."

"Well, get your head right. I'm counting on you on Saturday. Both squads could use your talent. But if you are going to play like this, I'm not risking you on varsity. Those girls deserve a teammate who is consistent. Can you do that, O'Neill?"

"Yes, Coach."

Ember jogged over to the water fountain. She knew what the problem was. She had shut off her connections to everyone in the gym and could no longer anticipate their thoughts and emotions or where they were going with the ball. While no connection meant fewer distractions for her, it also meant she was operating at a lower level. Her confidence decayed. Slower and unsure, she was the worst player out there.

Ember bent over, taking a cool drink from the fountain. She turned to face the two players she was teamed up with. She opened herself up, connecting to their auras. Instantly, she heard their conversations from across the gym. She could see and feel their frustration as they looked over at her. She took a deep breath and exhaled. Next, she linked herself to Ashleigh. Her aura was rolling with confidence as she stood with her teammates, laughing. Ember bit her lip, crossing the gym, and connected to them as well. Coach blew the whistle.

"Again," he yelled across the gym.

She jogged back into position at the net. She ignored the amplified noise and smells and, instead, focused on the volleyball that sailed over the net. She tracked the ball as it bounced between each player's volleys. When the ball flew to Ashleigh, Ember mentally commanded, "Miss it."

Ashleigh jumped up, pulling back her arm to spike the ball over the net; but as her hand fell forward, she missed the ball completely. The ball fell to the court on their side. Ashleigh's eyes widened in disbelief. She shook her head.

Ember's teammate yelled, "Point!"

She turned to see their smiling faces and soaring, lemon-yellow auras. A small voice inside her head urged her to stop—that it was cheating. But she didn't stop. It felt good to stretch and test her abilities. Just like with Wayne, she didn't just compel—she commanded. She could control people.

Maybe it was wrong, but it felt good to win. A small smile played at her lips. Adam would be proud, she thought.

When her side overturned the ball, Ember distracted the girl serving, causing the ball to go wide of the net. She helped her teammates by slipping into their minds and pushing them to dig when the ball fell deep into their zones or to leave it if the ball was going wide. By the end of practice, the varsity girls were giving her high fives and celebrating their come back. She overheard Ashleigh talking to Coach Greene.

A sliver of guilt snaked across her mind as he chewed Ashleigh's ear off for not trying harder. She cringed, disconnecting herself. Instead, she let herself savor the appreciative auras of the team and cut her ties to everyone else.

****

Logan leaned against his car in the high school parking lot, waiting for her. Ember allowed herself to connect to his aura. His head swung in her direction. A smile stretched across his face, causing both dimples to pop. Ember sensed the familiar buzz ignite between them. She inhaled deeply, allowing his delicious odor to consume her. A rush of warmth engulfed her as she watched his aura blossom magenta.

He walked around, opening the passenger door for Ember. "Nice glow, O'Neill."

"Thanks."

She loved the way he made her feel as his eyes appraised her. She wiped the sweat off her brow with the back of her arm. "Practice was intense, but it got better towards the end."

He turned the keys in the ignition, and the car hummed to life. He drove onto the county road in front of the school and let his hand drift to her knee. She swallowed hard as the tingle of energy from his fingertips sizzled down her thigh.

His eyes darted to hers and back to the road. "So,

I'm curious to know…what was so important today that Erick and Hallee needed to talk to you?"

She studied his aura and connected to his mind. He was, in fact, curious, but also very much annoyed at being left in the dark. She released the connection to his mind and shifted her gaze to the blurring landscape as they drove past brown combined fields and half naked trees that'd lost their leaves to the autumn winds.

She had toyed with telling him everything hundreds of times; but each time she imagined the conversation, Adam's pale face and piercing green eyes made her stop. Adam was right. She couldn't trust Logan with that information, not yet. And besides, she didn't want to tarnish what they had, not if she could hide being Nephilim a little while longer.

He squeezed her leg. "It's okay if you don't want to talk about it."

Ember sighed. She didn't want to keep secrets from him, though. She was a terrible liar.

"Really, O'Neill. Whatever it is…you don't have to tell me. I get it. Some things you just can't tell other people about." A muscle ticked in his jaw as he pulled his hand away from her.

"Logan, if I told you, you'd think I was crazy and wouldn't believe me." She turned away and slumped back in her seat.

"How do you know that, O'Neill?" he asked.

"Because I wouldn't believe me."

"But Erick and Hallee believe you…" he said.

"Yeah."

"Someday, I hope you will trust me with your secrets."

She glanced back at Logan. His aura bloomed a

sincere midnight blue. She felt herself on the tip of capitulating and telling him everything, but the thought of losing him was too much. Without thinking, she clutched her dad's chain hanging from her neck. Maybe someday, when she had all the answers, she would let him in on her secrets.

Logan reached over and squeezed her hand. She returned the gesture and eased back into his mind, connecting to his aura.

"Logan?"

"Yes?" His voice fell flat.

"There is no secret. Erick and Hallee just wanted to talk about a project for school."

His head dipped in a nod. "There is no secret," he repeated. "You were working with Hallee and Erick on a school project."

"Yes." Ember broke her connection with his mind. A small pang of guilt poked her conscience as he blinked rapidly and pulled his hand away.

Ember sighed, letting her eyes slide away. *Someday, Logan, I will tell you everything.*

Even if it was a lie, she chose to believe it.

Chapter Thirty-five

For as long as she could remember, the night terror was always the same.

When Ember noticed that the leaves on the trees had changed colors, she knew the timeline of her premonition dream had changed. She reached out and fingered the golden leaf hanging from the branch of the oak tree.

When a voice in the distance called her name, she looked down. She was still wearing a Wilson County High volleyball jacket. A partial sense of relief flashed through her as she realized that she still had not received a team jacket—at least, not yet anyway. In fact, they weren't even going to get their jerseys till Friday, the day before the game.

She scanned the woods with her enhanced senses. She reached out, trying to latch onto any auras nearby. Inhaling deeply, she sniffed the air. He was out there—along with the girl. They were too far away for her to use compulsion. So, Ember ripped off her jacket and ran.

Branches cut across her arms, leaving stinging welts. Bear charged through the woods behind her. The roar of a boat engine rang through the air. She broke out of the woods and into the clearing. She sensed a presence in the cabin. Her nostrils flared—a male—that

was new. Tempted to go to the cabin, the muffled
screams of the girl pulled her towards the water instead.

Ember jerked as a boy materialized next to her.
Adam. His intoxicating scent of chocolate and whiskey
swirled around Ember. He reached out and touched her,
sending an electrical current down her arm and straight
to her core. His emerald eyes sparkled in the moonlight
as his lips jerked up to one side.

"As much as I'd like to see you wet, angel, I know
how this ends. It will totally ruin the mood."

The riverbank evaporated, and Ember's secret
garden took its place.

Her eyes rounded as she noticed Adam's aura. A
prism of colors surrounded him, only to be outshone by
the most glorious golden light. It was beautiful. His
aura flared magenta as he caught her admiring him.
Annoyed by his reaction, she pulled her arm from his
grasp.

She crossed her arms, glaring daggers at Adam.
"Why did you take us out of my dream?"

"Tsk. Tsk, Eve. Don't get mad. I was just trying to
save you from a losing battle. You can't change the
future," he said and sauntered over to the swing.

"What happens...happens." He shrugged and
pumped his feet, sending the swing into motion.

Ember's hands formed into fists. "This dream was
different, though."

"Different how?"

She squeezed her eyes shut as she recalled the
changed scene. "It wasn't spring anymore." Her eyes
connected with Adam. "It was fall."

"Okay." He let the swing drift slowly to a stop. He
cocked his head. "Anything else?"

"I think there was someone in the cabin. I've sensed no one there before."

"Maybe they have always been there, but your abilities are getting better."

"Maybe…"

"Anything else?" he asked.

"No. If you hadn't barged in, I might have learned more."

He shrugged. "You were late. I was concerned."

Ember feigned a shocked expression, placing her hand on her chest. "You were worried? About me?"

"Trust me…I have more important things…people I could be doing. If you don't want me—" He stood.

"No." She cut him off and blushed when she saw the smile crawl across his perfect lips. "I mean…since you are here…I have a few questions."

"Shoot." He sat back down.

"Do you ever feel guilty? You know…using your abilities on people?" She looked away.

A small chuckle rumbled in his throat. "What have you been doing, angel?"

"Nothing. I mean, I may have slipped into people's minds a few times."

His dark brows raised. "Been naughty, angel?"

"What? No. Just…Wayne Wilson was released. He was at school and…."

The whites of his knuckles shone as he squeezed the rope on the swing. She noticed a muscle tick rhythmically in his jaw. "I thought he was taken care of," he muttered.

"Taken care of? No. He was in juvie, but apparently a lawyer from Cincinnati took his case and proved to a judge that he was framed." She shook her head. "So, he was released. And now, he is back at school."

His eyes darted to hers. Head cocked to the side, he asked, "So, what did you do, angel?"

She swallowed, looking down. "I got in his head and commanded him to stay away from my home and to leave me and my friends alone."

She furtively looked up, surprised to see Adam's eyes glowing at her words.

"You didn't command, angel. You compelled."

"Compelled?" Brows drawn together, she knew what she did. She didn't just suggest an action. She was able to control Wayne and her teammates. "Right. Compel." *Could I be more powerful than Adam?*

"We can't control people, angel. I told you this before. We can only strongly suggest. Humans have free-will." He watched her as she processed his words. "Don't feel guilty." He looked away. "We do what we must do to survive. It's our instincts."

"Why do you refer to other people as humans, as if you are not? Aren't we part human?" She took a step closer. Mentally, she reached out to the invisible string tied to his aura, but it quickly evaporated.

His lips tilted to one side. "You are so adorable, angel, when you try to be sneaky."

"I wasn't trying to be sneaky." She shifted her gaze and walked over to the roses, studying their soft petals.

She could feel him watching her. She looked up, catching his stare. His tongue darted over his lips. Eyes locked, she wondered what he was thinking. She broke the silence. "So, are you going to answer my question?"

Suddenly, she felt Adam's warmth behind her. She turned. The charged air buzzed between them. She looked up into his dark green and golden flecked eyes. He was only inches from her.

The smell of his black leather jacket mixed with his arousing scent. She bit her bottom lip. Her gaze slowly slid to his mouth. A low growl escaped from his throat. His head tilted slightly. He reached out, shifting a stray hair off her temple. Her lips parted at the tingle of his touch.

He leaned in to whisper in her ear. "Answer my question, and I'll answer yours." His fingers trailed down from her temple to her lips, tilting her chin up.

"Okay…" Flashes of Logan kissing her flooded her mind. Butterflies took flight in her stomach.

He released his hand and stepped away, leaving her cold and wrecked. Despite knowing very little about him, she desperately wanted him to kiss her. She watched him saunter back to the swing. His dark raven hair slid over his brow. He looked up, their eyes met.

"Do you love him?"

Ember blinked. Of all the questions she thought he might ask; this was not it. "Love who?"

"Logan." He said his name like a curse word.

"Logan? What? No. No, of course not. Not at all." Ember felt heat rise to her cheeks. "You were in my head again."

He shrugged and pumped his feet. "Can you blame a guy? I lean in and you're practically screaming his name."

"I wasn't screaming his name."

"Yes, you were. In here." Adam tapped a finger to his head.

Frustrated, she turned her back. "I was just thinking about the dance. He kissed me."

Before she turned to see his reaction, his hard body slammed into hers. His powerful arms wrapped around her torso, turning her to face him. Fire scorched her entire body. He lowered his head. Her mouth parted. His lips were millimeters from hers.

"He shouldn't have done that." He growled. "You are mine, angel."

His possessive tone snapped Ember from the hypnotic trance of his eyes. "Let go of me."

Instantly he moved back to the swing, leaving her flustered and confused from his embrace. He ran his fingers through his hair and let out a breath. "I will never hurt you, Ember."

Her eyes rounded at the sound of her name on his lips. "How did you..." His eyes flashed. "Right, you were in my head," she said. He knew everything about her. Everything. And she knew practically nothing about him. Yet, somehow, she trusted him more than Logan.

She walked towards him, eyes connected. "That is the first time you've said my name." The gold in his emerald eyes sparked. "What is your name? Your real name, Adam?" They were now just a few feet apart.

He cocked his head. "Is that really the question you want me to answer?"

Her gaze shifted to the ground. If she was being honest, it really wasn't the most pressing question she had. For one, who are the Covenant Knights?

Before she could finish her thoughts, he grumbled, "Stay away from them."

She looked up to see that his face had turned stony, eyes hard. "You were in my head again." Her hands fisted. "Stop, Adam."

His lips twisted into a smirk. "Block me."

"I will. Someday," Ember hissed, frustrated. "You heard my question in my head. Who are the Covenant Knights, and what do they have to do with us?"

"That is two questions, angel." His emerald eyes danced. "But I am a man of my word."

He stood and pulled on the low hanging willow branch. He pinched off the thin leaves, twirling them between his fingertips. She admired his tall frame, the way his jeans hugged in all the right places. She shook her head, trying to erase where her thoughts were headed. He glanced up, catching her roving eyes. His lips tilted into a delicious smile.

She bit her lip, forcing herself to look away. "So, who are the Covenant Knights, Adam?"

"All you need to know is that they are hunters. And they will stop at nothing to eradicate us."

Ember looked up, shocked. That was not what she expected to hear. "I don't understand."

"It's not complicated, angel. To them, we are an abomination. We shouldn't exist."

"That doesn't make sense," Ember thought back to the papers Hallee tried showing her.

"So, the Order of Saint Michael?"

His pupils narrowed. "Assassins."

Ember gulped. "Assassins?"

His chin dipped in a nod.

"How do you know all this?"

His lips twisted in a smirk. "My father and grandfather trained me in all things Nephilim, angel."

"I still don't get it. Why would these knights want to hurt us?"

"Humans fear power. And we are very powerful."

"I don't feel powerful."

His lips slid into a small smile. "Not yet, but you will." His face shifted. "Keep your father's blade close and keep practicing."

"Wait. You're not going. Are you? You haven't answered all my questions."

"I think you have met your quota for the day, angel."

"But how do I know if one of these knights or Order guys is after me? Do they have a different aura?" Her mind flashed to her premonition dream.

Adam closed the distance between them. He tilted her chin up and studied her eyes.

"You have nothing to worry about, angel. I will always protect you." He spoke, fading from her dreamscape.

Her limbs became liquid at the intensity of his words. She believed him.

****

Ember's eyes fluttered open. She turned over in the bed and looked out her window. The Kentucky night sky was beautiful as millions of sparkling stars shone twinkling above. A small shiver danced down her spine as the thought of assassins lurking pulled her senses into high alert. Her hand slipped under her pillow, clutching her father's blade. She released the dagger from its sheath and studied the etchings in the moonlight, wishing she knew what they meant. Her finger trailed along the engravings, sending a tingle along her fingertip.

"An angel blade..." she whispered. Bear's ears twitched on the floor beside her. "Why didn't you tell me, Dad? Why didn't you tell me we were different?"

Her fingers drifted to her father's military chain, now a permanent fixture around her neck. Her eyes landed on the picture of her father and the mysterious soldier sitting on her nightstand. "I will find him. I promise."

Chapter Thirty-six

Ember should have seen the dark clouds as an omen of the storm coming her way. Charcoal gray clouds hung low in the sky. The local TV station forecasted severe weather throughout the day as a cool front moved into the area. She threw her hair up in a ponytail. It was the Friday before her first volleyball game; Coach had told her she would start on JV and sub in on varsity.

Her nerves were on edge as she slipped into Logan's black sports car. His lips curled into a smile, revealing his dimples. "Hey, O'Neill," he said.

"Hey, yourself, Lauder." She inhaled his chocolate and berries scent as he leaned in and kissed her temple. Despite the hungry roar of his aura when they were together, he had yet to kiss her again on the lips. It frustrated her that he didn't do it again, but then the echo of Adam's words sent tingles down her spine. *"You are mine, angel."*

The first raindrops splashed against the windshield as they pulled out of the gravel drive. The water streaked in little rivers down the glass.

"Tried to call you last night," he said.

"Oh, sorry." She rolled her eyes. "Birdie Mae sometimes takes the phone off the hook when she's had a long day at the beauty shop. She doesn't want anyone disturbing her after hours."

"That's cool."

"What did you need?" She looked over, studying his aura. He was nervous. She connected to his mind, then pulled herself back. It was becoming too easy to slip into people's minds. No wonder Adam read hers so easily. Like breathing, it had become an unconscious habit for her.

"Nothing major. Just Kale and I were thinking about maybe doing a double date with you and Katie?" He searched her face.

Other than a casual nod of acknowledgement at school, Katie had kept her distance since the bonfire. "Katie," she asked, surprised.

"Yeah, Kale says she really admires you and has a lot of regrets…about the past."

"Okay…" Ember watched as his fingers drummed on the steering wheel.

"So, it's a yes?"

"Sure. When?" she asked.

"Saturday night, after your games…if you're not too tired from kicking ass, that is?" His brow arched as his lips twitched into a smile.

"I think I can handle it." Her heart skipped a beat as his aura turned magenta. Maybe he would kiss her again on their date, she hoped.

"Looking forward to seeing those skills, O'Neill."

"Yeah?" She smiled.

"Yes." His eyes darted to hers. The heat from his desire sent the hairs on her arm to attention as he reached over and slid his hand into hers. "No pressure, though."

Ember gulped and stared out the window, releasing

her connection to him. She was already feeling the immense pressure from Coach Greene and her teammates. Knowing Logan was going to be there watching, felt like someone put a pile of bricks on her shoulders. She sighed as they neared the school and he squeezed her hand.

Be brave, she told herself.

****

Ember clipped her connections to her schoolmates as they walked down the hall to their lockers but her back stiffened when she saw Erick and Hallee waiting by her locker. She had been avoiding them all week. Whatever their theories were, they were wrong.

Her father couldn't have been a Covenant Knight or a part of the Order of Saint Michael. She would have known. While he loved the brotherhood of the military, he hated war and taking lives. He had told her as much last summer when they were camping. Plus, after what Adam told her, she just couldn't imagine her dad as an assassin with one of the secret organizations.

She sighed when she saw Hallee's pinched brows behind her purple frames. Erick cleared his throat and nodded to Ember.

"Hey." Ember reached between them and opened her locker.

"Em, we really need to talk," Hallee pressed.

She glanced at Hallee who hugged the overflowing file folder of theories to her chest.

Erick leaned in. "You can't avoid us forever."

"I know—"

She didn't finish her sentence. Wayne Wilson's voice coming from the end of the hall made her lose focus. She looked over her shoulder. He was talking with Maddison. Alarm bells went off in her head. She turned on her connection to their auras, then instantly jerked from the negative energy radiating off the two of them.

"This can't be good," she muttered.

While Hallee and Erick both turned to see what she was talking about, Ember focused her enhanced hearing on their conversation. Anger ignited inside her as Wayne claimed it was Ember who framed him in order to get back at him for the pool party stunt. Maddison of course nodded in agreement, saying it just had to be Ember who set him up. She then raised her voice. "I'm so over the pity party everyone is throwing for that freak."

As if they realized Ember was listening, they both turned their heads and looked down the hall, locking eyes with her. Wayne's lips twisted in a sneer as he slammed his locker door shut and strutted out the hall doors. Maddison waggled her fingers, as if waving hello, and pulled her lips into a fake smile.

Heather and Jamie walked up to Maddison to get the fresh gossip. Ember's nails dug half-moons into her palm as Maddison told them Wayne's lies. Logan's tall frame blocked her view as he retrieved his World History book from his locker. She looked over his shoulder.

"Ember?" She heard Erick's voice, but it sounded far away.

She couldn't believe her eyes. Maddison looked at her and called Logan over. He turned and walked towards the blonde cheerleader. Maddison draped her hand on Logan's arm. He looked over his shoulder and gave Ember a reassuring smile. Shifting, he leaned in, giving Maddison his full attention.

The cheerleader's eyes darted back to her. Before she finished saying Ember's name, something snapped inside her. She slipped into Maddison's mind, forcing her to stop talking. Maddison's hands clutched at her throat. She gasped, like she was trying to form words, but nothing came out of her mouth.

"Help! She's choking!" Jamie yelled as her friend became blue in the face.

Logan dropped his books and immediately tried to perform the Heimlich maneuver on Maddison. But the cheerleader shook her head back and forth, eyes watering.

Someone slammed into Ember's side. The force broke her concentration, releasing Maddison from her control. She jerked her eyes around to see Erick's upset face. He had both hands on her arms, shaking her. He yelled for her to stop. She blinked rapidly, realizing what had happened. She had made Maddison to not only stop talking, but to also stop breathing. She almost killed her.

She pulled out of his hold. "Let go of me."

"Ember, you could have killed her." Hallee hissed.

"What are you talking about?" She glanced back at Maddison. Logan was consoling her. He rubbed her back. The fleeting shame she felt was overtaken by anger as Maddison turned and leaned in to thank Logan for helping her.

"That stupid bitch," she muttered.

"Ember, no!" Hallee reached out to stop her, but she pushed past.

"Get your hands off my boyfriend." The knuckles on her fists were white.

Logan's aura shifted to one of concern as Ember closed the distance between them. She clipped the connection with him and focused solely on Maddison's innocent facade.

Maddison's hands dropped to her sides. Her eyes rounded and her brows pinched in confusion as Ember latched onto her aura and entered her mind.

"It's okay, O'Neill," Logan said, raising both palms in a sign of surrender. "She was choking. I helped her. She was just saying thank you."

Ember sensed the presence of others closing in. She looked around. A crowd of onlookers was forming.

"Or what?" Maddison's high-pitched voice drew her back. "What are you going to do? You going to frame me for something? Like you did Wayne?"

"Shut up."

Maddison's lips clamped close.

Logan stepped closer. "What is she talking about?"

"It's nothing. She's lying," Ember said. "She's just jealous of us and that they voted me queen instead of her."

She reached for Logan's hand, pulling him away, then released the connection to Maddison and turned. Before she could take a step away, the sting of hairs being ripped from her scalp made gasp. Maddison had pulled her hair.

The crowd began to chant, "Fight! Fight! Fight!"

She spun on her heel. A stew of emotions erupted as she connected to Maddison's aura once more. Logan clamped his hands on her arms. Ember linked to his mind and made him let go.

"She's not worth it, O'Neill." Logan's deep voice barely registered in her mind as she stepped into the circle that had formed around them. She clenched her fist, ready to connect it to Maddison's perfectly symmetrical face.

"It was a pity vote, you freak," the cheerleader announced. "Everyone felt sorry for Bloody Ember and her poor dead dad."

Ember lunged. Before she could make contact, Logan wrapped his powerful arms around her waist and pulled her back, thrusting her up against the lockers away from Maddison.

At that moment, Mr. Greene parted the crowd. "Break it up!"

His eyes widened when he saw Ember struggling against Logan's embrace. The rest of the student body immediately dispersed. Maddison sneered and crossed her arms. Ember's eyes snagged on Hallee and Erick as they both stared in shock with mouths ajar.

"Everything all right?" Mr. Greene peered between her and Maddison.

"Calm down, O'Neill, or you're going to get yourself expelled." Logan whispered in her ear.

The severity of his words snapped her out of her anger.

Maddison flashed her pearly whites at the teacher and touched his arm. "Everything is fine, Mr. Greene." She waggled her fingers at her and bounced down the hall, flanked by the cheer squad.

The teacher tilted his head, studying her. "You good, Ms. O'Neill?"

"Yep."

"Good. Cause if there is a problem—" he said as the bell rang, cutting him off. His smile didn't reach his eyes. "Saved by the bell, I suppose. See you last hour,

Ms. O'Neill."

Ember walked back down the hall to her locker. The door was still hanging open. Erick and Hallee were nowhere to be found. Ember's eyes zeroed in on the fat file folder sitting inside on top of her books. Her shoulders slumped at the sight. Hallee must have placed it in there.

"Ember...what happened back there?" Logan leaned in. His deep voice caressed her ear.

"Nothing. It's over." She slammed the locker shut and brushed past him to first hour.

Erick and Hallee looked away as she entered the classroom. She clipped her connections to everyone, ignoring the searing stares of Heather and Jamie from across the room. She slumped down in her chair as the clap of thunder rolled outside. It didn't take special abilities to know that soon the entire school would be talking about the fight between her and Maddison.

Chapter Thirty-seven

Hallee and Erick gave Ember the cold shoulder the rest of the morning. Guilt overwhelmed her. The last people she ever wanted to upset were her best friends. The bell rang for lunch and she knew what she had to do and rushed to the library. Even if she couldn't stay, she wanted to apologize for the last few days. They were only trying to help, and she knew that.

She slipped her head inside the door. No one was there yet. She glanced at the halls to see if she could spy them coming, but they were nowhere to be seen. She walked over to the chessboard. Another wave of guilt washed over her. They hadn't played in weeks. She moved her pawn, setting up an easy advance for Erick. She turned, feeling people enter the library. Her best friends walked in holding hands and kissing. Her fingers accidentally knocked over a chess piece, clattering to the ground and startling the kissing couple.

"Ember!" Erick's voice cracked. She noted their auras shifting from magenta to an embarrassed carnation pink.

Hallee's face flushed crimson. "What are you doing here?"

"Are you two official now?" Anger laced through her. She knew she had no right to be angry, but it hurt to be left in the dark.

"Yeah, actually." Erick pushed his glasses up his nose and stood straighter. "Hallee is my girlfriend."

"Thanks for the update." Ember picked up the chess piece and placed it down hard on the board.

"I was going to tell you—" Hallee started, but Ember cut her off.

"Whatever, enjoy your lunch." She brushed past them to the door.

"Warrior princess, wait." Erick pleaded.

"You really should stop calling me that, Erick. It's a stupid nickname." Ember shot the words at Erick like darts as she turned her back on them and walked out of the library.

She felt like she was hyperventilating. Lightning flashed, and the sky rumbled. Ember leaned against the lockers, inhaling and exhaling shaky breaths. Tears stung her eyes. Erick's stunned face as she walked by haunted her. A group of students spilled into the hallway from the exit doors, laughing and dripping from the rain. She clipped her connection to them and threw her shoulders back, wiping the tears away with the back of her hand.

She ran to the cafeteria, desperate to get away from Hallee and Erick. The cold, wet drops stung as they pelted against her skin. She reached the awning faster than humanly possible. She smacked into the glass doors just as Logan was exiting.

"Hey, are you okay?" His eyes were as wide as saucers. "I swear I didn't see you there." His fingertips sent tingles down her arm.

"Of course, I'm fine." She brushed his hand away.

"Are you sure everything is okay, O'Neill? I was hoping we could talk about this morning." His chocolate brown eyes melted in concern.

She pressed against his mind. "I'm fine, Lauder." His pupils narrowed.

"Okay." He said robotically. She clipped the connection.

She looked over his shoulder at the volleyball team seated in the cafeteria. "I really need to hang with my teammates, Logan. Our first game is tomorrow."

His brows scrunched together. "Okay, cool…see you later?"

"Yeah. Sure." He dipped his head and left a soft kiss on her temple. Another spark of frustration seared through her as he once again avoided kissing her on the lips. It was bad enough that she had to witness her best friends making out behind her back. But no matter how badly she wanted him to, she refused to beg Logan Lauder for a second kiss.

She hissed her goodbye and brushed past him, eager to have a no-drama lunch with her team.

****

The attention of the entire student body shifted to her as she walked into the cafeteria. She unconsciously shut off the connections and ignored their stares. She waved and forced a smile at her teammates as she walked to get in line for food. Ember was late, and the line was short. She snagged a pre-made peanut butter and jelly sandwich and a water bottle and paid.

Nina and Missy flagged her down and scooted over, making room for her.

"What's up?" Ember's brows rose at the girls' giggles.

Missy punched her arm. "You tell us, slugger."

"We didn't actually fight." She looked down at her

sandwich, reliving the altercation with Maddison in her mind.

Nina's brown forehead wrinkled in concern. "That's not what Maddison is telling everyone."

Ember bit into the stale bread. "You shouldn't believe everything you hear, especially from her."

"She said you framed Wayne and flipped out when you caught her talking to Logan." Missy's brows danced as she relayed the gossip.

It didn't matter what she said or did. The cheerleader wouldn't stop spreading rumors about her. She gritted out, "Maddison is a lying, jealous bitch."

Missy's eyes lit up. "Oh, snap!"

"You should be careful, Ember." Nina jerked her thumb toward the other side of the room. "She might hear you."

Ember looked over to where she was gesturing. With her connections cut, she hadn't realized that Maddison sat two tables over with the cheer squad. Their eyes met. Maddison sneered, waved at her, and, then leaned in, whispering to Brittany.

Ember stood. She had had enough of Maddison Miller.

"What are you doing?" Nina hissed, trying to pull her down.

"Putting Maddison in her place, once and for all."

Missy rubbed her hands together. "Oh, this is gonna be good."

"Don't encourage her," Nina hissed.

"Maddison!" she yelled across the tables.

The perfect, petite-blonde's head bounced up, locking eyes with her. Her lips twisted in a fake smile as she lifted her middle finger to Ember. A gesture which everyone nearby found hilarious.

"Maddison Miller! I'm talking to you!" she yelled even louder. The buzz of conversation in the cafeteria dimmed as all eyes focused on her.

"What do you want, Em-ber O'-Neill?" Maddison emphasized each syllable.

She latched onto Maddison's mind, shutting down all of her thoughts. The cheerleader sat there and blinked as Ember walked over between tables to stand in front of her. She leaned across the cheer table and spoke low so that only those close by could hear. "Stay away from my boyfriend and keep my name out of your mouth."

Maddison's eyes sparked, but she didn't respond. Ember released her control and stepped back. Maddison blinked and stood up, crossing her arms. "I can't help it if Logan is finally taking his pity goggles off and seeing you for what you really are."

Her head cocked, "Oh, really? What is it I really am, Maddison?"

"You're just one of those attention seeking types…always getting the spotlight put on you."

"Me? You've got to be kidding."

Her eyes danced. "Shall I start from the beginning?" She ticked off a finger. "Wah-wah, I've got a medical condition." She ticked off another finger. "Wah-wah, no one will sit with me at lunch. Wah-wah, no one will play with me. Wah-wah, I don't have any friends."

Ember's fists clenched.

"Wah-wah, my mother is a drunken whore."

That was it. Ember lost all control. She reached over and took Brittany's chocolate milk, slinging it across the table, spraying chocolate milk all over Wilson County High's most popular student.

Maddison gasped as chocolate milk dripped down her face and onto her chest. "You bitch!" she screeched, then reached over and grabbed a burger off a tray and slung it at Ember.

But Ember's unnaturally fast reflexes caught the burger in midair. Maddison's eyes widened in disbelief. She latched onto her nemesis' mind one more time. "Remember what I said."

She clipped the connection. Maddison huffed and ran to the bathrooms. Ember suffered the angry glares of the cheer squad. Heather and Jamie got up and quickly ran to the bathrooms after their friend.

She pivoted to return to her lunch table only to face her coach and teacher, Mr. Greene, dripping wet from the rain and glaring at her from the gym doors. She cut the connection as he sauntered to her table, followed by Nina, who averted her eyes as she neared.

His steel grip wrapped around Ember's arm. "You can thank your teammate for coming to get me."

Nina mouthed "sorry" and slipped into her seat beside Missy.

Mr. Greene's hard face made everything inside Ember shrivel. "Outside. Now." He led her to the awning outside the gym doors. The rain fell in waterfall curtains off the edge. "What is going on, O'Neill?"

"Nothing."

He put his hands on his hips. "It's definitely not nothing."

She looked away, watching the rain as it slid along the blacktop, forming a small stream.

"Look, I'll do what I can to smooth things over

with Maddison. Tomorrow is a big day, and I can't afford to lose one of my best players over some tiff."

She nodded. He put his arm around her shoulders. "I know things are tough without your dad around." He squeezed. "You can trust me, Ms. O'Neill. If you ever need to talk, I'm available."

Ember forced a smile and nodded.

"Okay, good then." He released his grasp. "Go on and head back to the school. Lunch is almost over." He jerked his thumb to the doors. "I'll go in and clean up your mess." His lips slipped into a grin.

"Thanks, Coach."

Ember didn't bother to run to escape the downpour. She let the heavy rain wash over her, soaking her to the bone.

Chapter Thirty-eight

An uncomfortable silence settled between Ember and Logan as he drove her home after practice. Mr. Greene had excused Maddison for the rest of the day so she could go home and clean up and recuperate from her trauma. She smirked at her own reflection in the car window, remembering Maddison's face as the chocolate milk dripped down her perfect cheekbones.

It had stopped raining, revealing the devastation from the storm. Several limbs hung broken in the treetops, while the more vulnerable ones lay on the ground. Most of the leaves were now stripped bare, leaving branches exposed. I can relate, she mused. She felt raw and exposed after the day's drama.

Logan let out a sigh as he turned onto the gravel county road leading to Ember's house. She squeezed the plastic bag in her lap. Her coaches handed out uniforms and jackets at the end of practice. The muscles in her shoulders tightened. Receiving the team jacket put her one more day closer to her premonition dream becoming a reality. The car jostled as it hit a washed-out dip in the road. His eyes slid to Ember. "Sorry."

She adjusted the pile on her lap. She had sandwiched Hallee's file folder of theories between her notebook and math book. "You don't have to say you're sorry. I should apologize."

"I was talking about the pothole in the road."

"Oh." Ember watched as her house came into view. Logan turned up the drive. She winced, missing Lola's howl every time she came home now.

He shifted the car to park. "So, are you going to talk to me, O'Neill, or are we going to continue to play this game of pretend?"

She cocked her head. "Game of pretend? What are you talking about?"

He blew out a loud breath and released a tight, half-crazed laugh as his fingers drummed the steering wheel. "Okay, whatever…keep your secrets."

"Secrets? You want to talk secrets?" Her voice drifted an octave higher.

He jerked his head around to meet hers. The muscle in his jaw ticked rapidly. "What are you talking about, O'Neill?"

She reached for the door handle. "You know what, never mind."

He grabbed her arm, pulling her back in. "Ember, hold up."

"Why don't you ever want to kiss me?" Heat flushed her cheeks as the words spilled out.

He let out a sharp laugh. "Is that what this is all about?"

She jerked her arm out of his grasp.

"Ember, listen, I like you. I really do."

Her chin tilted as she studied his face. "But…"

"You wouldn't understand."

Ember was glad she had cut their connection before she got in his car. She didn't want to know what he was thinking or feeling. Her eyes stung. "You just want to be friends," she stated flatly.

"No. I mean...I shouldn't have kissed you. I moved too fast."

"Too fast?" she nearly shouted in disbelief.

"I'm old school?"

"Look, I'm not an idiot, Logan. I see how other guys are with their girlfriends."

Her mind drifted to how Derek made her feel. She shook her head. Even Hallee and Erick had more passion between them than they did. There was something that drew them together, a sort of electric magnetism, but that was it. That was all it ever was. Ember swallowed hard.

"Logan, I think maybe we should break up."

A soft whistle escaped his lips. "Wow. That is not how I saw this conversation going." His eyes locked with hers. "Okay."

His casual reaction to what she proposed flew all over her. "That's it? That's all you have to say about it. Did you ever really like me? Or was it just cool to date the Dead Girl? Was I just some curiosity or challenge for you?"

He sat there dumbfounded, mouth agape.

"You know what? Goodbye, Lauder." She exited the car.

"Ember!" She looked back. He stood outside the car. "I'm sorry."

As she marched up the drive, Bear bounded to her. She dropped her things and crouched, hugging the giant to her chest. "At least I know you really like me."

Tears leaked from her eyes as Logan drove away. *Maybe Maddison was right.* In her attempt to fit in, Ember had morphed from school pariah to the pity case.

Chapter Thirty-nine

Ember sat on her bed, trying to focus on her math homework. Bear snored loudly next to her. Birdie Mae, on the sofa, was already two drinks in while watching her music videos. Lightning struck, flashing light through the windows; thunder rumbled in its wake.

She glanced up at the list she'd made just before school started and chewed at her bottom lip. Things had been going so well. She was no longer the freak at school. She had friends...even a best friend in Hallee. She had a boyfriend. She was popular. She was on the volleyball team and had joined a club. Her grades were perfect. She'd even been voted Queen of the Sadie Hawkins dance. She got up off the bed and pulled the list down, ripping it in two and tossing it in the trash.

"None of that matters anymore, Bear." His ears twitched. "I'd rather people liked me for who I am rather than pity me because I am the Dead Girl or like me because I'm dating the new guy." She scratched behind his ear. "Did you know the only people, Bear, who truly liked me before any of this happened were Erick and Hallee?" Her eyes shifted to Hallee's folder. "I shouldn't have ignored them or snapped at them."

Her fingers trailed over the worn folder. Hallee had written 'Top Secret Mission' in purple block lettering surrounded by flowers and heart doodles. Ember swallowed back the guilt and walked down the hall to the phone. She dialed Hallee's number. After a few rings, Hallee's dad answered.

"Hi, this is Ember...can I talk to Hallee?" She nervously twirled the coiled phone line between her fingers.

"Hi, Ember...sorry, Hallee is at a sleepover," he said.

"Oh, okay." Ember cringed. "Sorry."

"I'll tell her you called."

"Thanks." She slowly set the phone back in the cradle. Her eyes watered. Even Hallee had moved on.

Back in her room, she shoved the folder under her bed. She glanced out the window and winced as more lightning struck. She snuggled in next to Bear and reached up, clicking off her light and sighing. As bad as the day had been, she needed to move on, too. She needed to dream and figure out her night terror, her premonition dream. Her eyes shifted to the red satin team jacket now resting on her desk chair. Time was running out.

****

Ember's nostrils flared as she inhaled the damp air. It had recently rained. Someone called her name in the distance. Heart pounding, sweat beaded on her forehead. The air was cool yet muggy. She shrugged off her Wilson County High Volleyball jacket and raced forward.

Branches slapped her arms as she sped inhumanly fast through the woods. A familiar voice yelled her name behind her. She focused her senses on the energies in front of her. The cabin wasn't far. She knew she could make it this time.

"Daughter of Eden." A deep, rich voice exploded all around her. The woods evaporated and transformed into a blank canvas. She froze as the Archangel Michael materialized in front of her. His aura glowed a blinding, golden shade. Her vision adjusted as she took in the perfect being. A warm feeling of love washed over her.

"Michael," she said.

"Ember." The archangel dipped his chin. "It is good to see you again."

"What are you doing here? I mean, it is good to see you, too, but why are you here?"

The archangel reached out and rested his firm hand on her shoulder, sending tingles down her arm.

"Time is running out." His face hardened. "You must choose, Ember."

Her brows pinched together. "Choose what exactly?"

"Have you not spoken to your Earth fathers?" His head tilted to the side.

"My father is dead." She bit her lip.

The archangel's forehead lined with concern as he pulled his hand back. She felt the familiar tingle of connection as he linked his mind with hers.

"I see." His brows pinched. "I am sorry, Ember. I have been busy. My soldiers have been under attack. The battle has once again intensified." Her secret garden materialized. "Come. Sit."

"How did you…?" Her eyes rounded. "Oh. Yeah, you read my mind."

"It seems to be a place of comfort for you," he said.

Ember sat on Adam's swing. The archangel steepled his hands under his chin and briefly closed his eyes. When he reopened them, she jerked back. His eyes glowed like an animal's irises in the dark. Slowly, they dimmed back to normal.

"Do not be afraid, Daughter of Eden." He raised his hands, palms out. Another wave of love washed over her.

"I'm not afraid." Her chin tilted up.

"Good." He relaxed his hands at his side. "I have just received a new mission." His fingers twitched. "And it involves you."

"Okay." Ember leaned forward. "What do you need me to do?"

His head cocked to the side. His back straightened. "Ember, I don't have time to explain everything to you, now. And I am sorry for that." His eyes softened as his golden sword materialized in his hand. His lips pressed together in a tight line. "There are those who would wish you harm, Daughter of Eden. I can protect you. I can teach you to become a great warrior in my army. But you must swear your allegiance to me and our God."

She slowly nodded as his angelic aura glowed brighter.

"How do I do that?"

"You must take the oath," he said.

Ember swallowed. "And after I take the oath, what happens then?"

"We will be linked. I will train you. You will go on missions for the Almighty and serve righteously under my command in His army."

"And if I don't take the oath?"

His pupils narrowed, and his face looked pained. "Then, I cannot help you. You have freewill, Daughter of Eden." His fingers tightened around the sword.

"Your 'friend' is trying to reach you." He gritted out the word, friend.

"Adam?"

The archangel nodded as a muscle ticked rapidly in his jaw. "I must go."

"Wait. Michael, wait." She jumped up from the swing.

The archangel looked torn as he searched her face. His chin dipped as his eyes filled with sorrow. "I know what you wish to ask."

"And?" Ember swallowed. "Who are the Covenant Knights?"

"Thousands of years ago, I petitioned the Almighty to spare the Nephilim who swore allegiance to Him and who vowed to serve in His army. The Covenant Knights are the descendants of those soldiers, the descendants of Noah. They fight for redemption. They fight for humanity, Daughter of Eden."

"And the Order of Saint Michael? Are they the bad guys?" Ember's brows pinched together.

"Bad guys? No. Misguided? Yes. Negative influences have infiltrated that sect." The archangel's sword glowed brighter. "Your friend is impatient."

"So, who are the bad guys then?" she asked.

The angel's face hardened. "Lucifer and his army."

"You mean, like Satan? He's actually real?"

"He's very real, Daughter of Eden, and so is his Earthly army, the Brotherhood of the Snake."

Ember crossed her arms. An icy chill ran down her spine. "Wait. So, am I a Nephilim? Is that why I can do things other people can't? Was my dad one? Is he one of the good guys?"

A soft rumble escaped his Adonis-like chest. "I

don't have time to answer all your questions, Ember. But, short answer, you are more than Nephilim. You are...unique. And your Earth fathers are indeed Nephilim."

Ember's eyes widened. "You said that again, fathers...as in plural."

"I must go, Daughter of Eden." His eyes softened. "*Eligere*." The archangel dissipated from the garden.

Her mind swirled with the new information. She slumped down onto the swing.

Suddenly, an angry, beautiful face formed in Michael's wake. Dressed in dark denim and a black tee, Adam's raven black hair shined above his brooding emerald green eyes. He crossed his arms and glared at Ember.

"What?" she asked, all innocence.

"What?" His voice rose an octave too high. "You are going to sit there and act like you didn't block me all night?"

"I did?" Ember's brows rose.

"I could sense you were upset all day, angel. I got here as fast as I could." The flecks of gold in his emerald eyes sparked. He walked forward and tilted Ember's chin up to face him. Electricity raced to her core. "Tell me what happened today, angel."

Ember shifted her gaze to the ground. "I almost choked out Maddison Miller in the hall this morning, and then later, at lunch, I threw chocolate milk all over her. And now my best friends aren't talking to me. And..." She looked up. "I broke up with Logan."

A chuckle erupted from his chest. "Is that all?" Eyes dancing, he brushed a stray hair from her forehead.

"It's not funny. I tell you I almost killed a girl, and you laugh?" She slapped his hand away.

He cocked his head as a crooked grin snaked across his face. "Tsk…tsk…don't get mad, angel. I'm the good guy, remember?"

She studied his face. "Are you, Adam? Are you the good guy?"

His smile spread, flashing his perfect white teeth. "Do I look like a bad guy to you?"

Her eyes fluttered closed as she inhaled his intoxicating scent of whiskey and chocolate. But then they flew open at the thought. She had no reason to trust him, yet…

"No, I don't think you are a bad guy, Adam." She chose her words carefully. "But I don't think you have been completely honest with me, either."

His hand drifted to his chest. "Ouch, angel, you wound me. I have done nothing but help you—teach you." He leaned over, his lips brushing her cheek as he whispered in her ear. "I promise you, angel, there is no one else on this Earth who wants to share the truth and protect you more than me."

A tingle danced down her neck and to her core from the warmth of his breath.

He stepped away and clutched his hands behind his back, pacing around the garden.

His eyes twinkled. "Tell me, angel, why did you let the Logan boy go?"

"That's none of your business." She pushed off with her feet and swung.

"Ah, I see." He chuckled as he paced. "Not enough kissing for you?"

"What? Stop. Get out of my head, Adam." Ember

planted her feet, stopping the swing.

"Stop me." He locked eyes with her. "Or, can't you?" His head cocked.

In less than a blink of an eye, he was in front of her. He pulled her off the swing, wrapping his powerful arm around her waist. His other hand gripped the back of her neck, eyes piercing hers. Both of their hearts pounded against each other's chests like twin drums. Her breaths came out ragged as his eyes searched hers. Energy buzzed between them where his hard body pressed, melting Ember to the core. She watched his eyes drift as she bit her bottom lip. His fingers tightened on her hip. His lips inched up.

"You are keeping secrets, angel."

Her head shifted slightly from side to side. "No, I'm not."

His pupils narrowed. Ember watched as his tongue darted over his bottom lip. Her head drifted forward to meet his. The heat from his breath sent tingles down to her neck. She wanted to feel his lips on hers. A soft growl escaped his hard chest. Her eyes rounded as he pulled away, leaving her cold and wanting.

Her fists clenched as he laughed at her. "Why did you do that?"

"Why? Why do I test you? Tempt you?" His smile didn't quite reach his eyes. "To prove a point."

Her hand landed on her hip. "And that is?"

He ticked off his fingers. "One, because you lied to me. You should trust me by now, angel. Two, because you like it. You like my touch. You like me. And I enjoy making you happy. And, three, I like it, too, angel." Her heart raced at his omission.

"I didn't lie," she insisted.

319

"No? Keep your secrets. I—" He stopped and closed his eyes. A pained expression flashed across his face.

"Adam, are you okay?" Ember rushed forward and wrapped her hands around his arms. His eyes flew open as a smirk lined his lips.

"Don't worry about me, angel. I'm okay." His eyes softened as his hands cupped her face. A wave of desire flashed through her entire being.

"I have to go, though." He leaned down, his lips pressing a feather-light kiss on her forehead, sending tingles down to her core as he dissipated from her dream.

****

Ember shot up in her bed, gasping for air. The storm clouds were gone, and the sun was creating a warm rosy glow on the horizon. Her eyes darted to Bear, where he snored softly. She looked at the clock. It was barely dawn. She knew she should try to go back to sleep, but her mind was a jumble of thoughts. Her hand drifted to the chain around her neck. Michael had said Earth "fathers." Plural. *Was it a mistake?* Her fingers trembled against the metal.

The puzzle pieces of her dream shifted into focus. She was Nephilim. No, she was more. Not angel, but not human. *What am I?* And her father was a Nephilim…or, rather, her fathers were Nephilim. Ember looked at her father's picture on her nightstand. Could she really have two dads? Is that the man her dad wanted her to find?

Careful not to wake the sleeping giant, she leaned over and reached under the bed. Her hands snagged the folder. She hoped Hallee and Erick's research had uncovered more information about the mystery man.

She flipped open the folder, rubbed the sleep out of her eyes, and scanned the copied pages. Ember jerked moments later when the phone rang in the kitchen. Bear's head lifted to attention as he watched her get up. She answered the phone by the third ring.

"Hello?"

"Yes, is this Birdie Mae O'Neill?" A female voice spoke across the static laced line.

"No, this is her daughter," she answered.

"Oh, is this Ember O'Neill?"

"Yes? Can I help you?"

"My name is irrelevant but know I am the patient care coordinator with ELL Pharmaceuticals based in Chicago."

An unnatural shiver ran down Ember's spine as the nameless woman continued. "We received your name from our associate, Dr. Kayce, in Murray. Based off the information he provided, you would qualify for one of our case studies. Would you mind answering a few questions?"

Ember's heart pounded in her chest. Images from her vision flooded her mind like a movie reel—Chicago, the woman giving birth, and the baby being taken away.

"Ms. O'Neill? Excuse me? Are you still there?"

She slammed the phone down onto the cradle.

Birdie Mae sat up. "Who the hell was that?"

"No one. Go back to sleep, Birdie Mae."

Chapter Forty

She glanced at the clock in the kitchen. She had two hours to find a ride to the game. Ember swallowed her pride and called Erick.

The call didn't last long. Mrs. Grossman informed her that Erick had left to go meet Hallee to work on club stuff at school. She sighed. She was down to just a couple of options and the last option…she did not want to do…call Logan.

Never in a million years would the *old* Ember do this, she thought. She wrapped her hand around her dad's chain and prayed while she dialed her backup plan. The phone rang.

"Hello," the cheery voice of Mrs. Oliver answered.

"Hey, Mrs. Oliver, this is Ember O'Neill calling. Is Derek home this weekend?"

"Oh, hi, Ember!" Her voice dipped low. "Oh, my sweet girl, how are you doing?"

She winced at the pity oozing from Mrs. Oliver's tone. "I'm okay. Thank you for asking." She swallowed. "Is Derek home? I was wondering if he could drive me to the game this afternoon. Birdie Mae has to work."

"Oh, yes, darlin', of course. He's here." She paused. "One sec, dear." She heard Mrs. Oliver cup the phone and yell for Derek. "Sorry, dear. He's outside.

I'm sure he won't mind. What time do you need him to pick you up?"

"In an hour?"

"Okay. I'll have him drive over and get you."

"Thank you, Mrs. Oliver."

"Yes, dear, and again, I'm so sorry about the pool party and…your father. If I could go back in time, I'd…well, I wouldn't let Wayne onto the property. And please tell your mother that if she needs anything at all to just call."

"I will. Thank you."

Ember slowly set the phone back on the hook and leaned back against the kitchen wall. At least she didn't have to call Logan. But Derek…she bit her lip. The last time she saw him was at the dance, and he was Maddison's date. Her stomach turned.

She went back to her room and eyed the folder still spread out on her bed. She closed it up and vowed that after the game, she would go through it thoroughly. It was time to stop ignoring the past and find out who she truly was. She planned to apologize to Erick and Hallee if they still showed up for her game. And even if it killed her, she would sincerely try to make things right with Maddison.

Her dad wouldn't want her to be the person she had become, vindictive and lashing out. And she didn't want that either. No matter what her investigation uncovered, Billy Joe would always be her father, and she would honor his memory by being the best version of herself she could be.

She pulled on her uniform and cringed at her reflection in the mirror. She was lucky, number thirteen. The white ironed-on block numbers stood in contrast with the red jersey trimmed in black. She threw on the red satin Wilson County High volleyball jacket on top. A shiver raced down her back as she looked at herself. Ember blew out a long breath and brushed her hair into a high ponytail. She bent down and scratched Bear behind the ears.

"Guard the house for me, Bear." He panted, letting his tongue hang crookedly to the side.

Her sensitive hearing alerted her to Derek's truck approaching the house. The truck came to a stop in the drive.

Her heart fluttered at the thought of seeing him again. She took a deep breath, stepped outside, and walked to the driveway. Derek stepped out of the truck. His indigo eyes sparked as they floated over her. Wrapped in a magenta aura, his dimples flashed as he bent over at the waist, bowing. "Your chauffeur has arrived."

He rose and brushed his hand through his sun-kissed hair. Ember inhaled his delicious scent, causing butterflies to take flight in her stomach. "Hey," she said as he rushed over to the passenger door to open it for her. The metal hinge creaked on the ancient red truck. "Thanks."

He slid onto the driver's seat. His hand paused over the keys as he looked at Ember. His denim eyes turned dark. "About the dance…Maddison just—"

She unconsciously clipped the connection and cut him off. She didn't want to hear his excuses or feel what he felt for the cheerleader. He was a grown man and could see who he wanted. "I don't want to talk about Maddison."

"Okay, then." He turned the ignition and pulled out

of the drive. Minutes ticked by as they drove in silence.

"Want some music?" A single dimple emerged as he cocked his head toward Ember.

She smiled and nodded. "Sure."

"You like country? Pop?"

"Whatever is fine with me." She kept her focus on the blurring landscape.

Derek turned the knob on the radio dial, landing on the Q. It was a station Ember was more than familiar with. Her dad always had his radio tuned in to the country station. Her lips tugged into a small smile, remembering their last summer together camping in the bottoms.

"Have you heard this one?" His eyes sparked as he cranked up the volume and sang along.

"Billy Joe liked this one too." She spoke softly.

"Oh, sorry." He reached over to turn the volume down.

She stopped him. "No, don't." His eyes darted to hers. "Please, it's okay. I'm okay. Please, sing.

He slipped his hand into hers. A gesture of friendship or something more, Ember wasn't sure. She recalled sliding into his mind at the dance. Derek certainly was interested in her then. She watched him from the corner of her eye. Maybe he still was?

His dimples popped as he belted out the lyrics, dropping his voice down on the low notes making her laugh. He squeezed her hand. She looked away and out the window as a tiny tear escaped. She swallowed, fighting back the sob she felt rising at the back of her throat. She missed her dad.

Something about Derek Oliver reminded her of him. Maybe it was how he made her feel safe and accepted. Whatever it was and for however long it lasted, she would cherish it.

Chapter Forty-one

Derek pulled the truck into the paved parking lot in front of the high school. Several cars were already there. Maddison's pristine red off-roader sat in sharp contrast to Wayne Wilson's green, rusty old sedan with its busted taillight. A sense of unease fell upon Ember as she scanned the parking lot for their drivers. The two people that she was sure hated her the most in the world were somewhere on campus.

She noted Erick's old white car parked in the front row. Maybe he and Hallee would attend her game after all. The brakes on Derek's older truck squeaked to a stop. She spied the cheer squad exiting through the gym doors. Heather, Jamie, and Brittany flanked Maddison. Her breathing quickened. As much as she wanted to avoid Maddison for the rest of her life, she knew she needed to clear the air and apologize for both of their sakes.

Derek noticed what she was looking at. He rubbed the back of his neck. "Hey…she and I are just friends. That's it."

"It's not that." She swallowed. "I sort of lost it yesterday and poured chocolate milk all over her."

His lips twitched. "Knowing Maddison, she probably deserved it."

"Yeah, well, maybe. But I shouldn't have done it." She grabbed her things. "Thanks for the ride."

"Hey, I'm staying and watching the game, if that's cool? I can take you home after?" His tan cheeks flushed.

"Okay, thanks. That would be nice." She stepped out of the truck and straightened her back as the clique of girls approached the parking lot. She felt like a weight was upon her chest as they neared. Maddison's nose wrinkled as if she smelled something bad when she saw her climbing out of Derek's truck. The girls' light chatter stopped abruptly as Ember put one foot before the other and walked towards Maddison.

"What are you doing here, Derek?" Brittany asked her brother.

Maddison planted her feet. Her eyes darted between Derek and Ember. "So, what's up, Pity Queen? I can't go near your boyfriend, but you can sleep with mine?" Her hands shifted to her hips. "Wayne was right. You are a whore," she spat. The squad stood behind her, mouths agape.

Her hand clinched. "It's not how it looks."

Derek cleared his throat. "Maddie, just stop. You and I are not together, and you know it. Ember needed a ride to her game."

"And besides, I'm not with Logan anymore, either." Heads turned at Ember's announcement. "We broke up yesterday."

"Glad he finally came to his senses," Maddison said, lifting her chin.

"Look, Maddison, I'm sorry about yesterday. I shouldn't have done that to you. Can you forgive me?" she asked, but Maddison just stood there and crossed her arms, staring at her.

"Maddie, have a heart…Ember's been through a

lot," Derek added.

Seconds ticked by and finally Maddison dropped her arms, saying, "Whatever." Her smile not quite reaching her eyes as she and her clique brushed past her.

"Oh, Derek?" Maddison called from her vehicle. He turned, running his hand through his hair.

"Yeah?" he asked.

"You coming to the bottoms tonight?"

He shrugged. "I don't know. Maybe?"

"I'll save a beer for you." A toothy grin snaked across her perfect face as her gaze flicked to Ember, narrowing.

Ember rolled her eyes and walked to the gym, ignoring Maddison's pointed remark. She could hold her head up knowing that she at least tried to make amends. And, after the game, she planned on fixing things with Erick and Hallee, too.

****

Between sets, Ember kept checking the bleachers. Despite the JV team playing well, her heart sank once she realized her friends weren't coming. Derek's blue eyes glittered with pride as he cheered for her and the team. Coach Greene yelled at her to step up her game when the score juggled back and forth. Tension from her teammates added to her stress, but she refused to use her abilities to win. She clipped all her connections and just focused on the game. Missy and Nina both, seemed to be frustrated with her, but they kept quiet and hustled, making saves when she faltered. Eventually, the JV girls won, and her shoulders slumped in relief.

After the game, Coach Greene pulled her aside.

"Look, Ms. O'Neill, I get it. You had a shit day yesterday. But if you can't leave it off the court, I will pull you out of the line-up for varsity."

Ember winced. She really didn't want to use her abilities. She wanted to play fair. Coach Greene put his hand on her shoulder and squeezed. Her gaze snagged on the gold chain around his neck. A medallion about the size of a quarter glinted under the gym fluorescent lights. She sucked in a breath. Etched on the surface outlined an angel holding a sword, reminding her of the Archangel Michael.

Mr. Greene's jaw ticked, waiting for her decision.

"Hey, O'Neill, you good?" Ashleigh Gardner yelled from the court, warming up with varsity.

Mr. Greene's grip tightened. "Ember?"

She nodded to Ashleigh. "Yeah, I'm good, Coach."

"All right, go get 'em." Coach Greene nodded to Coach C as she returned to the court.

Her brows pinched together as she concentrated on volleying the ball amongst her varsity teammates for warmups. If her dad was here, what would he say? Would he tell her to hide her abilities? To hide who she was? She grunted as she missed the volley, diving for the ball. Her kneepads saved her from a nasty floor burn. No, he would tell her to own who she was. Don't be afraid. *Be brave. Virtus vincit.* Her thoughts shifted to Adam. He would laugh at her for being so conflicted.

Ember took a deep breath as the ref blew the whistle to start the varsity game. She exchanged high fives with her teammates and slid into her position at the net. Opening herself up to her teammates, she could almost taste the adrenaline pouring off them. Everyone's nerves were on edge. Rapid pulses. Sweat beaded. The pressure for varsity to win was much higher.

Ember decided in that moment to use her abilities to help her team, but she wouldn't do anything to harm the opposition. Her dad would be proud of her for embracing who she was and not hurting others.

She shifted into the ready position as Ashleigh served the ball over the net. Ace. The Hickory High Varsity girls looked stunned from the power of Ashleigh's serve. Their lips pressed in straight lines and their faces hardened as Ashleigh set up to serve again.

Ashleigh went on a rally—serving six unanswered points before they overturned the ball. Then it was Hickory's turn to serve. Ember swallowed back the overwhelming tension rolling off her teammates. The tall blonde across the net from her sneered. She shook her fingers out and turned her attention to the server. The pop of palm on the leather ball seemed to echo throughout the gym as the girl jumped and served, sending the ball straight to Ember. Without hesitation, she jumped up, blocking the ball, sending it directly into the girl's face on the other side.

The girl screamed out as the ball smacked her nose, sending blood spraying down her orange and black jersey. Ember stood frozen in shock as the ref blew the whistle. The stands filled with parents and fans fell into silence. The iron tang of blood filled the space between her and the injured player.

The Hickory High coaches rushed over, administering first aid. She jerked, startled, as Ashleigh put her hand on her shoulder. "Hey. It was an accident. Take a knee while they get her off the court."

The hairs on her arms stood on end when the blood

scent merged with a familiar male odor, wafting across the court. Nostrils flaring, she tracked the scent to a boy making his way down off the bleachers. It was Chad, from the bonfire. She would never forget his acrid odor. He was the one who forced himself on Katie, nearly raping her. She instinctively latched onto his aura. His gaze locked with hers, an unblinking stare, as he walked over to the wailing girl.

If looks could kill, she would be dead. Chad consoled the girl as he helped her to the sideline. Ember clipped the connection. He was an asshole, but she felt bad for hurting the girl. Whatever connection the player had to him; she truly hadn't intentionally tried to hurt the girl. She looked down at her hands, palms red and blotchy, still stinging from blocking the ball.

The ref cleaned the blood off the floor and the game resumed shortly thereafter. Ember shook off the incident and played at half her strength to be safe. She didn't want to hurt anyone else. The strategy worked. They continued to dominate and won the first set.

Paramedics eventually arrived. Chad escorted the girl to the ambulance. He turned and shot daggers at Ember before he exited the gym doors. A chill ran down her spine as he pointed a finger gun at her and pretended to pull the trigger.

She shook off the threat and checked the stands one more time for her friends. Erick and Hallee were still no-shows. The weight on her chest increased. She took a deep breath and reconnected with her teammates as the ref blew the whistle to start the second set. She slipped into an unconscious rhythm as her team dominated against Hickory. Ember lost track of the score and was shocked when the ref called the game.

The home crowd cheered.

Coach C proudly explained it was a mercy ruling. The score was too far out of reach for Hickory to catch up in the time that was left to play. Ember allowed herself to enjoy the soaring feelings of her teammates for just a moment, then she pulled away. She didn't bother to change in the locker room. She wiped the sweat off her brow and took a drink from the team water bottles. All she wanted to do was make things right with Erick and Hallee.

Still clapping, Derek sauntered towards her. His smile reached ear to ear, causing his dimples to flash. "Congratulations."

"Thanks." Ember blushed. She felt a familiar pull and turned. Logan stood leaning against the gym doorframe, arms crossed, studying her from afar. She glanced away.

"You haven't seen Erick or Hallee, have you?" she asked.

Derek shook his head. "Nope."

"I really need to talk to them. I sort of lashed out at them yesterday, too." She shrugged.

"Hey, it happens to the best of us."

"I saw Erick's car in the parking lot. I'm hoping he and Hallee are still here. Mind if I take a few minutes to look for them?" She looked up hopefully.

"Of course, take as long as you need. Want me to help you find them?" he asked.

"No, it's fine. I'll meet you at the truck." He nodded, leaving her to walk across the gym. She watched Derek noticeably stiffen as he passed by Logan.

"Hey, good game, O'Neill." Missy interrupted her

thoughts, beaming as she and Nina exited the locker room.

"You coming out to the bottoms tonight? We got to celebrate!" Nina did a little two-step across the gym floor.

"I don't know...maybe." She didn't feel like celebrating. She grabbed her jacket and bag.

Missy linked elbows with Nina and joined in the dance across the gym floor to the door. Logan laughed and moved out of the way of the dancing duo. He walked towards her. Her muscles tensed. She slammed the door on their instant connection as her body betrayed her. She would no longer think of him in that way.

"Ember, can we talk?" he asked.

She averted her eyes and threw her shoulders back. "Later, Logan. I need to find my friends." She walked with purpose to the door leading up to the stage.

"Ember, please." The sincerity of his tone made her pause.

He caught up to her. The familiar pull buzzed between them.

"Logan..."

He brushed his hand through his thick blond hair. "Please, hear me out."

She shifted her weight. "What is it?"

"Look, I'm sorry."

Ember winced. She didn't want his pity. Not now, not ever. She crossed her arms. "Is that it?"

He let out a long sigh. "You were right. It's complicated, but you were right to break up with me."

"Okay, thanks for clearing that up." Ember huffed spinning on her heel.

He tugged on her arm, forcing her to face him. "Wait."

"What else do you need to get off your chest, Logan?" Ember gritted out.

"There's more." He whispered as Coach Greene exited the coaches' office.

"O'Neill. Lauder." Mr. Greene's eyes darted to Logan's hand, gripping Ember's arm. "Everything all right?" he asked. Logan released her.

"Yep. I was just leaving to find Erick and Hallee. What are they working on for the club?"

The teacher's brows pressed together in confusion. "I haven't seen either of them today."

"But Erick's car is out front," she said.

Mr. Greene shrugged. "You're welcome to go look, but I haven't seen him or Ms. Wilson."

He brushed by her. "Good game, Ms. O'Neill." He squeezed her shoulder.

"Thanks, Coach."

"I hear there is going to be a party tonight down in the bottoms." He winked, raising his palms in innocence. "I won't tell the parentals, but you of all people, Ms. O'Neill, deserve to go out and let off some steam. Go have fun. I insist. Coach's orders."

"Maybe." Ember shrugged.

"Mr. Lauder, I'm counting on you to make sure our star player has fun tonight." He eyed Logan.

"Yes, sir." He winked and saluted as Mr. Greene left them and jogged up the stairs.

She rolled her eyes at him. "I need to go." She changed course and walked to the exit.

"Ember, wait, there is more I need to tell you." Logan pleaded, matching her stride. "Can I take you to

335

the bonfire tonight?"

She didn't stop and exited the high school.

"Ember, please."

She saw Derek leaning against his truck, waiting for her. A flock of butterflies took flight in her stomach as he smiled at her approach. "Sorry, Logan. I already have a date."

She didn't turn around to see his reaction. But she felt his penetrating stare on her backside as she walked over to Derek's truck. She allowed herself to link up with Derek's warm aura. There was no doubt he cared for her. No mixed signals. *Why did I waste so much time on Logan Lauder?*

Briefly, her eyes darted to the cars left in the lot. Erick's car was now gone, along with Wayne and Maddison's. Derek walked over to the passenger side of the truck, helping Ember slide in. Her heart beat wildly as she watched his aura flare.

"Got plans tonight?" Ember bit her lip.

A devilish grin spread across his tan face. "I'm all yours."

Wherever Erick and Hallee were at, she hoped that their night ended in the bottoms, too.

Chapter Forty-two

Back home, the house was quiet. Birdie Mae was still at work. Only Bear greeted her as thunder rolled in the distance. She hoped the storm would pass through quickly. She was looking forward to hanging out with Derek and, hopefully, Erick and Hallee. She tossed her new sketchbook onto her bed, wanting to draw the medallion Coach Greene was wearing. Minutes passed and Ember analyzed her work. Something about it was familiar.

She reached under her bed pulling out Hallee's thick file folder. She flipped through the stack. Her eyes caught on the title of a yellowed paper, "The Order of Saint Michael," by Tom Wilkerson, Hallee's uncle. Lightning struck and thunder rolled as fresh raindrops pelted Ember's bedroom window. She settled back in her bed and read the paper. Her breath caught with the first line.

"The chivalric order was first recognized by the royal courts of France in the mid-1500s. Members wore the medallion of the Archangel Michael proudly around their necks as they became the feared assassins of the monarchy." Her fingers trembled as she read on.

"However, the Order lost its affluence by the 18th century and the French monarchy abolished the Order. But I contend that the Order is still around to this very day, operating worldwide under the guise of various

institutions and organizations. To understand the Order of Saint Michael you must first go back in time to their origins." She chewed her bottom lip as she scanned down the page.

"It is believed the Order can be linked back to the quiet secular organization dubbed the Covenant Knights. The Covenant Knights believe themselves to be descendants of the Biblical Nephilim as described in Genesis and elsewhere in theological texts. The Nephilim were described as giants, half-human and half-angel. They are the alleged byproduct of inappropriate relations between angels and man.

In the time of Noah, God sent a flood to eradicate the Nephilim. The Covenant Knights claim that not all the Nephilim were wiped out, and that God sent the Archangel Michael to finish the job. The Covenant Knights believe their ancestors made a deal with the archangel, a covenant. They would work with the archangel fighting against Lucifer and his dark army to earn redemption in God's eyes, also known as salvation, earning their way into Heaven. They became the Covenant Nephilim and later took on the name of Covenant Knights." She paused, tugging on the chain around her neck.

"It is my belief that the Order of Saint Michael splintered from this origin group and became heretical assassins for monarchies and the Catholic Church throughout the centuries." Ember's mind reeled, processing the information. She flipped ahead.

"Whatever happened to the Covenant Knights? It is my belief that the Covenant Knights discreetly operate around the world, just like the Order. It is difficult to distinguish between the two organizations

now, as they both seem to operate clandestine missions in the name of the Archangel Michael. If you look closely at the archives of the Freemasons, particularly the Grand Lodge of Scotland, you will see references to the divine, including the Archangel Michael himself.

Over the centuries, many world leaders can be linked to the Freemasons and their Masonic Lodges. It is my belief that these self-titled Nephilim continue to this day working for their redemption. The only visible distinction between the Order and the Covenant Knights may be in the symbols they wear. The Order seems to favor the medallion etched with the Archangel Michael on one side and his sword on the other, as mentioned earlier. While the Covenant Knights seem to be less overt in their symbolism, a few accounts suggest they may honor the archangel's avenging golden sword with tattoos."

Ember looked up as lightning flashed. Her gaze fell to her reflection in the mirror across the room. It was true. All of it. It had to be. Everything that the Archangel had told her was true. It was clear now that Billy Joe was a Covenant Knight. Hands trembling, she bit her lip and flipped through the file. A highlighted sentence from a newspaper clipping from the *Conservative Times* caught her eye.

"...The Brotherhood of the Snake was once considered a theoretical and fantastical conspiracy theory. But if you look closely at America's wealthy, the Von Holsteins, Rockefeller, Reynolds, and Lauder's, also known in secret as the Crimson Ring, you will see an undeniable connection to Satan himself. The Brotherhood of the Snake seeks dominion over this Earth, and they are doing it one generation at a time

with the world's wealthiest."

Van Holstein. I know that name from the picture on Dr. Kayce's wall, she thought. Her brows pinched together.

"And...Lauder. There is only one that I have ever heard of...Logan." Ember breathed the words as a haunting prickle ran down the back of her neck.

She turned the page and the hairs on her arms stood on end as she read the news clipping titled, "Chicago Fire," dated July 5, 1975. A black-and-white image of the crumbled remains of a city building filled the top center of the page with the caption beneath it highlighted:

"ELL Pharmaceuticals declare a complete loss of their premier research facilities as their 4th of July Gala turns deadly. Several fatalities are reported including the renowned husband and wife research team, Harold and Lindsey Lauder."

Her heart raced as she flipped to the next article. It was a copy of the front page of the *Chicago Times* dated January 1, 1974, titled, *"Billionaire Rings In The New Year With Boom For Chicago Industry."* Her fingers trembled as she looked at the black-and-white photo of an older gentleman who was flanked on either side by two younger men. Her eyes flashed to the photo on her nightstand. She took the picture and lined it up with the newspaper photo. It was the same young man. She read the caption:

"Billionaire Adolf Von Holstein and his sons, Asher and Dasher, break ground on premiere medical research facility in the Bridgeport area of Chicago."

She rubbed her temples. The pieces of the puzzle were fitting together. The soldier that helped her dad save lives in the war was the same man in that picture, Dasher Von Holstein. She flipped back to the previous article from the *Conservative Times*.

"Van Holstein," Ember said out loud.

The hairs on her arm stood on end. She peered more closely at the newspaper photo. If any of it was true, then that man could be with the Brotherhood of the Snake. Her pulse raced. *Why would my dad want me to find him if he was a Covenant Knight? Wouldn't they be enemies?* Ember carefully placed the papers back in the file.

No wonder Hallee and Erick wanted to talk to her about what they had found. Lauder. Van Holstein. The past and the present were connected and converging all around her. And how did Logan Lauder fit into all of it? She thought of his golden trimmed aura. He must know something, she thought. Ember glanced at her digital clock. It was almost eight-thirty. Derek would be picking her up at nine. She needed a plan.

Ember took some cleansing breaths, closed her eyes, and meditated on the one person whom she knew had answers, too—Adam.

Chapter Forty-three

Ember opened her eyes to her secret garden. Her pupils narrowed as they locked with Adam's. Sitting on the swing, his lips twisted into a smirk. Her nose twitched at his scent.

"What took you so long, angel?" He pushed off with both feet, sending the swing into the air.

"Adam, I need your help."

"Of course, what is it this time?" His emerald, green eyes sparked with curiosity.

"It's my dad." Ember spoke softly. "Adam, I want the truth." She emphasized each word.

The energy crackled between them. He inhaled deeply. His dark lashes dusted his cheeks as his eyes slid close.

"You smell so good, angel." A low growl resonated from his chest, eyes flashing a ravenous green.

She crossed her arms. "Don't change the subject, Adam. I want the truth. Now."

"Easy, angel." He lifted his hands in defense, lips twitching. "Whatever you want, Eve." He slowly let her name slide off his tongue.

"I want answers."

"What is it you wish to know?" he asked.

"Well, first, I want to know about my dad. Who sent that demon?"

"Did I not warn you about the assassins, Eve?"

"Are you saying that the Covenant Knights sent a demon to murder one of their own? That makes little sense."

"Are you saying that your father was an assassin?" He countered.

"No. Billy Joe would never murder anyone," Ember huffed.

"Well, those Michael followers have a bad habit of blowing up things that aren't theirs and killing innocents." His hands formed fists. "You want the truth, Eve? You really want to bite this apple?"

She slowly nodded.

His jaw ticked, but his hands relaxed. He shrugged. "Okay, I'll tell you everything, but don't hate me if you don't like the answers."

Ember turned and paced around the garden, deciding which question to ask first. "What is your real name?"

"Are we back to this again? Is that really what you want to know?" He stood, walking over to the roses. His lips tugged into a smile as he watched her walk in circles. He reached down and stroked the ruby red petals of a single rose.

"Adam." She stopped and hissed. "Answer the question."

"My name is Lucas." His eyes danced, watching her reaction.

"Your whole name, Lucas."

"Lucas Adam Von Holstein, at your service, angel." He bent at the waist, bowing.

Ember sucked in a breath. "Von Holstein."

"You've heard the name?" He cocked his head,

slipping into her mind. "Ah, I see. Someone has been doing some research."

"What? How did you—?"

He tapped his head with his finger. A low rumble of laughter escaped his chest.

"Get out, Lucas," she said his name with emphasis.

"You want me to leave?" He put his hand to his chest. "Ouch, angel, just when I thought we were getting somewhere."

"No. You know what I mean. Stay out of my head." Ember paced the garden once more.

Lucas smirked. "You're making me dizzy, angel."

"Good." She paused, looking at Lucas as if seeing him for the first time. "So, are you, you know, a member of the Brotherhood?"

"The Brotherhood?" His lips twitched. "Which one?"

"You know what I mean, the Brotherhood of the Snake, the Crimson Ring."

Lucas shrugged and began plucking petals from the rose. "In my world, there is pressure to rise into power. Am I a card-carrying member of The Brotherhood?" He did air quotes with his fingers. "No, not yet."

The tension in her shoulders eased, a little. "Good."

He laughed. "Good? Perhaps. But we cannot evade our destiny forever, Ember Eve O'Neill." A shiver ran down her spine as he said her entire name. He picked the rose, lifting it to drink in the sweet aroma.

"What do you mean by that?" she asked.

His eyes slid to hers, flecks of gold sparking in lakes of green. "I am yours, and you are mine. We are made for each other."

A warm tingle ran down her spine to her center at

the intensity of his words. The heat of his gaze was searing. Whether or not true, she was certain he believed it.

Ember broke the tension between them with another question. "What if my destiny is to become a Covenant Knight like my father?"

His head tilted back with laughter. "Your true father was never a Covenant Knight."

Her brow arched. "How do you know? What exactly do you mean by that?"

His face fell as he avoided her gaze. "Billy Joe O'Neill isn't your blood father."

Ember's chest tightened as his words confirmed her fears, affirming what the Archangel had implied. She swallowed. "How do you know that?" She crossed her arms. "If Billy Joe isn't my dad, then who is my father?"

"It's complicated. And I think we are out of time, angel. Someone is trying to wake you." His lips twitched.

Ember cocked her head. Bear was barking in the background. She bit her lip. Derek must have pulled up.

"Later, angel."

The garden scene dissipated, leaving Ember alone, clutching her father's chain.

Chapter Forty-four

Ember quickly checked herself in the mirror before answering the door. Wearing the purple tee that Hallee had let her borrow weeks ago and a pair of Birdie Mae's cutoff shorts, her long auburn hair was pulled up with the team scrunchie. She smiled. Despite the revelations, there was a lightness to her chest now. So much had changed in just a short amount of time. She was no longer desperate for everyone's approval. The old Ember would never have cancelled a date with Derek Oliver, but she had changed. She needed to sort through the new information.

She stepped into the hall, surprised to sense that Birdie Mae was home. Cigarette smoke and incense drifted through the house like a fog rolling off the river. Her mother sat hunched over the kitchen table, flipping tarot cards. Her aura was dark and muddled. A half empty bottle of rum sat beside an overflowing ashtray. She snapped her head up as Derek knocked on the carport door.

"What the fuck? Damned salespeople. We ain't buying what you're selling so go away!"

"Birdie Mae, stop. It's Derek," Ember raised her voice. "Just a second, Derek!"

Her mother's brows rose above her glassy eyes. "Who the fuck is Derek?" She flipped over a card and hissed audibly, not liking what she saw.

"Birdie Mae, it's Derek O'Neill, the boy who saved me at the pool party."

She looked up, her aura flared emerald with curiosity. "And why is he here?"

Ember bit her lip. "We're going on a date."

"What about that real cute rich boy? Don't tell me you fucked that up." She licked her fingers, flipping a new card over.

"It's not like that." Ember clenched her fist and slipped into Birdie Mae's mind. "Birdie Mae?"

"Yes?" She looked up expectantly.

"Was Billy Joe my real dad?"

"Yes, of course he was."

Noting her mom's confusion, she asked, "Have you ever been to Chicago?"

Birdie Mae's fingers trembled as she took a long drag on her cigarette.

"Answer the question," she compelled her mom.

"No. Maybe. I'm not sure."

Ember slid into her mind. Flashes of memories scrolled like a movie reel till she landed on one, causing her to pause. Ember recognized her dad. He and her mom were on a riverboat on the edge of a city. Then, the scene faded to black, as if the memory was erased.

Her stomach churned as she pulled back and saw the dazed expression on her mom's face. She was more skilled than Lucas. Not only could she compel, but she could also control people's minds: shuffling through memories like a deck of cards or make them stop breathing. What she did to Maddison came flooding back, making her ill. But in Birdie Mae's mind, it was as if someone had chosen to erase a memory…

Why would someone do that? Could she do that?

347

Someone else was out there with powerful abilities. The hairs on her arm stood on end. And they had altered Birdie Mae's mind.

"Never mind, Birdie Mae." Ember released her mom, clipping their connection. Her mother slumped forward, rubbing her temples.

Ember threw her shoulders back and answered the door. Derek's aura shifted from a concerned navy to a lustful cranberry as his gaze slid over her. She leaned forward, enthralled by his mouth-watering scent. Her will to cancel the date evaporated. She immediately clipped the connection and stiffened her back.

"Hey." He brushed the back of his hair with his hand. He had freshly showered and shaved. Her fingers twitched as she imagined caressing his smooth jaw.

"Hi." Ember swallowed. The wood in the door frame splintered under her tight grip. She winced, placing her hands behind her.

"I was concerned you had stood me up."

"Oh, sorry. I fell asleep." Bear nudged himself between her legs and pushed out through the door opening to Derek.

"Hey, big guy!" Derek bent down scrubbing behind Bear's ears and then his belly as the not-so-guarded guard dog rolled over submissively. "What's his name?"

Ember rolled her eyes and laughed. "That is Bear. He is supposed to be a guard dog. He's normally more protective."

She studied their interaction. Guess she wasn't the only one who found Derek to be like Billy Joe. "I think you remind him of my dad." Her eyes misted at the thought. Maybe he wasn't her true dad, but he was the only father she had known.

Derek looked up, seeing the sadness in her eyes, stood, and spread his arms out wide. "Come here."

She hesitated at first, but then let herself fall into his warm embrace. She didn't fight the tears any longer. Derek held her, letting her cry as he rubbed soothing small circles across her back. After a few moments, she pulled back, cringing as she eyed the wet stain left behind on his shirt.

"Sorry." She sniffed back snot as she pointed to the wet spot.

His lips twisted into a crooked smile as he lifted the hoodie over his head, revealing a tight white tee clinging to his muscled chest. Her body betrayed her as it instinctively linked up to his aura. The air seemed to crackle with heat between them. "Problem solved." He shook out the hoodie. "It'll dry before we get down to the bottoms."

"About that..." She averted her gaze and swallowed. "I don't think..." Her words caught. She thought she saw a glowing golden sword tattoo on Derek's wrist. Ember reached out. The warm buzz ignited at her touch as she took his hand and flipped it over, exposing the tattoo. Her eyes went wide as saucers as she looked into Derek's deep ocean eyes.

"What is this?" she asked.

He pulled his hand back and brushed the back of his hair. His brows pinched together. "You can see it?"

"Yeah." She clipped their connection as the feelings pouring off him became overwhelming.

"We should talk. I'll explain everything on the way to the bottoms."

"Derek...I'm not sure I want to go anymore."

His face fell as he let out a soft breath. "Okay."

"No, I mean, I want to talk about that." She pointed to his wrist. "I just don't feel like being around many people. My mind is just all over the place today."

"Cool. No, that's cool." He looked down at Bear sitting obediently at his feet. "It's stopped raining. How about we take the big guy for a ride?" He bent down and stroked Bear's fur, eliciting a happy, crooked tongue from the giant. "Would you like that, Buddy?"

Ember's heart melted. The last time Bear got to go on a ride was with Billy Joe.

"Okay." She smiled down at the fluff ball. "You want to go for a ride, Bear?" He barked and paced around Derek.

"I think that's a yes." His warm eyes smiled back at Ember.

****

Ember threw on her volleyball jacket and slid into the cab of Derek's truck while he corralled the happy canine into the back. It made her heart happy to see Bear so excited. She watched as the muscles in Derek's tan arm rippled as he cranked the ignition. Butterflies took flight as he leaned towards her. His dark indigo eyes pooled with warmth.

"First, I need to know something…" His voice dropped and his face turned serious.

"Okay?"

"Do you like frozen drinks?" His lips twitched, fighting a smile.

"Yes."

"Bardwell it is then."

He pulled out of the drive with Bear happily leaning his head into the wind. When they turned onto the paved county road, Derek drummed his fingers on the steering wheel and looked nervously at Ember.

"So, are you going to tell me how you got that?" She tilted her chin to his tattoo.

Derek cleared his throat. "It's sort of a long, crazy story. I'm not sure where to start."

"Trust me. It can't be any crazier than my day already." She picked at the hem of her shirt. "Just start at the beginning."

"Okay." His eyes darted to hers. "After your accident…"

"When I drowned?" She watched as a muscle twitched in his jaw.

"Yeah…" He gripped the steering wheel tighter. "I got a visitor…" His voice trailed, glancing at her.

"Michael?"

"Right. The Archangel Michael." His chin dipped. "I thought someone had slipped something in my drink at the fraternity house."

"I get it." She nodded.

"He showed me things, Em." He swallowed making his Adam's apple bob. "I didn't think it was real at first."

"Yeah. Same thing happened to me, sort of, when I drowned."

Relief swept across his face. "He said I had free will to choose my path, but the future world I saw, Em—I can't let that happen."

Her gaze drifted to the golden sword on his wrist.

"So, you took an oath?" His head bobbed yes. "Does that mean that you are Nephilim, then? A Covenant Knight?"

He rubbed the back of his neck and looked over at

Ember. "Nope. I'm just a regular old human." He blew
out air. "But the Archangel filled me in on everything."

"So, you know about me?"

"Yeah."

"So, are you like a soldier for him? Did he give
you a mission?"

His eyes darted to hers as a small smile stretched
upon his lips. "Yeah…"

"What is it? What's your mission?"

"You." His aura flared with pinks and reds.

"Oh." Ember felt a warm tingle as he reached over
and squeezed her hand.

"I am supposed to protect you, since your dad…"
He let the sentence falter.

He tightened his grip on her hand. She looked out
the window, trying not to cry.

"Billy Joe never told me about any of this. And, as
far as I can tell, Birdie Mae is clueless, too."

"I'm sure he was only trying to protect you, Em."

"So, you know everything? What do you know
about me?" She watched his profile as his jaw flexed.
He released her hand to turn the steering wheel as the
road snaked into a tight curve. "Can you tell me?"

"What do you want to know?"

"Is Billy Joe my dad?" She asked cautiously,
knowing the likely answer.

Derek blew out a breath. "Not by blood, Em."

She kept her face neutral as he watched her
reaction. The news was still fresh and felt like a punch
to the gut. But hearing it a second time took out the
initial sting.

She swallowed. "Is Birdie Mae my mother?"

"She carried you. Yes."

"So, you're saying she's not my blood mother?"

He sighed. "This is getting above my pay grade, Em. But no, I don't believe she is. I think she was used like a vessel to carry you till you were born."

"So, who is? Who's my mother? Who's my father, Derek?"

He kept his eyes on the road. "I think that is a question for the Crimson Ring, or maybe the Archangel."

"Why the Crimson Ring? What do you know about them?" Her pulse thrummed in her veins.

"I don't know all the details, Em. I just know they were involved in your conception at one of their labs."

She was tempted to link into his mind. But she could see he was being truthful.

"Okay." She let out a breath, staring out the window. "Why do you think I need protecting?"

His grip tightened on the steering wheel. He glanced over at her.

"The Brotherhood of the Snake, or rather the Crimson Ring, they thought you were dead until this summer." He paused. "The Archangel said that Billy Joe kept you hidden and unaware of your ancestry. He was protecting you from them."

Ember nodded, not wanting to interrupt.

"When news spread amongst the Nephilim that a human girl drowned and then came back to life, unharmed, well, it got the Ring's attention." He looked over at her. "The Archangel told me to protect you until you had made your decision."

"When exactly did he approach you?"

"I took the oath a few days after the Sadie Hawkins dance." A muscle ticked in his jaw. "It was the second time he came to me. He said there wasn't much time. I didn't know the mission was going to be you, Em, I swear. But I just couldn't live with myself knowing that I could help prevent that…that future he showed me."

"What did you see in the vision?" Her question came out barely above a whisper.

He reached over and squeezed her hand. "It was Chicago…sometime in the future, I think…it was like a hospital and babies were being tested and…and worse." He swallowed.

Ember nodded. "Same. Mine was like that, too, but I wasn't sure it was Chicago." She released his hand and studied the haunted outlines of the dark tree branches arching over the road. She chewed her bottom lip and asked, "What do you know about ELL Pharmaceuticals?"

"Not much. The archangel just told me to keep you away from there."

"I think they are behind everything." She tugged on the chain around her neck. "Did the archangel say anything to you about Logan? Or his uncle?"

A muscle twitched in his jaw. "Logan Lauder descends from a long line of snakes—his uncle, too."

"But can we trust him?"

"Trust him?" His head jerked around. "Trust no one associated with the Brotherhood of the Snake."

She stared at the yellow hashes dividing the road as they neared Bardwell. But her thoughts were a carousel of lies and revelations. Logan was more than he seemed. She was sure of it.

"I've changed my mind. After we get drinks, we are going to the bottoms, Derek."

He cocked his head. "What are you thinking, Em?"

"What all did the archangel tell you about my abilities?"

"That you are enhanced." His cheeks flushed as his eyes raked over her body. "You can do things most humans can only dream of."

He pulled the truck into the lone Bardwell gas station. Bear barked at a couple walking out of the store.

He raised his palm. "Pause that thought. What can I get you?"

"Soda flavor, please."

"Are you sure? Cherry is the best. I'm a connoisseur of fine iced beverages, and my recommendation is the cherry." His lips twitched.

"I'll stick with the soda, thank you."

"All right, suit yourself." He exited and stepped into the gas station.

Ember watched him order the drinks through the glass storefront. Moments later, he returned with two drinks and a plastic bowl piled high with vanilla soft serve. He shrugged, smiling at her, and placed the ice cream mountain in the back for Bear. He slipped back into the truck, handing over her drink.

She jerked her head back to Bear. "You didn't have to do that."

"What? I got to take care of the big guy, too. It's my duty as your protector." He smiled and started up the engine.

"So, what is the plan?" He cocked his head taking a long drag on his straw. He winced. "Ouch. Brain freeze."

Ember laughed, "Some protector you are."

"Hey, it hurts."

Ember proceeded with caution and just sipped on her drink not wanting to replicate his so-called painful experience.

Moments later, he glanced over at her. "So, enlighten me, Em, why are we going to the bottoms, and what are your enhanced abilities?"

"To be honest, I'm just figuring things out myself." She paused, not sure if she was ready to talk to him about Adam—Lucas—yet. It was unexplainable, but Ember felt the need to protect Lucas. She let out a breath. "Erick and Hallee were helping me research my vision. That's part of the reason I want to go to the bonfire—to apologize. I sort of went off on them when they were only trying to help. But I also want to see Logan." She watched as his hands tightened on the steering wheel.

"Listen to me, to it all, before you go Alpha-protector on me."

Derek rolled his eyes.

"Since the drowning, I learned they misdiagnosed me with synesthesia. I know I'm not broken or a freak. I am Nephilim. But for years, I tried to ignore or hide what I was seeing. Things got so bad freshman year that I started taking a lot of medications. I couldn't sleep." She paused, recalling her nightmare. "The pills helped numb everything that I saw and felt. They helped dull the pain and made the halls of school more manageable. Though some days…I-I just wanted to die."

"I'm so sorry, Em." His face hardened as he blew out a breath. "I had no idea it was so bad. Someday, Wayne will pay for all the shit he did to you. I promise."

"It's okay, Derek. Really. I think part of the

problem was that I was suppressing my powers. At the end of freshman year, I was in a really dark place. If I had only learned to embrace my abilities early on or tried to understand them, I think my childhood would have looked a lot different. I think I would have been happier, regardless of what Wayne could have said or done, because I would have known that I wasn't a freak—that I wasn't broken. I was just different."

"You are a way more forgiving person than me, Em." He cocked his jaw. "So, what are your skills?"

"Last summer, things happened despite the pills. My dad…" Ember looked away. "Billy Joe and I went camping down in the bottoms every weekend. He taught me how to fight, how to use weapons, how to track prey, survival skills—you name it. And it felt good. He said I was a natural."

Derek grinned. "Sounds like boot camp."

"At the time he said it would be good for me to get outdoors and out of my head about school. But now, I think he was also trying to prepare me—for this."

Derek nodded.

"I've never pushed myself fully, but I know I'm really fast and strong. My hearing and vision are inhumanly great. So is my sense of smell." She watched his reaction. "And I can dream walk, see people's auras, and slip into their minds. I can see memories and thoughts. And I can influence their decisions—compel them to do things. Even control them."

Derek let out a long whistle. "Shit," he said under his breath. Their eyes met, and he grinned "You left out the part about being immortal."

She laughed. "I don't know about that. I think technically I did die."

"Whatever." He shook his head. "You are a bad ass. Period. Stop."

"Thanks, I think." She looked at her own smiling reflection in the window. She never imagined telling a guy any of this and him not running the other way. "None of this freaks you out?"

He reached over and took her hand, squeezing.

"Look, Em, I'm not sure you really need my protection, but I'm here for you. I'm not going anywhere." His thumb rubbed across her knuckles. "And, yeah, I was a little freaked out when the Archangel visited me, but some things are bigger than yourself, you know? If we have the power to stop that vision of the future, it will be worth whatever goes along with it."

"So, what are you planning to do to Logan? Get in his brain? Force him to reveal the snakes' lair?"

Ember laughed, "Lair?"

"All the bad guys have lairs, Em. It's bad guy one-oh-one."

"Okay. Well, the jury is still out on whether Logan is a bad guy—or his uncle, for that matter, but I hope to get to the bottom of it tonight."

"And that's it? You find out what he knows and then what? Pretend nothing's changed?"

Ember bit her cheek as the truck neared the river bottoms. "It depends. What I find out tonight could change everything."

Chapter Forty-five

Derek's truck rumbled to a stop amongst the scattered makes and models parked haphazardly in the river bottom scrub. Ember scanned the vehicles for Erick's car. She didn't see it, but she spotted Logan's black sports car among some of the other familiar cars from Wilson County High. Bear immediately let his presence be known by barking passionately at the onlookers hovering by the bonfire.

"Quiet, Bear." She commanded. The dog twitched his ears and stopped barking.

Derek looked surprised. "You didn't say you were a dog whisperer, too."

She shrugged. "He's well trained. But, yeah, I can see their auras. I can tell when he's happy, sad, hungry…he's always hungry." That made him laugh.

"Well, he's a big guy, I get it." He stepped out of the truck; and before Ember could get out by herself, he opened the door for her. "Careful, the ground is still wet from the rain earlier."

"Bear, stay." The fluff ball let out a small whine and then lay down in the back of the truck.

He rubbed the back of Bear's head. "I should have brought some treats."

"Oh my gosh, stop. He's fine. And he just had a ridiculous amount of ice cream. He's good, I promise." Ember liked how Derek was already attached to Bear and vice versa. It was a good omen.

"All right, who's first? Erick and Hallee or Logan?" He said Logan's name like it was tainted.

She scanned the cars one last time, searching for Erick's white car.

"I don't think Erick and Hallee are here, yet. If they don't show up, I'll try calling them tomorrow."

Derek cracked his knuckles. "That leaves option number two."

"I can handle this, Rocky." Ember smiled at her muscled protector.

"Rocky, huh?" His lips twitched. "Your awesome meter just went way up."

"Thanks." She linked her arm in his, savoring the warm tingles that radiated from his touch. "Come on. Let's go find out where their secret lair is."

The night was cool yet humid from the earlier rainstorm. Ember was glad she wore her volleyball jacket. The clouds hung low as the front broke apart across the Kentucky night sky. Music blasted from speakers. She clipped the pull of the people hanging out around the bonfire. Missy and Nina spied her first and came running over before she and Derek made it halfway there.

"Geez! Finally!" They both embraced her in a warm hug.

"I knew she'd come." Nina smiled confidently.

Missy shimmied her hips. "You ready to get your party on, MVP?"

"Coach made us promise to show you a good time tonight." Nina hooked her arm in Ember's.

She looked back at Derek. The fire reflected little gold boats in his ocean blue eyes.

"Go ahead," he said, smiling.

Ember let Nina and Missy lead her over to the cluster of tailgates belonging to the volleyball team. She exchanged high fives and hugs with her teammates.

"Want a beer?" Missy asked, pulling a can from an ice chest.

"Oh, no, I'm good." Last time she was in the bottoms she had felt the need to drink to fit in, but not anymore.

"You sure?"

She nodded and watched Derek and Kale swap palms on the other side of the bonfire. Katie sat on the back of Kale's truck. Ember was happy that things were still working out for the two of them.

"I think you might change your mind when you see Logan." Nina gestured to Maddison's vehicle. Inside, Maddison had her tongue down Logan Lauder's throat. A flare of jealous anger sparked, then fizzled. Logan's love life was not her problem anymore. But she needed to get him alone. Her pulse quickened as she slipped into his mind.

"We need to talk." She emphasized each word slowly.

She watched Logan's lips jerk from Maddison's. He searched frantically through the windshield for her, the source of the voice in his head. Finally, his gaze met hers. He blew out a breath and nodded. Ember released her connection as she watched him talk his way out of the vehicle. Maddison's upset face developed into an incredibly pissed mask, her lips forming a straight line and her brows dipping into a *V*.

She slammed the door and stomped behind Logan, ranting. Ember told her friends she'd be back and met the no-so-happy couple by the bonfire.

"Hey." He smiled sheepishly.

Maddison stared daggers at her.

"Hi." She nodded. "Hello, Maddison. Mind if I talk to Logan…alone?"

"The pity party is over, Ember. He was only with you because you were the Dead Girl. So, move on. Enjoy your sloppy seconds with Derek."

Though Ember's blood boiled, she refused to take the bait. She was better than that. Besides, she didn't want to use her abilities unless she absolutely had to.

"Just one little conversation, Maddison. And then he's all yours."

She crossed her arms and huffed as Logan leaned in and whispered something in her ear.

"Fine. Whatever." She spat. Ember felt the heat of Maddison's stare as Logan took her hand and led her to his vehicle.

"This okay?" he asked as she pulled her hand away.

"Yeah, sure." She leaned against the hood of his car. Derek walked towards her, but she stopped him by connecting to his mind, letting him know she was okay. Startled, he grinned and nodded.

"You're a freaking bad ass." He mouthed the words and signaled with his fingers that he would watch her on the other side of the fire.

Logan observed their interaction and reached out to grab her hand.

"Nope." Ember let the "p" pop. "Don't go there."

He awkwardly pulled his hand back and let out a breath. "Okay."

"You didn't seem too surprised that I could speak

to your mind." She cocked her head, watching his reaction.

His lips tilted into a crooked smile, making a dimple appear. "Yeah, no, I'm not surprised. Cool trick, by the way."

"I think it's time for you to come clean, Logan Lauder."

He raised his palms. "Trust me, I wanted to. So many times, I wanted to tell you, Ember."

"I've got all night." She crossed her arms. "Why don't you start by telling me why you and your uncle really moved here, Logan?"

He took in a deep breath and looked up at the breaking clouds. His eyes held so much regret that she didn't need to use her abilities to know what he was feeling.

"Would it surprise you to know that my uncle isn't really my uncle?"

"Nope."

"And that we moved here to do recon on the Dead Girl?"

"I figured as much," she conceded.

He shrugged. "You know everything then."

"I'm piecing it together." Ember fingered Billy Joe's military tags. "Who do you work for, Logan?"

He tilted his head. "That's complicated."

"Un-complicate it for me," she pressed.

He looked down, as if contemplating his words.

"Tell me the truth, Logan."

He let out a breath. "Okay, okay. I am breaking a lot of rules here. And that can have repercussions—not just for me, but for my uncle as well."

"Right. Your uncle."

"It's not like that. Richard is like an uncle. When my parents died, my actual Uncle Jack took custody of me. But he was always busy with work. Richard was like his right-hand man. So, when my uncle bailed on commitments, Richard would step in. We became close. I call him Uncle Rich…but he's more than that…I love him like the father I never had."

He paused, his Adam's apple bobbing. "This assignment is technically my first mission. We only expected to be here a few days; but as more information came to light, we had to switch gears and come up with a new plan." He swallowed. "How much do you know about it all? ELL…the Brotherhood…Nephilim?" Logan asked.

She glanced over at the bonfire. Maddison twirled her blonde hair while talking with Brittany and Derek.

"I know some." She made a divot in the soggy ground with the toe of her shoe. "My dad sheltered me from all of it."

"I figured as much. My real uncle, Jack Lauder, is very involved with the Brotherhood, to put it mildly. He serves on the board of the Crimson Ring, which owns all of ELL Industries in North America."

"So, why come out all the way to Western Kentucky to investigate me?"

"Because…the same explosion that killed my parents was supposed to have killed you, too." His fist clenched. Ember didn't react. "But somehow you already knew this?"

Ember nodded. "I had some help."

"The Crimson Ring believes terrorists sent by The Order intended to destroy the lab at ELL and kill those who worked there."

"Why destroy a lab? What were they doing?" She leaned forward, eager to understand more pieces of the puzzle.

"Creating you—and others like you."

Ember's mind immediately thought of Lucas. *We are made for each other.* He didn't just mean that metaphorically. The hair on her arms stood on end.

"But somehow, I survived," she whispered. "Or...Birdie Mae escaped." Her mother's memory suddenly made sense. Billy Joe was helping her escape.

"Exactly. The fire marshal believed the blaze was so hot from the chemicals that no human remains could have been left behind."

She crossed her arms, ready to latch onto his aura. "So, again, Logan, who do you work for?"

He swallowed. "Unofficially, my Uncle Rich has been working both sides."

That was not the answer she was expecting. "Both sides? Explain."

"He helps the Covenant Knights sometimes...when it's convenient, but his paycheck comes from the Crimson Ring."

"So, you come here to check me out...what was the plan? Abduct me? Take me back to ELL?"

"We had received intelligence from both sides that the Order of Saint Michael was making a move." He swallowed. "Once we could confirm your identity, our mission shifted to protection. I had to get close to be sure—"

Her stomach dropped. She finished the sentence for him. "You became my boyfriend." Maybe deep down she already knew the truth, but it still hurt.

"The Order are murderers, O'Neill. Violent

heretics with a mission. I had to do something. But it's not only that, I do also care for you, Ember. I really do. You got to believe me." He looked away. "But, yes, it seemed like a great way to run protection, without it being too invasive."

"Did you ever get inside our house and take my things?"

He looked up, eyes wide. "What? No." His honest aura further confirmed in her mind that it was Wayne. "Listen, Ember—"

"So, if you came initially to investigate the Dead Girl, then you had nothing to do with the demon that killed my dad…that killed Billy Joe?"

"No. We had nothing to do with that. But that is also when our mission shifted. We believe the demon was sent by the Order." His lips pressed together. "It fits their MO. The sick fucks think they are saving the world and will do anything and work with anyone or any*thing* to accomplish their goals."

"So, should I be worried?"

He let out a long breath. "You stay off the grid until this whole Dead Girl thing blows over, I think you'll be fine. Between my uncle and me, we can help cover it up."

Ember slowly nodded as several pairs of headlights pulled into the bottoms. She glanced over at Derek, who was laughing with his old high school friends.

"Why would you protect me, Logan?"

He shook his head. "You have nothing to worry about from me or my uncle. I swear."

"And your uncle's boss at the Crimson Ring?" she countered.

"He would not allow any harm to come to you.

That is a promise."

"And I'm just supposed to believe you? Trust you, after everything?"

He didn't have a chance to answer when the sound of car doors slamming came from behind them.

"Where the fuck is she?" Ember tensed at the familiar sound and smell—Chad.

"That bitch is going to answer for what she did to my sister."

Logan protectively stood in front of her as a group of angry males made their way through the parked cars. Glass broke as Chad waved a bat, shattering taillights.

Ember pushed Logan aside. "I got this."

She had never tried to control more than one person at a time. But there is a first time for everything, she thought. *Virtus vincit.* Bracing for the emotional onslaught, Ember cracked her neck.

She stepped out into the open, planted her feet, and spread her arms wide. "Looking for me?"

Chad stood at the front of the mob. His aura was seething as he swung the bat loosely from his fingertips. His eyes locked with hers. He pointed the bat at her. "You're going to pay for hurting my sister."

She felt Derek's presence close in behind her. The crowd chatter dimmed, and the music stopped as everyone watched the heated exchange. Bear's loud barks broke the silence. Ember sent calming energy to her canine protector.

"What are you doing, Em?" Derek spoke softly behind her.

"I can handle this," she whispered back.

Logan smiled and put his hands up. "Hey, guys. Wait. You look familiar. Yeah, it's coming back to me now. Isn't this the guy whose ass you beat a couple weeks ago, O'Neill?"

"Logan—" She didn't get to finish the sentence.

Chad took a swing at Logan but Ember latched onto Chad's mind, making the bat miss. Logan took advantage of the errant swing and punched Chad in the gut. He doubled over, dropping the bat. Ember felt the pain and clipped her connection to Chad.

She reconnected to Derek, only to sense him struggle as he was taking on two of the larger guys in the group. She spun and instinctively began protecting her friends as Kale jumped in to help.

She stopped fists or made them go wide of their target, slipping in and out of minds. Like a pianist striking keys, Ember controlled the tempo of the fight. Just as she felt she had gotten it under control, the touch of cool steel met her neck.

"Blood for blood, bitch." Chad held a pocketknife to her throat.

Logan and Derek both stood by, helpless, as they watched the knife dig deeper into her skin.

"Come on, Chad. It's over. Let's go." One of the Hickory High guys pleaded.

Ember connected to Chad's mind. Without saying a word out loud, she spoke to him. *It was an accident. I swear.*

His eyes glazed over, but his grip tightened on the knife as his breathing came out ragged against her back.

Logan spit blood onto the ground. "Yeah, Chad, be smart and listen to your buddy."

"Ember." Derek's eyes pleaded.

She didn't want to embarrass Chad by disarming him. She wanted it to be his choice to walk away.

"I am sorry. You don't want to hurt me, Chad. It won't make things better."

She tried to pierce through his rage, but there was something there pushing back. Ember stilled. He really wanted to kill her. He wanted to see her hurt, bleeding out. Dead. She had encountered no one that angry before. An icy shiver ran down her spine. She pressed harder, but the oily darkness of his mind wouldn't let her in. She couldn't control him.

Ember watched Derek as he slowly eased his way around the crowd. He was maneuvering to get in Chad's blind spot.

"Stay back!" Chad growled.

If she couldn't command Chad to stop, then she had no choice but to muscle her way out of the situation. Using Derek's position to her advantage, Ember released Chad's mind and linked with Derek. *"When I force him to drop the knife, you take him from behind."*

Derek dipped his chin, ever so slightly, acknowledging her message.

Gritting her teeth, she sent him the silent count. *"On three... One...two...three!"*

Using supernatural strength she was able to overpower Chad and dislodge the knife from his grip. Derek stepped up, and brought him down with a chokehold.

Ember picked up the muddied knife, folded it into the closed position and slipped it into her pocket.

"What do you want me to do with him, Em?" Derek asked as Chad squirmed under his embrace, his face turning red.

Ember shook her head. "Let him go."

"You sure?" Logan asked, tapping Chad's bat against one thigh. "Asshole deserves to have his ass beat again."

"Yeah, I'm sure," she said.

After Derek released him. Chad staggered forward, flexing his fists. "This ain't over, bitch," he sneered.

"You and your buddies better leave before she changes her mind." Logan brought the bat up and slapped it agains his open palm.

"Come on, Chad." One of the few Hickory High guys that hadn't already left took Chad by the arm and steered him away.

Derek's warm hands cupped Ember's cheeks, sending heat down her spine. "You okay?"

She nodded. He tilted her chin and scanned her neck. His thumb brushed the tiny whisper of a wound. His eyes rounded. Derek leaned in close to her ear.

"I think it's already healed." The warmth of his breath tickled her ear. "Add that to your list of superpowers." He kissed the top of her head and pulled back. "I'm glad you are okay." His thumb stroked her jaw. "You're such a badass, Em."

"Oh my God, Logan! Are you all right?" Maddison's high-pitched voice rang through the night air as she pushed through the crowd. "Oh, no! You're hurt!" she shrieked. "Someone get us some ice!" She pulled him towards the bonfire, sending orders to the cheer squad.

A rumble of laughter released from Derek's chest. "You know, I actually feel sorry for him…a little bit."

"Yeah, me too, a little bit." She grinned.

Derek guided her over to his truck. A stressed Bear barked excitedly as they neared. "So, you…Logan…did you get the answers you wanted?"

"Yeah, I think so…"

"And?"

"Jury is still out. You were right, though. He and his uncle…they have ties to the Crimson Ring."

Derek's jaw twitched. "I'm sorry, Em. But he can't be trusted. You can't trust those snakes."

"He could have lied, but he didn't, Derek. He came clean about everything." Derek just shook his head.

Ember heard the rumble of a car in the distance. "Someone is coming." She turned toward the road.

"If that asshole is coming back for more, he's going to get more than his fair share." Derek spat.

She slowly shook her head. "It's not him." Headlights rounded through the trees and broke into the clearing. It was the sheriff.

Chapter Forty-six

The sheriff's car rolled to a stop. Everyone cursed and tossed drinks to hide the alcohol. Ember was glad she drank nothing as the sheriff stepped out of his car. He was tall with a slight bulge over his belt line. Tightly shorn blond transitioned to gray under his wide-brim hat.

The sheriff reached in his car and clicked on his radio, pulling the coiled speaker to his mouth. Static erupted as his deep baritone voice projected from the car. "All right, kids, relax. I'm not here trying to bust underage drinkers." He paused, eyeing the crowd. "Missy, that better be water, though."

Missy raised her cup. "Cheers, Dad."

He waved her off. "Listen, kids, we got a couple of worried parents. Any of y'all seen Erick Grossman or Hallee Wilson?"

The crowd murmured amongst themselves.

Ember's entire body tensed. Her friends weren't just avoiding her. They were missing.

"No? All right then. If you hear anything about their whereabouts, please call the sheriff's office. And, Missy, be home by midnight, dear." He clicked off the speaker and slipped back into his seat, closing the door.

Ember rushed to his car. She tapped on his window. "Sheriff, wait."

He rolled the window down. His brows arched as

he recognized her. "Ms. O'Neill. You know anything about the two missing?"

"No, not really. I just…Erick's car was at the school this afternoon."

"About what time was that?"

"It was during my volleyball game. But his car was gone when my game was over."

"And what time would you say that was approximately?"

"Maybe, between four and five? I don't really know."

The sheriff scratched his stubble. "All right, thank you. We'll look into it."

"Is there anything I can do to help?" she asked.

His smile didn't quite reach his eyes. "Just call us if you hear anything."

Ember slowly nodded as he rolled up his window and backed out.

"You all right?" Derek walked up behind her.

"No."

"I was just talking to Kale and Katie. Guess Hallee never showed up for her sleepover at Katie's house." He rubbed the back of his neck. "She wasn't freaked out, or anything, but when Hallee's parents didn't know where she was…shit got intense, real quick."

Blood pounded in Ember's veins as her mind raced through potential scenarios.

"And what about Erick? When did he go missing? When I called his house for a ride, his mom said he was at school. His car was there this afternoon."

Derek shrugged. "Maybe they're together and everyone is just freaking out over nothing." He put his hands on her shoulders. "Hey, look, there is probably a reasonable explanation. Em, I'm sure the sheriff will find them. Even if they ran away together, they can't get too far."

He pulled her in close, kissing the top of her head. She closed her eyes and breathed in his scent mixed with the muggy air.

None of it made sense to her. It was totally out of character for Hallee to run away. She seemed so happy. She and Erick were perfect together. A renewed wave of guilt washed over Ember as she recalled her last interaction with her best friend. Perhaps Erick realized something was off when Hallee didn't show up. Maybe he was driving around looking for Hallee, too. Maybe he was…

Ember's eyes flew open. She pulled back. "Derek! I know where they are!"

"What the—" His mouth fell open as her skin began to take on a soft luminescent glow.

"Get Kale and Logan…and take Bear. Go to the old cabins by the river. I think Erick is there."

"Wh—" Derek couldn't finish his sentence before Ember took off into the woods at a superhuman pace.

Chapter Forty-seven

Barking, Bear jumped out of the truck, following Ember into the woods. Derek yelled for her to stop. But she ignored him and the dog and leaned in to all her abilities. She ripped off her volleyball jacket as she ran. This was it. This was the moment her premonition dream had prepared her for. *Virtus vincit.*

Barely feeling the sting, she ignored her glowing arms and legs as branches lashed out against her racing form. She felt powerful. Invincible, even. After countless nights of reliving this moment, she didn't need to stop to get her bearings. She knew exactly where to go. The river.

Within moments, her body alerted her to the familiar scent of her prey. He was just out of reach for her to link to his mind and stop him. Ember pushed herself beyond any human limits as she zeroed in on his pheromone trail. An uncontrollable shiver laced down her spine. The sweet scent of honeysuckle hung in the air. But it wasn't the scent of old blooms from summer like she had assumed. No. How could she have been so wrong? She knew that odor. It was Hallee. And she was in danger.

The roar of a boat motor broke the silence of the woods. Panic sliced through her. She had to move faster. She reached the rocky beach within seconds, spying the boat which was now near the center of the

Mississippi River.

Without hesitation, she ran, feet splashing into the cool, rushing water. Ember took in a deep breath and dove. The water was shocking, as the current fought against her and pushed her away from her target. The fast-flowing river dulled her hearing, disorienting her while the murky water blinded her as well. But like a spider triggered by a fly in its web, Ember could still sense her prey. The boat was close, but still too far away. She fought her instincts to come up for air. Somehow, she just knew her Nephilim body could stay under longer.

Fear laced through her as a new disturbance hit the water. Hallee's body sank in the river just ahead of her. But the boat and driver were getting away. Without question, she knew what she had to do—save Hallee.

As soon as Ember was close enough, she latched onto Hallee's mind, telling her not to be afraid. She would save her.

"Help!" Hallee's mind screamed.

Her fears became reality. There was no mistake. It was Hallee. And she was sinking to her death. Ember steeled herself against her best friend's panic, trying not to let the fear overtake her as well. Hallee's consciousness slipped from her. Her heartbeat slowed.

In two quick strokes, she reached her friend, continuing her mantra that she was going to be okay. She clasped onto Hallee's torso as she sank. The current pulled her along the muddy floor of the river's bottom. She tugged up, but something was dragging them both back down like a weight.

Frantically, Ember searched her friend, running her hands along Hallee's limp arms and legs. Her hand caught on a rope hanging taut from Hallee's leg. Attached to it, a cement block dragged along the river bottom.

She reassured her friend that she was going to be okay as she fumbled to untie the knot. Hallee's heartbeat faded as water gurgled, entering her lungs.

Time was running out. Her mind raced, searching for a way to cut the rope when she remembered Chad's knife was in her pocket.

She pulled the knife out, flipped open the blade, and frantically sawed. The threads frayed; and within seconds, she had cut the rope in half. She dropped the knife and shot upwards with Hallee in her arms. Her friend hung lifeless as Ember broke through the water and pushed against the current for the shore.

The rocky riverbank was just ahead. Derek ran along the shore waving his arms, calling her name with an upset Bear on his heels.

As she neared the bank, she linked her mind with his. *"Help me! It's Hallee. She's dying."*

Derek kicked off his shoes and dove into the water. His powerful frame made quick work of the distance, and together, they carried Hallee's limp form to the beach.

"I don't sense her pulse anymore." Her lips pressed into thin lines as she watched Derek check Hallee's breathing and pulse.

"She's not breathing. No pulse." He began CPR.

Ember dropped to her knees beside them. Tears slipped down her cheeks and onto her soaked clothes. "She's not going to make it."

He looked up for a half-second but continued the chest compressions.

"Derek." Ember barely choked his name out as her nightmare became real. Hallee had no aura. She was dead. "Derek." She placed her hand on his shoulder. He looked up. She shook her head. "She's dead."

His brows pinched together. "I can save her."

He blew air into Hallee's still body.

"Derek. She will not make it." She bit her bottom lip as salty tears dripped off her chin. "I thought I could save her, but I was—"

Ember didn't get to finish her sentence as the distinct sounds of gunshots rang through the air. She leapt to her feet.

"Where are the others?"

"They went to the cabin like you asked," he said.

"Oh, no!" Her chest tightened. She was so consumed with saving Hallee that she completely forgot about Erick. "Bear, stay with Derek," she commanded and turned, running along the river's edge to the abandoned cabins. She couldn't fail him, too.

"Em, wait!" Derek called after her, but she was already gone.

Chapter Forty-eight

Ember climbed the steep muddy bank. Her fingers clawed to get a grip as her feet slipped. Using her supernatural strength, she pulled herself up, inch by inch, until she reached the top. Just a hundred yards away, she spotted the cabin. A light flickered from within, illuminating a single busted window in the dilapidated structure. She unleashed her abilities, surveying the exterior of the cabin and the overgrowth surrounding it. Two cars were parked outside. She recognized both. A shiver ran down her spine. Erick's white car sat alongside Wayne's rusted green sedan.

Her nostrils flared and the hair on her arms stood on end as she inhaled the dank smell of decaying leaves mixed with Erick's metallic fear. He was scared, not hurt. But there was something else. The iron tang of blood hung low in the surrounding woods. Her pulse beat wildly as she crept along in the underbrush towards the source. Her steps faltered as she recognized who was hurt. Kale. She scanned the surrounding area to be sure he was alone. Breathing labored, his chest rose and fell in bursts. She rushed to his side. Fear and pain coated his aura.

"Em-ber." Kale choked out her name.

"Shhh. Don't talk." She looked over his body. He was shot in the chest, possibly the lung. Ember pressed down on the wound to stop the bleeding. Kale winced at the pressure. She slipped into his mind.

"You're going to be okay. Show me who did this."

Instantly, the image of Wayne shooting a gun into the woods at Kale and Logan flashed like a movie reel in Kale's mind.

"Oh, God, Kale. I'm so sorry."

Kale's weak touch on her arm broke her concentration. "He didn't see me." His eyes fluttered closed. "Wayne took Logan."

She looked up. In the distance, footsteps ran through the woods. A flashlight illuminated the trees. "Kale! Answer me! Where are you? Are you okay? I heard gunshots." Katie yelled into the night.

Ember stood and hoped she could reach Katie's mind from that distance.

"Katie, stop. Be quiet. Wayne has a gun." She mentally sent the instructions. *"Turn around and go get help. Get the sheriff. And have them send an ambulance to the cabins."*

Ember watched as the light from Katie's flashlight bobbed and changed directions. She bent down and connected with Kale's mind again.

"I can't stay. Help is coming."

Kale winced, face pale.

"You're going to be okay."

Ember stood and peered at the cabin. Her fist clenched and unclenched. Her stomach recoiled at the rotten scent of decay that now leaked from the cabin's direction—a demon. She bit her bottom lip. She didn't have her father's blade. She would have to be enough.

Cautiously, she crept closer to the cabin's edge. She still sensed Erick, but now, Logan was in the cabin with him leaning against the far wall. She breathed in deeply. Wayne's bitter scent swirled on a current with the demon rot. Now certain of who was inside, she reached out to her friends' auras.

"You good?" Ember sent to Logan. She sensed his muscles tensing in pain.

"Yeah, I'll be fine. Wayne has a gun, and he's threatening to use it again." He mentally answered her.

Wayne paced back and forth muttering unintelligible words inside the cabin.

"I am going to ambush Wayne." She told Logan as she weaved her way between the tall weeds to the cabin's porch, tensing as the wooden planks creaked under foot.

"Wayne isn't himself, O'Neill." Logan relayed. *"He might be possessed."*

The door was ajar, allowing her to see in. Erick was tied up on the floor with a cloth gag in his mouth. A lens on his glasses was cracked. He seemed to struggle to breathe. She recognized her friend's physical duress. He was having a panic attack. Ember released her connection to Logan and linked to Erick's mind.

"Hey, warrior prince. Looks like you could use some help."

Erick's eyes jerked open, scanning the room.

"Shhh...don't say anything. Just relax. I'm here, and I'm going to get you out of this mess."

She sent soothing energy to him. Instantly, his shoulders relaxed, and his breathing became less labored. His eyes widened as he saw her glowing form in the door's crack.

Ember froze when she saw her ex-boyfriend. Logan sat pale beside Erick. His head slumped to one side. His gaze was unfocused. She swallowed. He had been shot, too. A bloody hole bloomed in the shoulder of his shirt. Running down his arm, blood pooled red onto the floor.

Wayne paced the cabin, waving the gun around, muttering. His aura was black and tainted a rusty red. "I had to do it. I had to do it." He said the phrase repeatedly.

She latched onto Logan's aura. *"Hang in there, Lauder. I am going to disarm him in three…two…one."*

Ember crashed through the door, sending it swinging on its rusty hinges. She launched herself onto Wayne, dropping him to his knees and pinning him to the cabin floor. The impact forced Wayne to release the gun, causing it to slide away back towards the door.

He struggled and bucked against her, trying to dislodge her from his back. "Get off me, you whore!" He gritted between his teeth.

She latched onto his mind. It was oily like Chad's, but worse. A strong demonic presence within pushed back so hard that her brain throbbed at the attempt.

"Be still." She commanded Wayne as he continued to resist.

"You're a fucking abomination." He tried to head butt her with the back of his head, but Ember shifted and put him in a choke hold, pressing her knee even harder into his back like Billy Joe had taught her.

He whimpered as she forced herself into his mind. *"I won't hurt you, Wayne, but you've got to be still."*

"Go to Hell," a demonic voice hissed from Wayne's lips.

She fought the desire to squeeze the oxygen from his lungs. It took a particular kind of evil to do what he did to Hallee. And he of all people didn't deserve to live, but she refused to kill him. Her father taught her self-defense, to protect herself. But, never, under any circumstances, was she to take a life. Combat didn't have to end in death, he had told her. She had to subdue Wayne and the demon living inside him.

Gravel crunched outside as a vehicle pulled up. It must be the sheriff, Ember thought. Headlights beamed inside the cabin as the car parked. Ember sensed the energy of the new person as they exited the car.

Erick frantically fought against his restraints, mumbling through the gag.

"It's okay, Erick," she said.

His eyes rounded as he looked beyond Ember to the cabin door.

"Let him go, Ms. O'Neill."

She stiffened. It was not the sheriff. The distinct scent of leather and licorice flooded the room. She turned her head. Mr. Greene stood in the door with Wayne's gun pointed at her head.

Wayne bucked and growled beneath her. Ember maintained her grip and tried to link her mind to Mr. Greene's, but she was met by a brick wall. His eyebrow arched as his lips slid into a menacing grin.

"Tsk-tsk, Ms. O'Neill. That may work on the unenlightened, but not on a trained soldier of the Order of Saint Michael. So, stop with your little mind tricks and get off him. Now."

She slowly shifted her weight. Wayne shrugged her the rest of the way off and jumped to his feet. He kicked her in the stomach. Ember gasped, slumping on the cabin floor.

"Stupid whore." Spit dripped from his lips as his

foot shot out again, kicking her in the ribs.

"Enough, demon." Mr. Greene's gaze slid around the room, snagging on Erick and Logan.

The lantern light glinted off his dark eyes. "I thought you'd be drunk at the bonfire, Ember."

"And I thought you were a teacher—my coach, not some evil assassin." She spat out blood.

He cocked his head. "Evil? Hardly. Assassin? Sometimes. I am a soldier, Ms. O'Neill, just following orders." He looked her up and down. "As you well know, looks can be deceiving."

"Why are you doing this?" She noted the medallion at his neck. "Why kill Hallee if it's me you're after? She was innocent."

"I agree. Losing Ms. Wilson was unfortunate." His head cocked to the side. "I'm afraid I quite liked that little Nancy Drew. If only *you* had not dragged her into all of this."

She couldn't deny the pang of guilt she felt for not being able to save her friend. His words conjured up the image of Hallee's pale, limp form. But it was Wayne who drowned her.

She pointed to Wayne. "Me? He killed her, and you are blaming me?"

A single brow arched as Mr. Greene leaned forward. "We would never make Wayne kill his own cousin, would we, demon?"

Ember looked over at Wayne. His hand trembled as a single tear slid down his cheek.

"I killed Hallee Wilson, Ms. O'Neill." He tipped his head to Erick and Logan. "What happened, Wayne? You were supposed to take care of the nerd. How did Lauder get here?"

Wayne's eyes sparked as an ugly sneer snaked across his face. "They were going to stop it. We had to shoot."

Mr. Greene's left arm swung out, back-handing Wayne across the face. "You were not called here to make decisions, demon." His eyes shifted to Ember. A small smile parted his lips. "You get what you pay for, I suppose." He tilted his ear to Wayne. "This vessel is not the brightest, either. How you ever let a dumb sack like him bully you, Ms. O'Neill, I'll never know."

Her mind scrambled for ways to disarm him. She needed to keep him talking. Logan released a groan behind her. He had lost a lot of blood. She didn't have time to waste.

The teacher shrugged. "Your boyfriend is not looking so good, Ms. O'Neill. Shall we just ease him from his misery?" He angled the gun.

"No! Don't! Mr. Greene, please. He's innocent."

"Innocent? He's a Lauder. Probably already has the snake tattoo." He shifted his gaze back to Ember, cocking his head. "Oh, didn't you know, Ms. O'Neill? His entire Nephilim line sided with the Beast. It was only a matter of time before he turned you over to the Crimson Ring." His lips slid into a grin. "I guess you could say I'm actually doing *you* a favor."

"Wait! I just…I just want to understand. You owe me that much."

He glanced at his watch. Ember gritted her teeth, preparing to launch herself on him.

"You've got thirty seconds. Wayne, go get the gasoline out of my trunk." Mr. Greene's eyes fell into slits as he motioned to Ember, Erick, and Logan. "Looks like this love triangle is going to get heated."

Wayne limped out the door muttering, "Barbecue. Eliminate the abomination. Barbecue. Eliminate the abomination."

"Yes, Wayne…eliminate the abomination…and that would be you, Ms. O'Neill, or should I say, Daughter of Lucifer?" His thumb pulled back the hammer on the gun. "Now, what was your question?"

Daughter of Lucifer? His words smacked against her skull. *I'm not evil.*

Ember's heart pounded in her chest as she ran through scenarios in her mind. She needed to take down Mr. Greene while Wayne was outside. She was fast—inhumanly fast—but could she move faster than a bullet? She didn't think so.

If she was going to die trying, she wanted to be on the right side of things—her father's side of things. Ember silently called out for the Archangel to help her.

She was ready.

Chapter Forty-nine

Ember closed her eyes for a split second, praying for help. Everything around her fell silent. No labored breathing. Even the smells of the cabin disappeared. When she reopened her eyes, it was like she was in two places at once. Her body was crouched there on the cabin floor. Mr. Greene pointed the gun barrel straight at her. Erick sat slumped against the wall, struggling to breathe while Logan's body continued to leak blood.

Then everything faded into a formless blank canvas. Her body glowed once more, only brighter, like the Archangel Michael's brilliant shimmer.

"Daughter of Eden, it is good to see you again." The archangel spoke behind her.

Ember spun. "What is happening?"

"Your soul called to mine."

"But I was awake...this isn't a dream walk...and Mr. Greene! He's got a gun!"

His eyes crinkled at their corners as a warm smile spread across his face. "Do not be afraid, Ember." He reached out his hand. "Time is not the same for them. When you return, it will seem as if only a second has passed."

"You don't understand. He's about to pull the trigger," she insisted. "He's about to kill me!"

"And in your last moments, you chose." He again reached out his hand. "Come with me."

Reluctantly, Ember slipped her hand in his, comforted by the familiar buzz of the archangel's touch.

"So, am I about to die?" The surrounding scene morphed into a luscious tropical landscape complete with a waterfall that carved a lazy river beside them. It was beautiful. Ember gasped. "Wait, is this Heaven? I died, didn't I?"

A low rumble escaped his chest. "No, Daughter of Eden. This isn't Heaven, and you didn't die." He spread his arms out wide. "This is one of my favorite spots. Do you like it?"

She nodded as she watched an iridescent butterfly drift by, landing on a red hibiscus bloom. The archangel studied her. His eyes seemed to fill with sorrow. "You have learned much since our last meeting." She nodded. "I wish that you could have experienced more life, Ember, before taking on this burden."

"The oath?" she asked.

"Yes, the oath." The archangel's sword appeared in his hand.

She took a deep breath. "It's okay. I'm ready."

"Let me see your left hand." The Archangel flipped her arm over, revealing the underside of her wrist.

"Daughter of Eden, do you rebuke the fallen angel, Azrael, his demons and his misguided followers?" he asked.

"I do." She trembled as the archangel dragged the tip of the sword down the length of her left arm. It burned but did not bleed as it left a glowing trail.

"And, do you, Daughter of Eden, consecrate yourself to God and swear to serve only Him?"

"I do." The archangel drew the blade across the

first line, making a golden cross. It looked exactly like the golden tattoo on Derek's wrist.

Ember's fingers tingled as a long, golden sword materialized in her palm.

Tilting his chin to her sword, the archangel intoned, "*Gladium redemptionem mendacii.*"

"And I, the Archangel Michael, do hereby vow to petition for your redemption on the Day of Judgement."

A warm feeling of love enveloped Ember as a slow smile spread across the Archangel's perfect face. He lifted his sword to the sky. "*In hoc signo vinces.*" His deep voice resonated through the garden air.

He leaned in. "Ready for your first mission?"

At Ember's slow nod, a true, teeth-revealing smile erupted from his face. "Good. You have everything you need. Now, live."

"But I—" Her words died in her throat as the Archangel's garden dissipated and the dilapidated cabin returned in its place.

The archangel's voice echoed in her head as Ember transitioned back into reality. The barrel of the gun still pointed at her face.

Live.

Chapter Fifty

Her mission: to live.

So simple, yet so impossible, as Ember stared at the gun pointed at her skull. Mr. Greene's finger pulled back on the trigger.

Virtus vincit.

Reminded of her father's words, she found her courage. The world slipped into slow motion as she kicked out and swept her legs, causing the bullet to go wide as Mr. Greene fell to the ground.

Derek burst through the door; eyes wild as he took in the scene. Ember didn't have time to explain as she wrestled with Mr. Greene. She grasped his wrist, trying to force the gun from his hand. Wayne entered the cabin behind Derek, raising a chair to hit him over the head. Ember, now with her angelic powers fully unlocked, pierced the demon's rusty, black veil and latched onto Wayne's mind, taking control of the demon. She redirected his aim and forced the chair to go wide of Derek. The teacher slipped his arms around her neck, putting her into a chokehold, cutting off her air supply. She had no choice but to drop her connection to the demon.

He spoke low into her ear. "*Caedite Eos. Novit enim Domius qui sunt eius*. Go to Hell, Ms. O'Neill."

Ember stiffened at the words. Somehow she understood Latin: Kill them all. For the Lord knows those who are His.

A burning sensation enveloped her body from head to toe as she struggled to breathe. Her body glowed as bright as the Archangel's. Mr. Greene jerked back, screaming, and released his hold on Ember, hands burned and blistered from touching her glowing skin.

"What are you?" he hissed between gritted teeth. "*Et abiit, Satanas!*"

Ember kicked the gun away. Derek took advantage of the demon's distraction and knocked him out with a solid uppercut. Wayne's body crumpled to the floor.

She looked down at the trembling coach, anger and loathing oozing from his aura.

"I am not an abomination, Mr. Greene." A golden sword formed in Ember's hand. "There is nothing wrong with me. This. This is who I was meant to be. *Condemnant quod non intelligunt.*" A small smile stretched across her lips as she spoke the words, tipping the sword to his neck.

His eyes bulged as urine darkened his pants.

"Everyone, not just the Order, people throughout history have condemned what they do not understand."

"Ms. O'Neill…" The teacher pleaded.

She pulled back, raising the sword above her head. With a conviction and power that she did not know existed within her, she spoke.

"*Gladium redemptionem mendacii.*" In the sword lies redemption.

"*In hoc signo vinces.*" In the sign, we will conquer.

Ember's golden tattoo blazed on her arm. She slammed the sword into the wood floor next to his trembling form. The cabin floor cracked and splintered in two.

Her angelic light encompassed his aura, overcoming his internal wall of protection. "Go to sleep, Mr. Greene." He instantly slumped to the floor, unconscious.

Her attention turned to Logan and Erick.

"Help Erick," she told Derek as she stepped around the slumbering coach to Logan's unconscious form. Ember pulled on the thin string connecting her to him. He was at death's door.

"Stay with me." She commanded him through their connected auras as she placed her hands on the bloody wound. He moaned softly. "This might hurt."

Ember didn't know how or why, but she knew she could save him. Her angelic light energy flowed from her body to his shoulder. The bullet had entered and exited, just nicking an artery. Heat flowed through her fingers as she concentrated on the weeping wound. The healing energy knitted and mended the torn tissue. Logan whimpered.

"Em…" Derek's anxious voice cut through her concentration. "He's dying."

"I can save him." Closing her eyes, she let everything around her dissipate, focusing solely on Logan's damaged flesh. She put everything into it as pure divine energy flowed through her and into healing his injury. She had no concept of how much time had passed. But when she opened her eyes, Logan's clammy hand grasped her wrist.

"Thank you." Color had returned to his face. "You saved me."

Bear burst through the doors, barely sidestepping Wayne and Mr. Greene, nuzzling her arm. She finished healing Logan as Derek untied Erick.

Logan rotated his shoulder in awe. "Pretty cool trick, O'Neill."

She wiped at the wetness on her cheeks and hugged Bear. Derek held out his hand, helping her to stand. Her supernatural glow had faded, leaving her looking like a normal teen.

"Hey, I'm the one who got shot." Logan's crooked grin forced a dimple to pop as he raised his hand for help.

Derek glared at him. "You look okay to me."

Logan shot up, clenching his fist.

"Hey. Stop. Enough. I think we've had enough fighting for one night," Ember said. Her gaze slid to the two males on the floor. "I'm sorry. I'm so sorry for everything, Erick." Her voice hitched.

Erick's lips pursed together. "It's not your fault. You didn't kill Hallee. He did." He pointed to the unconscious teacher. Anger flared throughout Erick's aura.

Derek scrubbed the back of his head. "What do we do about these two?"

"We're going to have to cover it up." Logan volunteered. "My Uncle Rich can help."

Ember shivered, looking at the rust-red soaked aura of Wayne and Mr. Greene's benign lavender sleeping shade.

"What about the demon inside Wayne?" Erick asked.

She walked over to Wayne's body and kneeled. The last time she confronted a demon she had her father's angelic blade. Ember closed her eyes and prayed for help. Instantly a loving warmth enveloped her. She opened her eyes and the golden angelic sword appeared in her hand once again. She pressed the tip of the blade against Wayne's chest. "*Relinquo*."

The rusty aura around Wayne ballooned outside his body, sizzled, and dissipated with a pop of dust. Wayne's eyes fluttered open.

Her lips fell into a hard line. "Go to sleep, Wayne." His lids snapped closed.

Ember stood and faced her friends. Her glow faded along with the angelic sword

Erick's Adam's apple bobbed. "My best friend is a superhero. Like a, for real, real life warrior princess." He pushed up his broken wire-rimmed glasses.

"Yeah, about that…" Logan's gaze shifted around the cabin as he waved his hand at Derek and Erick. "You should probably do your thing and compel them to forget what happened here."

Derek raised up his wrist, flashing his golden tattoo. "See this, snake. It's my membership card. And I'm on her side."

"Chill, dude." Logan raised his palms.

Erick's fist clenched. "Look, Ember, I don't want to forget what happened here. I want to help you figure all this out…for you and for Hallee."

She cocked her head. Sirens blared in the distance. She stiffened.

"Kale!"

Ember rushed out of the cabin. Before she reached him, she knew it was too late. Kale was dead. She fell to her knees and cried out. The pain of losing her father and Hallee ripped at her soul, and now, Kale.

Her whole being erupted in an angelic glow. Erick, Logan, and Derek stood back as an unnatural cry escaped from her as she grieved their needless loss. Her glow faded as quickly as it erupted, like a meteor exploding in the sky. But the pain weighed heavy on her chest.

Pale moonlight hinted at Ember's trembling form next to Kale's body as sobs rocked her. It was all her fault. Derek stepped forward and bent down, putting his arm around her. Headlights from the ambulance lit the cabin's exterior as it pulled into view. Blue and red emergency lights slashed through the woods.

Ember stood and wiped away her tears, locking away the pain. She turned and placed her hand into Derek's. The ambulance crew stepped out with flashlights scanning the area as the sheriff rolled up behind them. She looked at Logan, the boyfriend that she had once dreamed of at the start of the school year, and Erick, her best friend, who had stood by her side for better or worse.

She didn't know what the future held, but she knew she would do anything to protect them. No one else would die on her watch. She squeezed Derek's hand. She would use her powers to protect them. She would live. "Okay. Let's do this, together. *Uniti status division sumus.*"

Erick pushed up his glasses. His lips slid into a small grin. "More Latin? Trade you chess for Latin lessons?"

"Deal." Ember released Derek's hand and hugged her best friend, grateful that he was alive.

As the flashing lights of the first responders showed, she turned to Logan and Derek. "We need to get our stories straight."

Chapter Fifty-one

The halls were abuzz the following week with talk of Hallee and Erick's abduction. No one could believe that Mr. Greene was involved. He seemed so cool. But everyone bought Wayne's crazy. Some even believed in the teacher's innocence, that there must have been some mistake. Logan and Derek were being hailed as heroes, while the entire student body mourned Kale's and Hallee's deaths. It was a somber mix of gossip that Ember was quick to cut her connections to.

They had agreed to keep the story simple and leave her out of it. She needed to lay low and stay out of the news. Derek had tried to save Hallee in the river but arrived too late. And Kale and Logan attempted to rescue Erick at the cabin. Wayne shot at them both, but Logan overpowered Wayne and took the gun. Mr. Greene submitted once Logan had the gun. Then Logan knocked them both out, rescuing Erick. At least, that was the story they stuck to when interrogated by the sheriff. Logan's uncle pulled some strings, ensuring that the evidence matched up with their testimony.

The bell rang for lunch. Ember hugged her books to her chest. She had already told Missy and Nina that morning about her plan moving forward for lunch as the two waved at her in the hall.

Mama Jackson pulled a mop bucket from the girl's bathroom as she spied Ember. Her warm brown eyes glistened. "Ember girl, I am so sorry to hear about your friend."

She stiffened. With the abduction news swirling, Mama Jackson was the first to say anything directly to her about Hallee. "Thank you, Mama Jackson."

The older woman reached out, squeezing her arm. "And you lost your daddy, too. He was a good man. Did you know I went to school with him?"

"No." She shook her head.

"Yep, sure did." Her eyes lit up. "Your daddy was a lot like you."

"Really?" Ember swallowed back the tears that fought to erupt.

"Uh-huh...quiet boy, kind...never looking for trouble, but trouble always seemed to find him." One of her black brows arched. "But that wasn't necessarily a bad thing, Ember girl."

She gripped the mop handle with both her hands and studied the floor as if lost in a memory. She looked up at her and smiled despite the tear leaking down her cheek.

"Not everyone was kind to me growing up, either. But your daddy...he stood up for me when others looked the other way. You is good like him. I can see it. You have a light to you. There's evil in this world, but you and him...you bring the light to the darkness."

"Thank you, Mama Jackson." Her shoulders trembled. She couldn't hold back the wave of emotion flooding her.

"Oh, sweet girl, I didn't mean to upset you. Come here." The old woman let the mop handle fall and pulled her into a warm embrace. She let her sadness flow as she returned Mama Jackson's hug.

"Now go have lunch with your friends." She patted her back. She sniffed back the snot leaking from her nose. "They is lucky to be alive." Her head tilted. "Don't let that darkness get to you, Ember girl. Go live. Be a light. And go eat lunch." She added as Ember's stomach rumbled loudly.

"Thank you, Mama Jackson." She gave the older woman one last hug before she turned and headed to the library.

****

"Hey." Ember waved to Erick, already seated at their table in the back of the library. It was bittersweet to reunite for their lunch club without Hallee. Erick looked up, smiling through his old black-rimmed glasses from Middle School.

"It sucks not being able to see well." He popped open his soda can.

Her stomach rumbled as she eyed his sandwich.

"Want to share?"

"Yeah. Thanks. With everything going on…forgot my lunch money."

"No problem, warrior princess." He ripped his peanut butter and jelly sandwich in half and passed it over. "It's okay that I call you that, right?" His brows pinched together.

"Oh man, Erick, I feel horrible for snapping at you about that." She reached across the table. "I was rude and not a very good friend at all. I'm sorry."

"You don't have to apologize." He reached over and squeezed her hand.

"You and Hallee…" She bit back the sting of tears that threatened to spill at saying her friend's name. "You were both just trying to help me figure things out,

398

and I ignored you."

"No, you saved me." Erick spoke low. "And you almost saved Hallee."

"But you never would have been in danger if it weren't for me," she insisted.

"Look, none of us knew until it was too late who he was…what Mr. Greene was capable of." He shook his head. "And Wayne…" Erick noticeably shivered.

"I'm sorry," she said.

"It's okay." He slumped back in his seat, taking a bite of the sandwich. "Do you think the Order will still come after you…after…" He looked down.

She sighed. "After Mr. Greene and Wayne failed to eliminate me? Yeah…I do."

She broke off a piece of crust. "I think it's safe to say that the Order thought they eliminated me in the lab explosion back in 1975. But when I made the news after the drowning, it triggered an investigation and the Order sent their assassin, Mr. Greene, to check it out. It was him that ordered that demon to flush me out, killing my da—killing Billy Joe." Ember massaged her temples.

"It all makes sense now. That whole time, he pushed me in practices. It's like he was testing me. Looking back, I think he was the one who stole my pills and sketches, too. Or, he had demon-Wayne do it. Either way, Mr. Greene figured out who I was…what I am. He was going to kill me, Erick." A shiver ran down her spine. So many times, she had connected with his aura and not once ever did she pick up on his true intentions.

She shook her head. "The Order won't stop." She saw the worried lines on Erick's forehead. She gave him a reassuring smile. "Don't worry. For years, I always thought something was wrong with me." She squeezed the chain around her neck. "But now I know I am different, but it's not because I'm broken—or a freak." Her gaze fell on the chessboard under the window. "I was created for a reason. For what, though? That—I still need to figure out." She imagined herself as the queen on the chessboard. "I didn't know I was being hunted before…" She glanced back at Erick. "But now that I do…"

Erick finished her sentence. "It's not a one-sided game anymore."

"Exactly. And if I'm the queen…" She motioned to the chessboard.

He grinned and snapped his fingers. "You're the most powerful piece on the board."

"Yep."

His face fell flat as he pushed his black frames back up his nose. "The Order, though, they are not messing around." He cleared his throat. "Ember, if you hadn't figured things out when you did—I wouldn't be sitting here right now."

She clenched her fists. "But my dad—Billy Joe, Hallee and Kale, all ended up dying. That's not okay. Erick, the Order won't stop. And neither will I." She sat up straighter in the chair. Her hand drifted once again to the keys and Billy Joe's military tags around her neck. Pulse racing, she imagined the secrets the Bank of New Orleans held.

It was true the Order wouldn't stop. Maybe Logan and his uncle could cover up things with the Crimson Ring. But the Order had already proven more than once that they would kill anyone who got in their way until she was destroyed. To save lives and put the Order's pursuit to an end, she would have to stop them.

"*Inimicus inimical amicus.*" Ember whispered.

"Translation?" Erick asked.

She looked up, a small smile thinning her lips. "The enemy of my enemy is my friend."

"Meaning?" His chin dipped.

"Meaning, who does the Order hate, maybe more than me?" She drummed her fingers on the library table.

"The Brotherhood of the Snake...the descendants of Lucifer?" He whispered, glancing nervously at her.

"Azrael," she corrected.

"Yeah. I know. Lucifer—Azrael, same thing. But you can't be serious. The Brotherhood of the Snake are like the bad guys, Ember."

"Yeah, I know." She swallowed, fingering the bank keys hanging from her neck.

Billy Joe may have been a Covenant Knight, but he was obviously working closely with someone on the other side, or she wouldn't be alive today. Birdie Mae made it out of ELL before the explosion.

Someone knew it was going to happen. Someone on the inside. And that someone, she was certain, was in the army with Billy Joe. He was an executive for ELL Pharmaceuticals. He was the son of a high-ranking member of the Crimson Ring, the controlling North American branch of the Brotherhood of the Snake.

Ember winced. And he could be her true father.

She chewed her bottom lip as she peered at her best friend across the table.

"I need to find out what this bank key unlocks, and I need to find Dasher Von Holstein. I believe he's the man Billy Joe wanted me to find. He must have all the answers, Erick. And I believe Dasher Von Holstein can help me take down the Order."

She stood. "Help me find some maps of New Orleans?"

Chapter Fifty-two

Ember fell asleep later that night with maps of the French Quarter in her lap, and her fluffy protector, Bear, taking up more real estate on the bed than herself.

****

"Going somewhere, angel?" Lucas sat in the swing hanging under the willow in their secret garden. The familiar pull of his energy surrounded her.

Ember stiffened, realizing she must have fallen asleep. For two nights, she slept blissfully. No nightmares. No dream walking with Lucas. No dreams. Period. Nothing. Just peaceful, restorative sleep.

"Stop, Lucas." She imagined closing an invisible door to her mind and locking it with a key.

"Ha. Nice. You are a fast learner, Ember." He put emphasis on her real name.

"Yes, I am, Lucas." She scanned the garden. As nice as it was, she really didn't want to hang out with him. She needed sleep and to plan her trip to New Orleans. "And I'd really like to go back to sleep now." She started to clip the connection.

"Wait. I've been trying to reach you." He leapt from the swing, tugging on her hand. He released it instantly as blistering heat sparked at their touch.

"Ouch." He hissed as his fingers twitched from the burn. His eyes rounded when he saw the golden tattoo on her arm. Slowly, his gaze shifted to her face. "I

403

knew you had an interesting weekend, but I didn't know it was this interesting." His lips twitched.

"Does it matter?" She crossed her arms.

The golden flecks in Lucas' emerald eyes danced as he reached out twisting a strand of her auburn hair between his fingers.

"This changes everything, angel."

A word about the author…

A native Kentuckian, Kerrie Faye, writes from the shadows of the Rocky Mountain Flatirons in Colorado, pursuing her YA Fantasy author dreams one Nerds Gummy Cluster at a time. When she is not writing, she can be found hanging with her family or binge watching reality TV, sipping a glass of wine, and sharing her popcorn with her lovable, food-motivated Saint Bernard, Maggie.

Checkout her website, https://kerriefayebooks.com for updates on new projects.

Thank you for purchasing
this publication of The Wild Rose Press, Inc.

For questions or more information
contact us at
info@thewildrosepress.com.

The Wild Rose Press, Inc.
www.thewildrosepress.com

Milton Keynes UK
Ingram Content Group UK Ltd.
UKHW020814260224
438492UK00015BA/684